P9-DWJ-600

Playing Happy Families

mystery novels by Julian Symons

THE IMMATERIAL MURDER CASE
A MAN CALLED JONES
BLAND BEGINNING
THE THIRTY-FIRST OF FEBRUARY
THE BROKEN PENNY
THE NARROWING CIRCLE
BOGUE'S FORTUNE
THE COLOUR OF MURDER
THE PIPE DREAM
THE PROGRESS OF A CRIME
THE PLAIN MAN
THE END OF SOLOMON GRUNDY
THE BELTING INHERITANCE
THE MAN WHO KILLED HIMSELF
THE MAN WHOSE DREAMS CAME TRUE
THE MAN WHO LOST HIS WIFE
THE PLAYERS AND THE GAME
THE PLOT AGAINST ROGER RIDER
A THREE-PIPE PROBLEM
THE BLACKHEATH POISONINGS
SWEET ADELAIDE
THE DETLING SECRET
THE TIGERS OF SUBTOPIA AND OTHER STORIES
THE NAME OF ANNABEL LEE
A CRIMINAL COMEDY
THE KENTISH MANOR MURDERS
DEATH'S DARKEST FACE
SOMETHING LIKE A LOVE AFFAIR

JULIAN SYMONS

PLAYING HAPPY FAMILIES

THE MYSTERIOUS PRESS

Published by Warner Books

A Time Warner Company

First published in 1994 by Macmillan London Limited, a division of Pan Macmillan Publishers Limited.

Mysterious Press books are published by Warner Books, Inc.,
1271 Avenue of the Americas, New York, NY 10020.

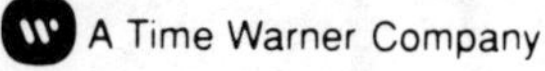

Printed in the United States of America

First U.S. printing: January 1995

10 9 8 7 6 5 4 3 2 1

Library of Congress Cataloging-in-Publication Data

Symons, Julian, 1912–
Playing happy families / Julian Symons.
p. cm.
ISBN 0-89296-578-9
1. Missing persons—England—Fiction. 2. Family—England—Fiction. 3. Police—England—Fiction. I. Title.
PR6037.Y5P43 1994
823′.912—dc20 94-15119
CIP

For
Harry and Sheila Keating

Acknowledgements

My thanks are due to Graham Ison, who gave me expert advice about details of the police background. But what should one do with expert advice but absorb and then forget it? Mr. (ex-Superintendent) Ison is not responsible for any passages that outrage probability. Recipes for all the dishes described or mentioned may be found in Jane Grigson's excellent *English Food*.

Contents

PROLOGUE
The Camera Sees a Happy Family 1

1.
The Disappearance 13

2.
On the Box 55

3.
The Telephone Call, the Sightings 64

4.
Roads to Nowhere 80

5.
The Arrest 90

6.
The American Connection 123

7.
Family Occupations 147

8.
The Trials 174

9.
Time the Healer 210

10.
Family Problems 242

11.
Final Resolutions 258

PLAYING HAPPY FAMILIES

PROLOGUE
The Camera Sees a Happy Family

First shot: the Midway home. This is halfway down Sapphic Street, which runs between the fashionable end of the Fulham Road and the King's Road. The house is Victorian, one in a row of eleven put up by a local builder a little more than a hundred years ago. They were of course not fashionable then, occupied by lawyers' clerks, foremen, under-managers, local shop owners, and skilled artisans who made good use of the workmen's trains on the Metropolitan District Railway.

The eleven houses were put up at a time when the tall grey brick buildings of mid-Victorian years were giving way to red brick. They are of three storeys with a gable, their tiny front gardens bright in the summer with lobelias, primulas, geraniums, shrubs in pots. The Midway home is one of only three that have preserved the original stained-glass front door panels. On this Saturday in early February the houses show their dull red brick fronts to a leaden sky, dark with the threat of snow.

The Midways have lived here for twenty years, graduating to Fulham from Wimbledon, which they agreed was pleasant but too far out. Like other occupants of now-fashionable Fulham they have effected improvements, making an extension at the back to enlarge the kitchen and change the shape of the bedrooms above it.

Move inside: John Midway, in dark red dressing-gown and striped pyjamas, is descending the stairs to breakfast. Descending is the word, his movements stately. He is fifty-eight, a lean lantern-jawed man with thick lightish hair, a prominent nose, and an out-thrust lower lip which suggests he is master in his home, not a man to be trifled with, et cetera. He is personnel director at MultiCorpus, and in spite of the lower lip is wonderfully patient and sympathetic with the staff problems brought to him. Reaching the bottom of the stairs he turns right for the kitchen, which offers a view of the thirty-foot back garden filled by Eleanor with plants and shrubs.

Now into the kitchen where Eleanor is already at the stove, trousered and shirted. A good kitchen, one which John has always been pleased with. He approves the logical placing of double sink and draining-board, Miele dishwasher and cupboards, while Eleanor likes the outsize cooker and its double oven with separate hob. Saturday is bacon and tomatoes day. John sniffs with his big nose and gives an appreciative nod. Eleanor is only a couple of inches shorter than her husband, big-boned but with a good figure, curly hair with blond highlights, pale rather prominent blue eyes. A discontented look passes occasionally over her face, a shadow over the sun. Why is this? No doubt about her loving and admiring John, who is a few years her senior, and her second husband. The first was a mistake. At twenty she married a handsome young Regular Army officer, who beat her up regularly as an enjoyable end to an evening of drinking in the Mess. She left him after three months, and had no problem in getting a divorce because he used to tell fellow officers of the pleasure that lay ahead at the end of an evening's drinking. During the three months he made her pregnant, and John Midway took on an eighteen-month-old boy as well as Eleanor. At that time he was no more than what he called a pen-pusher, and his father William, headmaster of the minor public school at which John and his elder brother Giles had been educated, helped them financially over the first difficult years. It has always been, as Eleanor tells women friends, a happy marriage. It was just that she sometimes felt—well—unfulfilled.

No sooner have such words been spoken, though, than Eleanor puts a hand over her mouth as if to cover an embarrassing belch, and says: "I'm terrible, I really am. What am I talking about when I've got a beautiful home and lovely children? And a wonderful husband," she adds after a moment. "It's wicked of me, I sometimes take John for granted, and he's so good." She opens her arms in one of the dramatic gestures natural to her and says: "Really, I love everything, I love life."

So we see them in the kitchen with its long narrow table covered with heat-resistant plastic, he tucking into bacon and tomatoes, she confining herself to coffee and dry toast. They present an image of English bourgeois life, a couple not at all self-satisfied, aware of their luck in being somehow remote from the problems that harass many of their seniors and juniors, problems about a place to live, children's education, money. They have no intention of leaving Fulham, the children are well past education age, they are not rich but there is enough money.

Today is a special day. John finishes his bacon, pushes aside the plate, says: "Thirty years." He shakes his head. "Seems like days."

"Oh, John." Eleanor is easily moved. A tear shows in her blue eye.

"You're the girl I married in that stuffy registrar's office." The lower lip out-thrust, he dares her to deny it. She shows no inclination to do so, gathers breakfast things for the dishwasher.

He watches her, not critically. "You've kept your figure. A fine figure of a woman." This is said not quite seriously nor quite jokingly, but somehow dilutes the earlier words. "So what's on the tapis?"

"We should get on. They're all coming to lunch."

"All?" A view now of John's eyebrows, previously unmentioned. Thick, curly, easily raised and lowered, they are used to express surprise, amusement, disgust, in lieu of showing such emotions on his wooden features. His face, one might say, is all eyebrows and lower lip.

Eleanor elaborates. "David and Mary. And Jenny of course, and she's bringing someone, perhaps two people, a surprise, she said. You know she's a girl for surprises."

Jenny and David are their children. Mary is David's wife. "You told them?"

"You know me, can't keep a secret. And I love to see them all. Oh, and I asked Giles." The eyebrows make no comment on this invitation to John's brother, who is a High Court Judge, but the lower lip shows signs of activity. "I feel sorry for Giles. I know he can be a bit of a bore, but he must be lonely. Besides, he's your brother."

"Nothing planned for this evening, I hope. We're going out. To the Reine Pedauque." In Fulham's clustered restaurant land La Reine Pedauque is somewhere new.

"John." She comes round the table. They chastely kiss. "About lunch, it's cold. Chicken with almonds, a special salad I've invented, cheesecake and another pudding, cheese." The eyebrows show slight surprise. "Cold food on a February day, I know, but the way Jenny spoke she might be bringing a platoon from the Brigade of Guards. Though it might be tramps from the Embankment. You know Jenny." Both laugh. Yes, they know Jenny. "You'll look after the wine. That's all you have to do, I promise."

John's moments of self-criticism are frequent, and this is one of them. "You'd have liked a bigger party, a proper celebration."

"Sweet thought, but I *love* my family, don't want anybody else. Only I wish Evers could be here." But Eversley Grayson, her son by the Army officer who long since drank himself to death, lives in Massachusetts, near Boston, with his wife and children.

Eyebrows and lip make no comment on that wistful wish. John goes up to shave, dress, and look at papers he has brought back from the office. Eleanor changes into a flowered dress that emphasizes her size, suits her less than the trousers. John's clothes are English male informal for his age, cavalry twill trousers, tweed jacket, cravat carelessly knotted. They are ready to receive.

An hour or two passes. A view now of the arriving guests. First, Jenny. The street is dense with parked cars, but she finds a space in which to manoeuvre her black VW Golf, as somehow she always does. She jumps rather than steps out of the car, and moves energetically towards her parents' door. At twenty-seven her loose-limbed movements still have the awkward eagerness of youth. She has her mother's pale blue eyes and is not beautiful, but her mobile features are attractive. Her male companion, warmly wrapped in a camel-hair coat, follows more slowly. He is burdened with a sheaf of flowers and a large brown-paper package.

Before Jenny can ring the bell the door opens. Mother and daughter are clasped in a whirling screaming embrace. "Darling Mumsy, happy silver anniversary or whatever it is, couldn't think what to get, here's flowers." The camel-coated man hands over the sheaf with the semblance of a bow. "Miserable flowers." Of course the roses are not miserable, but lovely blood-red buds. "Where's Pop?" Jenny got the names Mumsy and Popsy from some American film seen in childhood, and can't be persuaded to give them up, although the atrocious "Popsy" has been shortened.

Before her mother can answer she says: "Should have introduced, this is Louis. My boss."

Jenny has had several jobs, the most recent in an art gallery. Camel coat sketches another bow, says: "Louis Meyers." The coat removed, he is revealed as small, darkish in complexion, hair black and shining, jowl a little blue. He wears a grey pullover, reddish trousers that look to be made of canvas, sneakers. Eleanor prefers blond men like her husband, but greets him warmly. John appears. Jenny shrieks "Pop," there is another embrace. Louis hands him the large brown-paper package, from which John extracts a jeroboam of champagne. Louis says in a voice soft as melting toffee: "With the compliments and congratulations of Louis Arts."

John seems at a loss for words. He mutters something about cooling it, retreats. The others turn right into the living-room, two rooms knocked into one, the rear part used for dining. French windows lead to the garden and its shrubs. Round the walls are prints, Van Gogh, Cézanne, Gauguin. The little art gallery man dismisses them with a glance, gives closer scrutiny to an oil portrait of Pop done by his daughter during her two terms as an art student, abandons that and praises the ingenuity with which the two rooms have been made into one, yet retained an individuality established by the divider that separates living from dining area. Was it devised by—and he mentions a famous name? John Midway suspects this outlandishly dressed little fellow of getting at him, gives the eyebrows some exercise. But the man is Jenny's employer, and his "Did it myself, nothing to it" is polite enough. Little Louis congratulates him.

Upstairs Eleanor and her daughter are shrieking at each other as Eleanor shows Jenny a new dress, and Jenny tells her mother that the gallery job is really and truly the kind of thing she enjoys and Louis is really something, she's not just an assistant giving out chat about pictures and catalogues but does much more interesting things, when the doorbell rings . . .

And the camera moves quickly to catch Giles on the doorstep. The bachelor judge is much like his brother, same height, same cast of features but lacking the individuality given by the lip and eyebrows. Giles's appearance is milder, more cautious. He wears a Melton overcoat and carries an umbrella even though he has taken a taxi here. He holds a neatly wrapped package.

Eleanor opens the door. They kiss, dry lips touching cool cheek. They don't dislike each other, but warmth is foreign to Giles's nature. He thrusts the package at her, says it's nothing, a token. Eleanor takes him into the living-room, insists on opening the package, reveals a silver salt and pepper set, the price left on the bottom. Giles has already given a disapproving look at the canvas trousers. With the price of the gift revealed his embarrassment is considerable. There is a second embrace from Eleanor who says lovely *lovely*, and a cursory one from Jenny. Champagne is brought in, not from the jeroboam which is cooling, but a single bottle. There is chat about the weather. It has been a hard January, will February be gentler?

The camera leaves them, to look at David and Mary as they cruise slowly down the road in their six-year-old Vauxhall Nova looking for a parking place. There are no spaces. David is driving. The lines of cars seem to glare at him with mocking hostility, sneering faces appear between the headlamps. He turns right at the end of the road, then right again. "There," Mary says twice, gesturing at spaces he knows to be too small. "You could have got in," she says when they are past. He does not bother to contradict her. When they find a parking space at last they have a ten-minute walk.

"This area's just the end for parking," she says when they get out. "All right for your parents, they don't have a car." It's true that John says they don't need one, living close to the centre of town and with no garage, it's cheaper and more sensible to rent a car if they're going out of London. Eleanor would like to have one for shopping, but what John says goes. Where David and

Mary live in North London, away in Stamford Hill, there is no parking problem.

They trudge along, an ordinary couple. David works in an estate agent's office, Mary is a dental receptionist. They have been married three years. There are no children. David has the look of a perpetual absentee from the present. Two vertical lines between his brows give the misleading impression that he is thinking about something more important than what is under discussion. Mary is a doctor's daughter. She is small, dark, pretty, has aspirations to culture. She makes lists of new fiction favourably reviewed and gets the books from the library.

Neither has made any particular preparation for the occasion. David wears a raincoat, beneath it the tweedy jacket and flannel trousers that are his usual winter weekend clothing. She has on a close-fitting striped jersey and dark skirt, her outerwear a bright red mackintosh. She likes bright colours. As they near the house she suggests that they should have brought a present. David makes no reply. She emphasizes the point. "It's their wedding anniversary."

"Doesn't mean anything. Don't know why they're making a fuss, except that Mummy likes celebrations. Dad just goes along with it."

"Still, we should have brought *something*."

"Doesn't matter." She is about to say something more when he adds: "They're my parents, I should know." She leaves it.

They reach the front door. It opens, they are folded into Eleanor's embrace. She saw them last a couple of weeks ago, but is as enthusiastic as if it had been two years. "We're drinking champagne," she says. In the living-room the lack of a present seems unnoticed. John inspects husband and wife with lower lip menacingly stuck out. Mary seems lively enough, telling Jenny and the art gallery fellow some tale about a patient who fainted in the waiting-room at the thought of what she might suffer under the drill. David has gone into one of his brown studies, as if he weren't there. Considering this son, who doesn't resemble in character either father or mother, John wonders how they can have produced this. He asks how things are going, and David moves out of abstraction.

"Has been slack, but I think business is picking up. Dad, congratulations on the anniversary."

"Thank you. Eleanor and I, you know, we've never had a disagreement, not a serious one. I hope you and Mary will be able to say the same after thirty years."

David smiles, pats his father's arm.

Now the party is complete. So why is there a ring at the bell?

Eleanor moves to answer it, but Jenny stops her. The two women, both eager for pleasure and excitement, stand in the middle of the room. "Mumsy, what is it you'd most like today?"

"Darling, nothing. It's perfect."

"But Mumsy, if you had a wish, who would you most want to be out there?"

Eleanor is baffled. John, who disapproves of the excitement Jenny is generating, always generates, is about to say something when the bell rings again. At the same moment Eleanor catches on, cries: "It can't be." She hurries to the front door, opens it. There stand her son Eversley, his wife Sally Lou, and their children Frankie and Russell. Eleanor places a hand on her heart, falls into Eversley's arms. John, following up, kisses blond smart Sally Lou. The boys say, "Hallo Grandpa, Grandma, happy birthday." At seven and five they are understandably confused between birthdays and anniversaries.

After that everybody talks at once, the jeroboam is opened, other bottles too. Frankie and Russ demand to taste the yellow sparkling stuff, but say it's sour and clamour for Coke or 7-Up. Eleanor says and repeats that it's perfect, just perfect. John, brows working overtime, wants to know how and when Jenny arranged about Eversley. She tosses her almost coltish head, says she knew Evers had to come over soon and called him, said why not bring the family . . .

"And I thought, great idea." Eversley, darkly handsome, easy and elegant, resembles his father, as Eleanor once confided to her daughter. He has some connection with the world of art which neither John nor Eleanor fully understands. Perhaps he runs an agency or is connected with one. Whatever it is pays well enough for Evers and Sally Lou to wear their clothes in a way saying both that they're expensive and that money isn't really important. Evers came over with Sally Lou when they were honeymooning in Europe, John and Eleanor went out to the States a couple of years later to see their first grandchild, but otherwise Evers hasn't seen much of the family. Except Jenny, that is. One of her many jobs, when she was courier to a travel party, took her out to the States and she saw quite a bit of her half-brother then (she told the travel company she'd been taken ill and couldn't come back with the party), but Evers hardly knows David and has never met Mary. Within a couple of minutes, though, they are talking as easily together as if they had been friends for years.

The surprise of welcoming this Atlantic invasion over, Eleanor beckons her daughter out to the kitchen. With four unexpected mouths to feed (three if you count each child as half a mouth) will there be enough? Jenny inspects the dishes, exclaims with delight, says there's enough to feed another dozen. With that settled Eleanor gets down to what she really wants to know. How is everything going? Those are the deliberately vague words she uses, inviting the reassuring reply she wants and gets.

"Fantastic, Mumsy, just fantastic. Louis is truly amazing, it's an education just to hear him talking about pictures, he knows everything. And knows what *goes*, what's *in*, not just here but everywhere."

Eleanor listens with one ear, not much interested in Louis or the picture business. In the end she comes out with it. "How's Rupert? We thought he was very nice."

"Rupe? All right, nice enough. Yes, he's *nice*. Not seen much of him lately."

"You're not—" Eleanor gestures back towards the living-room.

"Louis? Of course not, I think he's gay." Eleanor sighs. Jenny giggles. "No good you going on, very likely I shall never settle down. I like playing the field." She puts an arm round her mother's waist. "But darling Mumsy, I'm pleased you and Pop stay married, that's wonderful. Come on, let's go back."

They return, and Jenny gives a little thump on the table for attention, and says she's not going to make a speech, only say the family, that's herself and David and Evers, wanted the best parents in the world to have a proper celebration, and so—and so she hands an envelope to her father. It contains two tickets for that evening's performance of a musical so popular it's booked up months ahead, and a reservation for an after-theatre supper at a restaurant only a hundred yards from the theatre. From your happy family, Jenny says, gesturing to Eversley and David so that they step forward. They all kiss their parents and John responds, says delightful surprise, look forward to the evening out, great thing to have the family gathered together. Then he says: "Quite enough from me. Let's have lunch."

Family and friends have lunch. No ripple of discontent shows below the surface of this company playing happy families, although some are revealed when they are parted late in the afternoon. Then John says to Eleanor it was a nice but typically scatty idea about the show and the supper, he'd sooner have gone to the local restaurant where he would now have to cancel the booking. Eleanor is delighted Eversley came, and pleased to have seen Sally Lou and the children, but thinks it a pity that Frankie and Russ apparently eat nothing but burgers and ice cream, and are allowed to say candidly that her chicken and almond mayonnaise looks like a dog's dinner. Mary, on the way back to Stamford Hill, complains that David told her nothing about the little surprise, rather as if she were an outsider. And on the way back to the Connaught Sally Lou tells Eversley that though it was all kind of fascinating, and John is rather a hunk of a strong silent man, his brother Giles had told her the details of some legal wrangle he'd presided over at unbelievably boring length. But Jenny is terrific, as she had been when she visited them. Hadn't Eversley recommended her to that rather slimy art gallery man? Eversley acknowledges that he had, and Sally Lou says she's the bright one in the family, no doubt about it. In the back of the car Frankie says they were all yucky, a word he has recently got hold of. Yucky little house, yucky food, yucky old Grandpa and Grandma, he says.

Afterwards all of them remembered that Saturday, for what happened on the following Monday changed their lives.

1. *The Disappearance*

On Monday morning John Midway left home at his usual time, just after eight-thirty, and walked from Fulham to the MultiCorpus office in St Martin's Lane. The walk took almost an hour and was not pleasant on this February day with the pavements slushy and slippery underfoot, and the grey sky threatening more rain, but as he often said, it was necessary exercise for a man who played no games and sat at a desk most of the day. Walking was healthy, and meant that he arrived at work with a clear head. Scarfed, raglan-overcoated, fur-hatted, he strode along nose in air, eyebrows occasionally working, observing the crowds queuing for buses, cars jammed bumper to bumper, congratulating himself on his healthy activity.

Of the several possible routes he chose this morning the quickest although not most attractive one, up the Fulham and Brompton Roads to Knightsbridge. There he hesitated—should it be along Piccadilly or through Green Park? He chose Green Park and was glad as, nose up, he savoured the thin clean air and uncrowded though icy pavements, and found himself spouting a bit of poetry as he sometimes did when alone. "She walks in beauty like the night," he said, and wondered who had written that. Why like the night? Was beauty not more like sunrise or full moon? Beauty is unpredictable like Jenny, he thought, not to be pinned down by any comparison with night or day. Out of the Park, up the steps, along Pall Mall to Trafalgar Square, up St Martin's Lane to the great grey monster with two hundred windows, ascension in the soundless lift.

"The top of the morning to you, Susan."

His secretary Susan Cook, a robust rosy-cheeked woman, protested. "I don't know how you can say that. Such weather. And the Tube. Talk about sardines in a tin."

"I came on Shanks's pony, Susan, can't beat it. The air in the Park was like wine." Nose up again, he sniffed in memory. A few words exchanged about the weekend, a brief reference to the family party, and John Midway opened the door with his name on it and *"Director of Personnel"* beneath. Then he settled into his day of chats with employees of MultiCorpus who were dissatisfied with their jobs or the food in the canteen or their superiors, those who suffered from mysterious allergies or from illnesses they attributed to conditions in the factory at Perivale, or—there was really no end to the variety of things he had to deal with, and Susan admired immensely the tact and good temper he showed when talking to what he called difficult customers. Today he settled down with his usual combination of good humour and authority.

Back in Fulham Eleanor was reading a recipe for turkey and hazelnut soup that called for raw turkey breast. She was a wonderful cook as everybody agreed, herself included. "Mumsy, you could earn real money out of it. You could have *fun*," Jenny said. Eleanor's response was that she had fun anyway. Yet there were moments when she felt she could do more than cook for John and herself and occasional guests, look after the house, and sometimes go to the cinema with Stella who lived a few doors away, or more rarely to the theatre with John.

The girl with whom Jenny shared her Balham flat, Patsy Malone, was still in bed when she left. She got her VW Golf out of the underground car park beneath Wellington Court and drove up to Louis Arts in Cork Street. It was an almost impossible area for parking, but Jenny had chatted up the owner of a local boutique who strayed into Louis Arts one day, and persuaded him to let her park occasionally in a delivery bay at the back of his shop. She said hallo to willowy Maurice, the other assistant at the gallery, and settled down to make notes for the catalogue of the next show. Louis came in around eleven, and said how much he had enjoyed meeting her parents.

"Your mother is delightful. I understand now her daughter's charm." Jenny laughed, said what about Pop? "Your father too, though I'm not sure he approved of my clothes." Today Louis was wearing thick trousers with a check pattern that looked like a cut-up carpet, a green shirt and a white jacket. He nodded approvingly at her jersey suit ending six inches above her knee, in a zigzag black and white pattern, and at her wooden earrings. "You look like a Bridget Riley picture. You remember the appointment, four o'clock this afternoon. And remember, you exercise your charm and give nothing away."

Jenny flashed a smile. "Can't give nothing away, can I, when I don't know nuffink."

Louis smiles too, a little uncertainly, not sure if this is a joke. Just before one o'clock Jenny goes out to lunch, says she will be back by two or a little after.

* * *

The dental practice of Howard Megillah, for whom Mary Midway worked, was in Harley Street, and she had never found any good route to it from Stamford Hill. She could go most of the way by bus, but gave that up because the buses were always full in the rush hour when she went to work, and eventually settled for a complicated route that took her to Liverpool Street by overland suburban train from Stoke Newington. From there she went by Underground to Oxford Circus and then walked. On the first part of the journey she had, as often, to stand, and thought she felt the man behind her exerting a meaningful pressure on her buttocks. Then on the Underground there was no doubt in her mind that a middle-aged man carrying a briefcase was pushing it between her thighs with every shift and jerk of the train.

"Do you *mind*," she said. He said sorry, and put the briefcase on the ground between his legs, but this had the effect that his knees replaced the briefcase. She bore this for a couple of minutes, then said: "Stop it, please." He said in a sarcastic tone: "Some people don't realize it's a crowded train." At the next stop she got a seat. She made a point always of being at the surgery before Mr. Megillah, and was opening the post when he arrived. He leaned over to look at it, a short dark eager man who carried with him a whiff of spices.

"Cheques, cheques, very good, they make the wheels go round. When people are in pain they come crying, saying, 'Urgent, urgent, Mr. Megillah he must see me at once.' Then I see them, no more pain, they get an account and think: 'This Megillah fellow he charges a lot, how long was I with him, thirty, forty minutes. I shall teach him a lesson, not pay him for twelve months.' "

"I don't think it's like that. I think they just forget."

"You have a kind heart, Mary, a nice nature." She felt his

breath come close to the back of her neck before he went into the surgery, chuckling as if he had made a good joke.

David's morning journey to Wayne, Mendelson, the estate agent's office where he worked, took little more than half the time of Mary's to Harley Street. He had a five-minute walk to Seven Sisters Underground, sat in the train to South Kensington, changed to the Circle or District line for the next station which was Sloane Square, and was then within five minutes' walk of the office.

David was a good salesman, or in estate agents' parlance sales negotiator, in part because of the diffidence in expressing enthusiasm that made him awkward or silent in company. He was likely to point out the defects of a property and its position before the prospective buyer had noticed them. "This may seem a quiet road now, but it's right to tell you a lot of drivers use it as a short cut in the rush hours . . . The vendor says the house has been rewired, but from the look of things he may have done it himself and I'd suggest you get a professional to look at it . . . My advice would be to have a full survey, not just a building society job based on the mortgage value, and I think you might tell your surveyor to have a careful look at the drains . . ."

A few were put off by this ruthless candour, but more were impressed, and felt confidence in a man who was so obviously refusing to try to put one over on them. On this Monday morning David showed three clients round houses in Chelsea, and one was so bowled over by David's dismissal of a house near the Chelsea football ground at Stamford Bridge ("Yes, it's a nice property, tip-top condition, but if you're looking for peace and quiet and you're upset by the possibility of a window or two broken when Chelsea have lost at home I should forget it") that they made an immediate offer for one in a dingy area off Fulham Broadway with which he found nothing wrong. The house had been on the Wayne, Mendelson books for some months, and the buyer was eager to exchange contracts quickly, so it was a minor triumph. "You did a terrific job," Barry Mendelson said to David, who replied that he had said just what he thought. Barry chuckled, said David had earned the right to a long lunch.

On that Monday morning Sally Lou took the boys to Madame Tussaud's while Eversley made some telephone calls. When they got back he asked if they had enjoyed it. Frankie, as usual, was more vocal than his brother.

"Kind of weirdo stuff, all those figures look like real but they're just wax, most of them nobody's heard of, who cares? Weird, wasn't it, Russ?" Russ agreed. "Then they got this Chamber of Horrors, all the people killed someone and they're dressed up in old clothes and stuff, and got axes and things, pretty yucky. I reckon all this town is yucky, Dad, when are we going home?"

Soon, Eversley said. Sally Lou asked how things were going, and he said pretty good, Meyers was optimistic on this side, and Jenny Midway was going along to charm Fraschini. Sally Lou said she didn't like it.

"I said before, there's nothing to worry about. Fraschini knows what he's doing, and so do I."

"I heard you, and I still don't like it. I don't understand what it is you're doing, but you said yourself Fraschini is trouble. And I don't understand why you want to bring in Meyers when you've got this buyer in the States."

"Maybe our man at home says no. Meyers has someone here could be interested."

"That isn't all, and you know it. I can tell when you're lying."

"The rest of the answer's in our bank statement, if you ever look at it. And don't say we'd have saved money if you and the kids hadn't come over. I don't mean we're on the breadline, and you wanted to do some shopping, remember? It's no use looking sulky."

"How about this, Hunchback of Notre Dame?" She screwed up her face, hunched her shoulders. "But it still gives me the shivers. You're supposed to be the moralist in the family, remember?"

"And the breadwinner. With butter and jam as well. I don't hear you complaining about the butter and jam. If this comes off, believe me, nobody will be any the worse. Forget it. Where are we taking the kids to lunch?"

"Burger King?"

He shuddered. They went to the Chicago Pizza Pie Factory.

The telephone rang at three thirty. Eleanor picked it up.

"Mrs. Midway, hallo. Louis, Louis Meyers. That was a delightful luncheon party on Saturday."

"Thank you. Having the whole family here, that was wonderful." She added as an afterthought: "We were so pleased to meet you."

"I suppose Jenny's not with you by any chance?"

"No." She almost said *of course not*, but refrained. "Hasn't she come in today?"

"Oh yes. It's just that she hasn't come back from lunch, and she has an appointment to meet somebody at four. It occurred to me she might have gone to see you, or you might have heard from her. I'm sorry to have bothered you, please think no more about it, I expect she'll come through the door at any moment."

Eleanor agreed to think no more about it, but began to worry five minutes after putting down the telephone. Little Louis, which was how she thought of him, must have been concerned to ring her. Perhaps Jenny had felt ill and gone back to the flat she shared with a girl named Pat something or other—Jenny was never one for surnames. She rang the flat, but got no reply. Perhaps she had been in an accident, taken to hospital . . . at that point she told herself not to be ridiculous. At four fifteen she rang Louis Arts and was put through to its owner. His voice was less liquidly soothing than it had been earlier as he said he had heard nothing. Perhaps, Eleanor suggested, Jenny had gone straight to the appointment.

"That is not so. She did not arrive."

"Was she lunching with somebody?"

"Not as far as I know. She went out at one o'clock and said she might be a little late back. But this is ridiculous. And most inconvenient."

Eleanor said it was not like Jenny. Should she ring the police? Louis deprecated the idea.

"I am sure there is a simple explanation. If we ring the police and she has gone home with a bad headache—"

"I rang her flat. She's not there."

"Perhaps she met an old friend." Before Eleanor could say meeting an old friend would not have made Jenny forget her afternoon appointment Louis had said they should leave it till the morning. He felt sure Jenny would be in touch before that.

Eleanor put down the receiver unsure what to do. The solution was one she generally found, to speak to John and do whatever he advised. She remembered too late, when put through to his secretary Susan Cook, that John had said he would be in a meeting all afternoon, and might be home later than usual.

"John said don't put any calls through, Eleanor. Can it wait?" Everybody in John's office used Christian names, just like Jenny. Eleanor asked how long he would be.

"I don't know. It's one of those departmental things, they do go on and on. He should be through by six thirty, he said, and asked me to stay till then in case he needed me." It was five thirty. Eleanor said it couldn't wait. "You're sure? He won't like it."

She felt irritation, anger, a touch of panic. "Just put me through, please, Susan."

"Okaaay. Here you go." A click and John's voice, loud and clear, said, "Midway."

"John, I'm worried about Jenny. Don't blame Susan, she said you shouldn't be disturbed, I made her put me through."

"Eleanor, pull yourself together. What's this about?" When she told him he was silent a moment, then said he would take her on another line. When he spoke again his voice was pacific. "Sorry to sound sharp, we're in the middle of a battle about staffing. Of course you were right to speak to me."

"What do you think I should do? She had this appointment at four, someone she was meeting on behalf of the gallery. Surely she'd have told them if she couldn't keep it?"

"Yes. Still, there must be a simple explanation."

"But what shall I *do*?"

A pause. Then his voice, strong and decisive. "Very well. Tell the police. Stay calm, don't make too much of it. Back as soon as I can, but it might be a couple of hours."

She kept firm control of herself as she spoke to the Duty Sergeant at her local station, who said he felt sure it was some sort of mix-up that would sort itself out. It was not really a matter for him, he said, but no problem, Louis Arts was in the area covered by West End Central and he'd get on the line to them straight away, they'd take it from there. The gallery would probably be closed, did she happen to know Mr. Meyers's home address or phone number? She didn't? Not to worry, they'd find it. As soon as they had news they'd be in touch, and if she heard from her daughter no doubt she'd let them know.

Half an hour later the telephone rang. She lifted it expecting, or almost expecting, to hear Jenny's voice. But the one she heard was male, impersonal, official.

"Mrs. Midway? Sergeant Wise, West End Central. You rang with a query about your daughter, that's Miss Jennifer Midway, correct?"

"You've found her? Where is she?"

"We don't have any direct news as yet, madam. Your daughter's the owner of a black VW Golf, I believe." He gave a number, and asked if it was correct.

"I don't know the number, but yes, she has a black Golf. But what's that got to do—"

"We've been in touch with Mr. Meyers and Miss Malone." Miss Malone, who was she? The impersonal voice explained with worn patience that Miss Malone was the girl who shared Jenny's flat, the one she knew as Pat. "Your daughter drove her car to work this morning, parked it near the gallery. It was seen there this morning."

"I don't understand. What does it matter whether she took it in to work?"

"It's not there now. Presumably she went to meet somebody in it. I wondered if you had any idea who it might be."

She said she hadn't, and like the previous police officer he told her not to worry, odds were she'd turn up in an hour or two asking what all the fuss was about. He would be in touch as soon as there was news. She was pleased that when John came home she was able to give him the news without a tremor in her voice. He said she seemed to be taking it coolly.

"No use frightening ourselves. As you said, we both know what Jenny's like, liable to go off at a tangent if something takes her fancy, forget everything else."

"Forget an appointment? But you're right, no use worrying." When the second call came however, just after nine o'clock, it was he who picked up the receiver before she could reach it. She listened patiently to monosyllables. "Yes . . . yes . . . I see . . . No . . . No . . . I'd like to come . . . Right . . . You will . . . You'll let me know . . . Yes . . . Thank you."

When he put down the telephone his lower lip was working overtime. "They've found Jenny's car. About half a mile from her flat. In Balham." They had been as one in feeling it was ridiculous, almost degrading, that their daughter should have chosen to live south of the Thames in a suburb that not only had a silly name but was said now to be a dangerous area, almost as bad as Brixton, the home of one or another South London gang. Jenny had laughed at them, said it was all nonsense, Balham was up-and-coming, full of people from the media and showbiz. Neither of them had visited the flat she shared with the girl Pat, nor had Jenny seemed particularly to want them to do so. Perhaps they should have done, Eleanor thought belatedly, though what difference could it have made? She was aware of missing something John had said, and he repeated it.

"They're sending someone down to look at the car. I said I'd go too, but Sergeant whoever it is didn't want that. He'll be in touch again when they've examined it."

"She may be with friends down there."

"Without telling the man at the gallery? When she had an appointment? I don't like it, Eleanor."

The formidable lower lip trembled a little. She saw the trembling and felt a surge of confidence in herself and in Jenny, confidence that there would be an explanation reflecting well on her daughter. She said John seemed upset and he snapped back that of course he was upset, and so should she be. He made an irritated gesture when she said Jenny was clever, knew how to look after herself.

At ten-thirty he rang the police again, to be told there was no news yet, but they would be in touch when they had some positive information. An hour later the doorbell rang, and John jumped up to answer it. He returned with a square-jawed broad-shouldered man of medium height who introduced himself as Detective Sergeant Wilson. John said eagerly: "You've found her."

"Not yet. But we've made a preliminary examination of the car." Wilson looked from one to the other of them, addressed himself to a point halfway between. "It was clean. That's good news." They stared at him, not understanding. "No sign of a struggle, nothing to indicate it had been driven to the place where we found it by anybody but its owner."

"Are you suggesting Jenny drove to Balham when she left to go out for lunch? If so, why did she want the car at all, instead of going by public transport as usual?" John Midway's manner had the restrained belligerence Eleanor had heard him use on the telephone when dealing with an awkward point connected with MultiCorpus. The Sergeant replied patiently, an adult talking to a child.

"We don't know that, Mr. Midway. To be truthful, at the moment there's very little we know for certain. I'm here in the hope you can help me. We've spoken to Patsy Malone, who shares the flat with your daughter. She said she hadn't met you. Her view is there's nothing to worry about, Jenny's impulsive." Eleanor frowned as John interrupted to say she would have rung or left a message to say she couldn't keep the afternoon appointment. She wished he would let the policeman explain, then they could talk afterwards. "I asked Mr. Meyers about the appointment. She was acting for him in some preliminary negotiations about the possible purchase of a picture. He says he was using her because she was a fresh face, and didn't know too much, he didn't want to seem too obviously interested. At the moment that doesn't seem to have any connection with her disappearance. If we call it that."

John Midway said in a high strained voice: "She's been missing nearly twelve hours. What else would you call it?"

"There are various possibilities. She may be with a friend. Do you know a man named Rupert Baxter?"

Eleanor spoke for the first time. "She's brought him home. He's some sort of insurance broker. We liked him very much."

"Do you have his address or telephone number?" Husband and wife shook their heads. "Pity. What about Alex, Gabriel, Nigel? No surnames, I'm afraid. According to Patsy Malone they were all friends of hers. Unfortunately, if Jenny kept an address book it must have been in her bag. You don't know them?"

Eleanor sensed a restraint in the detective's manner when they told him they didn't even know the names. It was still with that restraint, as of one controlling a car with gentle pressure on the brake pedal, that he asked how often they saw Jenny, and whether any other member of the family was close to her.

"She's a wonderful girl, we know that," John said. He went on to tell stumblingly of the anniversary surprise. "That's her, that's Jenny, doing something like that, thinking of it, then arranging it all." The detective nodded, looked enquiringly at Eleanor.

"She'd come in for supper unexpectedly, ring up for a chat on the phone sometimes. She had her own life, we didn't intrude into it or try to." He nodded again. "She and David, that's our younger son, they never quarrelled but they were different kinds of people. David's serious. Jenny, you could say she fizzes. Her half-brother Eversley was here for our little party but he lives in America, doesn't see Jenny, though she did pay him a visit a year or two back."

Wilson thanked them, took David's address and telephone number, stood up. "I'll be in touch again shortly, or my governor Superintendent Catchpole will. I know you must be concerned, but believe me in nine cases out of ten there turns out to be a straightforward explanation for something like this. At present I see no reason to think anything else."

Five minutes later he was gone, taking a photograph of Jenny to make sure, as he said with the briefest smile, that they knew her when they saw her. Eleanor returned from showing him out and began to say it had been good of him to come round and on the whole he had been reassuring, when she saw John was looking down at the carpet, head in hands. When he looked up at her it was with a face that trembled. "She's gone," he said. "Our little girl has gone."

She told him to stop talking nonsense. The consciousness that at this moment of crisis he was reliant on her gave her a sense of power she had not known in all the years of their marriage. She felt at that moment capable of enduring anything, and at the same time confident everything would turn out well. When she said this or something like it he shook his head. "Don't you see why he wanted a photograph? He thinks Jenny's dead."

In the next forty-eight hours the wheels set in motion ran along customary lines. A girl assistant at the boutique had seen the car driven off just after one o'clock with Jenny at the wheel. Nobody else was in the car. So she had driven the car away, but where she had gone, and just when the car had been parked at Hazelrigg Road in Balham remained uncertain. House to house enquiries in the road produced contradictory evidence. A woman living opposite was positive the car had been there at three in the afternoon. She had seen a man park it, get out, and walk away hurriedly at "about three." She described him as of medium height, wearing hat, scarf, and overcoat, and keeping his head down as he turned out of Hazelrigg Road, making towards Balham High Road. On the other hand, a man returning home after work to his house farther down the road was almost sure it had not been there at five-thirty, although he noticed it later around seven o'clock.

The detective who interviewed the woman thought she was a little too confident about her identification in view of the fact that she was in her living-room on a dark, rainy day, and the nearest street lamp was several yards away. Wilson had been to see Rupert Baxter, who agreed that he was what he called "very fond" of Jenny. He hadn't seen her for a couple of weeks, although there had been no quarrel. He admitted that their relationship was not a casual one, or in other words that they had slept together.

"He kept telling me what a nice girl she is." Wilson was talking to the man in charge of the investigation, Detective Superintendent Catchpole, known to friends as Catchers. Catchpole thought of himself as a modern police officer and also as a middle-class man which, he would readily have admitted, meant he had a particular set of beliefs and prejudices. He thought the best police officers came from the middle class because they understood the problems and attitudes of the classes above and below them, landowners and the recently rich at one end of the scale, the unemployed, unemployable, and ethnic minorities at the other. If pressed he might have agreed that his sympathies went more naturally to the neatly dressed and apparently law-abiding than to those who flouted authority by their noise, untidiness, and refusal to accept what seemed to him obviously sensible rules and regulations. He would still have insisted, however, that he did his best to be impartial.

Catchpole was not given to introspection, but it occurred to him sometimes that his way of life might have been adopted in reaction against a family tradition. The Catchpoles had for three generations been miners of a traditionally militant kind. Hilary's grandfather Joe had been one of the Yorkshire leaders in the General Strike of 1926 and the long miners' strike that followed. He had moved down south after being sacked as a troublemaker, and had found a job at the Kentish mine of Betteshanger. He died of asbestosis at fifty, which did not stop his son Joe junior from following his father in what both said was the finest and toughest job in the world. Joe junior married a local girl named Mary Walsh, and Joseph Hilary Catchpole was their only child. His mother called him Hilary because she thought it would be confusing to have still another member of the family called Joe, but perhaps also because she disliked the crudeness of miners' talk and habits and the danger of their lives, and was determined her son would not follow his father.

Not that Hilary (the name of his maternal grandmother, one to which Joe junior had most reluctantly consented saying it was a right name for a sissy) showed any inclination to follow his father's occupation. He was a quiet self-contained boy, who after being taken once by his father to the miners' club shook his head vigorously when asked if he wanted to go again. When he went with his mother to see the men coming up above ground after their shift was over his first comment was that they looked very dirty. He was not, however, a sissy, as his father acknowledged when he came home one day bloody and bruised after trying to stop three other boys from torturing a kitten. He did well at the village school and the local comprehensive. His A-level passes in English, maths and French were good enough for the headmaster to say he should get a university place without difficulty, perhaps even might try for one at Oxford or Cambridge. Joe junior refused even to consider such an idea. He was not spending any of his bloody money, he said, to have his son stuffed with book learning. Mary said there were grants that covered costs, the state would pay for Hilary's education.

"You telling me it'll cost me nothing? Get away." He addressed his son. "It's life you want to know about, boy, you've had enough of books and talk. You know what Herbert Smith, the finest leader we've ever had, said in 1926 when he was sick of all the talk? 'Git on to t'field,' he said. That's what's to do now, lad, get on to t'field, get some time in." A photograph of Smith, cloth-capped and hands on hips, was on the wall behind him.

Joe junior was a short, square man. His son already topped him by an inch, and his manner was cool as his father's was warm. "I'm not worried about university, Dad. Could be you're right, it'd be a waste of time. But you might as well face it, I'm not going down the pit."

"My dad went down the pit, his father too. But it's not good enough for you, that it?"

"I don't say that. Thing is the pits are dying, I've heard you say it yourself. How long will they last in Kent, d'you think? Twenty years?"

"They'll last as long as there's men ready to fight to keep 'em open and work in 'em. Shaking your head, are you? Think you know better?"

"I'm not going down, that's all." He paused, then came out with it. "You might as well know now as later. I've put in to join the police."

Joe junior stared at his son, drew back from him as if an apparently harmless bit of wood trodden on had turned into a cobra, said, "I'll be down the club," and was out of the door. He came back late that night, late and drunk which was rare for him. From that time on he never addressed more than a sentence or two to his son. Mary, who had been a silent witness to the confrontation, said to the boy that he knew his father like many miners regarded the police as enemies, he shouldn't have broken the news the way he had. Catchpole replied that it was best to have things out in the open. In fact he was too young to be accepted, and spent the intervening time doing a variety of jobs, in a brickworks, a car-repair shop, waiting on table in a restaurant.

That was twenty years ago, and the Kent coal pits no longer existed. Five years after that conversation his father died of pneumoconiosis, the lung disease associated with pit soot, and a couple of years later his mother was dead too. Shortly before she died from leukaemia she told her son Joe junior had always hoped Hilary would change his mind, and that his heart was broken the day he saw his son come home in a police uniform. When he asked what she thought about it she spread her hands in a gesture of resignation.

"You did what you wanted to do. I'd have liked you to go to university."

"I did go."

"Aye, through the police. It wasn't the same." Then she put her hand out to him. "I'm proud of you, you know that."

It was true even in those early days that Catchpole's progress through the force had been successful, almost triumphant. He was determined to get into the Met and managed it by leaving home and taking the job in the car-repair shop. This was in Brixton, where he mixed with all sorts, particularly blacks and Asians. His three months' training included street work, visits to courts and mortuaries, and dealing with domestic rows. He was spotted as unusually bright, and found it to be a positive bonus that he was not a graduate, the Met tending to be wary of those already highly qualified. He won a police scholarship from Bramshill, and might have gone to Oxford or Cambridge but chose to stay in London which he recognized as the city where he wanted to live. He read sociology and psychology at London University, and emerged confident in his ability to deal with most people and most situations, although he recognized some discomfort when meeting those who had the sort of confidence through birth that he had acquired by an effort of will. He had risen fast in the Met, and those who disliked his easy urbanity and the smile that had in it a touch of condescension called him Miss Hilly.

He smiled now at Wilson and said, "What do you think, Chas?"

"They all say how nice she is, then in the next breath tell me she's impulsive, might do anything. Talked to her young brother David, he said it too, told me when they were young she'd drop anything she was doing if something that looked more interesting turned up. He works for an estate agent, doesn't see much of her. No more do her father and mother for that matter. My guess is she met some new man, fell for him, in a couple of days she'll turn up and ask what all the fuss is about."

"The car?"

"Did not, repeat not, show any sign whatever of anything out of the way. No bloodstains, no sign of a struggle, just been driven from somewhere to Balham. Quite a lot of prints, most of them hers no doubt, no sign of anything unusual in the boot, and of course nothing that says who the last driver might have been."

"What about the missed appointment? She could lose her job over that. And the gallery man, Meyers. Isn't it odd he should use her as a negotiator rather than acting himself, when she knows so little about it?"

"Just using her for preliminary negotiations because of her looks. That's his story."

"A bit thin perhaps." Catchpole made a note. "What's the boyfriend like, Rupert Baxter?"

"Pretty much a Hooray Henry. Talks like you, guv'nor, only more so." Wilson reckoned he knew just how far he could go with Catchpole. He grinned now, and got an amiable grin back. "If there was any trouble, what he'd call unpleasantness, my guess is he'd be hotfooting out of it. This girl she shares with, Patsy Malone, wasn't saying more than she had to."

"Irish, I presume."

"You'd think." Wilson chuckled. "Black and highly polished. Like your shoes. A looker, s'posed to be a model. Jenny's parents have never met her, obviously don't know Jenny's sharing with a black."

"They'd have minded?"

"Wouldn't have said so in a million years, but might have minded. Very likely Patsy knows more than she told me, maybe could give us a lead to those others, Gabriel, Alex, et cetera, if she wanted." He anticipated an objection. "I didn't push it because I doubt if it matters. I'll lay odds she turns up in the next twenty-four hours."

Catchpole did not contradict him, simply said he would see Patsy Malone himself and talk to the parents, but Wilson sensed an implied rebuke. He had been made temporary manager of the inquiry, which meant coordinating the paper work already piling up. Jenny's disappearance made the midday radio and TV news, and reports of sightings were already coming in. As the day progressed without any hard news of her he was glad Catchpole hadn't taken up those offered odds. If Catchers had won the bet he would have expected Wilson to pay up.

That was Tuesday. On Wednesday Jenny's photograph appeared in the press, one head and shoulders, the other showing her at the wheel of the VW Golf, with a description obtained from Meyers of the clothes she had been wearing. Her black and white jersey suit was distinctive, and so were the wooden earrings, each shaped with a tiny man pendant from the ear. In the following seventy-two hours more than fifty sightings of Jenny were received in places ranging from Edinburgh to Penzance. Most were quickly dismissed as the products of imagination or a desire for notoriety. Several accounts of women obviously in trouble or distress who had been noticed or helped by passers-by proved to have no connection with Jenny.

There remained three logged as possibles. One was a woman seen by the owner of an antique shop in Portobello Road. The woman had been wearing the right clothes, the jersey suit glimpsed under a black coat. She had enquired about a ruby ring in the window, but shook her head on being told the price. The shop owner, however, was uncertain about the identification when shown a photograph, the time was around three o'clock which seemed neither here nor there in the way of giving any clue to

Jenny's actions, and the potential customer had been in the shop only a couple of minutes.

Another possible had been seen arguing with a cab driver in Parliament Square, the third noticed by a man in a Brixton pub where the putative Jenny was with a big black man. Both these sightings were between two and four in the afternoon. There were dozens of reports of the black VW Golf, seen either parked or being driven by a woman. All sightings made a long way out of London were dismissed, because the car had been found in Balham at nine o'clock in the evening, and had been there for at least two hours if either of the Hazelrigg Road witnesses was correct. One other sighting seemed possibly significant. It was in Parsons Green, a district adjacent to Fulham and no more than a mile from John and Eleanor Midway's home. The driver of a milk float making a delivery in Rodders Road, Parsons Green, between one-thirty and two, had noticed a black Golf drawing up with a man and woman in it, the woman in the driver's seat. She got out, and the milkman thought she looked like the photograph of Jenny, though he was not sure what she was wearing. The man got out too, but with his back to the milkman who didn't notice him particularly. The float then moved on up the road, and the milkman saw nothing more of the couple. House to house enquiries in the road brought no results. This was not surprising, because most of the houses were divided into flats, and the occupants were out at work.

Catchpole had an orderly mind. Almost from the beginning of his career he had found it useful to make notes, not only about the work he was doing but also commenting on the people involved, the villains he was trying to nail and their characteristics, the attitudes of colleagues and rivals, even his own reactions in situations of emotional or practical difficulty. He had been surprised by his own coolness when facing a gunman who had just killed two people and seemed ready to make him a third, and noted with detached interest the fact that bereaved women seemed to find him more sympathetic than similarly bereaved men.

That did not apply when he went to see the Midways, for Eleanor Midway was plainly determined not to regard herself as bereaved. After talking to them Catchpole's notebook entry read: "Interesting relationship with daughter, close, even intense, yet plainly neither of them knows much about her. Don't want to know perhaps, frightened they may find out something that will destroy the image they've built up in their minds. Certainly true of husband. Wife seems tougher. Little use to inquiry at this stage."

When Eleanor Midway had gone out to make coffee her husband asked the detective in a low voice what other news he had. "No need to keep anything back. We're prepared, or I am." Catchpole replied truthfully that he was keeping nothing back. "But you think she's dead, don't you?" His lower lip quivered, he looked ready to cry. It was a relief when his wife came back with the coffee.

No joy, then, from the Midways. Catchpole went on to Patsy Malone in Balham, which was no more than five minutes' drive from where he lived in Clapham, with his wife Alice and two young sons. As they passed Clapham Common thick flakes of snow were falling. His driver WDC Blake, Betty Blake, said: "You live around here, sir, don't you? Nice area."

"And handy. I can be at the Yard in fifteen minutes. With luck." When they left the Common and went down Balham Hill he commented on the change in the area. "A dozen years back this was just a nice dull inner suburb. Now look at it."

"Sir?"

"Clapham's mixed and I like it, but here half of them are brown or black or yellow. Explosive mixture. Look at the shops, every second shop saying special bargains, sales on all the time, those that haven't packed it in altogether. Know how many takeaways we've passed in the last hundred yards? Six. Two

Chinese, two Indian, one Greek, one Thai. Plus the Casablanca Nite Spot."

"I've known you eat a cheeseburger yourself, sir."

"Different." Catchpole gave her his practised but engaging grin. "Here it is. Better than you'd expect." He got out, shook his head when she opened her car door. "Better I go in on my own. Two of us, she could clam up."

"Nothing on record?"

"Not important at this stage. She attacks me or starts confessing I'll call for help." He gave her the grin again. It might be automatic, Betty Blake thought, but it was better than the scowl you got from some.

Wellington Court dated back to the thirties, hence was no more than five storeys high. It showed signs of wear, but the entrance was clean and tidy and the lifts worked. Catchpole, however, took the stairs to the third floor, noting approvingly the lack of graffiti. The girl who opened the door of flat thirty-three was in her early twenties, tall and slim. She wore a skin-tight bright yellow dress. "Hi," Patsy Malone said. "The top fuzz, right? Come in."

He noted automatically details of the living-room, its untidiness, the two sofas, TV and record-player, rack full of videos, another of cassettes, photographs of pop stars round the walls, others of Patsy in a bikini, in matching briefs and bra, at an outdoor restaurant table with a handsome young white, glasses raised, a bottle on the table. She followed his glance.

"Publicity shot. Non-alcoholic drink called Romantico, horrendous. You want to book me for the policeman's ball I can show you an album. Otherwise, what? Want to see Jenny's room? Feel free. Outside, turn left, her room's ahead, mine on the right, bathroom left. Look at 'em all, why not, your boy did."

He smiled, thanked her, did just that. His note read: "Jenny's room tidy, neat, unlike rest of flat, shoes in rack, drawer with jerseys, bras and briefs. Passport, cheque-book, bills in another drawer. Dressing table with rabbit's foot. Double photograph of parents on bedside table, no other photographs. No diary or notepad." Patsy's bedroom was as flamboyant as Jenny's was discreet, with a row of tiny china horses in different colours on a narrow mantelpiece, a black and yellow striped duvet, a wardrobe crammed with bright dresses, and a shelf containing half a dozen wide-brimmed hats. He returned to the living-room.

"How about the kitchen? Wanna see that?"

"Why not?" It was surprisingly large in relation to the rest of the apartment, narrow at one end, then opening out into a space large enough for a round table and four chairs. Back in the living-room she said, "You drink on duty? Gin or beer is the offer."

He opted for beer, not because he particularly wanted it but as a way of easing conversation along, sat on one of the sofas and asked where and when she'd met Jenny, and how long they'd been sharing the flat.

"Met her at the Motor Show, she was doing some PR job, I was on top of a car being photographed for an ad. How's it help to sell cars to have a black girl standing on top of a yellow car in a white dress? You tell me. She was fun, we got along, couple of months later I knew Jenny wanted to get out of the dump she was in, asked if she'd like to come here, share the rent. She did. We got along."

"Did she bring friends back to stay the night? Men friends."

"Not your business."

"Put it another way. She's been here how long? Three months, right. Has she done this kind of thing before, disappeared for a while?" She shook her head. "Right then, she's a missing person, may be dead. This stuff about men friends is the kind of thing we need to know. It is my business."

She shook her head. "I don't buy that."

"Don't buy what?"

"That she's dead. Jenny's not like me, I do crazy things now and then, get it from my father maybe. You check him out? He's IRA, you've got him locked up doing fifteen long ones for what you call terrorism. Right enough, I don't hold with blowing up people. My mum's from Jamaica, she brought me up, he was mostly on the run though he never forgot my birthday. So I do crazy things now and then, specially when I'm stoned. But Jenny, she didn't do drugs, not at all. She could be impulsive but she was in control, you get me? I'm clever but I'm a fool. Jenny, she puts on a bit of an act sometimes, but she's nobody's fool."

"She liked men?" She shook her head again. "She didn't?"

Patsy laughed, head back, breasts sharply defined in the yellow dress. "Not saying that. Not your business."

Catchpole enjoyed the to and fro of an interview like this, which was partly why he'd come in on his own, although it was probably true too that the girl was talking more freely than she would have done if Betty Blake had been making notes. He had guessed from what Wilson said that persuasion might be more effective than threats, but still it was time to put on a little pressure. "Look," he said. "I don't care what you think. She's been missing two days, not a sniff of where she may be. You gave my Sergeant some first names, no surnames, no faces. You're holding back information, and it's stupid. Now we can do it the easy way, you talk to me. Or the hard way, I take you down to the station. We do that and I'll make sure you get some publicity, some that won't do your modelling career any good. Your choice."

She got off the sofa, stood looking down at him. "I hate the fucking fuzz. Specially when they cuddle up to you."

He grinned at her. "So you want it the hard way?"

She sat down again. "All right. But Jenny and me, we weren't mates. We got along all right, that was all. Matter of fact she was thinking of moving out, getting her own place."

"Alone or with a man?" She shrugged. "These friends, the ones you knew only first names, they stayed the night?" A nod. "We've checked Rupert. How about Nigel, Gabriel, Alex?"

"Rupert's a sort of steady, keener on Jenny than she is on him. Nigel's a merchant banker or something, looked at me as if I was a bad smell, only came once. Alex is Alex Garrod, runs a betting shop in the High Street couple of minutes away, picked up Jenny somewhere. Gabriel's name's Lewis, he's a boxer, heavyweight. Black like most good boxers, not that he's good, or so they say." She paused. "That's it."

"They all stayed the night in her room?"

"Not Nigel. The others, you think they slept on the sofa?"

Scenes sometimes flashed before Catchpole, clear as film stills, and at this moment he saw the flat in the early morning, a scene from a farce, respectable Rupert slipping away early, another male head appearing round the corner of Patsy's door, different heads appearing twice a week. And these weren't drop-outs but capable, intelligent women. The way this lot live now, he thought, it's beyond me. He said, "She had other friends too? Men, I mean."

"Shouldn't be surprised. Can't be sure, those were the ones I saw."

"So she likes sex."

"Not exactly. She was interested. Don't know how much she *likes* it." She looked at him mischievously. "She likes cocks."

"What?"

No doubt her intention had been to startle him. She laughed now at the look on his face. "Cocks. Penises. The equipment. Me, I just like whatever it takes to get me going, but Jenny's different. She's always talking about shapes and sizes, blind pigs and bald heads. You know what a bald head is?" Catchpole nodded. She looked disappointed. "I sometimes think if she could have a tape measure and jot down the measurements that'd be enough for her, she'd say thank you and goodbye. Sounds like a cock teaser, but Jenny's not that either. How much she enjoys it I don't know, but like I say, she's interested." She paused, gave a sideways glance from big brown eyes. "Jenny's an oddball, one on her own. Like I told you, I don't believe anything's happened to her. She could be off on what you might call a man hunt. And why I'm telling you all this I don't know. You must be a persuader, Mr. Policeman."

Was there an invitation in that glance? Catchpole was not immune to the attraction of such an invitation but knew the unwisdom of giving way to it, and in any case the circumstances were unpropitious. He thought of WDC Blake in the car below, and the possibility that Patsy Malone might think it a good joke to scream for help after removing that skin-tight dress. So he called Betsy Blake, she came up in the lift, and Patsy Malone made a statement embodying what she had told him. In his journal Catchpole noted the details, then underlined his comment: *"More to tell?"*

Alex Garrod was a small rat-faced man. Catchpole talked to him in the back room of the betting shop, but learned little beyond confirmation of what Patsy Malone had said. Garrod had met Jenny in the saloon bar of the Duck and Goose just up the road. She was on her own, he asked if she'd like a drink, they chatted, she had been interested in the fact that he ran a betting shop. He had seen her again two or three nights later, had a drink or two, she asked what the shop looked like and how it worked, and he brought her back, showed her. And then?

"We was talking like, I was telling her about laying off bets when you're in for too much on one horse and that, and I felt—you won't believe this, guv—"

"Try me."

"Her hand on my crotch." Ah, the equipment, Catchpole

thought. "So, well, I was in. It was a surprise I can tell you, I mean she was class. Up against the wall of the shop we did it. Next time she took me round the corner, Wellington Court, flat she shared. Black piece there too, said something like, 'Where did you find that one?' Didn't take to her, I mean you got your pride, ain't that right?" Alex Garrod never stayed the night, and after a couple of weeks saw no more of Jenny. He had telephoned several times, but she was either out or said she was busy. To his regret he never saw her again in the Duck and Goose. Why hadn't he come forward when he read she was missing? He didn't know her surname, couldn't be sure it was the same girl, anyway he was married and didn't want to get involved. Catchpole asked what he thought might have happened to her.

"Asking for it, wasn't she? Picked up a wrong 'un, he did for her. Cut her up very likely, lot of that goes on now."

Catchpole also talked to Rupert Baxter, described by Wilson as a Hooray Henry, and certainly in manner he might have strayed out of Wodehouse's Drones Club. At the same time his ingenuousness had a sort of charm. He shook his head in admiration of Jenny.

"Wonderful girl. Never met anyone like her. Didn't care what other people thought, just did her own thing. Wish I could be like that. Used to live in a studio flat off Ladbroke Grove, very convenient though rather falling to bits, but then what did she do but move to Balham. Balham, I ask you, why would anyone move there from Notting Hill?" He was taken aback when Catchpole said he lived near Balham himself. "Yes, well, but still. I mean, living there with a coloured girl, too. Not that I've got anything against them, and she seems nice enough, but really not my style. Jenny's marvellous, though. And offly clever too, more brains in her big toe than I've got in my whole anatomy." He beamed at Catchpole, who had never heard anyone say "offly" instead of "awfully." The detective believed Rupert when he said he had been put off by what he called the Balham establishment, and hadn't seen Jenny for two or three weeks. "Not that she'd mind. She doesn't mind about anything like that, part of why she's so wonderful."

Since nothing was known of Jenny's movements after one o'clock on Monday, there was no question of providing or checking alibis. If something unpleasant had happened to her then, as Catchpole said to Charlie Wilson, everybody was a suspect, even a young insurance broker who said "offly" for "awfully." The answer to her disappearance, he told his journal, lay in the personality of the young woman who delighted in surprising her parents by arranging an evening out for their anniversary, kept her room meticulously neat in a way they would have approved, but had a reckless yearning for men, or if Patsy Malone was to be believed for their equipment. It was in pursuit of a personality rather than in hope of finding leads that he talked to Jenny's brother David and to Louis Meyers.

Catchpole talked to David in a café in the King's Road, where they ate ham sandwiches and drank weak coffee.

"Not much I can tell you," David Midway said. "Jenny and I aren't close, never were. Different sorts, I suppose. She's what they used to call extrovert, I'm an introvert. And she was always the family favourite. I don't mean I was neglected, just anything Jenny does they say how clever, how funny, how interesting, my father especially. Things I do they just take for granted. It's faded away now we've both left home and I'm married, but at school I used to resent it." Catchpole asked about boyfriends. "She always had plenty, used to bring them home when she was at King's—that's King's College, London. She lived at home then, read history of art, dropped out after a year and got some job or other. Never has trouble getting jobs, Jenny, or boyfriends. Only they never seem to last. Sounds as if I don't like her but that isn't so, the two of us get along all right if we don't see too much of each other. She does annoy me sometimes even now. We gave a surprise present to my mother and father on Sunday."

"I heard about that. Nice idea of Jenny's."

"That's it, you see. It was my idea. Jenny took it over, arranged somehow for Eversley to be there as well. In the end it looked as if she'd thought of the whole thing. She didn't mean it to be that way, mind, it just happened, but it was typical. As I say, I don't mind much about it nowadays, I have Mary."

He looked as if he did mind, but perhaps the lines of worry on his face were habitual. He had never been to the Balham flat, never heard of Patsy Malone, knew none of the boyfriends except Rupert, who had been around quite a while. When Catchpole mentioned her intention of moving, however, it struck a chord. "Right. She's asked me about places in a vague sort of way, hasn't looked at anything as far as I know." The detective said he thought this area would be rather pricey, and for the first time David smiled. "You might be surprised. The King's Road and the streets off it, yes, but there are some shabby streets and some cheap places." He told Catchpole about the house he had sold off the Fulham Broadway that Monday morning on the day Jenny disappeared. "Least it's north of the Thames, not Balham." Catchpole's journal note ended: "Inadequate personality. The kind that can bear grudges, but no sign that he's got a real grudge against Jenny."

In Louis Arts a young man wearing a green turtle-neck sweater and baggy trousers cut off at the knee with grey stockings below them looked up from a catalogue, smiled, and led him through to a back room where Meyers was making notes in another catalogue. The gallery owner asked eagerly whether there was any news. "Jenny's so delightful, so full of life. She's been here only three months, and to tell the truth she doesn't know much about paintings, but she has enthusiasm. I have seen her sell a picture because she likes it so much herself. The man who looks at it begins to see it as she does."

What was she then, Catchpole asked, a saleswoman? The little man laughed. "Not exactly. The process of buying and selling pictures proceeds by—what shall I call it?—a kind of osmosis."

"Perhaps you could call it something else."

Meyers stared, then laughed. "You're making a joke. Well, there's buying and selling, yes, but it is because somebody sees that the Kitaj on the wall will look well beside his Lucian Freud, or because he has two paintings in a series by Patrick Procktor and feels he must have the third one. Do you understand?"

"What about Jenny Midway?"

"I gave her a job because her brother Grayson—no, he is her half-brother—recommended her. I have sold him one or two pictures, she came to see me, she is young and attractive. So I gave her a trial. And I told you, she's enthusiastic, people like her, they are amused by her."

"You'll keep her on?" Meyers nodded. "And you've sold pictures to Grayson. He's an art dealer?"

"Not exactly," Meyers said again. He had the air of a teacher enlightening the ignorant, something Catchpole found annoying, in part because he was in fact ignorant. "He is a buying agent. That is, you might say, a middleman. He has clients for whom he acts, perhaps they don't wish their name revealed for one reason or another. The agent looks at the picture, reports back to his client on its condition, the provenance and so on, and if his client wishes carries through the deal. The eventual owner may only see a photograph, so that he relies on the agent. He gives the agent a top price, and the agent does any bargaining that may be necessary."

Catchpole made a mental note to ask an art expert at the Yard if this was in fact common practice. Meyers went on. "Last week Eversley had to come over in connection with a picture that may be of interest to me, and Jenny arranged for him to see his family on their anniversary, a delightful surprise for them. She took me along. I felt I was almost one of the family."

It seemed unlikely to Catchpole that they felt the same about Meyers, but he ignored this. "What do you mean, it *may be* of interest?"

"The matter is confidential."

"I don't betray confidences. Trust me."

Meyers showed no sign of recognizing any irony. "It is a matter of a private sale from Italy. Altogether private, you understand, there must be no publicity. It happens that I have a client who might be interested, but Eversley thinks he has one already, in the States, and he has the first chance. If he says no, or doesn't meet the asking price, my client may be interested. The agent from Italy is now in London." He shrugged. "But it is all preliminary, early days."

Catchpole had one of the flashes of intuition or guesswork that made him a good detective. He said, as a statement rather than a question: "Jenny's Monday appointment was connected with this picture? Who was she going to see?"

"It can have no possible connection with her disappearance."

"Tell me. Let me make up my own mind."

"I have been told of a Renoir, said to be a fine picture. It belongs to an Italian family who wish to dispose of it privately. Their representative, Ettore Fraschini, is here to negotiate. The appointment was with him."

"Why send her? Why not go and look at the picture yourself?"

"My dear Superintendent." The little man permitted himself a smirk. "The picture remains in Italy." Catchpole cursed himself for stupidity in even momentarily thinking anything else. "As I said, this is a preliminary stage."

"Even so, I don't see why you sent Jenny, when you said she knows little about pictures."

Meyers spread his hands. "At present that isn't important. Jenny is enthusiastic, charming, intelligent. Fraschini I know a little, he is susceptible to charming ladies. I sent Jenny to test the water, as you say. She was to emphasize that I know somebody willing to meet the conditions imposed by the seller, that the sale is to be completely private, not to a museum or gallery who will put it on display, and of course no newspaper publicity. All this, naturally, if he wishes to buy the picture."

"Isn't a restriction of that sort unusual?"

"Unusual, but not unknown. Of course it restricts the market, and might affect the price."

Was that the whole truth, anything like the truth? For the moment he let it ride, and asked if in the upshot Meyers had kept the appointment himself. No, he had sent Maurice, the young man outside. And the result?

"No *result*. I did not expect one. Some talk about possible problems, however. They say England is a free country, Italy is another free country, yet it is wonderful how difficult it can be to sell something you own. Ridiculous, don't you think? But we survive or try to. Fraschini brought a photograph of the picture."

Catchpole looked at a photograph showing two men presumably at a circus, one holding up a trapeze. He handed it back, asked if Grayson had seen it.

"Of course. He agrees with me it looks like a fine Renoir, he is interested on behalf of his American client. Americans have all the money in the world, and if Grayson's client wants the picture badly probably he will get it. We shall see."

"You mean Grayson's client might buy the picture without seeing it, even though it cost half a million?" Catchpole was interested, even if this had no apparent connection with Jenny's disappearance.

"Certainly. He will rely on his agent. Eversley will consult an art historian expert in Renoir, he will give his opinion, authenticate the picture if he thinks it genuine. And if the picture is authentic the price will be a good deal more than half a million." He spread his hands again. "But all this has nothing to do with Jenny. Let me tell you something. Jenny lives for her emotions and her fantasies. She likes being here, but if she met a man who caught her fancy and he asked her to go with him to look at the Inca ruins in Peru, she would go."

"Without telling anybody? Not even her father and mother?"

"She might give them a telephone call from Peru."

Back in the office Catchpole rang the man he knew best in the Art and Antiques Division, a genial wheezing Yorkshireman named Higginbotham.

"What's up, Catchers? Somebody pinched another Goya?"

"Just something sounds odd to me." He told the story of the Renoir. "I can't see it's to do with what I'm after, but I'd like to know what it's all about."

"Who'd tell the truth to a policeman? Sorry to disappoint you, laddie, but nothing you've told me sounds unbelievable. I'm not saying it's true, but it's the kind of thing happens. Mind you, the picture could be a fake, it could be someone'll be using it to smuggle drugs, reframe it and make hollows in the new frame to fit little bags of dope. But from the info you've given me it could be a straightforward deal, maybe a little unusual."

"Why send Jenny to see this Italian when she knew nothing about pictures?"

"But did she know about men, Catchers? Would she be ready for a little hanky panky with a lustful Italian in the hope he'd spill secrets along with his seed? Did that thought not cross your mind?"

"Sounds a bit crude. What about Meyers, does his name ring a bell?"

"You think I'm a dealers' encyclopaedia? I never heard of him, which is to his credit. And the crude approach sometimes works best, never forget that. The best of luck with the missing girlie." He gave the wheezing chuckle known as the Higginbotham special. "I hope you find her in bed with someone, not with her head chopped off."

"I expect you're right, and there's nothing in it. But perhaps you'd ask around, see if you get wind of anything that might be connected with Jenny's disappearance."

"Since it's you, Catchers, I'll do it, though I'm thinking you'll be wasting your time, and what's worse wasting mine."

Catchpole remained unsatisfied. He called Eleanor Midway, asked her for Grayson's telephone number in the States. She gave it him, asked if he had any news. He said they were still following several leads, and advised her not to worry.

"Thank you, Mr. Catchpole. Of course I worry because I don't know what Jenny's doing. But there's one thing I *do* know. Jenny and I have a very special relationship and sympathy, and if anything terrible had happened I should know. I feel sure of that."

She did not ask why he wanted to talk to Grayson, and he did not mention the Renoir. When he put down the telephone he wondered if she believed what she was saying, or had some knowledge she was keeping to herself. He got through to Eversley Grayson in Massachusetts within minutes, and the man seemed more concerned than Jenny's mother had been about his half-sister's disappearance. It was Friday now, and Jenny had been missing since Monday lunchtime. Grayson and his family had flown back home on Wednesday. He confirmed what Meyers had said, that he had come over to talk about a Renoir that might be of interest to a client in America.

"And is it?"

"Too soon to say." Grayson had a slow, easy American voice. "These things take time to set up. You say there's still no news of Jenny, I'm sorry about that. But as I said to John and Eleanor, Jenny's a smart girl, and she can look after herself. I'm not sure why you're telephoning."

To check on Meyers' story would have been a truthful reply. Instead he asked if Jenny had said anything at the weekend that might have provided a clue to her disappearance.

"Nothing at all. We talked on the phone before we came over, and she said it'd be fun if I paid a surprise visit to John and Eleanor on their anniversary. Sally Lou wanted to do a little shopping, and then we thought we'd bring the kids. Jenny said she was loving it at Louis Arts—I'd mentioned her to Louis Meyers, I dare say you know that. And that was about it. She stayed with us a few days a while back when she was over here." He paused. "She's great fun, you know. Gets sudden enthusiasms, then cools off fast. But she's tough, emotionally I mean."

The journal note on this ended: "Most interesting thing is how everyone says Jenny's impulsive but tough. But where does that lead?"

Quite possibly, it seemed, to Gabriel Lewis the boxer. His criminal record was slight, a fine for driving without a licence, and conviction for an assault outside a pub that left the other man in hospital and earned him a suspended sentence. There were associations, though, with more serious stuff. He had been in the dock for participation in a supermarket robbery at Peckham where the thieves got away with several thousand pounds. Lewis had been acquitted because the shop manager was unable to pick him out on an identity parade but the Inspector who handled the case, Gerry Mount, had no doubt the manager had been told not to make an identification if he knew what was good for him. Lewis, Mount said, had been involved for sure in a couple of other cases of robbery with violence that couldn't be pinned on him. He was not clever but not stupid either, thought he could always outsmart the police. A nasty piece of work, Mount said.

And an evasive one. He seemed to have no permanent address, and hadn't been in touch with his agent Nat Saxon for a couple of weeks. He had also not visited the gym where he trained, and if he had been to the half-dozen pubs and clubs he frequented nobody had noticed him. On Friday, however, Wilson got a tip from a snout that Lewis was holed up in a flat off the Old Kent Road belonging to one of his girlfriends, and he was brought in.

Lewis was very big, four inches over six foot and broad with it. He looked like an oversize black statue. He wore jeans and a thick workman's shirt. His feet, cased in bovver boots, were gigantic. His face was unmarked by boxing damage, his manner confident. He had a slight constant smile that was perhaps meant to irritate. Catchpole, who believed he had no prejudice against people of another colour, was duly irritated. Part of the interview, recorded on tape, went like this:

"You're a hard man to find, Gabriel. Why have you been hiding yourself away?"

"Hiding? Me? Who says?"

"Come on now. Nat Saxon's got a couple of things lined up, waiting to hear from you."

"OK, he can wait. I don't feel like fighting I don't fight. No problem."

"And you're not training. And nobody's seen you around in the usual places. You've been hiding out, why not admit it?"

"I ain't admitting nothing. I wanta fight I fight. I wanta train I train. You like to know what I been doing, OK, I'll tell you. I meet this chick Daisy, she goes for me, we been shacked up for days. Maybe I don't know I'll be able to stand up in the ring, my legs is too shaky. 'Less I stood up with you, of course, could manage that." (Laughter on the tape.)

"I see you've got a sense of humour. Let's try your memory. What were you doing on Monday?"

"Monday, this last Monday? Told you, shacked up. With Daisy. Since Sat'day. I tell you, she's *de*manding."

"Not been outside, not even for an hour, to see your pals?" (Pause.) "Yes or no, Gabriel, head shakes don't sound on the tape."

"I tell you, no. How many times you want it? What's it all about, what you bring me in for?"

"Wait on, you'll find out. Something that could put you away for a long time, I'll tell you that." (Pause.) "You should be calling for a brief, telling me you won't say any more till you see him."

"Don't want no brief, I done nothing. Just you bring in Daisy, that's Daisy Dean, she'll say where I was Monday."

"I'd sooner talk to you, for now. My money says Monday afternoon you were in Brixton, pub called the Iron Duke. You know it?"

"Could be I know it. But you lose your money."

"You were *seen* in the pub, Gabriel, we've got a witness who'll say yes, that's Gabriel Lewis the boxer. You were with someone and it wasn't Daisy Dean. You just say yes to that, no harm in having a drink in a pub, say yes and we can get on a bit, I can ask you some real questions."

"I don't know what you're talking about. You looking to fix me up, Mr. Catchpole?"

"Gabriel, I never fixed anyone up. What I'm telling you is, this is serious. You give me the wrong answers and you could go down for ten long ones or more, you help us and maybe we can help you."

"That's it, I'm saying it."

"Saying what?"

"You don't tell me what it is you pulled me in for, I don't say nothing 'cept I was with Daisy. I want my brief so he can stop you fixing me up. Till I see him, that's it."

Catchpole's sidekick Inspector Bertie Minnett thought it would have been better to come straight out and ask about Gabriel's connection with Jenny. Later that day Daisy, a hat-check girl at a club in Camberwell called the Californian, was brought in and confirmed Lewis's story. She had told the club she was ill, and they had spent five days from last Saturday in her flat. Under pressure she admitted she had gone out two or three times to shop and once to see a friend, though never for more than an hour or at the most two hours at a time. Minnett, who conducted the interview, thought she was frightened and probably lying. The Inspector, whose methods were a good deal more vigorous than Catchpole's, also conducted a further long interview with Lewis in which he accused the boxer of knowing all about Jenny Midway's disappearance. Lewis, who had at first maintained his silence, broke it when told the reason for questioning, and said he had not seen Jenny for some weeks. In the end he was released.

"He knows about it," Minnett said to Catchpole. The Inspector, a red-faced paunchy man, thought Miss Hilly was soft-handed and perhaps lily-livered. "Ask me he knows all about it. Break Daisy down, then give him to me for twenty-four hours and we'll get a result."

"You said he seemed to relax when you told him it was Jenny you wanted to know about."

"And why?" Minnett wagged a fat finger. "Because he could see we had nothing to hold him on. I hate to see bastards like that one getting cocky."

Catchpole sighed. "You know as well as I do we can't charge him. There isn't even decent identification." Fenwick, the man who had seen the couple in the pub, had been shown photographs. He had said the man looked a dead ringer for Lewis and the woman could have been Jenny, but he wasn't certain.

By the weekend sightings were still coming in and being investigated, most of them obvious duds. It seemed Jenny Midway had walked out of Louis Arts that Monday and simply vanished.

Catchpole spent a frustrated weekend at home in Clapham with his wife and family. Home was an early nineteenth-century house that had once been a Methodist chapel in one of the roads off Clapham Common's South Side. Catchpole was pleased with it, even proud of it, in part because it was so unlike the flats or semi-detached nineteen-twenties or thirties suburban houses which most of his colleagues nested in like homing pigeons. His wife Alice had spotted the semi-derelict chapel, persuaded him to buy it, and then found an enthusiastic builder who took an interest in the renovation and did it without charging the earth. The builder's bright ideas and Alice's amendments of them had produced a long high open-plan living-room with a raised dining area-cum-kitchen at one end. Open-tread stairs led out of the living-room to a long galleried space used as a study, a great arched main bedroom with its own bathroom, and three small ones for the boys and any chance or invited visitor, plus another bathroom. From outside the place still looked like a chapel, and Bertie Minnett expressed a general feeling about it by saying only Miss Hilly would want to live in a bleeding church.

The effect of frustration on Catchpole was to make him irritable at work, unusually concerned and helpful at home. Alice recognized the signs when he went up to the gallery to help their elder son Alan with his homework. "Trouble at t'mill?" she asked after he came down. "The girl who disappeared?"

"What else?" Catchpole had married her because she seemed a suitable wife for a police officer. Her family was comfortably off and Alice had middle-class standards of behaviour, and both were important to him. Catchpole believed in and adhered to standards of behaviour. In a force not renowned for scrupulousness he had never done a deal with a man he positively knew to be guilty of a serious crime. His view was that you mixed with villains, and there were some things you allowed yourself to do and promise in relation to them, others that were outside the limits. You might not be able to define the limits precisely, but still you knew when there was danger of going over them.

It was his belief that Alice like himself recognized limits of behaviour. He considered that she was not beautiful, but had a liveliness of manner and mind that complemented his. He had met her at a youth club dance, and it was obvious that she liked, even admired, him. Marriage to her was also a step up for the son of a miner. Her father Manfred Longley owned a small chain of clothing shops in Kent, and was a leading member of the local Chamber of Commerce. Her mother was a member of what she called a county family, the father having been an impoverished farmer who was pleased to marry her off to a tradesman. Laura Longley felt she had lowered herself by the marriage, and did her best to preserve her daughter from taking the family still further down the social scale. Her dislike of Catchpole had not been lessened by his success, or by the fact that he made little attempt to conceal his reciprocation of the dislike.

Manfred Longley died three years after his daughter's marriage, and his widow retired to a flat in Hove so that, fortunately from Catchpole's point of view, he saw little of her. There was an erratic younger brother named Brett, who occupied the spare bedroom of the one-time chapel rather more often than Catchpole would have wished, but he regarded himself as very lucky in his wife. He admired particularly the uncomplaining coolness with which she accepted the chores of being a copper's wife, the dances and get-togethers and back-slapping boozy cheerfulness that probably jarred on her more than on him. He liked the way she was able to brush off oafish jokes without offence, and to talk with apparent seriousness about subjects in which he knew she had only the slightest interest. He had been pleased when he heard a sergeant say: "One thing about Miss Hilly, he's got a wonderful wife."

Most of the time he took Alice for granted, but occasionally he wondered if she was as content with him as he with her. He knew she loved the boys, Alan and Desmond, but did she also love him? A detective sees so much apparently unlikely human behaviour that he is forever considering motives and possibilities. Suppose he found she had gone to bed with one of their neighbours, not looking seriously for another partner but simply in search of a little excitement, how would he be affected? To his surprise he decided he would be very upset.

It was with something of this at the back of his mind that he said: "Sorry, shouldn't be carrying work around with me and making it obvious. Do you mind?"

She laughed. "Why should I? Half my friends envy me, getting the lowdown on all the juiciest scandals. I say your lips are sealed, but they don't believe me."

"But it's all right? When I've got something going like this disappearance I can't really concentrate on much else. I can see it's a bore for you, and I'm sorry."

"When I feel hurt you'll hear me cry out. How's Alan's homework?"

He spread his arms. "Finished. With the master's help."

2. On The Box

Journalists had buzzed around the house since Jenny's disappearance became known, asking for interviews, photographs, views about what she was like. Say nothing, John told Eleanor, don't let them get indoors, they're all thieves and liars. She would have liked to tell them, or one of them, what a lovely girl Jenny was, but as usual she obeyed John and just said there was no news. On Thursday the *Banner* carried an interview with Patsy Malone and a picture of her modelling a bra and briefs, alongside a head-and-shoulders shot of Jenny. Under the heading DID MISSING JENNY HAVE SECRET LIFE? the paper gave an account of some of her men friends, which expressed more mildly what Patsy had told Catchpole. "She was interested in men, enjoyed their company, that's why we got along so well," Patsy was quoted as telling a reporter, Ruth Leader, who then added her own gloss: "The picture I got was of an outgoing fun-loving girl, always eager for a new experience. At the same time a private person who maybe didn't tell all her secrets even to a good friend like Patsy. Did Jenny perhaps have friends of a kind unknown to her art gallery employer and to Patsy Malone, friends of a different kind from the yuppies she brought home and introduced to her family? Her friendship with Alex Garrod, manager of a local betting shop, suggests that may be so. Handsome, sharply dressed Detective Superintendent Catchpole, in charge of the investigation, would say only that all possibilities were being considered."

Similar stories appeared in other tabloids, and they increased the tension in Sapphic Street. Eleanor's instinct was to ring the papers, talk to Ruth Leader and the others and tell them what Jenny was really like, but John's response when she suggested this made her refrain. "You don't understand how they twist things," he said. "They'll ask questions, whether you know this girl she shared with, why didn't Jenny bring her home, did she think you might not approve. They won't actually say you're a racist, but that's the way it would come out. Keep away from them."

The effect of Jenny's disappearance was to make John and Eleanor almost exchange personalities. Throughout all the years of marriage she had done what John said. He had decided where the children went to school, where and when they went on holiday, when it was time to have the house repainted and buy a new sofa. All this had seemed to her natural. She had acquiesced without much thought in the fact that John decided things and she then arranged for them to be done. She had been almost surprised to find herself taking over once when David was knocked over by a car on his way home from school. John was away on a course arranged by the firm, and it was she who not only took David to hospital where it turned out that he had suffered only shock, but also dealt with the police and the car driver, and decided not to press charges even though the driver acknowledged that he was to blame, because she didn't want David to go through the traumatic experience of giving evidence in court.

She was pleased when John on his return said he couldn't have handled it better.

Jenny's disappearance, however, seemed to be something he couldn't handle at all. On that Thursday, three days after she had vanished, when the stories appeared in the tabloids, he came home early saying he had found it impossible to work. A few minutes after his return he was almost in tears. Our little girl, he repeated, our little girl has gone. The famous lower lip quivered, not menacingly but with a hint of blubbering, his whole face seemed to be falling to pieces.

It is said that times of crisis are tests of personality. What is certainly true is that they often reveal strengths and weaknesses unknown to their possessors. After the first shock of Jenny's disappearance Eleanor was conscious of a kind of bounding energy and enthusiasm that demanded an outlet. She had an itch to be doing something, and a belief that no matter what it was her actions would somehow be keeping faith with Jenny, even in some mysterious way preserving her from possible harm.

Optimism was not quite the word for it. She felt she was experiencing a crisis in her own life. It brought back a memory of adolescence when she had been running in the half mile at school, saw the leader several yards in front as the bell went for the last lap, and was conscious of a power in her mind that could drive her body to the tape in front of her rival. She knew now a similar access of power, unused for years, that would enable her to cope with anything that might happen.

In some strange way this power seemed to have been transferred to her from John. She found it astonishing that someone so sympathetic and skilful in dealing with the troubles of other people should be so little able to cope now that they had come to his own family. She felt no doubt that the faltering was only temporary, and was glad she had the strength to carry the burden of worry for them both.

Something of this feeling was communicated to David and

Mary when they came round to supper on Friday, along with Stella and Harry Landis, who lived a few doors away and had been asked by Eleanor in the hope that the presence of someone outside the family might be a good thing. Harry, sales director of a food-processing firm, was often away on business trips, and in his absence Stella had become, as it were by stealth, Eleanor's best friend. Stella was a mouse-like creature with a delicate thin nose and a delicate thin voice that at times descended to a whisper. She admired what she called go-getting men, a category in which she put both John and her husband.

Stella mentioned the press stories and Eleanor, following John faithfully, said they should be ignored. She said they should have faith in Jenny's ability to deal with any kind of situation. "Although I feel I should be *doing* something, not sitting at home all day."

"But what is there to do?" Stella whispered. Some discussion followed about the intelligence, acuity, evasiveness, helpfulness of the policemen, Catchpole and Wilson. Were they doing all they could? Neither John Midway nor his son said anything as Eleanor and Mary, with Stella as an occasional chorus, talked about the missing Jenny in the long living-room where Jenny's portrait of John looked down on them, and a log fire shone and spat to remind them of the hostile world outside.

The two men looked into the red and orange flames with their occasional tinge of blue, as if in the hope that the flames might contain a solution to the question being turned around in the women's mouths. John's lower lip pushed in and out, his eyebrows were raised occasionally. David's inexpressive face was set in the gloomy expression that often inhabited it except when looking at his wife, when the gloom softened to tenderness. The men seemed ready to let the Jenny-related speculations burn themselves out until Stella, in her role of humble enquirer, said: "What do you think, John?" At that John Midway raised his nose in the air like some pursued animal seeking escape from tormentors, and said: "I don't know how you can talk like this. Last Saturday Jenny was here laughing and joking, now—I think it's obscene."

Silence. The reply is left to Eleanor. "You shouldn't say that, John. She'll come back to us." There are murmurs of approval, emphatic from Mary, muted from Stella. David looks up at his father with the unimpassioned sympathy a spectator at a hunt might give to a cornered fox. John turns his head from side to side and then says quietly: "You're fooling yourselves." Eleanor is about to respond again, but he anticipates her. "She's gone, don't you understand, what does it matter how or why?" He blunders across the room, opens the door, slams it behind him. A choking sound can be heard. Is it John Midway weeping?

A brooding presence has been removed. David suggests that one of them should try to console his father, but Eleanor shakes her head. He will be like this until there is some firm news, she says, then he will pull himself together. David subsides, as if aware of the way power in the house has shifted.

Half an hour later, when David and Mary have gone, Stella suggests timidly that David shows little concern about his sister.

"He never did show his feelings. You can't tell what David is thinking. When he was quite small, seven or eight, he had an imaginary friend he called Galloway, goodness knows where he got the name from. At that age he used to take things sometimes from shops, just little things, a packet of sweets, a pair of socks, some little toy. He didn't eat the sweets or play with the toy, just put them away in a drawer. If we found them he'd say they were for Galloway, Galloway's feet were cold, Galloway hadn't any toys to play with. Then he began to put some food aside at dinner, saying it was for Galloway, he didn't get enough to eat. In the end John had a long talk with him, said he was growing up and had to stop pretending and playing games, Galloway didn't exist."

"And that did it?"

"Yes, no more Galloway. They're different kinds of people, Jenny and David, but it doesn't mean they aren't fond of each other."

"I don't believe you care what's happened to Jenny." On the way back to Stamford Hill in the car Mary voices the same thought as Stella.

"Just because I don't talk about it, or shout and cry like Dad." David is driving, doesn't take his eyes from the road. The wipers are on, little pebbles of hail hit the windscreen and are wiped away or dissolve. "He was awful tonight."

"He's upset and shows it, that's all."

"You don't have to make that sort of display. I hate it."

"Nothing wrong in showing emotion. I'm right, though, aren't I?"

"What about?"

"You don't care. Sometimes I think you have no human feelings."

They stop at a traffic light. The wipers swish. Outside their range the hail blurs another part of the windscreen. He looks at her. "I love you, you know that."

"Yes." The light turns green, he drives on. "Yes, I do know that."

"All right then. That's enough."

They do not speak again before getting home, but Mary is used to his silences.

Eleanor had refused to put the telephone out of commission because that would have meant Jenny couldn't get through if she called. So there were dozens of calls, from journalists offering money for an interview, from friends and acquaintances, a few from people saying they knew where Jenny was or might be. She told these last ones to give their information to the police, and found most of them were concerned with money too, asking for instead of offering it. But she listened to Dennis Lacy, whose name she knew vaguely as a TV interviewer, when he said he thought she should appear on the box and make an appeal for information, and that the police approved the idea. Superintendent Catchpole would probably join in the TV appeal himself. He said it should be done quickly, they would send a car to Fulham, and it was not until they were almost at the TV studio that she realized she had not said anything to John. By that time it seemed too late to speak to him.

At the studio Dennis Lacy turned out to be as likeable as his voice. He had a long humorous face with untidy hair that kept flopping over his forehead, and he greeted her with just the right mixture of pleasure and seriousness. When she told him she had no idea what to say he told her the words would come, and that although Superintendent Catchpole couldn't be there because he was following a likely lead, he knew all about it and had said an appeal from her might be a great help. She would have liked just to be able to talk to Dennis, which was what he said she should call him, but she was whisked away and introduced to the producer, who said there was no reason to feel nervous, and then to a girl younger than Jenny who asked if she'd like to rehearse the exact words she would say, to which she responded that there was no need, the words would come. There were two or three others who smiled and shook her hand and said something sympathetic, and a make-up girl who combed and patted her hair, added what she called a touch of colour to her cheeks, and powdered her forehead. And at the end of it all she was under the lights that made her feel extremely hot, with the camera in front of her that she was told to look at all the time, and the producer saying again there was no need to feel nervous, and . . .

And she was perfectly at ease. The unrehearsed words flowed naturally and were the right words, even though she could not have said afterwards just what they were. Nor could she have said how long she spoke, but when it was over she did not need them to say she had done well, although that did not stop them. When she looked at the studio clock she could hardly believe the hands had moved such a little way. Afterwards Dennis took her to the canteen and talked while they drank coffee.

"You were wonderful. So composed, yet such feeling, I don't know how you did it." She said truthfully that she had just said what seemed natural. "If Jenny sees it she'll be in touch." He hesitated. "It won't upset you to talk about it?" She said no. "You know, you really are wonderful. My name doesn't ring any bells? Obviously not, or you'd have said something. I'm what you might call—"

She half listened to what he was saying about being a TV investigator who looked into all sorts of things, charities which siphoned money into private hands, companies offering time shares on estates that had been only half built—and disappearances. Only a few months back a girl who had left home at fourteen had learned of her mother's TV appeal in an interview with him and got in touch . . .

The half of her that did not listen was reliving those few minutes in front of the cameras, recalling her total calm, the ease with which she had spoken the right words. She saw Jenny called by a friend from whatever she was doing, told to watch TV, looking and listening, saying, "It's Mumsy, doesn't she look smashing, what have I been thinking of, I must get in touch straight away, where's the phone . . ."

"What have you been doing?" Those were John's first words when he came home and found her preparing supper. Yet although the words were meant to be indignant they were spoken with none of his usual vigour. Even when he repeated his injunction about journalists and asked why she had ignored it, he spoke not with the authority of raised brows and out-thrust lip, but in the low tones of dejection. She explained what had happened, and asked what possible harm she could have done.

"None, I suppose. No good either."

"If Jenny sees it, or someone tells her about it, she'll get in touch." She took his hand, kissed him. "You mustn't despair. It does no good."

He simply shook his head. He ate little supper, afterwards went to his study saying he had work to do. She waited for the telephone to ring. It did ring, more than once, but not with the voice at the other end she hoped to hear. Instead Mary, Stella and other friends told her she was a natural performer on the box, and that the broadcast was a wonderful idea. At eleven o'clock she went to bed. There was brandy in the study, and when John joined her she smelt it on his breath.

3. The Telephone Call, the Sightings

Catchpole watched Eleanor on TV and admired her composure, but thought there was only an outside chance of her appeal producing any results. On the following morning Charlie Wilson rang while he was shaving.

"She's been heard from. And seen. Not by the same person. She called the black Irish tart last night around midnight to say she'd seen her mother on the box, sorry she was worried, would get in touch in a few days, explain everything. Tart didn't tell us till two ack emma, duty officer thought it wasn't worth anyone losing beauty sleep, called me half an hour ago."

"Why didn't Jenny just call her mother?"

"Good question. Maybe you'd like to put it to the black tart, though why should she know?"

"And the sighting, was that in London?"

"Canterbury. Couple watched the TV, saw a picture of the girl after the mother had said her piece, recognized her as someone who'd been at a meeting about animal rights a couple of nights before, rang the locals."

"Animal rights?"

"Sounds crazy, guv, I know, but the Inspector there says he knows this couple, name of Andrews, they wouldn't be saying it for fun. They're pretty certain about the girl, same sort of clothes and wearing the earrings. The Andrews go every month to these meetings, never seen her before or the boy she was with, lots of hair, beard, sweater, old trousers. What's more, they say the man called her Jenny. Locals are looking into it, trying to get hold of the group secretary, see if he can tell us any more. You want me to bring in black beauty, talk to her?"

"Yes, bring her in. I'm coming in now. And her name's Patsy Malone."

"I'll try and remember."

Catchpole finished shaving and dressed with his usual care, but passed up breakfast and told Alice he would be home late, perhaps not at all. She made a face, and asked if she should put off their bridge evening on the following day.

"Could be. Hope not. Can't say for sure. You wanted a tidy life you shouldn't have married a copper."

"It had occurred to me." She considered him as he stood in the doorway in trilby hat, single-breasted overcoat, brightly shining shoes. "You may not have too many brains, but you look like a male model."

"Compliments come cheap." He kissed her and the children, then opened the door on a white world. The snow had stopped, frost had hardened the ground, ice crackled under his feet as he walked to the Tube station, the Common was an expanse of white. The train was packed, and stopped outside Stockwell for a quarter of an hour. The guard relayed apologies so distorted in sound as to be unintelligible. As he walked from St. James's Park station a lorry splashed mud onto his trousers. He arrived in a bad temper. Wilson greeted him with a grin, said the lady was waiting and seemed quite pleased they took an interest in her story.

Today Patsy Malone wore a sky blue jacket and dark blue trousers, and he was impressed again by her powerful sexual attraction. He asked if she would like a cup of coffee, joined her in drinking one, said he had come out without breakfast.

"You want a medal? Passed up breakfast in the course of duty? My, my."

"Just telling you," he said mildly. "Thank you for coming in. This telephone call, when was it made?"

"About midnight, just after."

"And you're sure it was Jenny? Couldn't have been someone who knew her, imitating her voice?"

"Sounded like Jenny is all I can say. Somebody else? Never crossed my mind. I think it was her all right."

"Good. Now, I want you to tell me exactly what she said. Not just the gist of it, but the precise words as near as you can get to them."

"Here we go then." The manner was assured, but her long fingers laced and unlaced as she talked. "There isn't much. I lift the phone, she says, 'Pat, it's Jenny, I haven't much time, so don't talk, listen. I heard my mum's broadcast, and I'm OK but I don't want them to worry, my mother and father. Will you call them, say I'm all right, may have to go abroad for a few days but if I do I'll be in touch, great thing is they shouldn't worry. And stop looking for me, that may foul the whole thing up.' Then she gave a kind of little gasp, said, 'Got to go now,' and hung up." She paused, considered. The fingers laced tightly. "Some point, I dunno just when, I started to break in, ask where she was, what she'd been doing, that kind of stuff, y'know. But she stopped me, said something like 'No time' or 'Can't explain,' not sure just what. That was the sense of it."

"She didn't say why she was calling you and not her parents?" The girl shook her head, said yes when he asked if she could be sure she hadn't heard a recording. "I told you, I broke in on what she said."

"Doesn't it seem odd to you?"

"What?"

"From what you've said, the only purpose of the call was to reassure her parents. Why should she ask you to do it, instead of calling herself?"

Her dark eyes glared at him. "You wanna call me a liar? I can't stop you."

Wilson, standing by the door of the interview room, moved forward. Catchpole frowned at him, spoke gently.

"You want to find her, we want to find her, we're on the same side, agreed? I'm saying it's odd, that's all."

"OK then, it's odd." Fingers unclasped, fidgeting with her bag.

"And did you ring Mr. and Mrs. Midway?"

"Yeah. Talked to him. Didn't seem to take it in."

"Now, Patsy, you say Jenny was hurried. Did you get the feeling someone else was there?"

"Coulda been, I s'pose. Only it wasn't quite like that, more like—"

"Yes?"

"More like there was someone near by, next door or something, 'cause she didn't speak in a whisper, only hurried. As if she'd snuck off to make the call." She nodded, as if reassuring herself. "Yeah, it sounded like that."

"As if she was in trouble?"

She laughed. "How does that sound? Me, I'm always in trouble."

"I can see that." When she laughed, head thrown back, there were darker patches on her neck. "Bruises."

"Hey, you ever heard of love bites?" With a deliberate change of tone she said, "Smart shirt you got on. I bet that sends 'em, Hampstead, Wimbledon, some place like that. You know what my dad woulda said? You dress like a pox doctor's clerk."

He ignored this, ignored Wilson's cough. "No impression of

distance, no background sound?" No, she said. "But when she gave the gasp, said 'Got to go now'—you sure they were the words?"

"Something like that." Hands clasped tightly.

"You got the impression she had to cut short the conversation, right?"

"S'pose so."

"Why didn't you ask what she thought she was doing, giving her friends and family so much grief? Ask where she was, how you could get in touch?"

Again she blazed at him. "You make it sound so fuckin' easy. Look, it was around midnight, I'd gone to bed, half asleep, right?"

From the door Wilson said, "On your own?"

"On my own, smartarse." She spoke again to Catchpole. "Maybe you'd been there, given me a hint what I should ask Jenny if she called and I was half asleep, maybe then I'da asked some of your questions and maybe she'da said just button your lip an' listen, but I didn't have no hints, I just heard what she said an' then she was gone. Then I tell you and you give me a hard time, maybe I shoulda just kept my lip buttoned. Tell the fuzz anything, they give you a hard time."

Wilson chuckled. "You think this is a hard time, you're dreaming. This is a friendly chat." Five minutes later she had gone. He asked Catchpole: "What d'you reckon, guv?"

"She's uneasy about something, that's for sure. Could be lying or the story may be true, though I doubt it. You noticed how she tried to shift the subject when I asked about those bruises. If they were love bites it was a very big set of teeth."

"Could be another reason why she changed the subject, guv. I reckon she fancies you. Straight up." He grinned. Catchpole grinned back, said they'd wait on Canterbury before bothering any further with Patsy Malone.

The word came through after lunch. The odd couple at the

animal rights group weren't known to the secretary. He had spoken to them, they said they were staying in the area, were interested in the movement. Their names were Jenny and Leo. When the secretary asked for an address so that he could let them know about future meetings Leo had said, "No fixed abode." Was the girl Jenny Midway? The secretary, shown a photograph, said he hadn't looked at her much, but she might be Jenny. She had looked what the secretary called "a bit fraught," but not intimidated by the man. Enquiries were continuing. Thank you for nothing, Wilson said, and Catchpole agreed.

He spoke to Higginbotham and learned that he still had enquiries out about Meyers. Then, brooding on possibilities in his office, he had one of the moments of understanding very little connected to rational thought. He had to wait until the evening before he found Patsy Malone at home. When she heard his voice her tone was exasperated. "You again. Why don't you leave a working girl alone?" When he said he was coming down to see her and asked her to stay in, she said, "I can hardly wait."

Balham High Road was brighter but looked no better by night. The girl opened the door, looked at him with hostility, asked what he wanted. Catchpole looked round the living-room. "Where is he?"

"Who?"

"Lover boy. The one who told you to make up the story."

"I've had a hard day, I can do without this. There's nobody here."

He sat down on one of the sofas, looked at her appreciatively. She was wearing a striped red and white dress, buttoned high at the neck. "Undo it."

"What?"

"Those buttons."

"Go to bed, man? With the fuzz? I could never wash off the smell."

"Stop playing games, you know that isn't what I meant. Those bruises aren't just on the neck, right, and they're not love bites. And the man who made them told you to give me that little tale about the phone call. You don't need to show me the bruises, just tell me the name." She shook her head. "Or shall I tell you?"

"You can say what you want."

"Here's a name then. Gabriel Lewis. Your boyfriend as well as Jenny's, something you forgot to tell me. Maybe she took him away from you or maybe you shared him, I don't know. What I should have realized is it's more likely you'd know a black boxer than she would, she met him through you. When the penny dropped I told a couple of men to check up, and of course you've been seen around with him." She shrugged. "And Gabriel's in trouble over the disappearance, knows something about it, so he fixes himself up with an alibi from Daisy Dean. You know Daisy?" Another shrug. "Never mind whether you do or not, you know Gabriel, a couple of his friends say you're his girl. Or one of his girls. Jenny's another, agreed? No use arguing, the only answer is yes."

"It's the answer you're giving yourself, so why tell me? But I'll tell you something, in my book nobody owns nobody. If you're thinking I got anything to do with wherever Jenny is 'cause she pinched Gabriel you got another think coming, you're way out of line. That sort of thing don't bother me, or Jenny either. I need a drink, you want one? Scotch or gin is what there is."

When she had poured the drinks she sat down with a sigh in a shabby armchair beside the sofa. Bertie Minnett had said about another black girl, the mistress of a Hackney gangster, that she looked as if you'd get an electric shock if you touched her, and Catchpole for the first time fully understood what he meant. In the notes he made afterwards he said: "It was an example of a good interrogation and the essence of it, the nasty thing about it, you could say, was that I enjoyed it. Being a policeman is about having power. On a crude level it's physical, beating up a suspect. If you're careful, don't get your rag out or lose control, know just where you should hit and how far you can go without doing real damage, you can have what Minnett would think is a lot of fun. I don't like that, it revolts me, I stop it if I know about it. But to play a suspect mentally, see them wriggling and trying to get away, go on playing them gently till you finally reel them in exhausted, that's something else. I persuade myself it's in the cause of justice and maybe it is, but it's exercising power just the same, and that's why you do it."

So now, sipping the powerful gin she had poured, he said, "Nobody with me, I'm not wired up, no way this is on the record, but I want to know the truth about that call."

"I told you already."

"I know what you told me. It was crap." He looked at her benevolently. "You were nervous. My sergeant noticed it, and he's not the brightest over things like that. Why be nervous? Don't tell me it's because you were in a police station, you know your way around too well for that. Shall I tell you the way I think it was? You know Gabriel well and he's in a bit of bother even with his alibi, so he says to you help me out, tell this story. But you don't like the idea. Jenny's a friend of mine and she's disappeared, you say, I don't want to be involved. Then Gabriel gets rough, not too rough, just enough to make you change your mind. How am I doing?"

"You oughta write a book, you got so many ideas."

"You may be right. But think about this, Patsy. If you've been putting over a bit of kidology and expect to get away with it, think again. This is serious business. You liked Jenny, you say. She could be dead, and if you're lying to help Gabriel or for any other reason, you're not only more of a bitch than I think, you're also stupid. And I don't think you're stupid."

The moment of hesitation before she said she'd never sell Jenny short and every word was true, told him that there was a crack in her defences, that if he played her carefully enough she would tell him the truth. It took another two hours of questioning and drinking, mixed with threats on her part to have him done over and on his to take her down to the station and let her cool off in a cell until she was ready to talk, before she gave way. It was nearly midnight, she was on her fourth or fifth whisky, the room was very warm.

"Look." She stopped, said again: "Look." Then: "Nothing I said—I don't want trouble for Jenny. Nor for Gabby. But I don't want trouble for me, either."

"Agreed. Very sensible."

"Gabby, you've got it in for him."

"I've not got it in for anybody."

"You say. But you, I know you. You get a black boy in the frame you don't look no further. Is there a white boy around mighta done it, forget it, we don't need him."

"Did what, Patsy?"

"How the fucking hell should I know?" She was screaming at him now, out of control. "I don't know what's happened to Jenny, do I? Don't know a fucking thing about it."

"I hope you don't." He said nothing more. Suddenly she nodded, said *all right*, and he knew he had won. "Did you get a phone call from Jenny, from anybody?" She shook her head. "It was Gabriel who asked you to tell the story, yes?"

"Yes." She glared at him. "He said you had him down at the station, you and some other copper playing softie and rough, says he doesn't know anything about Jenny but if anything's happened to her you're planning to plant it on him. If I said she spoke to me it would take the heat off. It was stupid, I guess. I knew it was, but Gabby, he wanted it."

"It was stupid," he agreed. "And caused you some grief. And wasted my time." She shrugged. "I'll want you to come down tomorrow and make a statement. There won't be any charges."

"What about Gabby?"

"I said nothing about him."

"You're a real cold bastard." She stood up, close to him. She smelled of sweat and whisky. "You want to fuck me, don't you? Admit it, bastard."

"Perhaps."

"Well then."

She stood between him and the door. He pushed her aside. "Don't be stupid. I'll send a car for you, ten o'clock."

The lift was no longer working, and the sound of her laughter rang in his ears as he went down the stairs. Snow was falling again, the flakes refreshing on his face. The car was lightly coated, and when he went to brush away the snow he saw that somebody had written on his rear window: *Cunt.* With one quick wipe the word vanished, but it stayed in his mind as some sort of comment on the investigation.

"More than two weeks gone now, and it's back to square one," Wilson said.

"Not quite. We know Lewis has something to hide, or why did he put her up to the story? So it's a fair bet he was the man in the Brixton pub and Jenny was with him. You said the pub identification was good by what's his name, Forgan?"

"Fenwick. Yes, a bit too good maybe. Seems a reliable character, but might be one of those who know what you want him to say and says it. But he identified the photograph of Jenny as well as Lewis."

A tail was out on Lewis without any useful result. He was still staying with Daisy Dean, saw his manager Nat Saxon twice, did some training at a boxing club in the Old Kent Road, spent evenings in the Californian talking to the local hard boys. All this was nothing out of the way, but Catchpole kept the tail on in hope rather than expectation. In Kent all the known animal rights groups had been contacted, but none admitted knowing the Leo and Jenny who had turned up just once in Canterbury.

Nor was there any better news from Higginbotham. Enquiries about Louis Meyers, made in the bars where art dealers meet in and around Jermyn Street, had turned up nothing to his discredit. He had escaped from Czechoslovakia as a teenager after the false dawn of 1968 along with his parents, who were both now dead. He had been living for some years with an actress named Zoe Downing. He had no criminal record.

Higginbotham was more informative about Ettore Fraschini, the man handling the possible sale of the Renoir, whom Jenny should have met on the day she disappeared. To say he had a reputation for shady deals would be an understatement, the Yorkshireman said. He had been associated with the disposal of several stolen pictures, without anything ever being actually proved against him. "The way it generally works is this. Some bad boys steal a picture. Often a museum employee, or if it's a private owner an ex-servant, is in on the deal. It's disposed of quickly, usually in the same city, at ten percent or less of the market price. Then our Mr. Fraschini is brought in, approaches a dealer who's prepared to close his eyes to where a picture came from if it's cheap enough. Or maybe he knows a collector who's prepared to keep the picture locked up for a few years before showing it to friends. He might even get it slightly altered and fake a new provenance for it. You'd be amazed what they get up to." Higginbotham agreed reluctantly that this sounded like a straightforward sale in which the Italian owner was using Fraschini. "But anything our friend's concerned in you want to watch out. How's that for helpfulness, Catchers?"

"Wonderful. Except that it seems to be no help."

"There's no such thing as gratitude nowadays."

The Midways were told that the telephone call had been a hoax, but not that the inquiry was becalmed. Catchpole said as much to Alice, who asked if he wanted to talk about it. Oddly enough—oddly because the hard facts were so few and he knew them by heart—that was what he did want. One of the things he liked about Alice was that although she rarely asked about his work she gave concentrated attention when he did talk about it. She did so now, then asked what he expected her to say.

"I don't know. I suspect I just want comments, thoughts. If she has gone off on her own account and doesn't want to get in touch I doubt if we shall find her, so let's forget that as a starter. Assume she was taken somewhere by force, how did it happen? And what should I be doing that I haven't done?"

She nibbled at a nail. "You don't seem to have thought much about the art gallery. Could she have found out something crooked about this man Meyers?" But she shook her head. "That won't do, will it? She was seen driving off in her car. So she went voluntarily to meet somebody. From what you've said she sounds like an amateur tart, so probably the somebody was a man. She picked the wrong one, he killed her. Not much help."

"Not much. And she wasn't exactly any kind of tart. Anyway it's an out-of-date word. We don't talk about amateur tarts any more, only about people having a lot of partners. Jenny had a lot of partners."

"All right, it was a *partner*. You just have to find which one. I think you should let your imagination go a bit. Trouble with detectives is they have no imagination. Official detectives anyway, not those in books." When she had no useful suggestions to offer Alice was inclined to take refuge in flippancy, and he recognized the signs. "I fancy that Hooray Henry myself, the one she took home, Rupert. Rupert found out another of her partners was his best friend, went mad with jealousy, killed her, put her body under the floorboards in his flat."

No good, he said, they'd checked Rupert's movements on that Monday. He'd been in the office all day, even at lunch, couldn't have been involved. She considered again, frowning. "All right then, but from what you've said they're what's called a close-knit family, and that always makes me shiver a bit, thinking of my own. You liked my father, didn't you? But he was an absolute bastard to both of us, me and Brett, when we were young. Dead mean, and always telling us we were no good, would never amount to anything." She shuddered. "It's that close-knit family I'd look at. If it was a detective story I'd fancy the stepbrother in the States."

"You're not taking it seriously."

"You haven't given me much to go on. But from what you've said, especially about the mother and father, I really think it could be a family affair. I saw the mother on TV, in a sort of way she was very good, in another way she gave me the creeps. That intensity—brrr. Now say I'm not helpful."

He said she had been, in a kind of way. What kind? "Just because you didn't mention him you've made it clear I haven't concentrated enough on the obvious. Gabriel Lewis. Why was he scared enough to put Patsy Malone up to telling that story, what's he hiding? Time to put some real pressure on him."

"You call that helping? Let's go to bed." Later she said: "Everyone says you're a cold fish, Mr. Catchpole, funny you're so warm in bed."

Later still, much later, he recalled things she had said about the close-knit family, but the immediate result of the conversation was that he paid a visit to the Californian the following night. That provided the first break in the case.

"When there's a problem you talk it out, have a family confab." That maxim of John Midway's had been adhered to throughout the years at moments of crisis. There had been a confab when David was found to have paid another boy at school for the correct answers to an exam paper, when Jenny had been accused of shoplifting, and later when David had wanted to go to university and Jenny to leave home as soon as schooldays were over. All these things had been talked out. The school scrapes had been settled by apologies and the payment of money, David had been told his A-level results simply didn't justify the drain on the family finances that would be caused by his attendance at the third-rate university which had tentatively accepted him, and after long discussion Jenny had been allowed to move into a flat with two girls who like her had just left school, on condition that she came home every weekend.

Perhaps the decisions did not leave everybody happy, but John at least was pleased that they had talked it all out in a confab as families should do, and what satisfied John left Eleanor happy. It was natural therefore that at this time of crisis there should be a family confab. It was prompted by a telephone call from Giles, asking if there was any news of his niece. Eleanor had been told of the possible Canterbury sighting and of the hoax perpetrated by Patsy. She told all this to Giles.

His voice was dry as a water biscuit. "I understand also that you have appeared on television." Eleanor agreed that was so. "It won't do, that kind of thing. No use, and damages the family."

The deference Eleanor paid to her husband's opinions had never been extended to his brother, and she found within herself a geyser of anger bubbling up, aimed at the callousness of the phrase about damage to the family when her concern was exactly what might have happened to her daughter. The geyser splashed out with a phrase about Giles's indifference to actual human beings and then died down, not extinct but simmering. The dry-biscuit voice made no apology but suggested it was a matter for discussion. For this reason David and Mary, John and Eleanor and Giles sat one night in the living-room looking at each other.

An atmosphere less of gloom than of dullness pervades the room and its occupants, a contrast with the cork-popping enthusiasm of that luncheon party from which it was separated as by an eclipse. David and Mary sit together on a sofa, he with his usual air of being emotionally absent though physically present, Mary staring at Jenny's portrait of John, who sits in his usual wing armchair which has fitted side pieces on which a plate or book can rest. The chair faces the blank TV screen, but John looks instead at the flickering coals of the fire, lower lip thrust out. Giles, the only one of them formally dressed, is a little apart in an upright chair, looking down at his shoes which have lost some of their polish because he has walked here through the slushy streets. Eleanor brings in coffee and biscuits, waits for John to speak. It is always John who starts and usually dominates a confab.

He does not speak, however, the coffee stays untouched at his side. So she speaks herself. David gives a jerk of the head at the sound of her voice, evidently brought back from whatever distant country he was inhabiting.

"The detective, Superintendent Catchpole, has talked again to the girl who said Jenny had telephoned. It seems she made up the story, I don't know why, but she's admitted lying. Apart from that he says there is no definite news." She looks at John, but he does not respond. "The question is what can we do now?"

At that John does raise his head and speak, in a voice whose dullness belies the authority of his words. "Anything that might happen has happened. Nothing we do can affect it."

"That's being, how shall I put it, altogether too drastic, John." This is Giles. "As the only person here who has some personal knowledge of police procedure, I can tell you they will be pursuing all sorts of lines of enquiry energetically. Most energetically." He then addresses himself directly to Eleanor. "My dear Eleanor, I'm sorry if I distressed you when we spoke, but I feel strongly that to advertise the worry we all feel, to make the affair public, can do no good and merely makes us look like—"

He pauses. Eleanor supplies words for him. "Sensation seekers?"

"A harsh term. Meddling with things that should be left to the police is what I should call it."

"Do you feel that too?" Eleanor looks at David and Mary. It is the latter who speaks.

"Surely anything, anything at all that might reach Jenny and help to bring her back is worth trying." She waits for comment, and when none comes turns to her husband and says almost savagely: "Don't you agree?"

David mutters some words which sound like agreement, lapses again into contemplation. Again Eleanor waits in vain for her husband. His silence makes her words sound, even to herself, more emphatic.

"I refuse to believe anything awful has happened to Jenny. She may be in trouble, but if it was anything worse I should know." She looks at them all challengingly but gets no response except an irritated sound from Giles. "If I'm asked to make another appeal on TV I shall do it. And we must try and find out things, trace her movements."

John looks up from the fire and says simply: "How?"

"You're overwrought." That of course is Giles. "I make allowances. But I do strongly deprecate the idea of your appearing again on television, writing articles in newspapers, being interviewed. Or of course playing amateur detective. Something like that might expose the family to ridicule."

The words sting David into speech. "The family, that means you. Do you think the rest of us care about any of that?"

Now John Midway speaks at last, with something like his old authority. "Eleanor will do what she thinks right, and I shall support her, no matter what it may be." It sounds like a final statement. "Unless any of you have other ideas—"

Nobody has. When the rest of them have gone Eleanor tries again to infuse him with her own optimism, uselessly. It is as much as she can do to get him away to the office in good order on the following morning, after he has dawdled over shaving and dressing, so that he leaves almost half an hour late. When he has gone she feels relief, as if a dragging weight attached to her has been removed.

4. *Roads to Nowhere*

The Californian was like fifty other clubs of the kind. Two or three small rooms had been knocked into a large one which contained a bar, several tables, and at one end a raised platform where a rock band made a lot of noise. A small space in the middle of the room offered the possibility of dancing, but theory rarely became practice, the noise generated by the Beasts being made chiefly because the people at the tables felt comfortable with some kind of background sound covering the things they were talking about, even when these did not concern criminal activities. Blackjack, dice and the humble brag were played in a back room, brag but rarely poker because the users of the Californian were mostly petty crooks and gamblers not well enough stacked for an evening of serious poker. The place was owned by a Greek named Lefty Venglos, named not because of his politics but because he had only one arm. The bouncer was an ex-pug known only as Rusty, who had a squashed nose to show for a mostly unsuccessful career in the ring. He recognized Catchpole, who asked if Gabriel Lewis was in.

Rusty's weakness in the ring had been the slowness of his reactions, and the years had made them slower. He considered for some seconds before saying no, and took longer to say whether Lewis had used the club lately.

"Nah," he said eventually. "Not Gabby. Nah. Leastways, I ain't seen him. Or if I seen him I misremember." Catchpole nodded, made to pass him. "Who you want? You wanna talk to Lefty, I tell him you're here."

"You'll tell him anyway," Catchpole said pleasantly. "I just want to look round, admire the scenery, have a word with Gabby if I see him. Tell Lefty that, tell him he's in no trouble." He hung up his own coat since there was no sign of Daisy, ordered a vodka with ice and chatted to Roger the barman, who confirmed that Lewis hadn't been around for a day or two. And where was Daisy?

"I dunno, shoulda been there, take your coat." He leaned over the bar, a shrimp with bad breath. "Look, Mr. Catchpole, no offence, you mind I don't talk to you, clients don't like it, get ideas in their heads. Anyway I'm busy." A memory stirred in Catchpole's mind that Roger had been used as a snout by Bertie Minnett, and he moved away, strolled among the tables, nodded to three or four men he knew. The darkness of the room and the noise of the Beasts had not concealed his presence. He was aware of movements, a couple of men got up and slipped away, papers disappeared from a table leaving three men and a woman staring silently at their drinks, carefully failing to notice him. He mildly enjoyed this, feeling it was the kind of respect crooks should pay a police officer, but there seemed nothing in the club for him. When Lefty came down from his upstairs office he greeted the club owner amiably, and asked for the word to be put around that he had come looking for Gabriel Lewis.

"OK, Mr. Catchpole, OK. Look around all you like. I run a straight club, no drugs, nothing like that."

"I'm sure that's so, Lefty," he said, although he was sure of no such thing. "Just put the word around I'd like to have a chat with Gabriel." It was no more than stirring the water, but who knew what might be brought up when you stirred? "I thought Daisy worked here, Daisy Dean."

"Sure does."

"She's not checking coats."

"Should be. Let's go see." There behind the counter was Daisy. Lefty jerked a thumb at Catchpole. "When he came in where were you?"

"A girl can't go to the toilet now? And what you come in here for anyway?" As she saw the detective's stare she cried out: "What you looking like that for, I done nothing wrong."

From each of Daisy's elegant ears depended a wooden earring, carved in the shape of a miniature man.

They brought Lewis in the next day, smiling. He was still smiling several hours later after interrogation by Catchpole and Wilson, Bertie Minnett and a tough sergeant named Stenhouse. He did not deny being given the earrings by Jenny and passing them on to Daisy. He said he had remarked on them to Jenny as real fun things. She had replied that since he liked them so much he could have them, took them off on the spot and gave them to him. It was an unlikely tale, as Catchpole pointed out. "What did she expect you to do, get your ears pierced and wear them?"

"I couldn't say, man."

"Can you think of any reason, any reason at all, why a woman should take off her earrings and give them to a man?"

"Hey, ain't you noticed, men wear 'em too? Can't give no reason, she just did it. I thought, you know, they were kind of cute and kind of like her, thing she did, keeping a man dangling. Sort of stuff she enjoyed, get me? Unexpected like." He said she had given him the earrings several days, maybe a week or two, before she disappeared. So how, Catchpole asked, could she have been wearing them on that day? Lewis suggested whoever said that was mistaken.

"Not so. Patsy Malone said she was wearing them, so did her boss at the art gallery where she worked."

"OK, then she musta had two pairs. Maybe more. Maybe she was really stacked with little man earrings, handed 'em out. *I* don't know." He lit a cigarette. The ashtray in front of him was full.

"Nasty habit," Catchpole said. "And you a boxer."

"Yeah, I agree. But when the filth is trying to fit you up you gotta steady your nerves somehow."

"Gabriel, I never fitted anybody up, and you won't be the first."

"OK then, I got nothing to worry about." And he gave a bigger smile than usual.

"These blacks, they're not like you and me," Minnett said when they conferred during a break in the questioning. "Lying just comes natural to them even when the truth wouldn't hurt. Is the Malone girl sure Jenny had just the one pair?"

"No, she's not. She had three or four pairs of wooden earrings, all different. There were a couple of animals, giraffe, rhinoceros, couple more she can't remember. She doesn't recall another pair like these. Which is not to say they don't exist."

"What are you, defence counsel?" Minnett picked up one of the earrings. "Perfectly formed, ain't he, like the man says." The little carved man had a tiny erect penis. "Think that's what she liked about them?"

"Could be. They look as if they're machine made, not hand. It's worth putting someone on to try and find where she bought them, Wilson's doing that. In the meantime, what's to do about our friend?"

"Try taking the smile off his face. Half an hour with Jerry Stenhouse and he won't be smiling, might be talking."

The boss, Bertie Minnett told Stenhouse later, just smiled slightly, shook his head, asked if the barman at the Californian was one of Bertie's snouts, and when he heard the answer was yes apologized for getting across him. "He's not a fairy, Miss Hilly, times I wish he was. He can be tough. Trouble is he wants to do it all by the book, and that way you don't get results."

The upshot was that they let Lewis go again. He was still in the frame as chief suspect, but the earrings and the fake call he'd told Patsy to report weren't enough to hold him. And within hours of his release there was another trail to follow. A man had reported to Canterbury police seeing a couple resembling those at the animal rights meeting. They had broken into a caravan in a caravan park, and the man who saw them had been threatened with a shotgun.

Catchpole and Wilson picked up the local Inspector and two constables at Canterbury. They all wore Smith & Wesson .38s and the constables carried M16 rifles. The two Londoners were unarmed, only local forces being allowed to carry arms on their own pitch. The Inspector's name was Rolling, which he wisely pronounced with a short "o," and he was loquacious.

"Nice part of Kent this, but run down since they closed the mines, Betteshanger, Snowdown, Tilmanstone," he said as they went down the A2. "Lots of unemployed miners, half of 'em unemployable, wonder we don't have a bigger increase in the crime figures. This man who's made the complaint, name of Adams, started off with a haulage business in Canterbury, bought some land near what used to be Betteshanger Colliery, got approval to open it up as a caravan site. Think you may have been told it was a park, not strictly correct, park you bring your own caravan, with a site they're all fixed and rented out. 'Course, some places combine the two."

"I know it," Catchpole said. "My father was a miner at Betteshanger."

"Is that so?" Rolling stopped talking about the miners. They turned off the A2 onto a side road. No snow was falling, but the banks on either side were white, and there were ruts in the untreated road. Wilson said he wouldn't have thought it was weather for living on a caravan site.

"Right on." Rolling beamed at Wilson. "Because it's a site and not a park it's closed up in the winter, services cut off. Unoccupied," he added unnecessarily. "Adams lives a couple of miles away, takes a look at the place every so often, make sure there's no vandalism and so on. This time he sees a woman coming out of a caravan, shouts at her, she runs back in, slams the door. Adams goes up to it, calls to her to come out, door opens, man's standing there with a shotgun, woman just behind him. Adams says they're trespassing, he'll give 'em till dark to get out, man points the gun says they're staying put. Woman asks what harm they're doing, says something about research into wildlife. Adams repeats he wants them out, he'll get the council to evict them, man raises the shotgun. Adams legs it out of it, gets on the blower to us at Canterbury. That's about the size of it."

"It's the woman who interests us," Wilson said. "Did Adams get a good look at her?"

"He says good enough. Sure it was the woman whose picture was on the telly. Mind you, he's the kind of man who's sure about everything. Here we are."

The house was red brick, detached and ugly. Adams, fittingly, was a small ugly man. He wore a duffle coat and a check cap. He looked pleased when he saw the rifles. "That man's dangerous. No use wearing kid gloves."

Rolling began to say soothing words. Catchpole interrupted. "Mr. Adams, we're not looking for a western shootout in which anybody's killed or injured. If it's simply a matter of a trespasser on your land there are procedures you can follow. My sergeant and I are here because it's possible the girl is Jenny Midway. What I'd like to know is how near you got to her, how sure you are she's the girl you saw on TV, and whether you saw any sign she's being held against her will. From the fact that you saw her going back to the caravan alone that doesn't seem likely."

Adams agreed he'd seen no sign that the woman was being kept by force, but said he'd been within a few feet and he was almost certain it was Jenny Midway. He added triumphantly that she was wearing some long earrings which he thought were wooden. He glared at Catchpole. "You've said nothing about the man. I tell you he's a bloody lunatic."

There were some twenty caravans in a muddy, snowy field. They looked very dismal. You would have to be eccentric or desperate to want to break into one, Catchpole thought. They all got out of the police van at the edge of the field.

"Last one on the left, second row." Adams stamped on the ground like an excited horse. When the detectives began to walk towards the caravan he stayed by the car. Rolling looked at Catchpole, who said, "It's your show." Rolling asked Adams: "Are all the caravans the same, two windows either side of the front door, one at the end, two at the back?" When the answer was yes, he told Catchpole and Wilson to stay where they were, sent one constable round the back of the caravan and approached with the other, one on either side. At a few feet's distance from the door Rolling produced a hailer and shouted through it: "This is the police. The caravan is surrounded. Throw out any weapons, then come out with your hands above your heads."

No sound came from within the caravan. Rolling had begun to repeat the message when the door opened. A shotgun was thrown on the grass. It was followed by a tall young man wearing torn jeans and a thick ragged sweater who looked at Rolling in bewilderment and said: "Jesus Christ, what's up?"

Adams made a grunting noise and approached at a trot, the two Londoners more casually.

Rolling said: "Where's the girl?"

"Jenny? Inside. She's got a touch of flu. What's it all about?"

Adams, up with them now, pointed at the shotgun. "You bastard—trespasser—you were going to shoot me."

"With that? I won it at a fair."

Wilson picked up the shotgun. It was a crude replica, of the kind sold in many toy shops. Catchpole went into the caravan.

It stank, less of human beings than of animal blood, shit and urine. At one end, in wooden boxes with wire stretched across them, were a fox, a dog and a cat. The fox had dirty bandages wrapped round the back of its body, the dog made a feeble effort to rise as Catchpole came in but collapsed, the cat had only one good eye and a bloody crust round the other. In the middle of the caravan wooden boxes served as table and chairs, and at the far end a girl lay, covered by old rugs. She propped herself on an elbow and said: "We're trying to save them."

The girl was perhaps eighteen, but looked older. Her face was so gaunt that her eyes seemed sunk in her head. She wore an expensive jacket and skirt now crumpled and dirty, and dangling silver earrings. She had a slight resemblance, no more, to Jenny Midway.

"Dead waste of time," Wilson said. "Bloody awful place. Glad to get away from it, guv, were you?"

"I was."

Catchpole said nothing more, and Wilson returned to the couple in the caravan. "They get on my wick. I mean, what do the stupid gits think they're doing? Ask me there's too many animals around anyway, but they want to save some, all right, take 'em to some animal welfare clinic, plenty of those around. Ask me they've just got no sense."

Catchpole said very likely he was right. He did not think of himself as a particularly sensitive man and indeed thought too much sensibility was a drawback in a policeman, but the hopelessness of the couple in the caravan remained uncomfortably in his mind. The girl who was not Jenny Midway had been turned out of the family home by her stepfather when she wanted to add an injured goose to the collection of damaged animals she kept in the garden of their home at Eastbourne. She was nineteen. She had met the man, who was twenty-five and called himself a peaceful anarchist, when they joined a group of animal activists who specialized in raiding laboratories and freeing animals used for experiments. They had decided to live as nomads, existing on an allowance sent to Jenny by her mother. Recently the stepfather had found out about the allowance and stopped it, which was why they had broken into the caravan. Without the allowance they had no money to live on.

What harm were they doing, the girl had asked Catchpole. Governments allowed cigarettes to be sold and at the same time put out advertisements saying they damaged health, farmers were allowed to spray harmful chemicals, car drivers killed or injured people and animals and were often given trivial fines. They were trying to save living things, not hurt them. It was not the whispered arguments but the mournful look in her great eyes that made the detective wish he could have done more than use similar clichés, telling her that she and her companion were not being punished for anything but damaging and breaking into private property. Do you really want to charge them? Rolling asked Adams. The little man said he certainly did, and repeated that he had been threatened. Catchpole told Rolling to try to persuade Adams that he would make himself look foolish by pressing charges, but the image of the thin-faced girl with beautiful eyes, the wrong Jenny, stayed with him. When he got home and Alice asked how it had gone, he shook his head. That morning he had told her he thought they might be on the right road. When she reminded him of this he laughed and said: "The road to nowhere."

On that same evening Eleanor had begun to prepare dinner when Stella rang up, wailing that she was in awful trouble. Harry was bringing people to dinner, important clients, she'd meant to give them a cassoulet, gone out and left the oven much too high, the cassoulet was burnt and uneatable, what was she to *do*?

She abandoned her preparations, wrote a note to John telling him where she was, saying he would have to manage with cold meat and salad, and gathered together a bagful of items from the food cupboard, the refrigerator and the freezer, including most of a large chicken, prawns, scallops, almonds, cream, broccoli and the remains of a Camembert. Making an impromptu meal was almost her speciality, and she was able to give Harry and his guests broccoli and Camembert soup, followed by what she called a Fulham paella, and syllabub. Stella insisted that she should not stay in the kitchen but come in to meet the company, to whom she was introduced as a miracle worker. A week later one of the guests, Bryan Connors, rang to ask if she would be willing to devise and prepare a meal for a small luncheon party he was giving in the boardroom at Purafood, the company of which he was managing director. She agreed. It was, although she did not know it, the beginning of a new kind of life.

5. *The Arrest*

Business was slack at Wayne, Mendelson, but in the afternoon David showed houses to three prospective purchasers. The first two had property to sell before they could buy anything, and in the sluggish state of the market that meant their enquiries were tentative. The third seemed a better prospect, a couple recently returned from some African state where the husband had been employed as an adviser to the government on ways of increasing food production. The Lovells therefore had no house to sell, and the husband spoke confidently of needing only a small mortgage. They were accompanied by their son, a talkative boy of seven.

David the estate agent was not the reclusive character known to his family. He knew when to point out the qualities of a property and when to stay silent, and could distinguish those seriously interested from those looking around to pass the time or in the hope that they might somehow manage to find the purchase money if a property was an obvious bargain. He quickly summed up the Lovells as serious buyers. The husband was an easily pleased pipe smoker, his stringy blonde wife the possible stumbling block. Wayne, Mendelson were basically Fulham and Chelsea agents, but had a few properties in Battersea and Wandsworth. Mrs. Lovell refused even to look at these.

"South of the river, no thank you," she said. David explained that old ideas about the inferiority of South London were now out of date, and that they would get better value for their money in Wandsworth than in Fulham. Mrs. Lovell gave a brief whinny.

"We may have been out of the country, but we're not as green as we look. Forget your Wandsworths and Batterseas, what have you got in civilization?" She added that she knew it was a buyer's market. Her husband chuckled approvingly into his pipe.

They looked at five houses in Fulham, Parsons Green which is really Fulham, and Chelsea, and after the third David revised his view of them as serious buyers to the effect that Mrs. Lovell would never find a house that suited her. Two were dismissed as poky, another as too noisy. The boy, whose name was Eric, took a hand.

"I don't want to live in any of these. I want to go back to Monagonga."

"You just be quiet, Eric."

"But Ma, I shan't be able to ride my bike. I could ride my bike in Monagonga."

Mrs. Lovell turned a dead-fish eye on David. "Your name's Midway. Are you any relation to this girl who's disappeared?"

"She is my sister."

"*Is* she now." The fish eye showed signs of life, even of interest. "Did you hear that, Granville? This young man's sister is the girl who disappeared."

Her husband removed the pipe, nodded encouragingly. "Very interesting."

"I saw your mother, I suppose that's who it was, on television. What do you think has happened to your sister? How long is it she's been gone now?"

"Just over a month."

"What do the police think? She must be dead now, I'd say, wouldn't you, Granville?"

Her husband puffed on the pipe. "Don't know about that. Remember that woman disappeared on a safari, turned up a month later in Kenya, safe and sound?"

"That was different. She was with a man. Could be the same with this girl. Still, gone over a month." She shook her head.

For the final half-hour, while they looked at the last two houses, she battered David with questions about what Jenny was like and what might have happened, the vibrant harshness of her voice twanging in his ears like false notes on a piano. At length he said: "We're supposed to be looking at houses, Mrs. Lovell, not discussing my sister."

She stopped what she was saying, pulling up like a horse refusing a jump, and did not speak again. When they got back to the office she complained to Barry Mendelson about David's rudeness, and the hopeless houses shown to them. Mr. Lovell put away his pipe and looked down at the floor. Eric broke in at one point, saying, "Ma, can we go? I like Monagonga better than London, Ma."

Afterwards David said he was sorry. Barry laughed, slapped him on the back, said Mrs. Lovell had given him a pain in the arse in two minutes, and he wondered David hadn't exploded after an hour and a half with her.

The work of a dental receptionist is less straightforward than the title suggests. For Mary it involved of course the making of appointments and the fitting in of urgent cases who said they were suffering agony from an aching tooth, an abscess or a dry socket. Beyond this, though, it was her role to reassure the surprisingly large number of patients who were terrified of the reclining dental chair and the masked face looming over them with what they felt to be instruments of torture in his hand.

She was gentle with new patients, telling them they would find Mr. Megillah ready to give a numbing injection at the first hint of a patient suffering pain. With regulars she had a brisker approach, saying they knew Mr. Megillah's skill and delicacy, and suggesting in manner though not in words that they were foolish to worry about what lay ahead. On the rare occasions when patients emerged from the surgery shaken and miserable she made them coffee, sat with them in the waiting-room and talked to them about things like the state of the housing market (she was well informed through David) and the increasing difficulty of getting around London by public transport. Few things are more cheering than the miseries of other people, and Howard Megillah was full of praise for her quality as what he called a cheerer-up. After three years as his receptionist Mary had little idea whether he was a good dentist, but liked his enthusiasm.

On the day David was exposed to the questioning Mrs. Lovell, Mary too had a reminder of Jenny. It came in the form of a new patient whom she recognized at once as Rupert Baxter, the friend of Jenny's she had met two or three times in Sapphic Street. He showed no sign of making a similar identification, but sat in the waiting-room nervously turning the pages of *Time*. When she told him Mr. Megillah was ready to see him he nodded and walked past her straight-backed and head up like a soldier going to a court martial. Twenty minutes later he emerged, and gave her a toothy smile.

She smiled back. "Not as bad as you expected?"

"Not half as bad. I say, I thought I knew you, and the penny's just dropped. We've met with Jenny, haven't we? I should have remembered before, but I'm the most awful coward when it comes to the old drill, I positively quail and everything else goes out of my mind. Look here, I wonder if you're free at all, there's something I'd offly like to talk about."

It was midday. She said she would be free for lunch in a few minutes, but that for her it was a sandwich and a cup of coffee.

"Sounds just the thing." Fifteen minutes later she sat opposite him in a Wigmore Street snack bar. "It's something Jenny said to me the last time I saw her. Not that it seems important, but I haven't told the police. Frankly, I'm more nervous of them than I am of your Mr. Megillah, and that's saying something." When he laughed, as he did now, he looked no longer vacant but attractively boyish.

"No secret I'm keen on Jenny, think she's a wonderful girl, never met anybody quite like her. Not sure she was ever so keen on me. She's been out to Chislehurst, met my people, they thought she was lovely. Then going along to be vetted by John and Eleanor, I like them and seemed to me they liked me. But Jenny, I don't know." He paused, shook his head, looked at the glass of wine he had ordered. Mary refrained from telling him to get on with it.

What he had to say turned out to be something that embarrassed him, so that he did not look at her but at the sandwich and the glass on the small round table in front of him.

"Expect you know I stayed once or twice at that flat she shared in Balham, can't imagine why she lived there, but then that's Jenny isn't it, part of her charm." He expected no reply, and she made none. "Last time I saw her, three weeks before she disappeared, we went to some film she was keen on, supposed to be the latest thing. Then had supper and I thought we were going back to Balham, but she said—" He stopped, began again. "She said there was no point going on, she'd done with all that."

Mary said she was sorry, and at that he did look at her. "You don't understand. The way she spoke it wasn't just that she'd finished with me, though that was part of it, but as if she'd done with some particular sort of life."

"You mean she was giving up her job?"

"More as if she was giving up one sort of life for another. And it was something I had no place in, she was saying goodbye to me. At the time, you see, I thought it was just one of Jenny's moods. Now I think she meant it."

"But you haven't told the police?"

"It didn't seem to matter, just rather humiliating for me. But if she was really thinking of making a complete break and doing some different sort of thing like going on an Arctic expedition or mountain climbing, perhaps I should say something, though I don't want to. Apart from anything else it might upset John and Eleanor, and I wouldn't want that. I don't know them well, but I like them both very much. How are they taking it?"

"She's marvellous. I think John's still in a state of shock, and Eleanor's being what they call supportive. Though I think what he really wants is a shoulder to cry on."

"It's awful for them both." He flushed. "I mean—don't think I'm callous, but after this time I think something must have happened."

"You mean Jenny's dead?"

"I—yes, I suppose so, though I don't even like to think of it. Perhaps she's doing something outrageous, and wants to keep it secret."

"Perhaps."

"Funny, isn't it, I can talk to you, you're sympathetic."

"So Mr. Megillah says. Really I just listen."

"Mr. Megillah? Oh yes, the dentist. Anyway, what do you think, should I go to the police?"

"I don't see why. They already know Jenny may have gone off on some wild-goose chase, and you'd certainly be asked a lot more personal questions. My advice is, stop worrying about it."

"I'll try. And you can tell Mr. Megillah I said you're not just sympathetic, you're wise too."

It did not occur to Rupert, then or later, that she had not expressed an opinion about whether Jenny might be dead.

* * *

Giles Midway's life had for years been conducted according to a satisfactory routine. He had never married, never felt any inclination to do so, nor to live with another person, male or female. Harkland Court, the block of flats in Pimlico facing the Thames where he lived, had a restaurant and a swimming pool, and he used both almost every day of the year. He swam several lengths of the pool on rising, and then breakfasted on wholewheat toast and marmalade, with strong Darjeeling tea ordered specially for him. When Court was sitting his arrival was always punctual. Lunch was brought to him in chambers, and when the day's duties were over he returned to find his rooms cleaned by Mrs. Entwhistle, whom he had employed for five years. He usually ate dinner in the Harkland Court restaurant, listened to German or Italian opera (his taste ranged from Wagner to Verdi), and looked at the papers relating to whatever case was before him. He watched little television, had no interest in sports, and saw no newspaper but *The Times*, which he read thoroughly every day.

Giles's appointment as a High Court Judge had come after a fairly undistinguished career as a barrister, mostly concerned with fraud cases. There was a joke, not really believed but often told, that his name had been confused with that of a much brighter and sharper QC named Midship when the time came for making a judicial appointment. To the surprise of his critics, however, Mr. Justice Midway had made no serious mistakes in his time on the bench, and there were few appeals from his judgements. He might be a dull dog, as Eleanor often said to her husband, but John was right in his reply that the dull dog was a persevering one.

The dull dog had one recreation, which he thought of as a little private game. Three or four times a month, though there was nothing regular about it, the little game was played. He took off shoes and socks, plain grey suit, vest and briefs, and put on silk panties, a different vest and the unnecessary brassière. He made up his face with care, putting on a touch of rouge and turning the almost colourless pink of his thin lips into an attractive red bow. A fairish wig fitted neatly on his grizzled head, and then came the absorbing problem of choosing one of the dresses he had bought over the years. He chose one that fitted the season and his mood, added sensible but not flat-heeled shoes, and the result was that a pleasant rather sharp-faced middle-aged woman looked at him in the mirror.

This woman then went out for an evening's entertainment. It might include a visit to a cinema where the person Giles in his mind christened Gilda would always sit next to a man, even when there were plenty of vacant places. This could be followed by dinner alone at a quiet little restaurant, followed by a visit to a club where the sound was deafening, the drinks expensive and the mostly youthful clientele paid no attention to the odd-looking woman who walked a little awkwardly. Sometimes the club was obviously used chiefly by gay people. Once or twice, in such a place, there had been an invitation to a party by somebody, man or woman, who said: "We're *all* cross-dressing tonight," an invitation that prompted an instant retreat.

But that was unusual. There would often be a good deal of walking around in the area of King's Cross and Victoria railway stations, ideal places for that part of the game Giles privately called Watching. The streets near by, rather than the stations themselves, were places where prostitutes paraded and were picked up by men, often in cars, sometimes by men who went with their pickups straight to a nearby hotel. Walking these streets, standing around in the stations, was done simply as an observer. Men leaned out of cars and called to the middle-aged woman occasionally, prostitutes sometimes gave warning of trouble if they thought an attempt was being made to use their pitch, but it was easy enough to walk away. Only rarely was it necessary to apologize to the girls and disclaim any intention of causing trouble, and this was done in a voice whose cracked falsetto made them look oddly at the respectably dressed woman. Once a girl, one with a skirt that ended at the top of her thighs, had said: "We're on to you, you bleeder, get out quick if you don't want to be cut." Behind her a figure conjured out of darkness had appeared, a small dark man whose hand showed a glint of steel. That had been a stomach-turning moment, yet in retrospect one to be savoured for its danger, for the look of hatred on the girl's face and the ambiguity of her words.

Back in Harkland Court, with his Watching gear off, soaking in a bath, Giles would reflect on how much it was possible to learn on such expeditions about the kind of human beings who came before him in Court. If he wore fancy dress when out Watching, did the wig and robes he wore when sitting on high constitute another kind of fancy dress, a kind that found its echoes in the clothes of those who solemnly pleaded cases before him? There were moments when he wanted to say to the petty gangsters, thieves and prostitutes who came before him: "I understand your activities, I know the kind of lives you lead, and how easy it is for you to slip into an existence ordered by the need for drugs, fear and love of the pimp who runs you, or simply because there is no way at all in which you could make a living honestly." But of course he did not say anything of the kind. The fact that he had never responded to the occasional suggestions made in the street and in clubs, never brought anybody back to Harkland Court, was a triumphant proof that temptation could be resisted. He tended to be if anything a little more severe on such transgressors from the underworld or under-class than on apparently respectable citizens who came before him on charges of commercial fraud or domestic violence. Watching was, after all, only a game.

* * *

Horton Lucas, the member of the MultiCorpus Board responsible for everything related to staff matters, was a much feared man. It was said he had his snooper in every section of the firm, office and works, who reported weekly to Horton on problems in their departments and on such matters as power shifts within them.

To be called in for what Horton called a little chat about their work was for many a preliminary to their departure from MultiCorpus. Some were so shaken by revelations of how much Horton knew not only about their office work but also their private lives that they left rather than (this was said to be hinted at) becoming Horton snoopers themselves. Horton, who in person was soft-spoken and a frequent smiler, said that he rarely sacked anybody, and that was true. It seemed that often they dismissed themselves, so that perhaps all the tales about Horton were untrue, but still John's secretary feared the worst when one morning John was asked if he could spare time to have a chat with Horton. He had arrived late, as was often the case now, late and looking what she thought of as woebegone. There was a little dandruff on his collar, which she brushed off.

Horton was a small man behind a big desk in a large office. He greeted John with a smile, and his manner was gentle as he asked if there was fresh news of Jenny, and received a negative reply. Had the police made any progress? Dully, John said not so far as he knew. Horton expressed the deepest sympathy with John and Eleanor in their time of trial, and then moved smoothly into a different gear as he said John had been late every day that week. He waved apologies aside. "My dear fellow, it's quite understandable. Nobody suggests you should have a time clock. And you'll remember I suggested you might like to take a week off, but you said no. Really the time of arrival or departure is of no importance, what matters is that the work gets done." His sigh, his sympathetic smile, his sad headshake, were masterly. In his gentlest voice he said: "And that isn't happening. Is it?"

John watched mesmerized as Horton pushed papers across his desk. "This is an assortment—a selection, I should say—of matters awaiting attention which have been brought to my notice. Some of them are urgent, others less so, but what is our Director of Personnel doing about them?" John began to say something about them being in hand, a little delayed, but his voice trailed away at the sight of Horton's shaking head. "Here is one Mrs. McCabe threatening action over what she claims is our medical negligence, which has caused her illness, something for which she says we are responsible. Has our Director of Personnel seen her?" The question was rhetorical, Horton's sad smile its answer. "Has he asked our Dr. Dennis for his views, found out if she has been treated for whatever it was before she joined us? No, our Director of Personnel has done nothing. We do have a problem, John, I'm sure you'll agree . . ."

In John's office Susan, a well-fleshed rosy-cheeked woman, anxiously awaited his return. She had been John's secretary for three years, and had always adored the masterful quality of his manner. When he returned she asked what had happened. He said Horton had just called him in for a talk, but his extreme pallor and appearance as of a sleepwalking statue told her it was more than that. It seemed natural, inevitable, that she should open her arms and he sink into them. Awkwardly, shuffling like boxers in a clinch, they moved around his desk.

She sat in his chair and he sank gradually to his knees, face buried in her skirt, body heaving with hiccuping sobs. She stroked his thick hair, murmured words of consolation, tried to find out what had happened. At length he raised a tear-stained face, gave her a watery smile and said Horton had given him a month to get things straight in the department, it had been no more than a warning. But tears came again as he told her his whole life now seemed meaningless, with Jenny gone and Eleanor somehow changed. How had it happened, he asked, how could it all have happened? To that she had no answer, but when he stood up she stood too, and said with a slight giggle that it was the first time she had sat in his chair. Their faces were so close that the kiss seemed inevitable. Inevitable, yes, but Susan was surprised to find her lips opening, a furious flickering of tongues, his mouth mashed on hers.

No words were spoken, but the moment was decisive. They worked throughout the day and made a start on the cases he had neglected, although he was still only a shadow of the forceful figure she admired. When they left the office they went without discussion to the flat in Stoke Newington Susan had lived in since parting from her husband. John Midway returned to Fulham at ten-thirty in a state that blended exhilaration and guilt. Fortunately Eleanor was so intent on telling him about the luncheon she had prepared for the businessman she had met through Stella that she seemed hardly to notice his lame words about lateness at the office.

"To sum up the position, Catchers," the Big Man said, "this boxer Gabriel Lewis has got one girlfriend to try some kidology about a phone call, given another a pair of earrings belonging to the missing woman, been seen with her in a pub. So why is he still walking around, not banged up?"

"Primarily lack of a body. And there's not enough we're sure will stick."

"You think there is a body? She's dead?"

"After this length of time the odds must be on it. If she's alive she's done a wonderful job of vanishing into thin air for several weeks." He hesitated. "About Lewis, sir, I still have a tail on him, making himself obvious. Doesn't seem to faze Lewis, he seems to regard it as a joke."

"Do something he won't think is a joke. Spread the word around he's the one we want, get him going. Get a warrant, turn over his drum."

"No permanent address, stays mostly with girlfriends."

A little impatiently the Big Man said: "Then turn over the girlfriends' drums. Kick up some dust, make a fuss, let friend Gabriel see he can't just cock a snook at us and get away with it. Mind you, Catchers, you know your man and I don't, this is only advice. The last thing we want is parades of bleeding hearts clamouring about racism."

And that means if there's trouble you step out from under, leaving yours truly to be sprayed when the shit hits the fan, Catchpole thought. But advice of this kind was a sort of instruction, and he got search warrants for Daisy Dean's and Patsy Malone's apartments. They found nothing in Patsy's, which as she pointed out had been informally searched before by Catchpole himself. She viewed the proceedings coolly, asking them only not to smash up the furniture. Daisy, however, protested all the time. She lived on the ground floor of a tall, narrow house in a street off the Old Kent Road. Her place consisted of a small front room with a bed in one corner, a couple of old armchairs, a TV and some new-looking audio equipment. There was a similar sized bedroom with pictures of black sportsmen and pop stars pinned to the walls, and a kitchen with a small table with three chairs, and a dresser containing chipped cups and plates. A lavatory on the half-landing was shared by those on the next floor.

"What you lookin' for? You tell me what it is I tell you if I got it," she said. "First you take my earrings, then you just 'bout go around wreckin' everything. It's persecution, I'll complain to the Town Hall."

"You do that, Daisy," Wilson said equably. He pointed to the audio equipment. "Drop off the back of a lorry, did it?"

"You think a girl don't ever buy stuff? I paid good money for that, I tell you, 'cause I like to listen to hot rock and stuff, what's wrong with that?"

"No need to get your knickers in a twist, it's not what we're looking for." They emptied drawers and turned over bed-clothes, but found nothing more than some cannabis which Catchpole told Wilson to forget. He asked if Lewis was staying with her.

"Not since you come round, he don't stay with Daisy now. I don't know why he left—" She stopped, looked frightened.

"Left what?" Wilson said. "Come on, what did he leave? It's here in this flat?"

"No no, just mean he left here, don't know why, 'cept you're persecuting him and me too."

"That's not the way you said it. He left *something*, what was it? You want us really to do this place over, we can do that if you want."

"No, ain't nothing here. He kill me if I tell you, he hurt me bad."

Catchpole stopped Wilson, spoke quietly. "Daisy, you're going to tell us. If you say nothing we'll take you down to the station, lock you up and throw away the key. If you've done nothing there's no cause to worry, but if you try and hold out on us it won't be Gabriel you'll have to worry about, you could be up as an accomplice to murder. It's murder we're talking about, am I getting through to you?"

A few minutes of this, with Wilson chiming in, and they did get through to her. What Gabriel had left was a car. A lock-up garage went along with Daisy's apartment, one not adjacent to the house but a hundred yards away, down a side turning. Daisy used it only as a storage place for junk, but a few weeks ago Gabriel had said he wanted to store a car there for a while. She had given him the key, he kept it, and when she asked for it back said he needed to keep the car there a few more days.

"There's no car registered to Gabriel," Wilson said. "What's the make?"

"I dunno. I never seen it."

"So you don't know it's a car in there, it's just what Gabriel told you." She agreed. "Now think, be careful. What day was it he asked you for the key?" It was the day of Jenny's disappearance, something she was able to confirm because before that he had not been to see her for two or three weeks. Gabriel had arrived on the Saturday as he said, but the rest of her story about being shacked up until the following Wednesday was fiction. Gabriel had been out all day Sunday, then come back early Monday evening and asked for the key to the lock-up. Then he had stayed with her until Wednesday.

"I got some stuff of mine round there," Daisy said. "Stuff I'm looking after for a friend, see."

"What kind of stuff?"

"Dunno, I'm only looking after it, doing a good turn."

"Oh, Daisy." Wilson shook his head. "Could be you have something to worry about, never mind Gabriel."

The side turning was a cul-de-sac, no more than a large yard. On either side of the yard were numbered lock-ups, three or four with metal doors, the others rotten-looking wood. Daisy's lock-up had a metal door with a thick padlocked bar that made it firmly shut. Wilson put in a call for a crew with oxyacetylene equipment, and they then stood around for half an hour.

"You reckon she's in there, guv? He killed her, panicked, put her in the car, maybe got rid of her since then and still worried about bloodstains in the car?"

Catchpole shook his head. "Doesn't add up. If this was the car, who drove her Golf back to Balham? And where did she go in it when she left the art gallery? The lock-up's a place for parking stolen stuff, no question about that. Daisy gets an occasional present like the audio equipment for letting them use it."

While the oxyacetylene boys got to work on the bar, and Wilson told several watching teenagers to move on, Catchpole felt the uneasy twinge of excitement he had experienced before, when persuading a man who had shot and killed his wife and still had the revolver in his hand to give himself up rather than try to use it again on the detective. In the moments of waiting he visualized with surrealist clarity a body wrapped in sacking in a corner of the lock-up, only partly concealed by various boxes put in front of and around it, and with a telltale bloodstain trailing across the floor. The image was so strong that he recoiled in momentary disbelief when the bar was severed and Wilson lifted the up-and-over door to reveal a car. Of course this was no surprise, it was what they had expected to find, yet the image of sacking and bloodstains was so strong that the actuality came as a shock.

The car was a green Rover, the lower door panels thick with mud. Wilson stated the obvious, that it looked as if it had recently been driven quite a distance. "Ten to one it's been half-inched," he said, called through with the number and asked for a check on the owner. With a gloved hand Wilson tried the door handle. The car was unlocked, and a torch shone inside showed no sign of a struggle, no sinister stains. At the back of the lock-up a number of packing cases were stacked. Wilson opened two of different shapes. One contained a new TV, the other a music centre. Catchpole shook his head, murmured, "Daisy, Daisy." The car had been backed into the lock-up, and they went round now to the boot. Wilson lifted it, shone the torch on cleaning rags, a deicing pack, a bottle of windscreen wash, jack and tyre lever. "Hallo, hallo," he said. "Do you see what I see?" Under torch light the tyre lever, which like the jack lay loose in the boot, looked stained.

"One for forensic," Catchpole said. "Just shine that torch a bit closer, will you. Yes, I thought so." Adhering to the stained patch on the tyre lever were several hairs. In the dim light it was not possible, even with the torch, to be sure of their colour. Catchpole repeated: "Definitely one for forensic." The tyre lever was wrapped in plastic and lifted out, Catchpole ordered a guard on the car, and they went back to the Yard.

A few hours later he was in possession of more facts. The Rover was registered to H. K. Simpson, who lived in Hertfordshire just outside Hemel Hempstead, and had reported the car stolen on the Sunday before Jenny disappeared. Simpson was a salesman for a firm who sold bathroom accessories, and had been attending a weekend sales conference at the head office in Highgate when the car was taken. He was quickly cleared from the investigation, and became indignant about the delay in returning his car. Three sets of Gabriel Lewis's prints were found inside the car. There were no prints on the tyre lever, but forensic were able not only to say that the marks on the lever were human bloodstains but also to identify the grouping as B rhesus negative. Only 15 percent of people are blood group B, and of that minority no more than 8 percent are rhesus negative. The grouping B rhesus negative is thus found in slightly more than one percent of the population.

To avoid alarming the Midways unnecessarily Catchpole told Wilson to see if Jenny's doctor had a note of her blood group. He had, and Wilson returned triumphant. The group was B rhesus negative. He was surprised to find Miss Hilly less elated.

"We've got the geezer who saw 'em together in the Brixton pub, got Lewis getting one girlfriend to tell a fairy-tale about a phone call and trying to fake an alibi through another, we got the stolen car with his dabs, we got these stains on the tyre lever that are her blood group, and there's one in a hundred in that group. What more do we want?"

"A body, Charlie. We want a body."

"Rest of the case is strong enough you can manage without.

Remember that chap pushed a girl out of a ship's porthole, thought he was safe enough, she was in the deep blue sea, can't convict without a body. So he thought. But he came unstuck."

"Camb, yes. Lucky to get a conviction."

"Seems to me if we bring Lewis in again, tell him we've got the car and the rest of it, odds are he'll cough."

"It isn't just that there's no body. There are too many holes. Why should Lewis steal a car if they were going somewhere, why not use her car? If they had a fight and he killed her, it seems to me it would most likely be by strangulation, not with a tyre lever. And the pub doesn't seem to fit. Say they're in the Brixton pub, all right, what happens next? Do they go off in his stolen Rover rather than in her Golf, and if so why? And what happens to the Golf?"

"Could be he's doing a job, she goes along because she gets a kick out of it. Something goes wrong, she loses her nerve, starts screaming, he gives her a tap with the tyre lever, only means to knock her out, panics . . ." Wilson's voice trailed away as he saw Miss Hilly's amusement.

"Charlie, I never knew you had so much imagination." He raised his hands in a gesture of mock resignation. "You've made your point. Let's have him in again."

They brought Lewis in once more, a Lewis at first loudly indignant, then distinctly worried and clamouring for his brief. They worked on him in relays for long sessions with only short intervals between, Bertie Minnett and Joe Stenhouse, Catchpole himself and Wilson, and a couple of others. In relation to Jenny Midway they got nowhere. Lewis admitted taking the car on the Sunday before Jenny's disappearance, saying he had an impulse to see an old friend down in Portsmouth and needed wheels. He failed to find the old friend, spent the rest of the day drinking, slept in the car Sunday night, spent Monday in Portsmouth, most of it with an ex-boxer named Sammy Grizzard and his girlfriend, returned to London on Monday. Sammy Grizzard, whose record included stretches for fraud, extortion and receiving stolen property, confirmed the story, but what else would one have expected? Lewis explained the attempted alibis through the invented phone call and the five-day stay indoors with Daisy by saying the police had it in for him.

Why had he hidden the car on returning to London rather than just abandoning it? Because he liked having wheels, he said, and thought he might get a respraying job done, have new plates fitted and keep it. With the smile that maddened all his interrogators he said: "Nice job that Rover, surprised me. And I'm a patriot, like driving British." The stains on the tyre lever? He knew nothing about them, had never even opened the boot.

It was a thin story, and there were times when Lewis showed uncharacteristic signs of unease when telling it, an unease particularly related to the day of Jenny's disappearance. The time came when he had to be charged or released, and he was charged with being concerned with the abduction of Jenny Midway. He made a two-minute appearance in Court and was remanded for further enquiries.

In his journal Catchpole wrote:

"Today the Big Man congratulated me on having got the right man banged up. Then he asked with lifted eyebrows: 'Sure he is the right man, are you?' If I'd been totally honest I'd have said I was sure of no such thing, certain only that Gabriel was our principal and in fact only suspect, and that he wasn't telling the truth. But officialdom wants certainty, not honest doubt, and who can blame it? When I outlined the case against Lewis the Big Man nodded, though hardly appearing to listen, and said what we all know. Until we find Jenny Midway we don't have a case likely to convince a jury. No matter what happens, the Big Man's covered his back.

"Is Jenny dead? Even now I wouldn't bet on it, nor am I certain Lewis had anything to do with her disappearance. The story of what he did in Portsmouth on that Sunday and Monday has some support, not just from Grizzard and his girl but also from four people who saw him in pubs on those days. After midday on Monday, though, we have only the word of Sammy and his woman Carla who knows only a few words of English that he was in Portsmouth, not London or somewhere else. They're probably lying, but even if they admitted it we haven't got a cast-iron case.

"There are times when I have to fight against the knowledge that our methods of interrogation are like fighting one-handed. When I see Lewis's smiling, sneering face I feel—I *know*—that much rougher methods would probably be effective, force the truth out of him. What realism says is that when confronting crime-hardened cases we should be harder than they are. What society asks is that we should be *better* than them and still put them behind bars.

"True, no doubt. By doing what society asks, shall we get a result? Not so certain, not by any means. After those sessions with Lewis it's easy to understand why detectives fake notebooks when they *know* a man's guilty. Do I approve? Of course not. But the fact remains: the balance of what's permitted and what's denied is too much in favour of the suspect, and should be changed.

"Here endeth Hilary Catchpole's lesson. But who's he teaching?"

Catchpole rang the Midways himself to give them the news about the blood group on the tyre lever. He spoke to John Midway, who made no comment. *Yes*, he said when the detective told him, and *yes* again when Catchpole said it might still be a coincidence. Then Midway did say something more than the single syllable.

"You think you've got the right man, but he's not admitted it."

"All I can tell you, Mr. Midway, is that he's been charged in relation to her abduction."

"But he's not—" Midway stopped and resumed. "Not told you what he did with Jenny's body?"

"At present he's made no admission at all in connection with her." Catchpole found it hard to express earnestness, but tried to do so as he said they were still following several leads. This was true enough, although none seemed likely to produce results.

"Thank you for keeping us informed. My wife is out at present, but I shall tell her when she comes back."

Catchpole put down the telephone, relieved that at least the man hadn't burst into tears, as had seemed likely from the sound of his voice.

This was a Friday. Eleanor had been involved in some way with arranging a drinks party for what John thought of as her pet businessman, and didn't return until after eight o'clock. She heard the news calmly, while putting a casserole to heat up in the oven.

"I'm sorry to be late. This shouldn't be more than half an hour."

"Is that all you have to say?"

"What else? There's nothing certain about it. The blood similarity may be a coincidence."

He thumped the kitchen table. "What else can possibly have happened? Why won't you face facts?"

"I will, when we know them."

The two people who faced each other across the supper table were changed from the couple who had celebrated their wedding anniversary a few weeks earlier. It seemed to him strange that she should be unaware of the astonishing and disturbing things that had happened, and by this he meant not only her refusal to accept the loss of Jenny, but also Eleanor's imperception of his unfaithfulness. How could the woman to whom he had been married for so long lack understanding of the need for that sympathy given by Susan, how was it possible she should show so little feeling? And Eleanor, as she looked at the man shovelling food into his gut without a word of appreciation, was conscious that the decision-maker whose words she had accepted as law had perhaps never been more than a façade concealing the uncertain figure whose occasional glances from under his thick brows now seemed, like the jutting of the lower lip, to be pleading for some response she was not able to give or even to understand. Between them, separating them, lay the shadow of the missing woman whom they thought of as a girl. The gap yawned in the indifferent words they exchanged, in the image of Susan that stayed in his mind as he lay in bed beside Eleanor, and the bitter contrast she felt between his lack of interest in what he called her cooking service and the appreciation expressed that very day by Bryan Connors. Both were aware of future possibilities they did not quite consciously contemplate.

On Saturday Alice farmed out the children to friends who had boys of similar age, preliminary to spending the day with her mother in Hove. Catchpole went with her, not from any desire to see Mrs. Longley, but chiefly because they both knew his absence would be remarked on unfavourably. It was raining as they left London, but streaks of sunlight appeared as they reached the Sussex border, then suddenly the clouds cleared. He opened the sliding roof, late April sun warmed them. Catchpole felt, as always, a lifting of spirit with the spring.

He began to talk, began to fantasize. They had got rid of the kids for the weekend, were on their way not to a valetudinarian in Hove but off on a dirty weekend in Dieppe via Newhaven. He elaborated on the hotel, told her exactly where it was just off the front, described the suite he had booked in such detail that for a moment she almost believed him.

"Hilly, you haven't really—"

"The letter from them is in my wallet. Dinner tonight. There's a hundred and twenty franc menu, but I went for the two hundred and fifty. We start with langoustines—"

"Now I know you're kidding, you'd never spend that much on dinner."

"Just coming to the Newhaven turn-off. Here we go, we'll call your mother from Dieppe."

"Hilly." The turn-off safely past, she sighed. "It would have been lovely. I know you don't like Mother, it's good of you to come."

"It isn't so much I don't like her, more that I know if we go to a restaurant she feels I should be waiting on table instead of sitting at it."

"It makes things easier for me when you're there. And sometime we'll manage that Dieppe weekend."

"Indeed we will. Before long."

"How's the disappearance case?"

"In the hands of Bertie Minnett. He'll do some more grilling, but until and unless we find a body Lewis'll be laughing. They'll call me if anything surprising happens."

"I ought to tell you. Brett will probably be there."

"You've made my day."

"Why don't you like him? Just because he's my brother. I believe you're jealous."

"It's not that."

"What is it then? You've got to admit he's bright and quick and clever."

He avoided saying he had seen a lot of men with just Brett's quickness and cleverness go down for a variety of frauds. Instead he replied pacifically that perhaps it was because Brett seemed so much the apple of his mother's eye, or perhaps he was envious of someone whose wits were sharper than his own.

"Now you're putting me on. Trouble with Brett is he's got no staying power."

He could not resist saying that the trouble with Brett was that he wanted to make a lot of money quickly without working for it.

"Like all those Stock Exchange yuppies you hate?"

"Perhaps."

It was as near as they got to bickering.

Mrs. Longley lived on the sixth floor of a big block of flats in King's Avenue. Brett opened the door, spread his arms wide. In the living-room Mrs. Longley offered her cheek to be kissed. She was a stately, handsome woman who wore rimless glasses that enhanced a general air of disapproval. Her grey hair was faintly tinged with blue.

"Now you've arrived we can celebrate," Brett said. He went out of the room, returned with glasses and a bottle of Veuve Clicquot. At thirty, with a marriage, a divorce, several affairs and various abortive enterprises behind him Brett was still resolutely boyish, his manner innocent and confiding. As he popped the cork and poured, Alice asked what they were celebrating.

"The birth and success of Ivorine Traders." Over the next ten minutes Brett explained that Ivorine was an amalgam with a metal base that looked indistinguishable from ivory but could be produced at a fraction of the cost of the genuine article. The ashtray and small figurine he showed them certainly looked and felt like ivory. Brett seemed to get younger by the minute as he explained how while acting as a travel courier he had met a scientist named Prenzyle who was looking for a backer to market this fantastic product he had patented, and how Brett had put him in touch with a couple of men who had money available, and . . . Catchpole found his attention straying.

". . . go into full production next month. With the ban on ivory hunters making the price of ivory go through the roof the market's wide open." And he told them the estimated turnover for the next three years. Alice listened with the indulgence an adult might show to a child, blended with pride in the child's cleverness. She gave an occasional glance at her husband to see how he was taking it. Brett spoke to him, his manner part wary, part mocking.

"What do you think? Feel like investing and making your fortune?"

Catchpole repressed a desire to ask what had happened to Brett's enterprise before last, as European representative for a Taiwanese firm selling high quality china at prices far below those of Wedgwood, Minton or any other English rival, and instead asked what made Brett think a policeman had any money to invest. Laura Longley made a sound that in somebody less genteel might have been called a snort. Brett laughed.

"Just kidding. Santoro, who knows a gold mine when he sees it, has provided the necessary. Now, ladies and gentleman, your carriage awaits."

Catchpole looked at Alice who said: "We'd booked a table for lunch, but I expect we can cancel it."

"Of course you can," Brett cried. "Just tell me the phone number, Sis, and I'll say you're ill, rushed off to hospital by ambulance, husband who's Assistant Commissioner Crime at Scotland Yard has been called to the Palace to investigate bomb left by IRA man posing as footman, whatever you like. I said this was a celebration, and it's all laid on."

When Alice had made the call Brett offered his mother an arm. The car was a Volvo. "I got it to try to convince the police I'm a solid citizen," Brett said, and winked. Alice laughed, even her mother raised a smile. A free day, Catchpole thought, what a way to spend it.

The restaurant was not Wheeler's nor English's, but a little place Brett knew, where the proprietor welcomed him with literally open arms. Catchpole was brooding on the way Alice became a different person with her family, one transformed into meek subservience to her mother and brother, when he became aware that Mrs. Longley had spoken to him, almost for the first time that day. What had she said? Through the rimless glasses she looked at him and found him wanting.

"I asked if you attributed the present wave of crime to the foreigners who are flooding into the country? You must see a great deal of it. No doubt you have an opinion."

My opinion is it's a bloody stupid question, you old trout. He said he thought it was impossible to attribute the increase in crime to any single source.

"Really?" The word conveyed a heavy weight of disbelief. "You are right in the middle of it. That must be most distasteful."

Brett chimed in. "The girl who's disappeared, Jenny whatnot. You're in charge of that, I read. Sounds as if there was a lot going on we didn't hear about. What's the inside story?"

Alice looked at her husband. Control yourself, she seemed to be imploring, I know you detest questions about work but this is my baby brother. Before he could reply his bleeper sounded.

"Good heavens, what is that noise?" Mrs. Longley watched with distaste as he listened to Wilson's voice. "Sorry if I'm breaking in on anything, but I thought you'd want to have the news."

"You've found a body?"

"No guv, no joy there. Thing is, he's coughed."

"Lewis?" He did not believe it.

"Lewis, yeah. Saw the game was up, I s'pose, only a matter of time. Coughed, anyway. The lot."

He left them at the luncheon table. Alice kissed him, patted his cheek. Brett said it had been good to see him. Mrs. Longley's glance expressed her feeling that policing was not an occupation for a gentleman. Catchpole returned to London by train, leaving Alice the car.

In the office Wilson blotted out a smile when he saw the look on his boss's face, and simply handed him the sheets Lewis had written and signed. Catchpole did not look at them. "How did you get word of this, Charlie?"

"This morning Lewis saw his brief. It was Maddox. Soon's he'd gone Lewis says he wants to make another statement, come clean. This is it. Admits he killed her."

"After talking to *Maddox?*" Maddox was one of the sharpest briefs employed by villains. "Who'd been with Lewis before then?"

"I told you, he saw Maddox and—"

"Who *interrogated* Lewis before that is what I want to know, and when."

"Last night, late. I talked to him an hour and a half—"

"And he stuck to his story?"

"Right. Then Bertie Minnett and Stenhouse. They got nothing, it's all on the tape."

"So he sees Maddox and coughs. Come on, Charlie."

Wilson moved uneasily. "May sound dicey, OK, but it happened. All written down, hangs together."

Catchpole sighed. "Last time I saw Lewis was like the last time you saw him, so why did he change his story? He's smart enough to know what we've got is thin till we find a body, and if he didn't know it Maddox would have told him. How long did Minnett and Stenhouse have with him on Friday night?"

"Fair time, couple of hours or so. I said, it's on the tape."

"And you saw Lewis after that? No? Anybody see him between Minnett and Stenhouse on Friday, then Maddox on Saturday morning? To talk to and look at, I mean, not just shove a plate in the cell?" Wilson said not so far as he knew, but what then? "What then is we don't want to drop into any holes kindly dug for us by Curly Maddox. Get a doctor to look at Lewis, see if he's got marks on him that could mean he'd been roughed up. And I'll talk to Inspector Minnett."

Wilson was deflated. He indicated the sheets on the desk. "You don't rate this, not worth reading?"

"I didn't say that, Charlie. Of course I'll read it. Trouble is you can't believe everything you read." But when he read Lewis's statement he saw Wilson had some basis for his enthusiasm:

> I now wish to change my statement about what I did on Monday February 25th. What I said before about stealing a car on Sunday and going to Portsmouth was right. On Monday, however, I did not stay in Portsmouth as I said, and asked Sammy Grizzard to confirm. On Sunday I telephoned Jenny Midway and told her I wanted to see her and talk. We'd been having arguments, she said she wanted nothing more to do with me, and I couldn't take that, it got me down. She said she was busy and thought it would be no good, but in the end agreed to meet me at her flat in Balham the next day, Monday, after lunch. When I got there just before two p.m. she opened the door. I don't know if she drove her car back from her job, I know nothing about that. I left the Rover in the car park under her block of flats. I didn't notice her car there, but of course wasn't looking for it. I was wild about Jenny, never had such good sex as with her, thought if we went away together for a few days everything would be OK again. I was flush at the time after a good win at Catford dogs. But when I saw her she said we were all washed up, and there'd be no point in going away together. I got angry, we argued, I hit her, knocked her out. When she fell she hit her head on the edge of a table. After that I wasn't responsible for my actions. I mean, I don't really know what I did or why. I was still determined we'd go away together, suppose I thought she'd come round as she'd always in the past been keen on me.

I picked her up, took her down to the car park, put her in the Rover, and began to drive to Brighton, which is where I'd thought we'd stay. She was in the front passenger seat and I'd put on her seat belt. It must have been around half an hour later she came round, said she had an appointment and must get back to town. I think she was still concussed or whatever you call it, because what she said didn't always make sense. She was very abusive, kept repeating we were washed up. For a while she was only half conscious, but then she came round and tried to grab hold of the steering-wheel. Then she pulled on the handbrake to stop the car, and got out. This was on a road somewhere between Standen and Ardingly, I took minor roads not the motorway because it was a hot car. I can't place exactly where it was, but there was a field on the left with cows in it, another field on the right. She got out and made for the field with the cows. I followed and grabbed the tyre lever, which was on the back seat of the car, not in the boot, because I'd had a puncture on the Sunday and changed the tyre. I don't know why I picked it up, but I definitely had no intention of hurting her, just wanted her to get back in the car. I suppose I thought if I threatened her she'd do that. But when I caught up with her she struggled, called me names, tried to get the tyre lever. I was struggling to keep hold of it and suppose I must have hit her, though I don't remember doing so. She fell over then, and I went on hitting her, I don't know how often. She stopped moving, and I was frightened. I took her back to the car, put her on the back seat, a rug under her so the blood wouldn't mark the car seat, put the tyre lever back in the boot. I was wearing gloves because it was cold. I was meaning to take her to a hospital, say there'd been an accident, but when I stopped a few minutes later she'd stopped breathing. I decided I had to get rid of her, didn't go to Brighton, but got on the A22 and went to Beachy Head near Eastbourne, which I'd never been to but read about as a place for suicides. All this time it was bad weather, rain and mist. It had been misty when she stopped the car and ran off into the field, visibility was only a few yards. Because the weather was bad I reckoned there'd be nobody up there, and by the time I got there it was dark. I parked the car near the cliff edge, wrapped her in the rug, carried her to the edge, dropped the body over. Because of the darkness and also I don't know the area, I couldn't say the spot exactly. I was in a state, forgot the tyre lever, else I'd have thrown that over too. Then I drove back to London and put the car in Daisy's lock-up, asked her to say I'd been with her the whole week-end. I should like to say I definitely didn't mean to hurt Jenny, she provoked me and I just went crazy for a while. I must have been crazy or I'd never have done it.

There were unlikely points in the story, like the convenient placing of the tyre lever in the back of the car to make seizing of it impulsive rather than deliberate, and Jenny leaving her job to go back to Balham and talk to Lewis when she had an appointment in the afternoon, but nothing in it was actually impossible. It left unanswered the question of why Jenny would have parked her car half a mile away from her flat instead of in the underground garage. Of course she might have parked it in the garage, and then Lewis or somebody else driven it later to Hazelrigg Road to create a bit of mystification. All in all, Catchpole was inclined to think the story partly true and partly invented. No body had been washed up on the south coast that could conceivably have been Jenny's.

He was not cheered by the result of the medical examination of Lewis. The doctor found bruises and scratches on the prisoner's arms, legs and abdomen, and abrasions on the back of his head. They could have been the result of an assault, but could also have been self-inflicted. None of the injuries was serious. A fork with tines sharpened to needle point was found under Lewis's bed, along with a piece of wood shaped like a rudimentary truncheon. Lewis, of course, said they had been planted on him.

Catchpole talked to Lewis, asked if he was making an accusation about any of his interrogations. He glared at the detective.

"You got my statement. Nothing else to say."

"You're going up for murder, you know that." No reply. "You're not a fool, Gabriel, I'll give you that. If you want to add anything to this statement—"

"I told you, nothing else. You got it all written down, I signed it, what more you want?"

Bertie Minnett was cockahoop. Put on the pressure, keep it up for long enough and they crack, wasn't that what he had always said?

"You and Stenhouse are at him for two hours or more on Friday night. You get nothing. Saturday morning he sees his brief, makes this statement. What happened in between?"

"I'm not with you. It's all on the tape."

"Was he duffed up?"

"I said *it-is-all-on-the-tape*."

"It's what's not on the tape that worries me. Did you and Stenhouse go down and duff him up on Friday night? Not on the tape. In the cell."

Of course Minnett denied it, said the injuries must have been self-inflicted. Was he telling the truth? The Big Man was tolerant, ironical.

"A prisoner beaten up in his cell to get a confession. Can such things be?" He tapped Lewis's statement. "You're not happy?"

"I don't understand why he made the statement at all, not even if he was beaten up. He's a boxer, used to taking punishment. But it's obvious the defence will be that a confession was beaten out of him."

"Not only a boxer, but a heavyweight. And these injuries aren't serious, no question of need for hospitalization. I doubt if that defence will stick." The Big Man steepled his fingers and spoke in his most reasonable tone. "We have a confession, he's our number one suspect. Unless there's some overwhelming argument against it I should say we're bound to charge him with murder, although of course the decision is up to you. No denying it would be nice to have a body, and by the time the CPS have delivered their verdict about whether we should go to trial I hope you'll either have the actual corpse or something else our boxer can't wriggle out of. This"—he tapped the statement—"commits him more thoroughly than he may have intended. Well done, my dear fellow."

Which again is the art of covering your back, Catchpole thought. If it goes smoothly we both come up smelling of roses. If it's a cock-up I carry the can and he's still smiling, saying I was in a position to evaluate the confession, he had faith in my judgement, I was the man in charge. He put down in his journal: "When you get to the Big Man's position you need never admit to a mistake if you're shrewd enough, it's always a subordinate who's wrong. But how do you get to that position?" A couple of minutes later he added: "The art of passing the buck, is that what I want out of policing? If not, what *do* I want? Nothing high-flown, that's for sure, but more than passing the buck."

He rang the Midways to keep them in touch with what was happening and this time spoke to the wife, who sounded much calmer than her husband. Even so he was surprised by her reaction.

"You haven't found a body, Superintendent. Has it occurred to you that is because there's none to be found? I know Jenny is alive, I can feel it. The man you have, Lewis, is lying for some reason, I don't know why."

This echoed Catchpole's own fear, but he had to control irritation when he asked if her certainty meant she had heard something from or about Jenny, and she replied that some things were inside oneself, things a woman and a mother simply *knew*.

A few minutes after he had put down the telephone Higginbotham's head appeared round the door.

"Something you might like to know. Your smooth Italian operator is in one of those wonderful flying machines, winging his way across the Atlantic. My information is he's given up the prospect of an English sale or perhaps never intended one, and is on his way to set up a deal in the States. Don't suppose it matters now you've got your man banged up, but I thought you'd like to be kept up to date."

Irritation was restrained with greater difficulty. He asked Higginbotham to tell him whatever he was saying straightforwardly.

"Is it too difficult for ye, laddie? One Signor Fraschini, whose ill repute I have apprised ye of, is away over the sea, in hopes of selling a picture by that famous painter of large ladies in the bath known as Renoir through a gentleman name of Eversley Grayson, the said gent acting as agent for some American person or persons unknown. Plain enough, Catchers? Good. No use you asking questions, my information goes no further and may be of no interest, except that as I've already told ye, anybody who does a deal with friend Fraschini and comes away without losing his jacket and trousers deserves a medal."

6. *The American Connection*

A recurrent unease was stirred in Catchpole by Higginbotham's words about Fraschini and his possible American sale of the possibly fake Renoir. Did he really have the right man banged up? And wasn't it odd that a relative of Jenny's should be involved? He thought about it for half an hour, then made three telephone calls.

The first was to Louis Arts, where Maurice said Mr. Meyers was out of the country. In America? Certainly not, he was in Cologne negotiating about a show of work by a very interesting German artist. Catchpole asked if he was still hoping to sell the Renoir being offered by Signor Fraschini. Maurice's tone was lofty as he replied that he couldn't say.

"You mean you don't know?" Silence. "Look, sonny, this is information I need in connection with the disappearance of Jenny Midway."

"I really don't see—"

"*You* don't see? What makes you think you see or know anything? Do you want to talk on the phone or in a police station, because I can easily arrange that? I want to know who owns this painting, and where it is now."

Five minutes later he had learned that the painting was the property of a count who, Maurice said in a hushed voice, came from one of the most distinguished families in Italy, and insisted that the sale must be absolutely private. He had been told also that Fraschini had been here only to test the level of British interest, and had said it must be offered first to a client of Eversley Grayson. The client wanted verification of the picture's genuineness and had insisted on this verification being made by a professor at Harvard who was one of the greatest living experts on Renoir. At this point Maurice's voice moved up a note. "There's been a lot of fuss about this, because Gifford's allergic to flying, he was involved in an accident once and nearly killed, so he just won't fly."

"I'm not with you. Who's Gifford?"

"Professor Gifford, Dale Gifford. He's the Renoir man."

"I'd have thought the Renoir man would be French."

"Oh well, perhaps. But this is the one the buyer wants."

"And who's the buyer?"

"Nobody knows. Or at least Louis doesn't. That's one reason for all the fuss."

"I don't understand. What fuss?"

Maurice's voice took on a note both superior and whining. "Gifford won't fly, and says he can't spare the time to come over on the *QE2* or whatever. The buyer, this American buyer, insists on Gifford. So the picture's been shipped across to the States for him to look at it."

"It's actually been shipped?"

"Oh well, no, it went by air. But they got customs clearance from Italy."

"I'd have thought that would be a problem."

"You don't believe anything I say, it seems to me." Catchpole did not deny it. "For Heaven's sake talk to the Count. Perhaps he can convince you. If he'll talk to you."

The second call was to the Count, a call made after checking up had shown that the Count was indeed from an ancient Italian family, and a famous one. He traced his lineage back to Gian Gastone, brother of the last of the Medici and himself the last Grand Duke of Tuscany. The professor of European history Catchpole spoke to proved only too eager to talk about the history of the Medici and the uncertainty of the Count's descent from them in view of Gian Gastone's homosexual preferences. Cut short, he reluctantly agreed that, whether or not his claim to Medicean descent was a good one, the Count was certainly a genuine Italian aristocrat.

An aristocrat who was quite ready to talk to an English policeman, and not reluctant to answer questions about the picture. Catchpole began the call in his serviceable Italian, but was relieved when the Count turned to English, in which he sounded amused and not in the least worried. He confirmed that the picture had been sent by air to Mr. Eversley Grayson in Massachusetts, and that he had been told of its safe arrival. Wasn't this an unusual procedure? Catchpole asked.

"I should think very unusual. Perhaps unique. But you understand I am not in the business of selling pictures. My ignorance is considerable."

"I'm not asking for figures, but would I be right in thinking you agreed to it because the amount mentioned as a possible purchase price is a high one?"

A pause, a chuckle. "You can say it is more than the estimate of the picture's value given by an expert here. And now, Superintendent, let me ask you something. You've told me this call has something to do with a girl who had disappeared. Do you have any reason to link Ettore Fraschini to her disappearance? Can you tell me any reason why I should not let Signor Fraschini handle these negotiations? You can't? Then I don't understand why you are asking the questions."

Catchpole explained that they were still not sure what had happened to Jenny Midway.

"But I have read something about this affair, that a man is arrested in connection with it. Correct? You see I read *The Times* and the *Guardian*, I am up to date. But you are still not satisfied, you think Ettore Fraschini perhaps had something to do with it. Believe me, you are mistaken. I have known Ettore a long time. You must be careful of him, but not in that way. He might take a girl to bed, but he would not make her disappear. He may cheat other people, but he will not cheat me. He knows it would not be wise." His laughter was loud down the line. "And now, you have been polite and not asked why I am selling the Renoir, so I will tell you. My father died recently, and this is what you would call an heirloom. It has been in our family for a century or something like it. My father and I we are alike, we enjoy ourselves and don't bother much about money. Money is just a bore when you don't have it, you agree? But now I am being hounded for taxes my father got out of paying for years, and this is a simple way of paying for them. Besides, to be frank I don't much like Renoir."

Afterwards Catchpole did some more checking, with an Ispettore in Milan. The Ispettore rather approved of the Count, who owned several racehorses and loved gambling, but was not at all surprised that he needed to sell a picture, nor that he had been able to come to an arrangement about an export licence quickly and without trouble. The Count of course had influential political friends, and in any case as the Ispettore pointed out, Milan was colloquially known as Bribesville.

Catchpole told all this to Higginbotham, who said it sounded above board, but it would be against Fraschini's nature not to be playing some trick, although perhaps not against the Count. His advice was not to worry. "Just as long as he's off our turf what does it matter? Let the Eyeties and the Yanks sort it out between themselves. I'll bet in the end they'll find Ettore's got away with something, but it's no skin off your nose or mine, laddie."

Very likely that was true, and it was hard to see any possible connection with Jenny, so why did Catchpole feel it might be some skin off his nose? Probably because his uneasiness about the case against Lewis would persist until Jenny was found, alive or dead. His third call was to Eversley Grayson, who sounded surprised to hear from him, but confirmed that the Renoir was in his possession, awaiting approval from Professor Gifford, who was busy with classes and would be coming out to inspect the picture on Saturday. Fraschini was in New York going round galleries. He would be coming up to Boston on the shuttle, and then out to the village twenty miles away where Grayson lived. Like the Count, Grayson said he understood an arrest had been made and was at a loss to know why Catchpole should be interested in the sale of a picture.

A truthful answer would have been that he did not know. Instead Catchpole said there were loose ends to be tied, even though they might have no direct connection with Jenny. He then asked if Grayson would have any objection to his being present when Professor Gifford examined the picture.

A longish silence. Then Grayson's voice, slower than usual, said: "I suppose not, if it will clear up any suspicions you've got, though I can't imagine what they are. But I can't speak for the other parties in the deal."

"You mean Fraschini? If you give me his number in New York I'll talk to him."

"There is also my client."

"He'll be there?"

"His representative. I don't know that he'll like it."

Catchpole said harshly: "We're talking about your sister. Half-sister."

"And you're really saying it might be helpful? All right. I'll talk to Fraschini and to the buyer's representative, and if there's any problem I'll call you back. Dale Gifford is another matter. He's something of an oddball. It might amuse him if you came along as his assistant. If he agrees, that's all I shall tell the others. If I tell them you're from Scotland Yard one or other of them will probably call the deal off."

"I don't know anything about pictures."

"That's why it might amuse Gifford. And me. You're putting me to a lot of trouble, Superintendent, you shouldn't grudge me a little amusement. And if you do, that's the end of it. Take it or leave it."

Catchpole took it, with the mental reflection that Grayson must be worried about something to consent to a police presence on any terms at all. Half an hour later Grayson called back to say Gifford was ready to accept the arrangement, and that he had told Fraschini and the potential buyer's representative that the Professor would be bringing an assistant.

Catchpole disliked flying, which he felt to be frightening, unnatural and uncomfortable. He travelled economy in a packed jumbo jet, with a fat Chinese on one side and a woman with an eighteen-month-old child on the other. The child took a fancy to Catchpole, kept trying to clamber on his lap, and when he succeeded left the detective's trousers damp. The Chinese kept up an only partly intelligible conversation about the supermarkets he owned in the Boston suburbs. Catchpole tried with little success to read a book on art forgery by a man named Kurz that Higginbotham had recommended.

In London it was spring. In Boston winter lingered, in the form of an east wind that made his thin raincoat seem nonexistent, and brought a memory of his father cutting beef with an electric knife. *Zizz-zizz* went the knife, *zizz-zizz* went the wind, slicing him in half. From an anonymous hotel room he rang Gifford and got no reply. Airline food had left him hungry, yet disinclined to contemplate exposure to that cutting wind in search of a restaurant. A Mountain burger in the hotel coffee shop did nothing to cheer him up.

His room was intensely hot, and there seemed no way of making it cooler. From an eleventh floor window he looked down on men and women leaning into the wind, then blown back by it as they turned a corner. He jotted down a few notes reflecting his mood:

> A good deal of police work is time wasted, not just the mountain of paper work indispensable from any bureaucracy, but time spent talking to people who have nothing to do with whatever one has in hand, chasing up possible leads that peter out perhaps without even learning whether they are directly linked with the investigation, so that they remain loose ends. What I'm doing here isn't good police work, if good police work means expecting a result. The way to get a result is to go after Lewis and bury everything that says no or perhaps. Common sense says that's the way to do it, and if you get a result four times in five you shouldn't worry about the fifth time when you don't, or maybe the result's wrong. Better a few possible innocents banged up than a lot of villains walking away laughing because a couple of loose ends weren't tied.
>
> Do I believe that? Or is the fact that this room might have been put together by a robot getting me down? "Catchpole, write out a hundred times 'I am not a bleeding heart.' " It's just the itch to be *right* . . .

He read what he had written, pulled the page from his looseleaf notebook, tore it up, went to bed.

In the morning the room had mysteriously cooled down, and he felt better. He rang Gifford again, and a voice answered on the first ring, saying: "Gifford."

"This is Hilary Catchpole from London. I—"

"Ah hah, yes. My assistant." Would a laugh have been in order? None came. "Where are you? Copley Square, right. Pick you up in an hour."

"Perhaps we should talk before—"

"I'm a busy man, Mr. Catchpole, sure you are too. We can talk in the car."

Catchpole believed voices were an index to appearances, and thought Dale Gifford's voice belonged to a short tetchy man, probably red-faced, and carrying too much weight. The man who met him in the hotel lobby was tall and slim, with a large aristocratic nose. He wore a double-breasted overcoat of a kind similar to those favoured in the winter by many of Catchpole's Clapham neighbours, and briefly inspected the detective through a monocle before saying: "So you're Scotland Yard's art expert. How much do you know about Renoir?"

The question caught Catchpole off balance. In any case, how could he have explained that although the Yard's Art and Antiques squad man would have known something about Renoir, he would have had no knowledge at all of the case to which this Renoir painting might (or might not) have relevance? His response was a weak *Not very much*, although at least he did not add to those words the feebler *I'm afraid*. Gifford gave a braying laugh, revealing large yellow incisors, put in the monocle and stared at Catchpole, dropped it again, shook his head, led the way out to a large saloon and opened the passenger door with a flourish. It seemed unlikely that they would get on.

"They send me a mock assistant who knows *not very much* about Renoir." Gifford shook his head. "No surprise. All, all of a piece throughout. Are you better on Dryden than on Renoir, Inspector?"

The time had come to put a stop to this. Catchpole said: "I'm not an art critic, and I don't read much poetry. I'm here to investigate a woman's disappearance, and the sale of this picture may have something to do with it. If it seems objectionable to you that I should be called your assistant, say so and I'll find another reason for being there when we arrive. Grayson seemed to think the assistant idea would amuse you, but plainly it doesn't. And by the way, Professor, it's not Inspector but Superintendent." He placed a very faint emphasis on *Professor*.

They approached a row of toll booths. "These are a unique way of squeezing money out of motorists that you haven't properly developed in England," Gifford said. He spoke again when they were through the booth. "I owe you an apology, I let annoyance get the better of my manners. The annoyance should have been with myself for taking on this preposterous assignment, but I transferred it to you. Unforgivable. But please forgive me. If you don't I shall be upset, start driving too fast, and very likely pile us up into another car. You've noticed there's not much traffic on the road and that we're all behaving unnaturally, keeping inside the speed limit? That's because there are patches of black ice, we're living dangerously. Of course you're used to that. Just remember I'm a professor who hardly strays out of his study or classroom. And please take it that you're my assistant. I'm amused, as Grayson said. But tell me more precisely why you're here."

Catchpole told him, and was surprised by another braying laugh. "I know what your occupation was before you joined the force. Shall I tell you? Chasing wild geese. And I bet you never caught one." This moved him to a paroxysm of mirth. Reflecting sourly that Gifford was easily amused, Catchpole asked why he called their mission preposterous.

"Good question. Here's why. I'm being dragged away from my comfortable home on a weekend to pronounce a verdict I may not be able to give. The truth about art fakes is they're either so obvious anyone who can tell a Picasso from an Edward Hopper can tell they're phoney, or else they're so well done it's a matter of opinion."

"But what about van Meegeren, baking paintings, putting in cracks, browning varnish, that sort of thing?"

"You've been doing some reading." The laugh seemed to fill the car. "But not to much effect. Van Meegeren everyone knows about, he was copying Vermeer, did a good job, but it was the time of the Nazis. In any other period his fakes would have been spotted, for all his expertise with putting in cracks and so on. Faking modern pictures is a different matter. It's easy enough to do, there are art students who can do you a good Picasso or Miró. Old masters are much riskier nowadays, what with X rays, infrared, microphotography, all those gadgets they call science. With something painted in the last century, if you take care, make sure the paper or canvas doesn't date your fake wrongly, then we're down to the skill with which a forger has imitated a style and he may get away with it, at least for a few years. As I said, it may come down to a matter of opinion. But with a classic painter like Renoir it's different again. I've been assured the provenance is authentic." A note in his voice suggested that he expected a question. Was he disappointed when the detective told him of the conversation with the Count? If so he showed no reaction, but asked: "Do you know what a *catalogue raisonné* is?" He looked directly at Catchpole, his eyes gleaming with malicious amusement.

"For God's sake."

They went into a skid that took them almost across the full width of the carriageway. Gifford righted the car. "Black ice. Your nerves aren't what they should be."

"I'm only up to facing villains with knives."

He was rewarded with the braying laugh.

"I like you, Superintendent. I think we'll get along. Well, do you know?"

"I think you're going to tell me anyway."

"Quite right. It has some bearing on our enterprise. A *catalogue raisonné* is a complete and methodical listing. It can be of anything at all, all the public lavatories in London or all the mail boxes in Boston, but it's meant to be complete, and for some reason it's usually applied to paintings. There's a *catalogue raisonné* of all the important classical painters, including Renoir. This painting isn't in it, and must therefore be suspect in spite of its provenance. Hence the reason, or one reason, for Grayson's approach to me. I know him slightly, he was briefly a student of mine. Now I'll go back to what I asked you before. How much do you know about Renoir?"

"Not a lot. I know he was a French Impressionist, second half of the nineteenth century, painted a lot of nudes. Mostly women in the bath, weren't they?"

"Bits of knowledge can be worse than ignorance. Renoir began as an Impressionist, broke with the movement in the eighties, said it was a dead end and he had to go back to the classics. Changed his method of painting altogether, started to use glazes over a white ground with the effect of making everything transparent, luminous. Marvellous. Original."

"So he wasn't an Impressionist?"

"Yes, but only for a time. He was unique. You know what he said about English painting? It doesn't exist, they just copy everything. Bonington was the only one he had any time for." Catchpole was ready for his quick malicious glance, and did not respond. "Full of theories, English painters. Renoir never had any time for theory, simply *knew* when he'd come to the end of a style, as he came to the end of Impressionism. You know what he said in old age to some fool who asked about his technique of painting, what materials he used, how he mixed the paints and so on? 'I paint with my prick,' he said. Very good, that. 'I paint with my prick.' "

Catchpole felt irritation, and saw no reason why he shouldn't express it. "Nice for you to show me how ignorant I am, but I don't see it has anything to do with the reason I'm here. Still, thank you for the lecture."

"Don't be so touchy. It just might have something to do with what you're after. In any case you should be pleased to be getting all this information. We turn off here. More interesting route than staying on the turnpike. May be more black ice though.

"Let me tell you what I know or have been told about this picture. Some time in the seventies Renoir used to go to watch a group of Spanish acrobats who set up a tent on a vacant plot in Paris. They called themselves the Cirque Fernando. There were the acrobats, their children who were part of the show, some horses and a rather famous donkey. The show became well known, Degas made a painting of it and so did Renoir. He was still an Impressionist then. He painted two of the young girls as well, a fine picture, in Chicago's Art Institute now. What we're going to see is supposedly another painting of the Cirque Fernando, previously unknown. It shows the chief acrobat Fernando, the clown, whose name was Medrano, and a couple of horses in the background. Of course, all I've seen so far is a coloured photograph, from which one can tell nothing important." Catchpole said he had seen the same photograph. "Have you now? Then there's the matter of tests. I don't set too much store by them, but I understand from Grayson that the picture's survived tests on canvas age, nature of the pigments and so on, and that he's got certificates to say so.

"So why isn't it in the *catalogue raisonné*? The answer's in the story told by your Count, which is reasonable enough, though that's not to say it's true. I'm not directly concerned with it. I shall simply give my opinion as to whether or not Auguste Renoir painted the picture."

"If you say yes, the buyer will accept it?" Gifford said he understood that was so. "And who's the buyer?"

"Not my business. If you want to know, ask your friend Grayson."

"It's my business though, or might be. And I've never met Grayson."

Monocle in, quick glance, monocle dropped, the laugh. "Touchy, touchy. Remember, if they start asking questions about art you may be in need of my protection."

"I doubt it. I may need your help in another direction, though. I'd like to stay on afterwards and talk to Grayson on his own. Do you think you can manage an excuse for me to stay on?"

"Rely on me."

"It may be difficult, since I'm supposed—"

"I said, rely on me."

The village—or what in England would have been called a village, here a small township—looked like a picture postcard. Houses were grouped in a semicircle round a pond. Beyond the pond was a patch of green grass, then a rambling building calling itself "The Pottery," and next to it a hotel with a sign in Gothic lettering saying simply "The Inn." The Grayson house stood well back from the road, fifty yards from its nearest neighbour, an elegant white clapboard structure. They drew up beside a station wagon and a Cadillac. The pushed bell brought a passage from "The Mountains of Mourne." The man who opened the door said, "I'm Eversley Grayson. Good of you to come out at a weekend, Professor Gifford. Hope it wasn't too bad a drive."

"My assistant here made the time pass. He's a great conversationalist."

Grayson took their coats, said the others were here. He merely nodded to Catchpole. Grayson was a dark slim man of medium height, his manner coolly pleasant, almost unnaturally calm. He led the way to a large room where two men and a woman sat with coffee cups beside them. Grayson introduced them as his wife Sally Lou, Ettore Fraschini and Len Fosskind.

The psychology course at university had led Catchpole to a habit of summing people up at first meeting. He put down grey-haired Fraschini, who wore his clothes with conscious elegance, as a professional charmer, and a salesman who would know when to start making his pitch. He said nothing now, only smiled and shook hands. Grayson's ease of manner seemed to the detective assumed, a feeling enhanced by the uncertain glance he gave his wife. Sally Lou was blond, small, expensively dressed, pretty as a doll but with a rat-trap mouth now turned down at the corners. Was it always like that, or was something going on of which she didn't approve? She glanced at Fosskind, then said she had things to do and would leave them to it. And Fosskind, the buyer's representative? He lounged back now in a tub armchair, a lean man with a thin face, jet-black hair flattened to the top of his head with gel, and eyes like two small dark stones.

As if he had heard Catchpole's thoughts, Gifford said: "You're the selling agent, Mr. Fraschini? And what about you, Mr. Fosskind, are you the putative buyer?"

Fraschini said: "I would prefer the term art adviser. I am the Count's adviser in this transaction."

"And I'm not the *putative* anything." Fosskind's voice sounded as if it was coated with rust. "I'm acting for a possible buyer. If everything's right."

Grayson said easily: "Len's an attorney."

The rusty voice asked: "Does it matter?"

"Not to me." Gifford inserted the monocle, inspected the lawyer, dropped the monocle, repeated: "Not at all." Catchpole admired the dexterity of a put-down all the more effective because not an objectionable word had been said. "The picture's here, I presume. So let's get on with it."

When the painting was brought in Catchpole was surprised and disappointed. He had seen the photograph, but somehow had expected a large painting, something around the size of the abstract that occupied a quarter of the longest wall in this room.

Instead, the painting was no more than fifty centimetres one way by thirty-five the other. If it had been hanging in the living-room at Clapham nobody would have taken much notice of it. One man held the end of a trapeze, the other had his face made up and wore a clown's hat. Two horses were vaguely shown in the background, and behind them was an even vaguer glimpse of spectators. Catchpole liked vivid colouring in a picture, and the greens and blues of this one seemed to him merely wishy-washy. It seemed absurd that this was what he had crossed the Atlantic to see.

The others took it seriously enough. Behind Fraschini, who carried the picture, came Grayson with an easel. The picture was placed so that light from the window fell on it, and Gifford approached the easel. He took down the picture, turned it over and looked carefully at the back, examining especially a label on the top right-hand side. Then he replaced the picture on the easel, took a large magnifying glass from a case in his pocket and examined the painting inch by inch, paying particular attention to the figures. This took a little more than ten minutes. During this time Grayson maintained his air of studied calm, Fraschini stood smiling slightly, Fosskind stayed in his chair and lit a cigarette. At the snap of the lighter Gifford turned and seemed about to speak, but refrained. It occurred to Catchpole that he should be taking some part in what was going on, or at least show interest. He approached, as if about to inspect the picture on his own account. Gifford turned and said peremptorily: "Fetch my briefcase from the car."

Catchpole felt a blend of relief and indignation, relief that he would not have to demonstrate any expertise, indignation at being ordered about. The drop in temperature outside the house made him shiver. He looked into the station wagon and the Cadillac, and turned the door handles. The Cadillac was open, but a quick glance inside revealed nothing except a copy of the *Law Quarterly Review* on a back seat that told him the owner's identity. The locked station wagon contained specially built racks for pictures. Perhaps the racks held other pictures Fraschini had bought or wanted to sell, but it was not possible to be sure because only the edges of the racks were visible.

He found the briefcase and took it to Gifford, who extracted what looked like a small telescope. He extended this and began another minute examination, less lengthy than the last. Then he closed the telescope, turned, and said as if announcing the birth of a healthy child: "My congratulations to whoever becomes the owner. They will possess a piece by Renoir, painted at some time between 1878 and 1880, in his best manner at that time. There is no doubt in my mind that this is a genuine Renoir. The mass of little multi-coloured brushstrokes making up the clown's clothing, and the fusion of blues and greens, are absolutely typical of Renoir's painting near the end of his Impressionist period. Of course they could be imitated, but they are done with a freedom that belongs to an original artist and not a copier, and a pleasure that again belongs to the artist and not to a faker."

While this was being said Catchpole took the opportunity to look at the painting more closely. Were the brush strokes multi-coloured? They seemed to him just a confused blend. On the back was the small hand-written label Gifford had examined. As he bent down to read the faded writing he became aware that the Harvard professor was talking about it.

"A label on the back of the picture says 'For M. Chocquet,' with the words then crossed out. That seems to me significant. Victor Chocquet was a customs officer with a passion for art, who began to collect Renoir when his work was totally unfashionable, almost unsaleable. Renoir was grateful, painted two fine portraits of the customs officer, introduced him to other painters. But Chocquet didn't like all Renoir's work, only the early paintings. The label suggests the picture may have been put aside for Chocquet, he rejected it, and it was then sold to the Italian family in whose possession it remained. This would explain why it didn't appear in any of the unsuccessful exhibitions the Impressionists held, that and the fact that I would date it at the end of his Impressionist period."

"The label could be a fake." That was the lawyer.

"Possibly. I am not an authority on labels and inks. I presume it has been checked as far as possible." He put in the monocle and looked at Grayson, who nodded. "It's unlikely that a fraudulent label would be attached to the back of a genuine picture. And as I have said, I have no doubt at all that this is a Renoir."

Fraschini exhaled. Fosskind said: "You'll put that in writing."

"Of course." With a touch of contempt Gifford said: "I can do it now if you wish, and one of you gentlemen can witness it."

Fosskind shook his head. "Not necessary. You just send a piece of paper with some official heading, putting down what you've said here. With reasons. All I need. My card."

Gifford accepted the card with an expression of distaste, turned to Grayson. "I have to go back. Happy to have been of help." He waved aside suggestions about staying to lunch, then spoke to Catchpole. "I want you to look up those details about the Hobbemas. Talk to the man at the Brooklyn Museum of Art, he'll know what I need. Come out to the car and I'll give you the details."

When they were outside he said: "Looks as if you've had a wasted journey. The picture's genuine, so where does that leave you? If I were your boss I should be asking was your journey really necessary? Phrase used a lot in your country during the War, I understand." He took out a handkerchief, blew his nose.

"If it's all above board, why is Fraschini mixed up in it?"

Gifford opened the car door, got in. "That's for you to answer, not me. Bear in mind, though, there's a lot of money involved, perhaps enough to make a crook turn honest." He closed the car door, opened the window. "Happy to have enlarged your artistic education. Not that it was difficult."

Sally Lou was waiting for him just inside the door. She took him into a room with a TV in one corner, two mobiles hanging from the ceiling, pictures occupying almost every inch of wall space. "They're in conference now. Evers thought you'd want to see him afterwards, and of course we'd love it if you can stay to lunch. Can I get you a drink?"

Catchpole told her the Harvard Professor had said the painting was an authentic Renoir, and asked if her husband often did deals like this.

"He certainly doesn't. And I'm not sure I like this one."

"They're not usually this big?"

"I'll say. I just hope he knows what he's doing. Dealing in pictures is dicey enough without—" She seemed to lose the thread, gave up the sentence. "I don't like that Fosskind, he makes me shiver."

"He's acting for the buyer?"

"That's what Evers says. And however much the money is, we can do with it. Evers says he's there to make money, me to spend it. Suits me." She cut off a laugh as if she had said something improper. "You're from the British police, Evers said." He put a finger to his lips. "You're here about Jenny, I suppose? I liked her, she was fun, real fun. Do you think she came out to the States, is that why you're here?"

He was saved from replying by the appearance of two small boys wearing baseball caps and plastic or rubber coats that made them look like miniature Michelin men. They told tales of riding bicycles down School Hill, and clamoured for crisps. When Sally Lou took them away Catchpole looked at the pictures on the walls, which confirmed his belief that he knew nothing about art.

In the living-room Grayson said to Fosskind: "That leaves you happy?"

"Happy enough."

"We can do a deal, talk figures?"

"Depends on the figures. And you'll be giving me the necessary bits of paper."

"Of course. I've got the results of all the tests, X rays and so on, that Ettore had done in Italy. And you heard Professor Gifford."

"Heard and didn't like. Snotty bastard, giving us a lecture."

"He's the greatest Renoir expert over here. If you want to consult somebody else—"

"No point. I just said he was a snotty bastard."

"Then let's talk figures. Like four and a half." Fosskind shook his head. "So tell us what you had in mind."

"Three."

Grayson and Fraschini exchanged glances. The Italian said: "That is out of the question."

"Okay." The lawyer unwound his long body from the chair. Fraschini protested.

"This is no way to do business."

"I didn't make it clear? I've got a figure, I told it you. You like it, that's fine. You don't like it, no deal."

"We should get more putting it up at Christie's or Sotheby's."

"Then put it up. But you won't, you know you won't. Your Count wants a private sale, we both know it. Which is why Grayson here approaches my client with whom he's done business before, satisfactory on both sides, right?" Grayson muttered what could have been agreement, took out a handkerchief, wiped his forehead. "We can do business again, but let's inject a little realism here. You know my client keeps what he's got to himself. You sell to him you'll never hear another whisper, and how many people can you say that about? Another thing. A picture ain't a refrigerator or my Caddy, no fixed price on it, it's worth what it'll fetch. You say four five, I say three. How many people you know ready to put down that kind of money on the spot for a picture? They're queuing up, you go talk to 'em." The little dark eyes looked from one to the other of them, the voice creaked to a stop.

Grayson and Fraschini looked at each other. Grayson said: "Excuse us a couple of minutes."

"Take ten."

When they returned Fosskind was at the window. Grayson said: "Look, we can show you the saleroom figures for Renoir in the last couple of years. The Japanese paid—"

"I don't want to hear. You want to fuck the Japs, go and do it. You want a deal or not?"

Fraschini said: "Three and a half. I couldn't go back to the Count and say anything less."

"And fuck your Count too." A pause. "All right. In consideration you had some expense, bringing the picture across the water, getting that glass-eyed professor to talk crap about being an original artist and that, I'll say three and a quarter. And think before you say no to that, because then I'm away and the deal's off. No more horse trading. I shouldn'ta said what I just said."

Fraschini nodded. Grayson said: "I think it's underpriced, I *know* it is, but all right. We agree."

Fosskind addressed the American directly. "Not we, *you* agree, it's you I'm dealing with. Far as I'm concerned this gentleman doesn't come into it." His manner relaxed a little. "You give me the papers you talked about say this wasn't painted last week, I take the picture with me. You get the money the day after my client sees the picture. You send on glass-eye's say-so when you get it."

Thirty minutes later the Cadillac had crunched away up the drive. Before that Catchpole and Sally Lou had been called in to drink a celebratory glass of champagne. Fraschini had smilingly proposed a toast to Renoir, then wrapped the picture and taken it out to his station wagon to fix it between wooden slats for safe carriage. Fosskind came out, took the picture from the Italian and placed it in the Cadillac. His goodbyes were brisk handshakes. A little later Fraschini also left. He kissed Sally Lou, patted Grayson on the shoulder, smiled as he shook hands with Catchpole.

"You had little to say, but I think nobody says much when Professor Gifford is around." Catchpole agreed, said he had only come in case the professor needed some fetching and carrying. When Fraschini commented on an American professor having an English assistant Catchpole explained he had come out on an exchange agreement. "But you know all about the seventeenth-century Dutchman, Hobbema," Fraschini said, still smiling. Was that a test he had failed, unaware even that Hobbema was a Dutch artist, let alone that as Fraschini told him his work was sometimes mistaken for van Ruisdael's? He still suspected the Italian was involved in some possibly dangerous scam, but was Grayson concerned? And had any of this a connection with Jenny's disappearance?

With the visitors gone Grayson insisted on opening another bottle of champagne. Catchpole said Fosskind seemed a rough diamond.

"If you could call him any kind of precious stone. He's a New York lawyer. I've had dealings with him before."

"Who is he acting for?"

"I'm not at liberty to tell you." He looked at Sally Lou, who was staring into her glass. "I've gone along with this little deception as you wanted, but I don't understand why you're here, how it can possibly have any connection with Jenny. I suppose there's no more news of her?"

Catchpole said the presumption must be that she was dead.

"Poor Jenny." That was Sally Lou. Grayson seemed about to say something, looked down at the carpet instead. "I said to you before, she was such fun."

"What sort of fun?"

"Well, she was scatty. You know she was acting as courier to a party over here, just gave it up like that, told them she couldn't go on. That was because she'd come here and loved it. Then she didn't mind what she did, or who she took to bed. Even the few days she was with us she found someone, and guess who it was? The mailman. Well, that sort of thing gets around in a little community like this. Evers asked her what she thought she was playing at, and I said if she was going to have a fling why in Heaven's name choose the mailman? You know what she said? He looked as if he was well hung."

"That's enough." Grayson's voice was harsh.

Catchpole asked if he had disliked her. "No, I liked her well enough, but she made trouble. I don't think she meant to, but she did. I liked her, but I was glad when she'd gone."

"And after the mailman, you know what?" Laughter rippled in Sally Lou's voice, but Grayson's mouth was screwed up as if he had tasted an aloe in the champagne.

"I said that was enough."

She shrugged. "You stop me talking, but you got her mixed up in deals like this." She stopped when she saw his forbidding expression.

"I didn't get her mixed up in anything. I told Louis Meyers she was bright, and so she is." He paused at the present tense, shook his head. "But that was all, absolutely all. And the kind of stuff you were going to say, there's no need to talk about it."

"If you say so. But I'll tell you one reason I liked her. She didn't have her eye on the main chance the whole time."

"Someone here needs to. I didn't hear any complaint when I said to you in London, go out and shop. And you certainly heard me, loud and clear." Sally Lou pouted, turned away. In her movements, the restrained turn of her arm as she put down an empty glass, the twitching of her fingers as she pressed one hand hard into the other, the detective sensed a repressed sexuality that made him wonder about their relationship. With a return to his usual easy manner Grayson said apologetically that tension built up with a big deal like this one.

Later, driving the detective back to Logan, he said again that he couldn't understand the reason for Catchpole's visit. He answered warily when asked if he knew Fraschini had a bad reputation.

"No more than others. If you knew the kind of thing that goes on—but it can't have anything to do with Jenny. You've got this man who's been arrested—"

"The case against him isn't watertight." Grayson made no comment on that, concentrating on driving, which he did efficiently, carefully. "I'll tell you something *I* don't understand. Fraschini is selling this picture for the Italian Count. Why should he involve you, why not deal directly with your client?"

"Because I'm the person through whom my client buys pictures. Fraschini has no access to him."

"But you're not very close to this mysterious client, are you? He does his dealing through a tough-talking lawyer. Why?"

"His privilege. Let's say he's careful."

"Suspicious might be a better word. And what made you decide to cut out Meyers's client in England? Correct me if I'm wrong, but it seems to me he didn't even get a chance to make an offer."

"I'll tell you. Because I know who Louis's client is, and I know he couldn't meet the figure being offered here."

"So you were holding Meyers in reserve, as it were, a sort of second string. Sounds hard on Meyers."

Grayson laughed. "It's a hard world, as I've been finding out the last few months. No secret, I'm strapped for money at the moment. I like Louis, but you know the old song, 'Money makes the wheels go round.' "

They had entered Boston. Grayson took out a handkerchief, wiped his forehead. It seemed the moment to turn the screw a little. "You say you don't know why I'm here. I'll be frank, and say I'm not satisfied with some of your answers. I don't know what connection this picture might have to Jenny Midway, but I suspect there could be one. I might have to ask you again, officially next time, to tell me the name of your client who bought that Renoir."

They were in a queue at the entrance to the Callaghan Tunnel. Grayson said: "I'm an American citizen, I've no need to answer questions like that. And I don't like being threatened." Before Catchpole could say no threat had been made he went on. "I have a wife with expensive tastes. Two kids I adore, but they cost money too. A house that cost me an arm and a leg. Sometimes I have to cut corners, grease palms, do things I don't like. From what I hear about Britain nowadays, corners are cut there, even the police do things they shouldn't." They were crawling through the tunnel now, and his voice had a hollow sound. "So get off my back, Superintendent. My Renoir deal had nothing at all to do with Jenny."

They parted with a nod on either side, no handshake.

7. *Family Occupations*

When Eleanor got the call from Mr. Connors's secretary asking her to come and see him because there was a matter he wanted to discuss, she thought it was probably to arrange a bigger than usual luncheon party. She had now cooked for Purafoods three times, giving the chairman's guests leg of lamb filled with crab, the leg boned and the crab meat plus mint, egg yolks and a dash of curry powder stuffed into the cavity; a simple Welsh chicken and leek pie with the surprise ingredient of sliced tongue added to the chicken; and wild ducks with apricot stuffing and a slightly bitter marmalade sauce. Puddings had been hearty as suited to those with hearty appetites: apple fritters from a centuries-old receipt which called for them to be soaked in sugared brandy before cooking; something called Poor Knights of Windsor which consisted of brioches sliced, soaked in sherry, dipped in beaten egg yolk, fried and served with a sherry sauce; and Sussex Pond Pudding, the standard suet pudding enlivened and sharpened by the addition of a large juicy lemon in its centre. All had been praised, and twice she had been asked to come in and receive the praise in person from between eight and a dozen flushed, well-fed and mostly full-stomached men.

Purafoods occupied a glass and steel block near Ludgate Circus. Around the walls of the large entrance hall were murals showing scenes from rural life. Labourers gathered the harvest, smiling girls milked cows, a farmer and his dog rounded up sheep, apples were picked in orchards. Above these scenes a banner said: "They all help to make PURAFOODS." In the centre of the hall a display case contained outsize models of Purafood products, poly-unsaturated Puramarg, cholesterol-free Puraveg, fat-free Pura-Ices, half a dozen others. Averting her eyes from the display case Eleanor reached the lifts, and took the one that soared past single digits up to the tenth floor. A dozen steps on thick pile took her to where Bryan Connors's secretary Janetta received her with a smile that showed a mouthful of perfect teeth. Janetta's teeth, unflawed complexion and slim figure seemed to symbolize the purity of Purafoods, and indeed there was something about the quality of air and light on this floor that differentiated it from the no doubt healthy but inferior regions below. And Bryan Connors, as he came bouncing across the carpet to greet her, seemed also almost impossibly germ-free. He was a small fresh-faced smiling man who looked as if all his visible parts had been scrubbed clean only five minutes earlier. His little hands were very clean, his cheeks had the almost transparent purity of texture often found in those who work under arc-lights, little patches of baby-pink scalp showed under his thinning, scrupulously parted hair.

"Eleanor, so good to see you. Sit down." She obediently sat in a large leather armchair. He walked across to the picture window that occupied one wall, stood looking down. "Astonishing that those little ants scurrying about down there are human beings like you and me, with the same hopes, disappointments, yearnings for the impossible. Amazing. You'd think they were a different species." He turned. "But they're not, Eleanor, they're not. Like us they live unhealthy lives, going from home to office, taking too little exercise. And we can help them, Purafood can help them. Help them to live better, more healthily."

She had heard him in this preacherly-philosophical vein before, when he had impressed on her that when possible only Purafood ingredients should be used at the luncheons, meat, organically grown vegetables, butter and cream, all from Purafood farms. Considerable quantities of all had been consumed, along with a good deal of alcohol, the final effect perhaps not conducive to health. However, she did not dissent when he launched into praise of her three luncheons, making them sound like a substitute for a two-mile jog. "Shall I tell you what I especially valued in those meals so cleverly devised and so perfectly cooked? Not the cooking or the presentation, admirable though that was, but two things: what we ate was *British* food and *healthy* food."

He smiled at her, and she smiled back. She had given up trying to guess why he had asked her to come and see him. He said in the same hushed voice: "Britishness and purity, they go together in my mind, they are the meaning of this organization. They are what Purafood stands for." He stood up, began to walk about, spoke again in his normal voice. "Eleanor, I have a vision, one I want you to share. Indeed, you are essential to it." He stood in front of her now, a clean smiling cherub. "I see a Purafood restaurant, one serving nothing but British food made according to old national recipes. According to Mrs. Beeton, yes, but we should go further back. I remember you saying one of the dishes at our luncheons came from a sixteenth-century recipe. I see a Queen Victoria meal, a Charles the Second dinner, a Prime Ministers' luncheon, everything according to what was eaten at the time and by those people. I see the Purafood British Restaurant, all dishes made from national recipes from our own pure materials. And the inspiration, the supreme designer of all this will be Eleanor Midway." He held out his hands. "What do you say?"

"Mr. Connors—"

"Bryan. Eleanor, this will only be the beginning. I see that first British Purafood Restaurant as the opening link of a chain, one in every great city, eventually in every large town. It will be a crusade for goodness and purity in eating, for the sheer superiority of our materials and the cooking of our national dishes. The London restaurant will be our flagship and you its captain. You will give us your genius for the planning of menus and their preparation, we shall make you famous."

"Mr. Connors—Bryan—I'm very honoured, but you must give me time to think about it. This would be a full-time job, and I don't know if I want that. And there's something else."

"Tell me."

"Some Purafood products are processed, some of the varieties of Puraveg for instance. I don't use them in cooking."

"Nor would I suggest it. Our basic claim for Purafoods is just that they are pure. If you prefer to use the organically grown vegetables in their original form for the restaurant, of course you would do it. This is not a passing thought, Eleanor, it has been in my mind for a long time, and now your wonderful cooking has made it a practical proposition." His smile reappeared. "Practical for you too. If we discuss terms—*when* we discuss terms—you will find it is a commercial proposition."

She said again she must have time to think, and must talk to her husband. On the way back to Fulham she felt more and more exhilarated, and inclined to say yes. This would be something she had done on her own, a kind of fulfilment. But what would John say?

John was late, as he often was nowadays, and he seemed really not very interested. The old John would have spoken decisively, either saying it was out of the question that she should give up so much time, or debating the pros and cons of the idea in the way that so much impressed her. Now she felt as if only half of him heard her, the rest being otherwise occupied. When she asked if he thought she should take the job, he said it was up to her.

"I know that, but what do *you* think? It would take up a lot of time, would you mind that?"

"No, why should I?"

She had wanted his agreement, yet found this unsatisfactory. When he said it would help to take her mind off Jenny she realized with a feeling of shame that she had not thought about her daughter for several hours. Weeks had passed, a man had been arrested, did she any longer believe Jenny was alive? She could not contemplate the question. She shuddered away from the thought that she would never again receive sometimes useless but always delightful little surprise presents, be told about a fabulous new job Jenny might get, or the absurd quirks of her present boss that she couldn't put up with for another week. Jenny had to be alive, because she could not bear to think of her dead.

And working for Bryan Connors helped. Was that true, or was she simply justifying to herself a wish to take the job? After two days she telephoned to say she accepted in principle, and was ready to talk about the details. When they did so she was astonished by what he offered, and realized that it was indeed from her point of view a commercial proposition. She told Stella, who said she was wonderful, which was the kind of thing she had wanted John to say.

There were times when Giles could not avoid meeting Mrs. Entwhistle, although he did his best to be out when she was there. This was not from any dislike of her, but because he did not want to talk to the woman who cleaned the flat. One Friday morning, however, she arrived at nine-thirty, an hour earlier than usual. He was dressing after breakfast when he heard the front door close, then her voice saying: "Only me."

He finished dressing, came out of the bedroom and said sharply: "This is not your usual time."

"Got my cousin Fergie staying. Came unexpected. Got to get back, make his lunch. Sure you wouldn't mind." Mrs. Entwhistle was tall and thin, with pinched features the narrowness of which were accentuated by the way her hair was pulled back into a bun, and even by her clipped voice that ejected only brief spurts of words. She never mentioned a husband, and he had always assumed her to be a widow.

Giles did mind, but he was a cautious man. He did not want the bother of showing another household help—as to his disgust charladies now had to be called—where things were and what she should do. He saw no reason why her cousin could not get his own lunch, but did not say so, only remarking that he hoped this would not happen again.

"Couldn't say. Not for sure." From the kitchen her voice told him: "Had a bit of bad luck, Fergus has."

"I'm sorry to hear that."

"Yes, well." The disembodied voice continued. "Had his own business, Fergie did. Secondhand cars and that. Outside Oxford." Giles said something about the recession and the bottom dropping out of the market and was, as he felt rudely, interrupted. "Nothing like that. His partner it was. Been cheating Fergie for months. Gone off now. Business is bust."

Giles repeated that he was sorry to hear it. Mrs. Entwhistle reappeared at the kitchen door, her manner curiously aggressive. Giles said he hoped the man was caught and prosecuted.

"Fat chance. They say he's in Spain." Her manner softened slightly. "He won't give up, Fergie. Start again. Never say die." There seemed no need to respond. "Only thing is the banks. Won't lend." Again Giles found no call for comment. He was about to say he had an appointment, and leave the apartment to get away from this unwanted chattiness when she said something else he thought he must have misheard. Yet even in the moment of asking her to repeat the words, he knew that he heard them correctly.

"I said, wondered if you could help." Mrs. Entwhistle faced him boldly. Her eyes were unusually close together, barely separated by the thin nose.

A judge is used to exercising authority, and Giles had a tone he had found effective in quelling the possible insolence of inferiors. He used it now. "I don't know your cousin. In what way do you imagine I could help him?"

"Only needs a start." She was not only unquelled, the woman positively sat down on one of the two chairs at his small dining table. "Just so he can start dealing. Can't start dealing on credit, Fergie says."

"You are seriously suggesting I should lend money to this cousin of yours, a man I had never heard of until this morning? What makes you think I would do that, Mrs. Entwhistle?"

"Because you've got a good heart." The reply disconcerted him for a moment, but the following words brought an awareness of danger. "And you wouldn't miss it. Not much, hundred or two. Start him off. Course he'd pay it back." When he said, still in the quelling tone, that it was out of the question, she did not seem surprised. He added that he wanted to hear nothing more about her cousin, who must solve his own problems.

"I'll tell him." She stood up. "There's this journalist might help." He asked what she meant. "Got a hobby, see. Fergie has. Likes taking pictures." The close-set eyes looked at him eagerly. "Some this journalist he knows might buy. Least he'd be interested. Very interested. Fergie says." She paused, waiting, but he said nothing. "Took them in some club. Don't know the name. Thought you'd be interested. See them. Keep them."

Photographs taken in a club? He tried to recall a snapping camera in one of the clubs visited on a Watching expedition and was unable to do so, but knew it was possible such photographs might have been taken. Possible also, he supposed, that a tabloid might use them as the basis for an article. He must decide what to do, but for the moment—for the moment he fixed Mrs.

Entwhistle with the gaze that left her unquelled, and spoke with what he hoped was effective boldness.

"Go back and tell your cousin that if I hear anything further from him I shan't hesitate to inform the police. He might care to pass that on to his journalist friend." He took out notes from his wallet. "Here is your week's money, Mrs. Entwhistle. Please leave now. I don't want to see you again."

That was unexpected, and he was pleased to see alarming to her, at least momentarily. She picked up the notes, glared, said: "You'll be sorry. I'll tell Fergus." She was shaken further when he said he doubted if Fergus existed. She did not reply but slammed the front door after her in what he hoped was a final gesture. He walked round the apartment humming with satisfaction, then looked in the cupboard containing his Watching clothes. He had a sense of triumph he knew to be illogical, as if he had vindicated the purity of his motives in the face of an unjust attack. The caretaker said he would have no trouble in finding another cleaner to replace Mrs. Entwhistle, and Giles left in a surprisingly good temper. His sentencing of the cases that came up before him, however, was no less severe than usual.

Mary told David what Rupert Baxter had said, and the advice she had given. He said she had done the right thing. "Jenny's dead, you know that, don't you?"

They were in the living-room of their Stamford Hill flat. The room was roughly triangular in shape, but in practice almost a pentagon because the conversion of the house into flats had been made so ineptly. There were five bits of wall, none more than seven or eight feet in length and all at awkward angles so that it was not possible to fit any sizeable piece of furniture into the room. The walls were plasterboard and so was the ceiling, and they could hear clearly the couple upstairs having one of their frequent rows. She was white, he was a Pakistani, a polite young man who smiled at Mary when they met and, whatever the weather, always said it was a delightful day. The girl had orange hair and worked at the checkout in a local supermarket. She ignored Mary, but said hallo to David.

A heavy object thudded on the floor above them. Mary said, "You don't *know*."

"If she was alive she'd have been in touch." She made no reply, and they sat for a minute or two, he staring into space as he often did, she reading the *Evening Standard*. The voices above rose, the girl's to a scream, then there was silence. He spoke again. "It won't always be like this. We'll get out of here soon."

"I'm not complaining."

"But you should. Christ, I hate it. I don't think I could stand it, except I know it won't be forever. I'll get another job, do something different. We shall have our own place, I promise. Somewhere away from all this."

She put down the paper. "The way things are we're lucky to be both in work. And saving money. I tell you, I don't mind it that much."

The sounds upstairs began again, this time a prolonged sobbing, the sex indiscernible. David too seemed on the verge of tears. "It's not what you expected. Or me. We haven't got a house, haven't got kids."

She went over, took him in her arms. She knew there were times when he needed such consolation, knew his customary detachment concealed not strength but weakness. She said over and over, "It's all right." After a few minutes he recovered, she put aside the paper, they watched a new sitcom on the telly.

The flight from Boston was delayed for three hours, and when Catchpole got back there was no further news of Jenny Midway.

He arrived at the Clapham chapel not exactly bad tempered but with the feeling of frustration that he knew was likely to occur at some time in any investigation. Awareness of this, however, didn't make it any better. Alice met him with the news that Alan, their elder son, had chickenpox.

"The spots are just coming out, his temperature's a hundred and two, he's feeling sorry for himself, been asking for you." She checked herself. "How did it go?" He made a face, shook his head, said he would go up.

The boys occupied the top rooms which had coved ceilings. They were hot in summer, cold in winter, even though they had installed large radiators. Alan had his eyes closed, but opened them as soon as his father entered the room. A low-voltage lamp made his face look blue. "Hello, Dad," he said. "I've got pox."

"Chickenpox. Pox is something different." He sat on the bed, took his son's hot hand. "I can't see any spots."

"They're on my chest. Millions of them. And my back. Shall I die?"

"Of course not. You'll just get some days off school."

"This afternoon I thought I was going to die."

"Well, you're not. You're just lucky. Desmond will be angry he's not got it when he sees what a good time you'll have in the next week or two."

"Have you had it, Dad? Will you catch it from me?"

He pretended to be appalled by the thought, got off the bed and made for the door, returned. His son did not laugh. Catchpole looked at the poster of the Arsenal team on the wall, the flag pinned above it saying "Up the Gunners," the photographs of Arsenal players cut out of a magazine. He shook his head. "You should be supporting a South London team, Chelsea, Charlton, Millwall."

"None of them are any good. Do you think Arsenal will win the championship?"

"No. But suppose they do, what would you like to have to celebrate it?"

"A new bike."

"OK, you're on."

"You mean I'll get a new bike? A *new* new one?"

"If Arsenal win the championship. I'll give you a chance. If they're in the top six."

"Fantastic. They can't miss, you've lost your bet, Dad."

"Wouldn't be the first bet I've lost. Now, have a drink and go to sleep."

Alan drank a mouthful of lemon, said, "Arsenal are magic," turned over and was still. Catchpole looked at his son's fair head, the slim arm outside the covers, and was moved almost to tears. He went downstairs, told Alice he had tried a little bribery, and said what it was.

"Do you know how much those bikes cost?"

"We can manage it if we don't eat meat for a week." She asked if he was hungry. "I ate on the plane. A whisky would be good. A big one. Straight, no ice." She brought it to him and he began to tell her about Gifford, the meeting, Grayson's refusal to name the buyer. Then he realized he had lost her attention, and asked what was wrong.

"Something I should tell you." She didn't go on and he remained silent, which he had found the best way of inducing the inhibited to speak. After a few moments she said, "I've invested some money."

Alice and Brett had each inherited several thousand pounds from a trust left by their grandfather. He did not doubt that Brett's was long spent, but when last Alice mentioned hers it had been safely lodged in a building society. He was about to say her investments had nothing to do with him, when instinct told him what had happened. "It's to do with Brett, isn't it? That Ivorine scheme." She said yes. "How much?"

"Ten thousand. It's a loan really, they just need backing, he'll pay it back in twelve months if I want. With the same interest I get from the Woolwich, only I won't have to pay tax on it.

Or I can leave it in the firm and take a share of the profits. It's all been properly drawn up, with witnesses." He said nothing. "It's my money, after all."

"It was your money."

She rarely swore, so he knew she was upset when she did so now. "That's a bloody mean thing to say. This is the first real chance Brett has had. He says it's bound to take off, and if it does it will make their fortunes. All they need is what they call start money."

"So what's wrong with a bank loan?"

"There's a recession, haven't you heard? The banks aren't lending." Again he stayed silent. "I know you don't like Brett, but he's my brother and I love him. And he really is clever, you don't see it because you don't like him, only things haven't gone right for him."

"You're wrong about one thing. I do think he's clever."

"What is it, then?"

He made a conscious effort, suppressed what he had been about to say. "Look, I think I've been wasting my time in the States, the plane was delayed, I'm not happy about that Lewis confession. It's been a bad day. So could be you're right, and in a year's time you'll have doubled your money. Anyway it's yours, you do what you like with it. You had no need to tell me, and now you have I've got no business to criticize. Argument over, all right?"

"And when I've doubled my money you'll agree you were wrong about Brett?"

"I'll agree you're a loving sister."

Higginbotham was, as often, inclined to facetiousness. "So you're an art expert now, Catchers. Vetting a Renoir across the Atlantic, where will it be next to spend the Department's money? I hear there's a big Art Expo coming off in Rio in a couple of months, do you fancy a trip there by any chance?"

Catchpole plugged the irritation fizzing within him, and asked mildly if Higginbotham didn't agree there was something odd about Meyers being discarded, and Grayson refusing to name his client.

"I've already told you, anything friend Fraschini's got to do with, odd would be the polite word. If he had a genuine picture to sell he'd pretend it was a fake, then he'd enjoy selling it more. But Dale Gifford, that's a respected name. If he says it's a Renoir you can believe him."

"What about the secrecy?"

"Nothing out of the way, laddie. Could be a way of laundering money, investing it in a picture instead of buying a chain of laundrettes. Or could be your buyer just doesn't want the press moseying around, wondering how he happens to have two or three million handy. As for Meyers I'd guess they were telling the truth, the Americans had more money than his client over here. Does that help?"

"If confusing the issue helps, yes."

"You want my advice, Catchers? Forget about it."

He did not find that advice easy to follow, or even acceptable. Back in his office he rang Louis Arts to be told by Maurice that Mr. Meyers was still in Cologne. "He's trying to arrange an exhibition over here of a really exciting German artist, Hans Kretschmer." There followed words the detective at first thought he must have misheard. "He works in dung."

"Why not in paint?"

Maurice was eloquent. "I think the medium is symbolic. Kretschmer uses material of all kinds, from humans and animals, even birds and insects. It is pressed so that it's hard but not too stiff for handling, and then made into symbolic forms, perhaps you might say sculptures. What's the symbolic relationship between black, white and yellow races? Or between the lion and the lamb? That's the kind of thing Kretschmer is getting at. I've only seen illustrations, but they look quite marvellous. You must come and see the show."

Catchpole said he wouldn't miss it. He learned that Meyers wasn't expected back for two or three days. No sooner had he put down the telephone than the internal line rang. The Big Man's secretary said he would like to see Superintendent Catchpole as soon as it was convenient.

That meant *at once*, but the Big Man would never have used words expressing that degree of urgency. Indeed, Catchpole had never seen him out of temper—he had not reached his present eminence by losing his temper, as he might have said himself. But the detective knew also that the geniality with which he was received meant little.

"Sit down, my dear fellow. Was your trip across the Atlantic useful?" He said he was not sure. "But pleasurable, I hope. And necessary?"

"Yes, it was necessary." He had long ago decided that a modified aggression was the best way of dealing with the Big Man. "I don't need to remind you of the trouble we've had in cases where leads haven't been followed through, or where forensic scientists have concealed bits of information that didn't fit into the case we were preparing."

"I take your point. It makes one wonder whether justice was not done more effectively before queries about notebooks and statements by suspects were raised by all these machines supposed to help police work. It could be said they tend to hamper it by telling us things we don't want to know about the way officers write up their notebooks. But such heretical thoughts must be whispered only between these four walls." He beamed at Catchpole. "No more Midway news? No body washed up off the Sussex coast or in Boston Harbour?"

"No, sir. Nothing at all."

"A pity. But I have what I hope you'll agree is good news.

Our lords and masters in their wisdom have decided that the case against Gabriel Lewis is strong enough for us to go ahead." He beamed again. "You look a little surprised."

"I am, sir. But it's their decision, not yours or mine."

"Very well put. We've presented them with the material, they've said go ahead. I think we should have a drink on it."

As Catchpole downed his single malt, and took part in conversation about Alice, Alan's chickenpox, the work the Big Man was having done to his house at Esher and the problems involved in getting a particular type of shower fitting, he was aware that this almost congratulatory chat could turn to cool disapproval if Jenny Midway turned up tomorrow alive and well.

Sometimes, in the crowded, tedious journey between Stamford Hill and the Wayne, Mendelson office, David closed his eyes and visualized the kind of house he and Mary would have one day. He saw it very clearly, a small Victorian terrace house, with original features like the fireplaces and plaster ceiling roses still in place, rooms not enormous but larger than those in their flat, and properly shaped. This daydream house was rather like his parents' Fulham home, but with those two ground-floor rooms back and front left as they had originally been, not made into one as in the Fulham house and a thousand others like it. The furnishings would be in keeping, old pieces bought secondhand at sales, inexpensive plain carpeting, prints and pictures on the walls, which would be papered with Morris designs. Upstairs would be their bedroom, a small guest room (though he was not sure he wanted many visitors), the bathroom, and of course the nursery. The house would be set in a side road with little traffic, there would be a small front garden and a manageable one at the back where Mary, who was believed to have green fingers, would plant annuals and rose bushes. Their next-door neighbours, a couple about their own age, would have a child just a little younger than their own boy . . .

He knew this was a pipe dream even before he opened his eyes in the Tube train and saw the dull, defeated or self-absorbed faces round him. There were houses in Fulham, Chelsea and Kensington that fitted the description and were on Wayne, Mendelson's books, but the prices were far higher than anything David and Mary could manage. South of the river, then? Battersea, Clapham, or—Balham? But Balham was where Jenny had lived, and he shuddered away from the thought of it. And the houses there of the kind he wanted might still be outside the price range David and Mary could afford. Their sort of house, the sort they might be able to buy, would be in a busy street, where most of the houses would have possibilities of improvement, to use a phrase often on his own lips when showing people round houses crumbling from dry rot or in need of total reroofing. A good many of the neighbours would be young and rowdy, the kind David simply did not want to find living next door, or even in the same street.

But you never knew . . . He spoke to Barry Mendelson, the exuberant Jewish junior partner in the firm, who showed the immediate enthusiasm built into every estate agent at birth.

"Something on our books, Davy boy, why not? You know me, I'd sell anything to anybody. And for one of our own we should be able to manage something special in the way of a deal. What did you have in mind?" His enthusiasm waned when David named two houses in Fulham and Chelsea, and mentioned the size of mortgage that would be needed. "If you'll forgive me, Davy, I'd say you were aiming a bit, quite a bit, above your financial station. Put it another way, if you want to do a deal on either of these you'd have to put down a fair amount of cash. Family cash perhaps, is that a possibility? Not? Then I'd say you should forget that kind of address and look elsewhere, lower down the price range. And even then, just tapping out the mortgage repayment details on the old ready reckoner, I doubt if you and Mary would be well advised to buy. Something newly built out in the sticks where the builder's backed by a mortgage company who's charging top interest rates yes or maybe, but the kind of house you've got in mind and the level of repayments you'd have to make, the answer has to be you'd be foolish."

When David said he had hoped the firm might be able to manage special mortgage terms, or in some way support his application, Barry's enthusiasm changed to sorrow. "I wish we could, Davy boy, I really wish we could. Help to get the asking price down, I'll do that with pleasure, but get involved in a loan to you which I think is basically what you're suggesting, no can do. For one thing Johnny Wayne would never wear it, for another as you know the market's dead quiet, and believe me it wouldn't be in your own interest. You want to get away from where you are, right, then what you should be looking at is a nice flat."

Of course he had really known something like that would be the answer before he put the question. It sometimes seemed to him that his whole life had been a series of defeats, from those schooldays when Jenny had been the favoured one, so much brighter and quicker witted, to his present dead-end job. But at least he had married Mary, that was the prize life had awarded him.

For John Midway these were days, weeks, when he felt himself to be a man who has committed himself to a decisive course of action that will decide his future. He felt this, although in some ways little had changed in his life. He still walked from Fulham to the grey monster in St. Martin's Lane, and the snow had gone, replaced by the bite of spring winds so that his big nose was raised more appreciatively as he strode through the park, humming, whistling, or spouting aloud the odd line of poetry. At the office his arrears of work had been cleared and Horton was quiescent, even amiable. At home Eleanor seemed involved with her cooking engagements and commitments, a hobby that occupied her time and apparently gave her pleasure. He was unsure if she had accepted the fact that Jenny was gone forever, but at least she demanded no kind of action from him, and talked about her daughter much less than she had done. The man who killed Jenny was coming up for trial at the Old Bailey.

Yet a great deal had changed. He said in his office one day, with a sense of wonder: "My secretary is my mistress." Before Jenny's disappearance he would have said such an idea was preposterous, yet it had happened. Three times a week they went back after work to Susan's flat. Her treatment of him there made him feel like a patient recuperating after an illness. She blended the qualities of nurse, housewife and servant. When, two or three times he had tried to make love and wept on finding himself impotent, she had hushed and soothed him as if he were a child. Later she expressed delighted surprise, almost as if he had won a prize at school, when he found himself in erection. She talked about her husband Greville, said she had married young and been shattered when after some years he went off with a much younger woman, leaving her with a teenage son who was now doing an engineering job, and had left home to live with his girlfriend.

"I was really desperate when Greville left me with Stephen to look after. It was only working for you that kept me from having a nervous breakdown."

"You never showed any sign of it. If I'd known—"

"I didn't want you to know. It was enough that I was working for someone I admired. You were so decisive, you always knew what you wanted, how to deal with people, what ought to be done. Different from Greville. He was no good, no good at all."

"I don't know what you must have thought of me lately."

"It was only natural. I could have killed Horton, going on at you. But you're better now."

It was true. He had recaptured his characteristic blend of

decisiveness and sympathy, and he owed the recovery to Susan, not Eleanor. When he looked round her flat he felt astonishment at his presence there. And Susan astonished him too. In the office she was anxious to the verge of fussiness that everything should be done in the right way and the right order. Every day the appointments list was ready, with notes on all the people who wanted to see him. At home she left unwashed plates and cups in the sink for days, and rarely made the bed. Occasionally he would find dirty panties in the living-room, stuffed under a cushion, beneath the sofa, or on one occasion wrapped in a tea towel. Why were such habits tolerable in her when they would have infuriated him in Eleanor? He had no idea.

Sometimes he felt a surge of guilt at his betrayal of Eleanor, and disgust at his cowardice in not telling her he was sleeping with another woman. And when his guilt was not, as it were, on the boil it was simmering menacingly, the consciousness of it infecting all he did and said. At times, when he was listening to staff talking about marital or financial problems he felt inclined to say he knew all about marital difficulties, was in the same boat, could do with a bit of advice from *them* about how to get out of an emotional tangle. He was not at all in love with Susan, although her blend of humility and motherliness combined with sexual inventiveness had proved surprisingly stimulating. She had made no demands on him, seemed content for the situation that had arisen to continue. Yet some sort of change was inevitable, but of what kind? He felt committed to decisive action without knowing what he wanted it to be.

It soon became clear to Eleanor that what had sounded like an agreeable sideline would be something like a major enterprise. It turned out that Bryan, as he insisted she call him, had already bought a long-established but recently defunct gentleman's outfitters patronized almost exclusively by the legal profession. The shop was in one of the side-streets off Chancery Lane, ideally positioned as Bryan said for the patronage of lawyers and those working in the many foreign enterprises—English branches of foreign journals, London offices of provincial papers—that still remained in or around Fleet Street. The place had to be gutted, furnished, fitted with up-to-date kitchens, and she was expected to advise on all this. She dealt sometimes with Bryan, more often with a Purafood executive named Maggie Lomas, a brisk woman twenty years Eleanor's junior, who was apparently some sort of financial adviser. She smoked small cigars, which seemed contradictory to Purafood principles. "Maggie will hand out the pounds and count the pennies," said smiling Bryan, adding that his culinary and financial geniuses were two of a kind.

Eleanor did not find that to be the case. It seemed to her that Maggie's instinct for saving pennies was much stronger than her feeling that purse strings should be loosened to buy the very best kitchen ware. There were battles over the seating (the Rustic English bought was much cheaper but also less comfortable than the plush-covered carvers Eleanor wanted), and also over what Maggie called the crocks. She said good quality china with the Purafood lettering PFP (for Pure Farm Produce) outlined in gold would be a waste of money.

"Let's face it, the crocks are going to get chipped and broken by the dopeheads and layabouts we hire to wash them," she said. "Buying that sort of stuff is money down the drain." Eleanor took her case over that to Bryan and got her way, but the battle over money was constant. She was disconcerted also to learn she would not deal with the Purafood farms direct, but place her requirements through Cliff Davies, a lanky Welshman who seemed always to have a cigarette in the corner of his mouth, and reminded Eleanor of minor villains in the films of her youth. Cliff's manner of speech was suitably mock-American.

"Yeah," he said when Eleanor handed him the list of materials for some of the meals she cooked before the restaurant opened, to try to eliminate possible hitches. "Can do, no problem." And although she would have preferred to deal with the farms direct, there were no problems of supply. Eleanor found she was not expected actually to cook, but to devise menus and supervise the two chefs who worked under her, both young enough not to mind being given orders, and skilful enough to carry them out as well as she could have done herself.

A lot of time was taken up also by meetings to discuss the range of menus, the prices, and whether to serve English wines. (The verdict went against them.) Although it was not what she had expected, it was all very enjoyable. There were hours, mornings, even days at work when she did not think about Jenny. The fact that John was busy at the office was also a blessing, since it meant she did not have to worry about him.

Catchpole's call must have alarmed Maurice, because Meyers rang to ask what he wanted. He said he wondered what the dealer thought about the sale of the Renoir for which he had a possible buyer to America.

"I hoped you rang with news of Jenny. I read a man had been arrested, but—are you sure she is dead?"

"The man's coming up for trial, and the charge is murder."

"That's terrible." A pause. "But then why are you interested in the picture, Jenny had nothing to do with it in the end. Anyway, what you say isn't right. The Renoir hasn't been sold."

"Hasn't been sold," Catchpole echoed stupidly.

"Correct. The buyer in the States didn't like the picture when he saw it, that's my understanding. I've told Fraschini I'm still interested, and he'll be bringing it over so that my client here can see it." Catchpole asked the client's name. "I can tell you this, it's a private individual, not a museum. And he wants to avoid publicity. If there is a sale there won't be a newspaper story. Ettore tells me that's what his Count wants, so it suits both parties. Provided the picture is validated, of course."

"It will be validated all right." He told the dealer he had been present when Gifford examined the picture and his verdict on it, although he did not mention his own role as assistant. He ended by saying he had seen the picture into Fosskind's car, and asked if Meyers knew the name of the lawyer's client.

"I have no idea. You would have to ask Grayson."

Catchpole did not say he had done that already, but repeated his request for the name of Meyers's possible buyer.

"It won't go any further?" Not unless some criminal activity was involved, Catchpole said. "Very well. It is Angus McCracken. You'll know the name."

"I do." McCracken Properties, founded on the basis of buying and renting out a slum terrace in Deptford, had been developed in twenty years through what was said to have been ruthless landlordism, with houses bought cheaply, existing tenants persuaded to leave by professional frighteners assisted by dogs, and the houses then split up into small rooms and packed with immigrants who could find nowhere else to live at affordable prices. When taken to court McCracken insisted he was performing a public service by providing Asians and West Indians with roofs over their heads when otherwise they would be a charge on the government purse. The firm was now one of the biggest property companies in Britain, and its founder among the hundred or perhaps even fifty richest people in the country.

"He may buy paintings as a hedge against inflation or a potential tax loss, I don't know," Meyers said. "Or to avoid death duties—you do that if you make your pictures available for public viewing on request, nobody comes to see them, a legal tax dodge. Whatever it is I've sold him several paintings, never anything risky, nothing recent, only what you could call gilt-edged securities as far as you can have them in painting. He never buys in the sale room, likes to do private deals. I am lucky to be one of the three or four people he uses to look out for things he might like."

"Did Grayson know you look out for things, as you say, on McCracken's behalf?"

"Yes, certainly."

"And you learned about this particular painting through him? He approached you?"

"Of course he did. Superintendent, I don't like the sound of these questions, and I don't understand why you're asking them. There was nothing odd about Grayson approaching me. We've done business before."

"With pictures you've sold to McCracken?"

"No, nothing quite like this."

"Weren't you annoyed when he told you the picture would be offered first of all in America?"

"Not particularly. If a rich American or Japanese is interested they'll usually outbid a European. Of course we're talking about individuals, not museums."

"But now you're being offered the picture again."

"Correct. And now will you tell me why you're asking these questions."

Catchpole said truthfully that he didn't know. He sensed disbelief in the silence at the other end of the line and decided to be conciliatory. "I'm poking around in the dark because something about this sale doesn't smell right. I got the strong impression that the sale to the American, whoever he is, was a firm one, and I'm very surprised it came unstuck. But I may be wrong about it all. I appreciate your cooperation, Mr. Meyers. When Fraschini gets in touch with you again about the picture I'll be grateful if you let me know. If everything's the way it should be, I promise I'll do nothing to get in the way of your deal. Will you do that?" Meyers said he supposed so. He did not sound happy when he said it.

Catchpole had the feeling he was being tricked, or Meyers was being tricked, although he could not see how. A couple of years earlier he had been in New York on one of those exchange visits laid on so that British and American policemen can see how hopelessly unsuitable their routines would be in the country they are visiting, although the object of the exercise was supposed to be precisely the opposite. He had got on well with a cynical, rawly humorous New York police captain named Rory O'Donnell. He rang the New York police department now, and to his surprise was put through to O'Donnell in seconds.

"Well now, if it isn't my old friend the Limey cop," O'Donnell said. "Are things so quiet in that little offshore island you're desperate to chat, that why you're calling?"

"Not exactly. But you sound as if it's feet up on the desk time yourself, I got through so fast."

"You should see the workload on my desk, Catchers." This abbreviation had never ceased to amuse O'Donnell. "You want something, why else would you be on the line? Tell me."

"I want everything you can tell me about an art dealer or agent named Grayson and a lawyer named Fosskind. Not just if they've been inside or have connection with villains. I'd like to know what sort of reputation they have, and how they're fixed financially." He gave Grayson's address and the name of Fosskind's law firm.

"Noted. Now the question one friend should always ask another. What's in it for me?"

"If I could tell you I probably wouldn't be calling. Perhaps nothing. I have a feeling some scam's being worked through the sale of a Renoir painting, and it would help to have the background. And the picture deal may have something to do with a girl who's gone missing here."

"My my, French pictures is it? Trust you to give a job a touch of class. Here we just worry about girls getting gang-raped in Central Park and the blacks and Jews killing each other."

"That's why your feet are up on the desk?"

This genial badinage continued for a couple of minutes, ending with O'Donnell saying he'd do his best to get back with some news before Labor Day. That afternoon Catchpole was summoned for a chat with Harvey Dayton-Williams, the Treasury Counsel nominated by the Attorney-General to prosecute Gabriel Lewis. Catchpole knew Dayton-Williams only by reputation as a good cross-examiner who didn't always read his papers closely. He was pleased to find a jolly red-faced man whose determinedly matey manner seemed designed to contradict any impression that might spring from his double-barrelled name. He shook his head when Catchpole said they were no nearer to finding Jenny's body.

"Pity, that. Lost at sea we have to assume, but no doubt about it a *corpus delicti* would come in handy. Have to rely too much on the confession, don't like relying on confessions. The other side are going to say it was beaten out of Lewis, what's our reply to that?" Catchpole told him of Bertie Minnett's denial that there had been any visit to Lewis in his cell. "And we can trust Inspector Minnett, no doubt. I mean, trust him in the box? He's liable to be put through it a bit, you know, a lot may hinge on the way he answers." Catchpole said he was sure Minnett could handle anything thrown at him without losing his cool. "Good, good. And the injuries were superficial, though of course they'll have an expert to say they weren't self-inflicted. We all know what experts are like, don't we, never wrong." He laughed heartily. "Then there's the matter of how the defence play it. Are you with me? How will they say Lewis spent that Sunday and Monday? With Daisy Dean as she said, or with his friends in and around Portsmouth? Which way will the cat jump? Could pose problems but we'll have a go, never fear, we'll have a go. And if the *corpus* should turn up, the sea give up its prey, so much the better."

"You're optimistic?"

Dayton-Williams bellowed with laughter. "I'm always optimistic."

No doubt about it the weather had improved, Catchpole thought as he made his way from Clapham Common station to the chapel. Spurred by the sun's benevolent warmth he cut the grass in their hundred-foot garden, and admired Alice's massed primulas and wallflowers, and the tulips scattered round in unexpected places.

Indoors too there had been a return to harmony. Alan had recovered, they had gone together to see Arsenal play Sheffield Wednesday, and the Gunners had won. Alan had received a special commendation for a project about the care of old people in Clapham, and although Alice had said she wished he understood what Brett was really like, she had admitted picking a bad moment to tell him about her investment in Ivorine. But what about the case? He noted in his journal:

> Improvement in the weather, irrationally cheerful. So why do I also feel like someone sickening for an illness? What in other people would be a rise in temperature is for me a sense of something left undone. In my private life? I do worry about Alice and Brett. Perhaps that's part of it, but loose ends in the Midway affair are the rest.
>
> Of course there are always loose ends in any case. Why did we never find the knife the witness saw the killer use, why were cigarette butts left in an ashtray when the two people using the room were non-smokers, and so on. This time we've got a good solid tyre lever as the weapon, and what looks like the decisive point about the blood group, no obvious loose ends, so why do I worry? Because Lewis's confession may after all have been beaten out of him? I don't think that's it, but I really don't know.

When Giles left London for the Crown Court in Sussex he deliberately put out of mind the problem of Mrs. Entwhistle. That there was a problem he acknowledged. He had received in the post a note containing a photograph and a sheet of paper which said in typewriting *More where this came from* and a telephone number. The photograph showed him sitting at a table in some unidentified club. He was in Watching gear, a delightful flowered dress and a thick gold chain worn to conceal the scrawniness of his neck. At the table with him was a young man also in drag and rather well made up. He could not remember the young man, but the photograph was authentic. It occurred to him that the young man might have been a plant, or at least the photographer might have suggested he should sit at the table.

So there would be other photographs, and this was an attempt at blackmail. Was it serious, would a newspaper really pay money for photographs of one of Her Majesty's judges in fancy dress? Since the gutter press was truly of the gutter that was likely, and something must be done about it. But not at this moment. The gift Giles possessed for ignoring all but immediate problems made it possible for him to take unalloyed pleasure in the train journey to Sussex, and look forward to the comfort and attention that would be his in Judges' Lodgings. Of course such things were not as they had been. It would no longer be a Court of Assize over which he presided but a Crown Court, there would be little of the ceremony he remembered from his early days on circuit, perhaps no more than an official greeting from the county's High Sheriff and a police escort to and from Court. But there was still the pleasure of wearing wig and robes, being announced as the Honourable Mr. Justice Midway and addressed in Court as "My Lord." The Honourable Mr. Justice Midway settled down to enjoy the train journey, of course in a first-class compartment.

8. *The Trials*

Anybody unfamiliar with the place must be impressed by the surroundings of the Old Bailey. Those long wide echoing corridors where witnesses pace uneasily or sit in urgent conference with solicitors seem to demand the respect of hushed voices, and for a neophyte the feeling of awe is increased by the minority who take it all for granted, treat the place as if it were an office, chat easily as they push open the doors leading into Court number this or that. Are they really the important people suggested by such casualness, or merely minor functionaries to whom the place is familiar? The neophyte never finds out.

And inside, inside Court Number One where Gabriel DuBois Lewis is to be tried for the murder of Jennifer Elaine Midway, the surroundings are also impressive, although we have seen mock-ups of them so often on television that they have an air of theatrical unreality. Can the little Judge—Mr. Justice Clements who is trying this case seems almost to be peeping out from his protective oaken barriers—can the little Judge up on high really be the person to whom everybody is deferring? And is that ordinary dozen of citizens, three black, one Asian, the rest white, four of them women and eight men, really the right body to pronounce a verdict on whether the crime of murder was committed? Perhaps that question occurs to the jury men and women themselves as they look at the man in the dock. It may occur to them, as it does to some of the spectators in the gallery, that much the most impressive figure in Court is the defendant. To an observer unmoved by court ritual it might seem that he alone was real, while the wigged barristers, paper-turning solicitors, ponderous and self-important ushers, anxious jurors, were fitting themselves for parts in a play. In the dock Gabriel Lewis looks enormous. He turns his head from side to side, staring at judge, jury, counsel about to attack and defend him and the acolytes behind them, as if suspecting he has let himself be led into a trap. When Harvey Dayton-Williams stands up to open the case for the prosecution Lewis is quiet, the only movement that of his large hands opening, then closing to shape themselves to formidable boxer's fists.

The opening is casual, the tone that of somebody chatting to his contemporaries about a subject of which they already know a good deal. And they *do* know a good deal, Dayton-Williams says, it would be stupid to pretend they won't have read of Jennifer Midway's disappearance. And—he spreads his hands to show there is nothing up his metaphorical sleeve—he will say at once that in this case there is no body, so that he cannot positively say Jennifer died in this way or that, or suffered these particular injuries, or died in such and such a place. All this red-faced genial Harvey admits, as he says, quite frankly. But the accused has made a confession, and in it explained that he threw the body of the unhappy woman off the cliffs at Beachy Head. The sea accepted her, and the sea has not yet given up its dead although it may still do so, counsel says in the sole rhetorical flourish of his opening.

Expressions of contempt or scorn for the opposing side are nowadays often thought self-defeating, and when Harvey admits that the defence is likely to claim the confession was obtained by force or under pressure he does so with a disarming smile, suggesting that both he and the jury know such things do happen, denial would again be useless. But, he goes on to say, although they will hear from the officers who interrogated the accused that no force or undue pressure was brought to bear, the prosecution does not rely merely on the confession. There is a witness who saw the accused and Jenny Midway together shortly before she disappeared, there are hairs and bloodstains on a tyre lever and the accused's total failure to account for them other than in the way suggested by the confession, there are his clumsy attempts to create an alibi by persuading one woman friend to say she had heard from Jenny and another to say she had been with him during the relevant period . . .

In this opening Dayton-Williams deliberately sketched Jenny's portrait as that of a fun-loving modern girl, who had as he had put it "enjoyed life to the full," the enjoyment including love affairs like one with Gabriel Lewis. So now he brought John Midway and Louis Meyers to the witness box only to confirm that Jenny was a loving daughter and an efficient assistant. Lewis's counsel Charles Golightly spent little time in cross-examination, establishing that she had worked at Louis Arts only for a few weeks, and that the Midways had known almost nothing of their daughter's private life.

"Did you know your daughter had formed an association with the defendant?" John Midway murmured something. "Will you please speak up."

"No. No, I did not."

"Or that she had sexual relationships with other men?"

"She brought some of her friends home."

"And you approved of them?"

"We liked them, yes."

"Do you accept that she had other men friends, men with whom she had sexual relationships?"

"Apparently that is so. I did not know of it."

"I suggest that she did not introduce these other men to her family because she knew you would have been upset."

"Eleanor and I are broad-minded. We would have welcomed any friend of Jenny's."

"But still, you never met some of them. You never met the defendant?"

"Never." With a flash of passion John Midway added: "I never knew he existed."

His brief ordeal over John Midway returned to MultiCorpus, and when Susan asked how it had gone he replied: "Hateful, simply hateful. They want to smear poor Jenny's name with mud." He spent much of the rest of the day trying to sort out the problems of a works engineer named Wainwright who had bought a house with the help of a large building society loan at the time when both he and his wife were working. She had lost her job as a remedial teacher six months back, they were unable to keep up the mortgage payments, the building society was threatening to repossess the house, and his wife was saying she thought they should let the house go, separate, and start again on their own.

To his own surprise John found himself wonderfully fluent and energetic in support of Wainwright. He talked to the building society and persuaded them it would be in their own interest to declare a twelve months' moratorium on the mortgage repayments and the interest due on them, telling them untruthfully that Wainwright was a militant character and would certainly publicize his eviction. He learned Mrs. Wainwright could type, and got the Contract Department to take her on as a copy typist. It was not in Wainwright to show gratitude, but he grunted words that could have been taken for thanks. Susan was wide-eyed with admiration. John said it had helped to take his mind off other things, but the truth was that after leaving the Old Bailey he had hardly thought about Jenny for the rest of the day.

Eleanor spent the morning battling with a Purafoods executive about the costing of meals. She spent a restless night before the trial began, wondering if she could bear to attend it, perhaps to hear Jenny's life dissected and her character travestied, so that a caricature of her was created and taken as the truth. She asked John if he thought she *must* go, whether it would be cowardly not to, and he said she must make up her own mind. He had to give evidence, but would not stay afterwards. What was the point? Jenny was gone. She tried not to believe that, but in the end took what she really thought was the coward's course and stayed away. Mary thought it unwise to desert Mr. Megillah, and although Barry Mendelson had asked David if he would like to take time off for the trial, something in his manner suggested it would be unwise. So after John gave his evidence there was no member of the family present.

Battle was not truly joined until the afternoon, when Jeffrey Fenwick entered the box. He was the man who had seen Lewis and Jenny in a Brixton pub on the day of her disappearance, at about two o'clock. Lewis's confession had said nothing about the Brixton pub, but Dayton-Williams thought it unwise to rely totally on the confession which would no doubt be retracted, and so miss the positive identification made by Fenwick. Bertie Minnett had interviewed him and said he would be a splendid witness.

Catchpole saw Fenwick now for the first time. He was a tall upright man in his forties, with a toothbrush moustache. His clothes were shabby but neat, speech clipped in what might have been a military fashion. He was the manager of a small Brixton supermarket, and went most days for a sandwich and drink at lunchtime to a nearby pub, the Spread Eagle. There, at about two o'clock, he had seen the defendant come in with a woman. When Fenwick left the pub about twenty minutes later the two were still there. The woman was drinking gin and tonic. They seemed in good spirits, laughing and joking. He had not seen the woman before, nor the man. He had identified the woman as Jennifer Midway when shown a photograph, and had picked out Lewis as the man at an identity parade.

All this Fenwick said without fuss or elaboration. It was easy to see why Bertie Minnett had said he would be a good witness.

Before Golightly began cross-examination he consulted Lewis's solicitor, who sat behind him. Curly Maddox, as he was called in reference to the billiard-ball bareness of his head, spoke rapidly, nodded and smiled. Long-faced Golightly nodded back, little Mr. Justice Clements showed signs of impatience from on high, Golightly gathered up papers.

Golightly spoke in a drawl, the tones melting, the voice almost liquid, as if the progress by which sounds reached the air had been slowed down and thickened by a mixture of oil and sugar in his throat. A question from him took a while to unwind, take shape, disclose its meaning. So now, as he sinuously revealed that Fenwick had managed other supermarkets in areas of North London, Haringey and Southall, it was not easy to understand his purpose. The almost liquid voice rolled on.

"Why did you leave those shops, Mr. Fenwick?"

"Didn't pay well enough. Moved to South London."

"Was there not an accusation of assault" (the word came out so slowly it might have had four syllables rather than two) "in Southall?"

"Found one of my assistants had been robbing the till. Gave him a cuff round the ear."

"An Asian gentleman, was it not? And the result of your cuff was that he suffered damage to the eardrum, and threatened to sue?"

"Put-up job. Had trouble with his hearing when he worked in the shop. Never came to court."

"Because a cash settlement was made?" Fenwick did not reply.

"And then in Southall, did you bar certain customers from the shop?"

"Correct. Young thieves, came in couples, one bought a packet of crisps, the other loaded his jacket pocket inside with all sorts of stuff. Of course I banned them, wouldn't anybody?"

"Am I right in saying all those you banned in Southall were black gentlemen?"

Fenwick's mouth twitched with amusement. "Certainly black. Don't know I'd call them gentlemen."

Golightly paused to let the reply sink in. Catchpole cursed Bertie Minnett for not checking Fenwick's background properly. Worse was to come.

"Would I be right in thinking you don't regard black British citizens as gentlemen?"

"No, you wouldn't. I only know about the ones I come across, but a lot of them are thieving, conniving—well, whatever I'd call them it wouldn't be gentlemen."

"I take it you wouldn't employ one in a shop you managed?"

"After what I've seen? Not in a million years."

Golightly consulted his papers again. "Now, you tell us you'd not seen the defendant before that day when you think you saw him in the Spread Eagle. Did you go to an evening of professional boxing at the Lewisham Theatre in Catford in November of last year?"

"Can't remember. Possible I may have done."

"I suggest you were present in the company of a friend named Gerry Winters. If he says you were there together on an evening last November, would you accept that?"

"I've been there with him, yes. Not sure of the date."

"The defendant was on the bill that night, according to the evidence Mr. Winters will give. He boxed a six-round contest which he won on points. Does that jog your memory?"

"No, I don't remember."

"What I'm suggesting, Mr. Fenwick, is that your identification of the defendant came from a memory of seeing his fight some few weeks earlier, and that when you saw another black man in the Spread Eagle you made a mistaken identification." Fenwick said no. "So that at the identity parade you recognized the defendant as somebody you had seen before, but in the boxing ring, not in the Spread Eagle pub."

"I saw him in the pub."

Golightly consulted again with Maddox, nodded, then said in his maddening drawl: "I suggest further that you are strongly prejudiced against the black people you meet every day as a shopkeeper."

Fenwick bit off the words. "Not true. I serve them."

Again Golightly waited a moment to let the precise words of the reply sink in, then said: "But not all of them. You have banned some from the shop, isn't that so?"

"Only if I think they're trying to nick stuff. I told you my experience."

"Have you called the police, have any of them been charged?" Fenwick did not reply. "I asked you, have any of them been charged?" Still no reply. The judge said: "Answer the question, Mr. Fenwick."

Fenwick's self-control went. "What would be the point? You charge 'em, what happens? They get a slap on the wrist, go away laughing."

The destruction was complete. Harvey-Williams did not try to repair it. Later Catchpole tore a strip off Bertie Minnett who was unrepentant. "How was I to know he'd seen Lewis in the ring? Or Curly's got someone to say so."

"You could have checked on what he felt about coloured people."

Minnett snorted with laughter or indignation. "You think he's on his own? You should get out there and talk to shopkeepers.

Ask any of them, any small storekeeper, they'll tell you petty thieving goes on all the time and three-quarters of it's done by blacks or Pakis. Not Indians, they're straight."

"Pakistanis are Indian too. They just live in another country."

"I'm not arguing, just telling you the way it is. The way they think it is, if you like. I checked on Fenwick's politics. He votes Tory like most shopkeepers, never belonged to any party, no connection with Left or Right groups. He's just a shop manager trying to make a living, doesn't like it when stuff is pinched and he can do sod all about it."

He had a point, although Catchpole still felt the check on Fenwick had been sloppy, and that perhaps he should have got involved in it himself. The rest of the day went well enough, with the evidence about the bloodstains on the tyre lever. Patsy Malone told how Lewis had persuaded her to tell the story about the telephone call, then resisted Golightly's insinuations that she had invented the story because of sexual jealousy. She was discreetly dressed in black jacket and white shirt, her manner was restrained, altogether she was an excellent witness.

So too was Bertie Minnett. He had been known to blow his top under questioning, and Catchpole was doubtful about what kind of show he would put up. In fact he received Golightly's lightly veiled sneers stolidly.

"Let me repeat what you are asking the jury to believe. You and Detective Sergeant Stanton—"

"Stenhouse, sir."

"I beg your pardon, Stenhouse. The two of you grilled my client for more than four hours—you don't object to the word, I hope—?"

"We interrogated him. Not the two of us for the whole time, others as well."

"Ah, you took turns. And we may take it the interrogation was intense, that you pulled no punches—"

"No question of anything physical, sir. It's all on the tape."

"My words were, ah, metaphorical, Inspector. In any case, as you say it's on the tape, and the tape makes it clear my client made no admission. None of any kind. We are agreed on that?"

"Yes, sir."

"Then, at twenty fifty-five hours, the interviews are terminated, and he is taken back to his cell. Not taken by you, Inspector, nor by your colleagues."

"No, sir. Taken down by the duty officer."

"Just so. And neither you nor your colleagues involved in the interrogation saw him again that night. Nor on the following morning early?"

"No, sir."

"So you must have been surprised, amazed even, when you learned on that morning my client had confessed to the crime. How do you account for his astonishing change of mind, Inspector, this sudden need to confess?"

"I don't account for it. But funny things happen."

At that Golightly changed from his sinuous drawl to a thundering indignation the more impressive because so rarely used. "*Funny things*, indeed, Inspector. Like the injuries found on my client when he was medically examined. Do those injuries come into your category of funny things, do they make you laugh?"

For a moment Catchpole feared Minnett would meet fury with fury, then saw with relief that he controlled himself. "Not my business to speculate."

"But you insist neither you nor your colleagues had any responsibility for those injuries?"

"I never touched him. Never went near him after the interrogation."

Golightly now gave a creditable impression of a man just managing to control his indignation. "I suggest to you, Inspector, that at some time late on that Friday night you and some companion went down to my client's cell, inflicted injuries that left him mentally confused and calling for a doctor, that you told him he would get no doctor but more of the same if he did not confess. You attacked him, threatened a more severe attack, and left him to think it over, isn't that so?"

"No, sir. That is entirely untrue."

"So how do you account for his injuries, and his remarkable change of mind?"

"As I've said, it's not my business to speculate. But Lewis saw his brief—his solicitor—Saturday morning. It was after seeing him he changed his story."

"Are you suggesting my client's solicitor suggested he should plead guilty, when the evidence against him was so flimsy? Come come, Inspector, you can do better than that."

At the end of a long cross-examination Golightly had made his point about the oddity of the changed plea, but Catchpole doubted that the jury had believed it was beaten out of him. He congratulated Bertie Minnett, who said with some satisfaction that it had been a pleasure to see off that bastard. Outside the Court afterwards he saw Patsy, and congratulated her too on the way she had given evidence.

"Thanks for nothing. I'll tell you something, though. Gabby's not your man."

"We have a confession."

"For what it's worth. How much do you think that is?" He said truthfully that he didn't know. "I'd say Gabby's playing some trick on you, got something up his sleeve. Sometimes he's stupid, Gabby, but he can be smart too." She touched him on the arm, smiled, and he was aware again of sexual attraction. "Does my reputation no good at all, talking to the fuzz. So long." And she was gone, moving with a turn of the hips, a natural style that delighted him.

When he told Alice how it had gone she tried to cheer him up by saying it was good to have the pub business out of the way because it contradicted the confession. Hadn't it been foolish to use it?

"If we hadn't, Maddox would have asked Golightly to use it, then accused us of concealing evidence because it didn't fit our case. Anyway, of course they'll say the confession was beaten out of Lewis."

"Could it be true?"

"Could be, though I don't believe it. I'm pretty sure the injuries were self-inflicted, they never went down to his cell. The trick is to get a jury to believe that too."

The first case heard by the Honourable Mr. Justice Midway had one unusual and interesting aspect. A girl of nineteen said she had been raped while walking the half-mile to her village home after getting off the bus from Brighton. She knew the alleged rapist, a man in his twenties who lived in the same village. Indeed, they had got off the bus together. It was dark, there was nobody about, he had dragged her off the road, threatened her with a knife, and forced her to have oral sex.

She had said nothing about this to her parents when she returned home, but had gone straight up to her room. She had done so partly to avoid distressing them, but also because of the unusual circumstance that the man was a policeman. Not only that, but he was one of the instructors on a training course she was taking, at the end of which she hoped to become a policewoman. She reported the attack three days later to the course director, and said the man had asked her to have sex twice before, once after a police dance, the second time when they were on their way home. She had told him she wasn't interested.

The policeman denied the attack, and said nothing at all had happened. Since oral sex and not physical penetration was involved, there was no useful medical evidence. The man attributed her accusation to the fact that he had given her low marks on two or three tests. She had somehow discovered the markings, which were meant to be secret, had said he had a "down" on her, and that she would get back at him. The girl denied knowing anything about her marks, and certainly there was no obvious way in which she could have discovered them. Her parents testified that she had seemed upset when she got home on the evening of the alleged attack, but they thought she had had a bad day on the course. Her course marks were given in evidence. They were below the required standard, so that unless she had improved she would not have been accepted.

Nothing was known against the defendant, except that he had a reputation for talking about how many girls he had pulled. He carried a knife on his belt, but it was of the multipurpose kind that could serve as a corkscrew, and seemed an unlikely threatening weapon. A drinking companion in the village pub gave evidence saying the policeman told him he liked to have sex every day of the week with a different companion "one way or another," and the girl's counsel made the most he could of this. How foolish people were to make such boasts, Giles thought, how much better the harmless pursuit of Watching.

His summing-up was clear and concise. If the jury believed the girl's story they should find the man guilty, but he pointed out that it was unsupported by any shred of evidence. She had said nothing about the alleged attack for three days, during which she had not only seen the accused but attended two classes in which he was the instructor. He invited the jury to put themselves in her place. If they had suffered such an attack, could they have borne to attend a class given by the attacker? Both accused and accuser were of unblemished reputation. The consequences for the girl would no doubt be the end of her intention to join the police service, but for the man they would be much more serious, certainly the ruin of his career. Apparently he had no difficulty in "pulling" girls, to use what he understood was a current phrase, and they must consider whether, that being so, he was likely to use the threat of force.

The jury took no more than three-quarters of an hour to bring in a "Not Guilty" verdict. The policeman stepped down from the dock smiling broadly, and there was a good deal of applause. The girl wept, her father shouted, "You call this justice?" and said to the policeman, "I'll get you, you bastard." The policeman laughed. The Honourable Mr. Justice Midway felt justice had been done according to the evidence.

The following case was one among several attacks on village post offices and sub-post offices in the area during the past few months. This one, in the South Downs village of Morling, had ended with three people in hospital and the arrest of two men involved in the raid, one other having got away. There was time only for the long-winded Treasury counsel to open the case before a halt was called to proceedings for the day. The car that took Giles back to Judges' Lodgings was a Rolls, and that was only the beginning of an agreeable evening in which he was entertained at dinner by the High Sheriff, his wife, and a group of local grandees. Giles told a number of legal stories, and the company laughed, either dutifully or with actual appreciation. Either way Giles enjoyed himself.

At the Yard Catchpole found a message asking him to call Rory O'Donnell. The New Yorker's voice brought to his mind for some reason an image of raw steak.

"Those two little birdies you wanted to know about, asking us to do a job of work for you. One a tame birdie, the other a bit of a vulture or one of those, I've forgotten the name, sit on an elephant's head picking out the ticks."

"Rory, you've been drinking."

"That's my boyo, thinks I only know about natural history when I have drink taken." He laughed richly. "I'll tell you, don't want you hanging up on me. The tame birdie, Grayson. Calls himself an art agent, sort of middle man, knows people with money, not like you and me, Catchers, people with real money who don't know what to do with it, ready to put it in pictures but want to know what the cash value's likely to be in ten years' time. He's in deep money trouble—"

"He said he had an expensive wife and was strapped for cash."

"You might call that the understatement of the year. He put a lot of money, half of it borrowed, into an investment bank that's gone bust. Also has a reputation for doing a bit of sharp dealing in the art agent line. Nothing concrete, mind you, but lots of rumours. Has a big house he hasn't paid for—"

"He told me that."

"OK, OK. I'm telling you two things. One, he's never been inside or in real trouble, so maybe he's smart, or maybe just lucky. But two, he's desperate for cash, doesn't know where to turn to pay off the people he owes money to. Which may be why he's mixed up with Lew Fosskind, our elephant bird." O'Rourke belched, the sound a small explosion in Catchpole's ear. "Lew's a Mafia lawyer. Not the only one, not the most important one, but one of a dozen they call on when they have a little problem about things like money they want to launder. Nothing violent, they don't use Lew for that, and you don't often see him in a courtroom. We'd be very happy if Lew was behind bars, his employers too. And strangely enough Lew has a habit. Not coke or H, what you'd call the gee-gees."

"I've never called horses gee-gees in my life."

"Pardon me for joking. Lew is a gambler on the horses, all right? And like most gamblers a loser. Now, the Mafia link. You heard of Carlo Matresca? I'll tell you anyway. Was a major boss in this great city, belonged to a family fell out with the Patreses, retired to a fortress outside LA where the only way anyone can get at him is by dropping a bomb. Carlo has a big bag of laundered money to get rid of, likes to turn it into pictures.

He's used Grayson before as someone he halfway trusts to tell him he's buying the right things, then runs a check on Grayson to make sure this East Coast gent isn't trying to put one over on him. And the man he uses to run the check is our Lew."

"Fosskind was acting for this Mafia boss Matresca?"

"Ex-boss." He belched again. "Onions. Remember Paddy Phelan's place I took you on Second Avenue? Never forget your face when you saw the size of the T-bone. T-bone, Paddy's martinis, my lunch. With some of the boys."

"I thought I saw a deal being done at Grayson's home, but my latest information is that it fell through."

"Well now, there you're more up-to-date than I am. I'm told Lew did a deal for Carlo, the deal was OKed, Carlo has the goods. I understand he takes a look at the pictures he buys after they've been unpacked, then sticks 'em down in the cellar, his own taste being more in the way of *Playboy* centrefolds."

"And it's the Renoir we're talking about?"

"Now that I couldn't say. My informant is pretty reliable but not into every detail of Matresca's establishment. What I'm telling you is Carlo's bought a picture, Grayson was the agent or what name you give it, Lew had it checked by some expert, made sure it was the genuine article. You want to know who painted the picture, tell me it was Renoir, I don't know any different. What I got comes from a couple of people, but ain't neither of them taken a degree in French painters. One's in the same bed with a secretary in Lew's office, says our Lew's a very sharp customer as if we didn't know. Useful to you, any of this?" Catchpole said it solved some problems, posed others. "Ain't that a bitch? You thinking of crossing the water again, let me know, understand, Catchers?"

"Rory, thanks for everything. You've been a lot of help. Tell me one thing."

"For you, anything."

"How many of Paddy's vodka martinis did you down?"

"After the first half-dozen I lost count." One more great belch and the connection was broken.

At the Old Bailey the prosecution case ended shortly after lunch. Golightly made an opening speech for the defence emphasizing that, the confession aside, there was no evidence any crime at all had been committed by his client. He was at his most oleaginous in describing Jenny Midway. "You have heard her father saying what a delightful girl she is, friendly, open-hearted, a loving daughter. I don't wish for a moment to suggest anything else. But did her parents know about her relationship with the defendant, or with other men? They did not. And when her father said she 'enjoyed life to the full' did it not occur to you, as it did to me, that she was the kind of young woman who might do almost anything on the spur of the moment, that she is a creature of impulse who could go anywhere that took her fancy? I hope, as I am sure you do, that she is safe and well. What I am sure of is that apart from the so-called confession, about which my client will tell you, there is not a shadow of a case against him. I suggest that the police picked on him as a possible suspect first of all because of his colour, and questioned him again and again, playing a cat and mouse game with him. If Gabriel Lewis had a white skin instead of a black one, their treatment of him would have been different."

It was a bold opening, although one made less plausible by Gabriel's appearance. There could be no getting round the fact that he was a very big man. He filled the witness box when he entered it, and looked far more like a cat than a mouse. But he responded well enough to Golightly's questioning as he described how he had been brought in for questioning, released, brought in again and released again.

"What did you think after the second time you were brought in?"

"Thought I gotta watch out, take care. They wanted to get me some way or other, thought I'd protect myself the best way I could." How had he in fact spent the crucial weekend? As he had told the police, in Portsmouth and then with Sammy Grizzard. He insisted he had not told Patsy to invent the telephone calls nor asked Daisy to say he had been with her the whole time.

Golightly had chosen this as the better of the stories available to him, although it contradicted the testimony of the two women. Now he faced the improbability of it directly. "Can you think of any reason why the two women should have invented those stories?"

Gabriel's features were made for menace rather than charm, but he lowered his eyes and murmured something inaudible. The Judge told him sharply to speak up. Eyes raised for a moment to look at the jury, then lowered again, Gabriel said: "Just saw I was in trouble, tried to help me, I s'pose. I never asked 'em to make up those stories, I know that."

Golightly left it at that, and moved on to the earrings his client had given to Daisy. Dayton-Williams had not made too much of this, because it turned out the earrings had been imported to England in quantity, and could be bought in several shops and stores. Golightly by contrast dwelt on the earrings, and asked just how it was Jenny had given them to Lewis.

"Why, I just said something like, 'Hey they're neat,' and she said, 'you like 'em you have 'em, I got plenty more.' "

"She actually used those words, 'I got plenty more?' "

"Can't swear they was the exact words, but it was her meaning. Then she took 'em off, said, 'Catch,' threw 'em to me, I put them in my pocket. All there was to it."

"Were these the only things she gave you?"

"No, she liked giving presents. Gave me this ring." He held up a large hand, a ring glittering on his pinky. "Said these here were sapphires and diamonds. I found out they was just—what you call 'em, blue stones, and the diamonds weren't real either. That was the way with Jenny, liked giving things, wanted you to think they were important, valuable."

Golightly assumed a puzzled expression that made him look like a bewildered duck. "Those earrings now, why would she give them to you? Not so that you could pass them on to a girlfriend, surely?"

The boxer's face split into a wide, attractive smile. "I think she had in mind I'd wear 'em. Men, they wear earrings, you know. I got some big gold ones. But wear these, with the little men, I thought they were neat but not for me. So I gave 'em to Daisy." A black juryman nodded approvingly.

After taking as smoothly as possible those two hurdles of the alibis and the earrings, Golightly moved on to the heart of the matter, the confession. If the jury could be induced to believe it had been obtained by force or the threat of it, the prosecution case would be destroyed no matter what anybody thought about the rest of it.

"Now, on Friday you were again interrogated by the police for a period of several hours. Is that correct?" The words rolled out slow and smooth like ball-bearings. "And you admitted taking the—ah—Rover car, said you slept in it on Sunday night, then spent most of Monday with a friend in Portsmouth. Was that story true?" In a low voice Gabriel said it was. "Yet on the following morning you admitted to killing Jenny Midway on Monday. Was that admission the truth?"

"No, sir. I never saw her that Monday."

"So why did you make the confession?"

Low-voiced, almost *sotto voce*, Gabriel said: "I was frightened."

The ball-bearings running perfectly, Golightly again anticipated the jury's natural scepticism when they looked at Gabriel's bulk. "You're a big man, a boxer. Just tell us what happened to frighten you."

Low-voiced still but perfectly audible, eyes cast low, the boxer told his story. "They came down to me, in the cell, two of 'em." Bertie Minnett sat with arms folded, red face impassive, as Gabriel said he was the boss. "He said, 'Now we're going to teach you, don't like liars,' something like that. Then the other one punched me in the stomach, and they beat me up."

"Did you fight back, hit them?"

"Nah, knew it would be no use, just covered up, tried to make sure they didn't hurt me bad. I'm a boxer, know about that."

"You've heard evidence that the injuries were superficial. It has been suggested you made them yourself. What do you have to say about that?"

"No way I'd do that. Superficial, right, I said I knew how to cover up. Another reason, like they said they was teaching me a lesson, didn't take that long, maybe no more than five minutes. Then they said what they'd do next time. Frightened me, that." With these last words, spoken head well down, his voice dropped to a whisper yet remained audible. Catchpole, who heard every whispered word, admired Gabriel's acting ability. The judge asked him to repeat the last words. He did so, then put his head down again.

Golightly affected surprise. "Why were you frightened?"

"What they said. Told me when they came back again they'd smash my hands. I'm a boxer, hands are all I got, smash my hands I'm finished. Told me how they'd explain it, say I went crazy, did it myself, broke the bones. That's what they said."

"And you believed them?"

Now Gabriel looked up, at his counsel, the judge, the jury. "Didn't know what to believe. Just knew they'd got it in for me and they'd fix me one way or another. Thought about it that night, reckoned my best chance was say what they wanted, go on trial, get myself acquitted, 'cause I know I never saw Jenny that day, and if I'd seen her wouldn't have touched her. Reckoned that was the best thing to do, only thing when they got it in for you the way they had for me. When they got you targeted they don't let go."

Would the jury swallow it? Minnett, talking to Catchpole in a Newgate Street pub later, was sure they wouldn't, said the cross-examination had shown how stupid the whole tale was. "Smashing his hands, what would we have used, a hammer? And how would he have broken the bones himself? It's stupid stuff, he's just a half-smart black bastard."

Catchpole said he hoped the jury would think so. That night he told Alice he was sure Lewis was lying. "Not that Minnett isn't capable of beating a suspect up, but I'm sure Lewis would have put up a fight, and if he had they'd have done more damage or left him alone." They were at the pudding stage of supper. He ate another mouthful, said reflectively: "Very good apple crumble. But if we allow Lewis wasn't beaten up, I still don't understand why he confessed."

He waited for comment. When it came he was surprised. She said: "You've changed."

"Come again?"

"Not so many years ago you'd have been beside yourself at the very idea anyone could be beaten up in the cells. Now you just say it could have happened. What if it did?"

"I don't follow you."

"Suppose you found out Lewis's story was true, what would you do about it?"

"Minnett and Stenhouse would go up before a disciplinary board who'd investigate the whole thing."

"And then?"

"If the case was proved they would be compulsorily retired from the force. The least would be they'd get their cards marked, never get promotion, probably leave, join a security firm." She looked at him, said nothing. "I don't make the rules, that's the way things are. You have to accept reality, then do the best you can."

"Please, it isn't me that's changed, it's society?"

He laughed. "Woman, you've got a wicked tongue. Actually I do have standards. Intuitions too. They tell me you want me to give a hand with the washing up."

Giles's enjoyment was carried over to the following morning. At the Judges' Lodgings he was fussed over, his bed had been turned down and an electric blanket offered and rejected. The copy of *The Times* that waited for him in the morning had been ironed, and at breakfast it was remembered that he liked his eggs boiled for exactly four minutes and ate only ginger marmalade, a pot of which appeared on the table. The Rolls and its chauffeur awaited him, along with a small crowd when he appeared, wigged and robed, ducking his head in acknowledgement of the murmur that greeted him. It was all gratifying, in part because it was so unlike the circumstances of life at Harkland Court. And on the way to Court he thought of how he should deal with the Entwhistle matter. He was in an excellent temper when the Morling Post Office case was resumed.

The post office was at one end of the village street, and served also as the local newsagent and tobacconist. The post office section was at the back of the shop, and only two customers were inside at ten-thirty in the morning when a car drew up outside and two men jumped out. The shop and post office combined to make a reasonable living for its owner, a one-time paratrooper named George Crossan, and his wife Mildred. There were few people about in the street, but the car was seen to draw up by a spinster in her sixties, Patricia Pender, who was walking her dogs on the other side of the road. Miss Pender, a devout royalist, carried admiration of the Queen to the extent of owning two corgis. She had given the dogs a run on the village green, and was going back to her cottage at the other end of Morling. She saw the men, noticed that they wore black masks over the upper parts of their faces, and vaguely imagined that they must be connected with the preparations for a fête that was to take place in a week or two. Morling was a peaceful place. It never crossed her mind that they might have violent intentions.

Inside the shop one of the men shouted to the customers to lie face down on the floor. The two, one a man in his mid-forties, the other a young woman, did as they were told. One man stayed near the door, the other came up to the post office grille and ordered Mildred Crossan, behind the counter, to undo the partition door separating this section from the rest of the shop. She pressed the catch releasing the door and at the same time put her foot on an alarm bell that rang in the nearest police station, at Ravenslea four miles away. The bell also rang in the shop and brought George Crossan in from the back, hastily pulling up his trousers after a visit to the lavatory. He grasped the situation immediately, and brought down the man who had threatened Mildred with a flying tackle, knocking the revolver he held from his hand.

The man near the door had what George Crossan identified as a Kalashnikov rifle. He shouted something, and began firing. Three shots went astray, peppering National Savings posters, but two others hit Crossan in the shoulder and chest, another grazed his wife's neck, and a fourth struck the raider on the floor in the leg. He pulled himself free of George Crossan, and the two ran out of the shop. All the time the alarm bell rang.

Outside the shop Miss Pender's curiosity had been roused. She crossed the road and approached the car, with the corgis on leads. As she did so a man in the driving seat jumped out, pulling on a mask, and the other men ran out of the shop. Miss Pender, realizing something was wrong, moved towards the three crying out the traditional words: "Stop, thief." The driver was behind her, and she received a blow that knocked her to the ground. The corgis, free from the lead, yapped wildly and attacked the raiders' trouser legs. The man with the Kalashnikov fired a short burst that killed one dog immediately. The other was also hit, and had to be put down. The men got into the car. It went away down the street with a scream of tyres.

The raid had taken six minutes in all, from the time the car pulled up outside the post office to the moment it roared away. No money had been taken. Neither George Crossan, who was in hospital for two weeks, nor his wife who was released within hours and back behind the counter on the following day, was able to say what they looked like. Miss Pender, who had fractured her skull when she fell, was unconscious for several days, and although she made a good recovery was at first unable to remember what had happened. She was much distressed by the deaths of the corgis, knew little about cars, and was able to say no more than that this one was big, and the colour might have been blue. Had she caught a glimpse of the driver before he put on his mask? If so, she could not remember what he looked like.

There had been a delay of a few minutes before the police at Ravenslea got on the track of what the papers called the Post Office Raiders. By the time they got to Morling the raiders were well away, and that two of them were caught was in part due to their own rashness. When a police car near Leatherhead in Surrey, some thirty miles from Morling, flagged down a Jaguar doing seventy in an area with a thirty-mile speed limit, the driver did not stop, and the car chase that followed ended with the Jaguar going off the road and crashing into a lamppost. The two men inside were too dazed to offer resistance, and were quickly identified as participants in the raid. One had a leg wound, and the Kalashnikov rifle was in the car, along with a Smith & Wesson that proved to be a dummy replica.

The wounded man was Ferdie "Peppermint" Mintoff, and the

man whose prints were found on the Kalashnikov was Pete Luciano, called Lucky after the gangster. They were both Londoners, although their parents came from Cyprus and Italy. They were of little importance in the metropolitan criminal world, no more than petty crooks. Nor were they particularly violent, although both had done time for burglary. The case against them looked open and shut, since forensic identified the bullets as coming from Luciano's rifle, and Mintoff's leg wound was presumptive evidence. Some gaps remained. It seemed unlikely that the Jaguar, stolen the day before in East London, was the car Miss Pender had seen, since its colour was a pale grey that couldn't conceivably have been called blue. The police thought it had been for use as a getaway car, after the original one seen by Miss Pender had been abandoned. Luciano and Mintoff denied any connection with the raid. Their story was that they had taken the Jag for a lark after having a few jars. They had driven out to Surrey, stopped, and had been taking turns at target practice on a tin can. Lucky, who never could master a gun, had accidentally shot his friend in the leg, and was taking him to hospital when the police chase began. Since their story was that they had nothing to do with the raid they were obviously not prepared to name the other man on it.

This was the case that unfolded before Giles, the hopeless defence being in the hands of a barrister named Lackington whose appearance, untidy, slightly grubby, and giving an impression of being unshaved, Giles distinctly disliked. It would have been foolish to show such dislike openly, and Giles prided himself on never being foolish. Even when Watching he had been careful not to stray beyond the grounds of what he regarded as proper behaviour.

He was now able to torment the unlucky Lackington with little *ohs*, raised eyebrows, sighs, and incredulous *Really, Mr. Lackingtons* that fell short of any possible accusation of bias, yet made his low opinion of the defence counsel clear. Lackington was aware too of his own impotence in the face of it, and it made him exaggerate a natural tendency to histrionic gestures. It also brought sweat to his brow and cheeks, sweat he wiped off with a handkerchief not altogether clean.

But still, Lackington hammered away at the single hopeful point in the defence case, the fact that neither of the accused could be identified. George Crossan reluctantly admitted that he had no idea whether the man he tackled was short or tall. Lackington referred to Crossan's first statement to the police, in which he said the man was about six feet tall, then asked Mintoff to stand up.

"Mr. Mintoff's height is five foot six. The man you tackled was six inches taller. I suggest to you that he was not the man you so courageously tackled."

"I don't know, it was all done in a moment, and I was that angry I just charged into him."

"Let me see, your own height is nearly six foot, I should say."

"Five eleven."

"So you were charging a man about your own height. Now, just look at the defendant—"

"Mr. Lackington." Lackington paused in mid-sentence, looked at Giles. "The man was on the ground, and the witness has said already he had no idea of his height."

"But he was not on the ground when the witness charged him. And he told the police—"

"We have heard what Mr. Crossan said to the police shortly after he had been shot. He has now had time to think again. I think you may trust the jury to decide which of his statements is more likely to be correct."

The day passed pleasantly in such minor tormenting of greasy Lackington. As the witnesses came and went, and the forensic men gave evidence that the shots fired in the post office had come from the Kalashnikov found in the car, Giles separated part of his mind from the case and dwelt on Mrs. Entwhistle, her so-called cousin, and the come-uppance he would get from young Kelsey, the man who would solve the Entwhistle problem. In his mind the cousin's appearance took on the greasy grubbiness of Lackington's, and he was taught a lesson by Kelsey, a lesson that would make him understand the unwisdom of trying to blackmail his betters. Another part of his mind, however, stayed aware of what was going on, and he continued to tease Lackington as the barrister plugged away at his hopeless task of trying to find a crack in the solid wall of the prosecution case.

So the witnesses came and went. It was not until late afternoon that Patricia Pender took the stand. A tall thin figure dressed in black, she walked to the witness box with the aid of two sticks, and told the story of what she had seen and the blows from the driver standing behind her that had rendered her unconscious. As she described it all her voice was raised.

"I thank God I didn't see what happened to Philip and Elizabeth."

Prosecuting counsel paused before saying: "They were your two dogs?"

"My corgis. When I recovered I asked to see them. I knew they would be unhappy without me. The villains had shot them both." She choked, wept a little. Some of the jury were visibly moved.

When Lackington rose to cross-examine he thought of making the point that there was no actual proof either of the defendants had shot the corgis, since there were no witnesses other than their unconscious owner. He decided such nit-picking would only alienate the jury, and concentrated on the lack of positive identification.

"Let me just go over again what you actually saw. You saw a car stop outside the post office, and its colour was blue. Is that correct?"

"I think it was blue. Or perhaps greeny-blue."

"Am I right in saying it was certainly not pale grey?"

"Oh yes. It was a sort of blue. Or a sort of green."

"And you don't know the make of the car?"

"I know nothing about motorcars except that they make a great deal of noise and pollute the atmosphere."

"Then you saw two masked men enter the post office. Can you say whether they were tall or short?"

"I'm afraid I didn't notice."

"And then they came running out. You realized there was something wrong and crossed the road. But the two men were still masked. Can you identify them as the two defendants?"

"No. I couldn't see their faces, and didn't notice their clothes."

"And then you were struck on the head from behind. Am I right in saying this couldn't have been done by either of my clients?"

"Oh yes. It was the driver, you see. He was behind me."

Lackington's manner was not naturally sympathetic, but he made it as nearly so as possible. "Would you agree that it would be fair to say you knew something wrong was happening and tried to intervene, but you are unable to identify your attacker or anybody else involved?"

Miss Pender asked for the question to be repeated. Giles intervened.

"I'm not surprised you were puzzled by that rather lengthy question. I think the nub of it is that you are unable to make a positive identification of anybody involved in the raid. Is that so?"

"No." Miss Pender paused. "I mean, I can't identify any of them. But I've seen a photograph."

Lackington looked bewildered and dismayed. Giles said: "Take your time, Miss Pender. Just tell us what you mean by saying you've seen a photograph."

"It was the driver. I saw his face as he was getting out of the car, just before he pulled on the mask. At first I didn't remember what he looked like, I think perhaps I didn't want to." She looked appealingly at Giles, who nodded benevolently, then asked where she had seen the photograph that jogged her memory.

"In a paper, an old paper. I didn't see the papers for two or three weeks while I was in hospital, but my daily hadn't been cancelled, and when I came home a lot of them were piled up. The lady who helps in the house never throws anything away. So I looked through them all and I recognized him." She paused. "He was coloured. I mean, black. He was a black man."

Mintoff, in the dock, said: "Fucking shit," then subsided. Giles contemplated further questions, decided against them, said: "Mr. Lackington, it seems I am doing some of your work. Does that answer prompt some further questions?"

"It does, my lord." Giles nodded graciously, and Lackington asked the name of the paper.

"The *Banner*. I've taken it for years."

"And what was the photograph you think you recognized? How did this man's picture come to be in the paper?"

"Why, it was because he'd been questioned about the girl who was missing, and then he'd been released. I can't remember his name, but I'm sure you'll know it."

"Was it Gabriel Lewis?"

Miss Pender leaned forward as if to congratulate the defence counsel. "Of course, that was it. My memory isn't what it was since the accident." She added apologetically: "I always think of it as an accident."

Lackington asked another question or two, then sat down. That the driver should be identified was of no help to his clients. Prosecuting counsel established that she had seen the driver's face for only a few seconds while he put on the mask. She agreed, but said she had been close to him, and felt sure he was the man whose photograph had been in the paper.

That brought the day's proceedings in Court to an end, but a great deal of activity followed that evening. Detective Inspector Havering, who had charge of investigating the Morling raid, was not the quickest-witted nor the most energetic man in the county force. The photograph in the *Banner* had been found, a head and shoulders that appeared after Lewis's second release from interrogation, but Havering's natural inclination was to assume the old spinster had lost the few wits she possessed after being hit on the head and learning her corgis had been killed, and hysterically assumed that a man wearing a black mask had a black face. Hence, he need do nothing about it. When his side-kick, Sergeant Savage, suggested it might be a good idea to let Scotland Yard know about the identification because Lewis couldn't have been in two places at once, Havering replied that up in London they seemed sure the man Lewis had been engaged in disposing of the woman who disappeared, and it would be a mistake to muddy the waters with Pender's silly story. He was dismayed when he heard an hour later that Mintoff was changing his plea to guilty, and had made a statement that Lewis was the driver of the car, that it was a green Rover, and that they had an arrangement to split up afterwards, using the stolen Jaguar to confuse any police chase. Mintoff also said he had been brought in by Lewis, and understood only dummy weapons were to be used. He added that the Morling raid was a copycat one based on the half-dozen earlier successful raids with which they had nothing to do.

Havering read the statement gloomily, said to Savage: "Trying to get out from under."

"Yes, sir. But it's true Mintoff's gun was a dummy. And in the other post office jobs they wore stocking masks not black ones, and they were much more professional. Morling was a real botch-up, the shooting just stupid, he could have given Crossan a tap." Havering grunted. "We should let the Yard know, guv."

"I suppose so." Havering picked up the telephone.

Wilson brought the news in to Catchpole, who told him to check on the computer for any possible links between Lewis, Mintoff and Luciano. Wilson came back looking unhappy.

"Mintoff and Luciano have both got plenty on their sheets, stealing cars, burglarizing houses after checking the owners are away, nothing violent. Knew each other as kids, went to the same educational establishments for making your way in life without working. Neither of 'em, Mintoff or Luciano, ever held a job for more than a few weeks. No surprise, what do they know about except thieving? Mintoff's got a girlfriend, Luciano a wife and a couple of kids. Another link. Lewis's manager Nat Saxon used to be a bookie before he took up making money by handling half-smart pugs, Luciano was a runner for him, knew Lewis that way."

He paused to draw breath. Catchpole said: "Charlie, you've spent more than a minute telling me nothing. I don't want to know what they did in the sheds behind the playground."

"OK, OK, there's more. That Peckham job Lewis was up for, when a supermarket was done for around six hundred nicker, Mintoff was in it, found guilty, went down for eighteen months. The supermarket manager said he'd been threatened, gave us a description, fitted Luciano to a T. Trouble is when the man came to give evidence he had a forgetful fit, couldn't say whether it was Arnold Schwarzenegger or a ten-year-old kid who had warned him off. Couple of other cases Lewis was mixed up in, robbery with a bit of violence when the people living in the house came back unexpectedly, Luciano was copped for one of 'em, Mintoff for the other. You want links, we got 'em. Something else. Fashionable gear nowadays and for some time back if you're shy of being seen is stocking masks, but our boys like to be different. For the other jobs they just wore those black masks you pull on quickly, cover nose and top part of the face. Like the Lone Ranger. And like this post office job. One more thing and that's it. Last time Peppermint, which is what they call Mintoff, was pulled in he swore he'd never go down again. Bertie Minnett tried running him as a snout, but found him too unreliable."

"So now he's trying to cop a plea by identifying Lewis."

Catchpole brooded. Wilson wondered what he could be thinking about. The answer came as he began to talk, using the Sergeant as a sounding board. "If we believe him and the woman Pender, Lewis was on this job, so he can't have had anything to do with Jenny Midway's disappearance. But she saw the driver only for a few seconds, and maybe Mintoff's nursing a grudge. So it could be he wasn't on the raid." Wilson made no comment on this statement of the obvious. "Even so, Charlie, why confess to a murder? The two things must be linked somehow. If you say A you must say B, you know that old line of argument." Wilson did not bother to shake his head. Miss Hilly was then silent for so long that the Sergeant was inclined to cough or sneeze. Instead he speculated on the possibility that this unwelcome development might involve changing his weekend plans. He almost jumped from his chair when Catchpole said loudly, and with an uncharacteristic edge to his voice: "The conniving bastard."

"Lewis?"

"Not Lewis, he wouldn't have the brains. Curly Maddox. Shall I tell you what happened when Lewis saw his brief that Saturday morning? Lewis said, look, here they are trying to land me with killing this girl and I never touched her, never saw her that Monday. But they want to know where I was, and I can't tell them because I was doing a job that went wrong and people got hurt. I had to tap an old lady on her nut, she'll be all right, but I can't say where I was, you get me? I don't say he spelt it out that plainly, that would have been the sense of it. So then Curly sees the best way of getting Lewis out of the job he did is a confession to the one he didn't do. He knows we wouldn't have enough to go against Lewis without a confession and tells him what to say, they'll get away with it. Lewis fakes a few bruises and scratches, goes for trial, retracts the confession, gets a verdict. And we'll still believe he killed the girl and got away with it, won't be looking to link him up with any other job done at the same time."

"Supposing he doesn't? Get a verdict, I mean?"

"If it comes to it, he can always admit to the Morling job. But the chances are he'll be acquitted and his pals will take their medicine, leave the wheelman still a mystery, no point in dragging him into it. They may even have thought they had a chance of getting off, specially Mintoff with his dummy gun, or being let down lightly. And that's the way it could have gone if it weren't for Miss Pender."

Wilson said: "Diabolical." Then: "Would Maddox do that?"

"Would a pig find truffles?"

"So what next, guv'nor?"

"Next you check Miss Pender's blood group, also see if forensic can check the hairs on the tyre lever against a sample of her hair. If they match, then Lewis is off the murder count and looking at five or more for the post office job."

"This blood group, it's rare, one in a hundred they say. So it's a hundred to one chance against Pender and Jenny Midway being the same."

"A hundred to one shot won the Grand National not too many years ago. My father backed it, one of the few bits of luck he ever had."

"So if it does come up, what then?"

"Then I put my neck on the block."

You had to hand it to him, Wilson said to his live-in girlfriend that evening, there his case was shot to pieces, he was in dead trouble, but when he said that about his neck being on the block it was like saying he'd be going round the corner for a pint. Not, Wilson added, that Miss Hilly was one for pints.

The hundred to one shot came up. Within forty-eight hours Patricia Pender's blood group had been confirmed as B rhesus negative, and hair samples from her head had been matched against those on the tyre lever and found to coincide in the nine components making it statistically certain they came from the same head. Jenny's hairbrush had been washed just before her disappearance, making a comparison impossible in her case, and the hairs from the tyre lever had decayed even though preserved under laboratory conditions, so that the presence of so many trace elements was remarkable.

And that was that. Dayton-Williams stood up in Court to say that in the light of further evidence that had become known to them the Crown was not proceeding with the prosecution. Mr. Justice Clements thanked the jury and discharged Lewis. Mr. Golightly looked cheerful, Curly Maddox impassive, the acquitted man gloomy. Lewis was immediately rearrested, charged with robbery and causing grievous bodily harm to Patricia Pender, and taken off to Ravenslea prison.

Outside the Court Catchpole came face to face with Curly Maddox, and couldn't resist saying: "So it didn't work."

"I don't get you."

"The little plan Lewis thought up *entirely on his own*," Catchpole said with heavy sarcasm.

Maddox shook his head. His bald pate gleamed. "You know as well as I do a solicitor has to act on his client's instructions, put up the defence he's given."

"So it was just chance Lewis was stonewalling Friday night and coughing Saturday morning. After he'd seen you."

"Must have been. Unless of course your boys did have something to do with making him change his mind." Maddox permitted himself a brief smile as they parted.

The Big Man's immediate comment was confined to two words: "A pity." Then: "You don't trust Minnett. If you trusted him completely you'd have known he was telling the truth and that Lewis must be lying about the attack. Then you'd have looked for a reason." He cut short Catchpole's plea or argument about the coincidence of the blood groupings. "You should have looked for a reason, done some digging."

Was this the same Big Man who had said unless there was an overwhelming argument against it they were bound to charge Lewis? But Catchpole knew the comment was true, and was not surprised when the Big Man said he might have got too close to the case. Although there was no question of an investigation, and he accepted there was a basis for regarding the confession as credible, he was turning over the case now to Bill Lowry. Catchpole knew he was being told, in the friendliest possible way, both that Jenny Midway's disappearance was no longer going to be top priority and that he had made a muck of it.

That evening Alice was indignant. "But you've told me Lowry's a deadbeat, just waiting for retirement."

"That's right. He'll go through the motions, wait for something to turn up. If nothing does, the file stays open." When she said that was awful he corrected her. "Not so. Just the way it goes. There's more crime than we can handle, too much time spent and too many bodies used on cases that make news. Who knows, maybe the girl is wacky enough to have upped and gone to Bolivia or Buenos Aires with a coke baron she fancied."

"You don't believe that."

"What I believe doesn't matter now. I had my chance and blew it, giving credit to that confession."

"I wish you weren't so bloody *logical*." They were in the bedroom. She was standing close to him, and suddenly punched him in the solar plexus. He gasped, they both laughed, collapsed on to the bed, made love. Afterwards he said: "How's your great investment?"

"Fantastic. Brett's in Germany or Holland now, negotiating with agents who want to handle it. They've got enquiries from a dozen countries. You'll see, that ten thousand will turn into a hundred."

"Good for you."

"The way you say it means 'I know you're wrong.' All because Brett's my brother."

"I give in. Let's work out ways to spend the hundred thousand." He put a hand on her breast.

"I'm an awful bitch, going on at you when they've just taken you off this case and you must be feeling miserable. I'm sorry. Truly."

"I'll survive," he said. "And I'll tell you something. The case was a strain. Not only on me, on us I mean. I know I'm sometimes a thoughtless bastard. It goes with the job, but sometimes worse than others."

"I'm not complaining. I've said before, when I do you'll know."

"Except about Brett."

She laughed. "Except about Brett."

9. *Time the Healer*

"This can't go on." The words astonished John Midway because they did not come out of his own mouth as they might and he felt should have done, but were spoken by Susan. She had been sitting astride him when they made love, a position curiously satisfying his need to be a body something was *done to* rather than doing, a continuation of his role as convalescing patient. She rolled off him and went to the grubby bathroom where the bath had a ring of grime round it, and spilt powder was trodden deep into the carpet because she had never bothered to clear it up. He looked at her plump wobbling buttocks and wondered why he was in this flat with a woman neither particularly intelligent nor wonderfully attractive. The boss and his secretary, he thought, what a cliché. How did I get into this situation, and why wasn't it me who said: *This can't go on?*

But it was Susan who now repeated the words as she came back, moving with a duck waddle reminiscent of Mrs.—no, Baroness—Thatcher. He watched with detached interest as she put on briefs, trousers, bra, jersey, doing it all a little clumsily. She said he had better get dressed, and while he did so expanded on the theme.

"Eleanor doesn't know about us, does she?" He acknowledged that was so. "I'm surprised she's noticed nothing, the time you spend here, but you should tell her."

"Tell her?" The idea shocked him.

"She must know, must guess."

"I don't think—she's never said anything, shown any sign, doesn't seem to worry whether I'm at home or not. All she talks about is her cooking job."

Susan laughed briefly, then repeated: "Anyway, it can't go on. Can it?"

"I'm not sure what you mean."

Her gesture embraced the rumpled bed, the carpet mysteriously stained, the untidy dressing table, perhaps the rest of the flat, even the roar of Stoke Newington traffic outside. "You coming here. Me seeing you at the office every day, just your secretary. Eleanor not knowing. The secrecy. I hate it, so must you. All the pretending, I can't stand it."

He was astonished. The idea that what had been for him something like a course of therapy could have been a strain on Susan had never occurred to him. Confronted by the thought he had no instant reaction, felt dazed as a boxer who has just received a punishing but less than knockout punch. He said he was sorry, asked what she wanted to do.

"It's not me, it's you, what *you* want to do." He stared at her. "All right, I'll tell you what I want. I want Eleanor to know about us, if you don't tell her I will. I want you to meet Stephen, know more about me. If I was someone at the office coming to you with a problem, you'd ask them all about their background, family life and so on. I know you would, I've seen you do it. Then we can decide what to do." In a slightly shaky voice she said, "I love you, you know that."

The word dismayed him. *Love:* surely the activity they had engaged in had nothing to do with love, which was—what, exactly? Of course if asked he would have said he loved Eleanor, as he had loved Jenny and grieved for her. If pressed he would also have said he loved David, unresponsive as he had been when a boy and now was as a man. Yet he knew those feelings to be quite different from what Susan Cook was talking about. The round rosy face, the slightly trembling lips, the determined yet yearning look—contemplating them he felt something, perhaps a stirring of *affection*, but not *love*. He took her hand, said, "I didn't know you felt like that." The hand was plump, the fingers stubby. He suddenly remembered the elegance of Eleanor's hands. "Of course I'll be pleased to meet Stephen. I'd no idea you wanted me to know—your family."

"I want you to know *me*, be interested in me. You've been going to bed with me, is that too much to ask?" She removed her hand, stood up. The lips no longer quivered, the plump face showed determination. "Something has to be settled. I want us to be together properly." She paused, but he said nothing. "If you say that isn't possible, it would be no good, I must get another job. I can't go on seeing you every day in the office and then here, the way we do. I just can't bear it."

It was the kind of moment when he might have expected tears, as women had wept in his office when talking of their marriage problems, but her gaze was firm, might even have been called implacable. They talked for another few minutes during which he heard with dismay the clichés dripping from his mouth: *think it over*, *do nothing we might regret*, *find out what Eleanor feels*, *decide in haste repent at leisure* . . . in the end she stopped him and said if he wanted to end it he should say so. "I shan't put my head in the gas oven, I'm not the sort. Anyway, the cooker's electric." No no, he said, it was just that they should give it a day or two, do nothing hasty. She acknowledged the words with a nod.

When he left her rain was falling, the streets shiny with it. He put his big nose in the air, relished the drops on his face as he waited for a taxi. On the way back to Fulham he was overcome by a wave of self-recrimination. How feeble it had been to fall into Susan's arms, how badly he had behaved just now in response to her declaration of feeling for him. As the driver kept up a flow of conversation about the recession, the petrol you used driving around if you didn't get a fare, the hard times getting harder, two kids under five and the wife always grumbling, a litany of complaint to which he seemed to expect no reply or comment, John felt a surge of admiration for Susan's courage in confronting him with that either/or statement of the way things were for her. Along with that, one could say parallel to it, went indignation at Eleanor's behaviour. If she had accepted from the beginning the reality of Jenny's death as he had done, they could have mourned together, each comforting the other. If that had happened, he would never have turned to Susan. Yet he knew this was only another evasion to escape the consequences of his own actions by blaming Eleanor. Tears ran down his cheeks. "Nobody's fault," he said aloud. "It was nobody's fault."

"I dunno about that," the driver said. "Ask me it's the bleeding government letting in all the foreigners. Take the minicabs, we got to have the knowledge before we go on the road in a black cab, but these minicab drivers they don't take tests, you get your Poles and your Pakis, Chinks and blacks and what have you, they can get behind the wheel though half of 'em can barely speak the bleeding language let alone know one bit of London from another. *You* got to tell *them* the route, can you believe it?" John made a sound to show he had been listening. Decisive action, he thought, that's the thing, I must speak to Eleanor. The driver took the sound for assent. "I tell you I reckon this country's finished, best to let the Jerries run it, they will in a few years, I'm off with the wife and kids when I've got the necessary. Australia's the place I reckon, they got a quota system there, you know that? Here we are, Sapphic Street. You ordered a minicab you'd been heading for Forest Hill instead of Fulham."

He gave the man too large a tip, but got no thanks for it. Then the gestures made so many times through the years, key turned in lock, feet wiped on mat, wet coat put on hanger. Voices from the living-room. Bright faces turned to him. Eleanor, David, Mary. He kissed the women on the cheek, put a hand on David's shoulder.

"Good news," Eleanor said. For a moment he thought of Jenny, wondered: Is it possible? Then Eleanor went on. "Mary. You say."

"I'm going to have a baby." She looked at David who smiled, put his hand over hers.

He said it was wonderful, but his mind was full of the problem of Susan and the need to tell Eleanor, and the words did not come out as they should have done from the personnel chief of MultiCorpus. Nobody said that was so, but David retreated into his shell of silence as Eleanor said what a perfect time late autumn was for a baby, summer was the worst, sweating out those last two or three months, but autumn was much better too than the dead of winter. Mary smiled occasionally, sometimes looked at David. There was a silence. John knew something was expected of him, but what? He stayed silent.

"When the baby comes your flat will be too small." Eleanor spoke to her son and daughter-in-law, but John felt the remark was directed at him. Mary said they could manage. Eleanor went on: "I said we might be able to help them get something bigger. There must be a separate room for the baby, otherwise it's hell."

Now David came out of the shell and spoke, the words conventional enough but said with a sort of contained violence. "Mary said we could manage for the first months."

"But where you live isn't—well, it could be better." Eleanor looked at John. "I'm sure we can help. And if we can it seems silly not to."

He felt passionate irritation. This was the kind of problem brought occasionally to him in the office, but what right had they to bring it into his home when his mind was concentrated on the problem of Eleanor and Susan? He said it had been a hard day, there was no need to settle anything that evening, it was something he and Eleanor should talk over. Mary looked bewildered, David retreated again into silence. He tried to put things right with David when they left, saying he was sorry to sound brusque, a bad moment, he had a lot of things on his mind. David responded with his rare but sweet smile. Mary said nothing more than good night.

Then it was back to Eleanor, who asked him what was the matter, he had sounded as if he wanted to know nothing about the baby and had no intention of helping them. "They didn't ask, of course not, it was my idea. When Mary has to leave her job they won't find it easy to manage. I thought we could put down the deposit they'll need for a bigger flat or a small house. We've got the money, haven't we?"

"I suppose so, yes. What does it matter?" She stared at him. "Time will decide it all, time heals everything. Jenny dead, a child coming into the world, one life for another. None of it matters."

"John, what's wrong with you?" He shook his head, his lower lip was thrust out but then retreated. "You don't like my having a job, is that it? You want me to be dependent on you, like the idea women are inferior to men, have to rely on them. I'd never have believed it was possible. Don't you *want* to help your son and his wife?"

He felt as if his mind had been sliced in two. One part was prepared to engage in discussion about Susan, discussion, explanation, argument. It would elaborate a position, explain what had happened and why, tell how near he had been to a breakdown from which Susan had saved him, a breakdown for which Eleanor had been in part responsible because of her foolish refusal to accept the fact of Jenny's death. Yet another part of his mind winced away from these agonizing subjects. The sense of guilt nascent when Susan first took him to bed was overwhelmingly present now he was confronted by the need to tell Eleanor he had cancelled out the thirty years of marriage as if they were so many days. You've changed, he wanted to tell the big-boned woman who stared at him now with what seemed muted belligerence, the shadow of Jenny has fallen on us. It has alienated you from me, like you I have become a different person and the life we lived is over, replaced by something neither of us has ever known.

This he found it impossible to say, and returned almost random replies to what was being said about the strain on David and Mary and also on her, Eleanor, as she tried to come to terms with a life from which Jenny was missing. Now that this man Lewis had been acquitted, charged apparently through a mistake made by the police, would the police give up looking for Jenny? she asked. And didn't they have some responsibility, she and John, for the fact that they hadn't really known Jenny, were they sure they knew more about David? When he said none of this mattered, they should simply accept that Jenny had gone, she cried out in anger and desperation: "You deal with people all the time, you're supposed to help them with problems, why don't you try to help *us*?" We have to help ourselves, he said, in this kind of catastrophe nobody else can help.

She glared at him. "Isn't that what I'm trying to do, help myself by doing this job? And help the rest of the family, David and Mary? What are *you* doing, may I ask?"

It was not possible to answer: I am going to bed with my secretary. That night, for the first time in years, they slept in separate rooms.

* * *

Giles returned from the Crown Court in excellent spirits. The flimsy defence put forward by greasy Lackington had collapsed with Mintoff's change of plea and his identification of Lewis as driver of the getaway car. Luciano had been found guilty of armed robbery and attempted murder, Lewis of robbery and causing grievous bodily harm, Mintoff of robbery only. They had gone down for ten, seven and three years respectively. Justice had been done.

On return to Harkland Court he prepared to see that it was done also in the Entwhistle affair. He telephoned the number he had for Jimmy Kelsey. A woman, one of Kelsey's ever-changing girlfriends no doubt, said Jim was out. Giles left his number, and when Kelsey rang back later that evening arranged to meet him in the snug at the Open Arms. This was a pub a few minutes' walk from Harkland Court, a quiet bar frequented mostly by men in pinstripe suits who talked about friends named only as the Colonel or old Bumpo or the Dreaded End. Sometimes the pinstripes were accompanied by gaunt well-dressed women who spoke little but downed their gins and vodkas fast and often. Giles used the Open Arms occasionally, perhaps at the end of a half-hour evening stroll he called a constitutional, and always sat in the little-used snug. He was on his own there, a whisky in front of him, umbrella by his side as guard against the wet and windy evening, when Jimmy Kelsey came in.

Jimmy was a fresh-faced boyish-looking man in his mid-twenties, who had been employed as secretary by one of Giles's friends, a building contractor named Fothergill. Giles had few friends, did not particularly wish for them, would not have counted Fothergill among their number although they had known each other at school, and was surprised to have his help invoked one day on the plea that they were old friends. Fothergill had discovered his young secretary had been, in his own phrase, robbing him blind by forging his name on cheques. The individual amounts were not large, but in total they added up to several hundred pounds. So why not prosecute? It seemed that Fothergill, trusting the young man as he put it, had used him as an agent in carrying out deals with some foreign companies which had, as the contractor put it, cut a few corners. What corners? Well, a reluctant Fothergill admitted, it was understood, absolutely understood by everybody, that wheels had to be oiled, paths to be smoothed, before a contract was signed and sealed. Fothergill had trusted young Kelsey, and Kelsey had betrayed the trust. Now if he was prosecuted, even if he was sacked, he was threatening to tell everything he knew. More and worse he was actually demanding promotion, an eventual partnership.

So what could Giles do? Why, talk to the young villain, make him see reason. Fothergill, a burly red-faced man, almost whimpered as he said he was prepared to make a reasonable deal, and had absolute faith in his old friend. "We were such chums at school." Giles remembered that Fothergill had rightly been called Bully Fothergill at school, although neither he nor John had been among his targets. On the basis that it would be interesting to see the young man prepared to take on Bully Fothergill he had talked to Jimmy Kelsey. When seen—this was a couple of years back—he had looked like a schoolboy, although his manner had a cockney brashness as he looked round the flat.

"You a judge, that right? Don't exactly live it up, do you?" Giles did not respond to this, but said he wanted to point out the seriousness of the young man's position.

"Serious? I don't see it, I'd call it a stand-off. He calls in the law, I tell all I know, and believe me I know enough, *and* I've got paper to show to prove it. Enough to put Fatso's head right down the pan. And he made it so easy, you know, so bleeding easy." Giles told him it wouldn't happen as he expected. "You just tell me why not, I'm listening."

"Very well. First of all, you are arrested. And you're guilty, as I understand it there is no doubt of that, the proof is irrefutable. You've been forging cheques, and you'll go to prison. The sentence will probably be three years, two if you're lucky."

"So? Go on."

"In prison—" Giles lingered over the next sentences. "You'll find your luck has run out. You are young, attractive. You'll be bought at auction. You know what I'm talking about? Of course you do." Kelsey said nothing. "You'll be the property of whoever buys you and you'll be raped. Buggered. If your owner is powerful enough he'll protect you. If not he may loan you out to other people."

Kelsey's lips moved in a sneer that, surprisingly, made him look more youthful. "You oughta write horror comics. What happens to Fatso? I'll take him with me. Others too maybe, but Fatso—I'd love to see that bastard get it."

"Don't be so sure you'd take him with you. First of all, to get him you have to dig a deeper hole for yourself, you realize that? You knew what he was doing, were part of it, said nothing. But now you're going to talk." Giles gave a small judicial cough. Kelsey's very blue eyes seemed to have grown larger. "But do you have absolute proof of your accusations? The man you're accusing has money, he will hire an expensive barrister, the other people you say have benefited from Fothergill's—shall we say generosity?—will deny it. If you've got factual material, the papers you mention, you should take care to keep it in a safe place. You understand I am speaking impartially, telling you the situation as I see it."

"But that fat bastard's a friend, right?" Giles said neutrally that they had been at school together, and the young man said, "Oh yeah." It seemed to Giles that there might have been some physical link between Fothergill and this young man so plainly not out of the top drawer. Had Bully Fothergill been that way inclined at school? He could not remember. Now Kelsey said, "So what?"

"You mean what course of action would I advise?"

"Yeah." He mimicked Giles's stateliness as he repeated the words. Giles merely looked at him. The wide blue eyes blinked, he muttered something that might have been *sorry*.

"You're looking at a prison sentence. I suppose you want to avoid it. If you forget the accusations you've been making I might be able to persuade Mr. Fothergill not to press charges."

"Like I said, a stand-off."

Giles ignored that. "You'd need to make a statement acknowledging the forgeries—"

"No way, no way I'll do that."

"—and making it clear you had no complaints of any kind against Mr. Fothergill and have no claim on him." Kelsey stood up, protesting. "Providing you sign such a statement Mr. Fothergill would agree to pay you an *ex gratia* sum of a thousand pounds in lieu of notice."

Kelsey sat down again. "That your idea?"

"Perhaps." In fact Fothergill had said it would be worth five thousand to get the young bastard off his back.

And that was what happened. The statement had been Giles's idea. The signing and witnessing had taken place in his chambers, and Fothergill had been happy for him to keep the document. Kelsey received the envelope containing the money with a radiant smile, and was almost embarrassing in his thanks.

"I owe you." The blue eyes looked deep into Giles's. "Good advice that was. It was out of order what I was thinking of, I see that now." Giles said he should keep out of trouble in future. "Yeah, right. Thing is I had an expensive girl, ditched her now, got a cheaper one." His smile was confiding. "But I owe you, I know it, I don't forget. Any time you got a problem let me know, I got friends. I'll keep in touch."

That was two years ago, and to Giles's surprise Jimmy Kelsey had kept in touch. Surprise and pleasure, for there was something about the fresh-faced audacity of the young fellow that he liked.

It was connected with the pleasure of Watching in some way, although he did not care to think exactly what the connection might be. Twice a year they dined together, once at Jimmy's expense, then at Giles's. (He had insisted that Giles should use his Christian name, although he made no attempt at similar familiarity.) The restaurants Jimmy chose were bright, flashy and new, and they served what to Giles seemed extraordinary food. When Giles was host he never moved outside the safe orbit of Simpsons, Rules and Wheeler's. Jimmy always brought a different girl, and introduced Giles as "my friend Judge Midway, who once kept me out of the nick." Jimmy always seemed to have money to spend and the girls, who had names like Jetta and Darlene, obviously adored him. Giles sometimes reflected that it was daring on his part to have any connection with Jimmy, but what harm could there be in it?

So it was with pleasure that the Honourable Mr. Justice Midway greeted young James Kelsey in the snug of the Open Arms. Giles was dressed soberly as usual, his clerical grey suit with turn-ups accompanied by a discreet striped shirt and neat bow tie. Jimmy was as stylishly casual as Giles had learned to expect, dark blue jacket, linen trousers of a different blue, cravat instead of tie, suede shoes, one gold earring. He was unaccompanied, Giles having said the occasion was one for private conversation. Jimmy drank only tonic water, saying he had to look after his figure, said, "Good to see you, Judge. What gives?"

"Judge" was the form of address Jimmy had settled on after trying out "sir" and "Mr. Midway," and Giles had found himself liking this as it were formal informality. When Giles said he had a little problem there was perhaps a relaxation in the young man's manner, as if he had been expecting something else. He listened carefully as Giles explained about the photographs without going into exact details. At the end he said: "These pix, just you in them, nobody else? So what's up, why not tell this cousin to get lost?"

"There is at least one of me at a table with another person. In any case they could be embarrassing if they appeared in a newspaper." Sensing another question he said firmly: "I want them back. And the negatives. You need not know anything further."

"OK, OK. But when this cousin hands over the negs he'll have taken photocopies, you're no better off. You thought of that?"

"Of course." Giles downed his whisky. "Jimmy, you remember you once said you owed me."

"Sure." The blue eyes looked straight into his. "I said it. Meant it too."

"Very well. Now I am—" Giles coughed. The phrase was not one that tripped off his tongue. "Calling in the debt."

It had been said, Jimmy had given his easy smile, the path was smoothed. Did Jimmy know a lot of people? He did, all sorts. They would understand what was needed, that the cousin should hand over negatives and photographs and be made aware how unwise it would be for him to approach a newspaper or magazine with the idea of selling copies of them for publication. Was it certain that Jimmy also understood what was *not* needed, what Giles would very much deprecate? He began to say something of this, a little haltingly, but Jimmy stopped him.

"No need, Judge, my friends, they'll know what to do." Giles gave him the piece of paper with the telephone number on it. He had already destroyed the photograph. Jimmy glanced at the paper, nodded, smiled, said: "And that's it?"

"You'll have expenses." Giles's hand moved towards his wallet. Jimmy shook his head.

"This one's on me. I said I owe. You go away, forget it, consider it done, no bother." A last flash of the bright smile, a hand laid light as a feather on Giles's hand, and he was gone. That virtuous action in helping both Bully Fothergill and the young man who had been tempted by Bully's carelessness had brought its reward. He had another small celebratory whisky before walking home.

To his surprise Catchpole found that being off the Midway disappearance left him feeling as if he had been cured of some small but worrying physical problem. An aching tooth had been filled, or perhaps a small ulcer healed. The sympathy of colleagues amused him, since he knew most of them were secretly pleased he had been, as they would feel, taken down a peg. Should he have guessed Curly Maddox's devious ploy? He acquitted himself of negligence and blamed the Crown Prosecution Service for deciding that there was a case to go to a jury. Of course it was fashionable to blame the CPS.

There was plenty of work to occupy him. Another man, the third in twelve months, had threatened to infect tins of baby food in a chain of supermarkets. He had specified the modest £100,000 he had asked for should be put into a particular street dustbin at precisely seven o'clock in the morning, and was caught when at seven-thirty he picked the parcel containing forged notes carefully out of the bin instead of tipping the contents straight into the municipal rubbish collecting van. He was a garbage collector employed by the local Council and might have stayed undetected at the time if he had been more careful, although he would have been picked up when he started passing the forged notes. There was a complicated credit card fraud to untangle, and a love triangle involving attempted murder by electrocution that couldn't have been more straightforward even though the three sides of the triangle were all feminine. Altogether, losing the Jenny Midway disappearance caused him no grief, although he did feel a twinge as of the nagging tooth suddenly playing up when Lowry said: "Not much to be done with this one except wait and see, eh, Catchers? You ask me, she's done a runner."

But he resisted the temptation to say no, he believed she was dead and there was more to be discovered. Let Lowry plant his heavy bottom on the case and extinguish it. There were enough pluses on his own card for one minus not to count against him in the long run.

So he was cheerful at home, playing Monopoly and a board-game involving racing cars called Speedo with Alan and Desmond. Alice said he was behaving as if he'd had a small win on the pools. Just that the pressure was off, he said.

"I don't know why you're not angry. I would be. You've got to carry the can and it's not your fault, that's what gets me. They put pressure on to get a result, otherwise you'd never have charged Lewis. Would you?"

"Probably not, but you know what the rules are, you play by them. If it'd been left altogether to me, yes, I'd have waited, probed around into the confession. But I didn't, and as you say I'm the one who carries the can. No use complaining, it's how the system works."

"It's a bloody rotten system. Still, it's made you good tempered so perhaps things should go wrong more often. Did I break the news I've arranged a dinner party for Saturday? It's the Peakes, their daughter Lucille's been babysitter for us a couple of times and they've got a son called Norman who's in Alan's class at school, Alan's best friend at the moment. They live down the road, very nice, longing to meet you."

He gave a mock groan, and said they were certain to want to know about things that had nothing to do with him, like why one man got ten years for fraud and another got only six months for careless driving when he killed a mother and her year-old child. Sure enough, Brenda Peake asked what he thought about a friend of theirs who'd lost his driving licence after being just, only *just*, over the limit when he was stopped doing eighty-five on a motorway, didn't he think it was a bit off when there was so much *real* crime around? Her husband Eric, who was a media consultant whatever that might mean, tried to change the subject but Brenda, who had drunk two large gins before dinner and her share of burgundy during it, was persistent. Think of Lucille, Alice said when he had brought out the dishes into the kitchen to escape the barrage, we don't want to lose our sitter. But Eric's voice, distinctly raised, could be heard in the dining-room, and when Alice brought in her baked Alaska Brenda was staring at the tablecloth. She said: "Eric tells me I've been making a fool of myself."

"Now sweetie, all I said—"

"But if you can't ask a policeman about police business, why not? You're the servants of the public, aren't you?"

God give me patience, Catchpole thought, no sitter is worth this. He said politely that the sort of crime dealt with by the CID wasn't the sort that concerned traffic police, they couldn't really be compared. It was a relief when the door bell rang, even when the unexpected visitor turned out to be Brett. A Brett full of apologies, returned to London unexpectedly, come as he frankly confessed to cadge a bed for the night. No no, he'd eaten on the plane from Berlin, but yes, he'd love a cup of coffee and a glass of brandy.

And he talked. Catchpole had never thought he would be pleased to listen to Brett, but now he blessed Alice's brother for diverting the attack from Brenda Peake, who sat silent and apparently fascinated as Brett told the tale of how wholesalers all over Europe, but particularly in Germany and the Netherlands, were placing orders, and how the only problem was going to be producing enough to satisfy the demand. Eric chimed in with chat about marketing needs and possibilities, the Peakes stayed until after midnight and both congratulated Alice on the possession of such a delightful brother. Over a nightcap Catchpole thanked Brett for saving him from verbal assault by Alice.

"And the marketing is really going well?" That was Alice, the words simple, the manner adoring.

"Just fantastic." But Brett's response was automatic, he was a performer who needed an audience that knew him less well than his sister and her husband. "You seen Mum lately? I talked to her on the blower and she sounded a bit low. Loves to see you and the kids, you know that." Alice said it wasn't easy in term time, the only possible time was at weekends. Catchpole added that weekends were the time she saw her husband, and suggested Brett himself might go down for a couple of days.

"I wish I could. Just not possible. Tomorrow's a conference with Santoro, that's my partner, then it's over to Amsterdam again, after that a swing through Scandinavia. It's a great life if you don't weaken." In the morning he was up early, ate a piece of toast, thanked Alice for his night's lodging, told Catchpole to keep catching those crooks, and was gone. You see, she said, all Brett needed was a real opportunity, and now he had one.

A couple of days later she rang him at the Yard to ask him to make sure he wasn't late home. He sensed tension behind her always equable voice, and said: "What's up? Is it Brett?" She said they could talk when he got home and it wasn't urgent, just don't be late.

She met him at the door, her face a little paler than usual, and took him into their bedroom. When he asked again if it was to do with Brett she said, "You've got Brett on the brain, nothing to do with him. It's Alan. They say he's been stealing money. At school. I've asked him. He won't say anything, just won't talk about it." Two large tears trickled down beside her nose. "I'm sorry, I'm being stupid."

"Not stupid at all. Tell me more."

It was straightforward enough. A boy called Melrose in Alan's class was given much more money than anybody else. He boasted that he had five pounds a week pocket money, and his parents confirmed that he had been given a five-pound note on Monday morning (it was now Wednesday), the note given because they had no pound coins handy. The note was in an envelope, and the boy also had some small change loose in his pocket. On Monday after lunch the class played football, and Melrose left the envelope and the small change in his locker. When he changed before going home the envelope had gone, but the small change was still there. Melrose shouted and wept, and the deputy headmaster was alerted. Some of the class had already left, but those who remained had their lockers opened, with no result. They were then told, or as the deputy head said invited, to turn out their pockets. The envelope, torn open and with the five-pound note in it, was found in the pocket of Alan's raincoat.

Alice was indignant about the turning out of pockets. "The deputy head, his name is Wallace, says they were 'invited.' Some invitation."

"What does Alan say?"

"I told you, he won't talk about it. The school head wants to see us. They hinted on the phone that perhaps Alan's kept short of money, asked how much we gave him, I said two pounds a week."

Alan was in his room, doing or pretending to do homework. Catchpole sat on the bed, asked the boy what he knew about the money. Alan's small handsome face was blank as he said nothing.

"At school they think you took it." Silence. "Maybe you did. You knew about it, Melrose boasted, you thought you'd show him, never meant to keep the money. How about that, is that the way it was?" Alan shook his head. "OK, we rule that out. You didn't take it, but you know who did. Or you can guess. Someone who doesn't like you, or a friend you've had a row with. It's a kind of mystery, we've got to solve it. What do you think, anyone like that?" Alan shook his head again, but for the first time showed interest.

"You're sure there's nobody who wants to get back at you for something you did?" Another head shake. "Then we rule that out too. Now, listen carefully and think back. You were all getting ready to go home, some had gone. Then Melrose cries out that he's lost his money, makes a hullabaloo, the deputy head comes in. Before he came, though, can you remember which boys went home?" Alan said he might be able to. "Might be able to isn't good enough. Think, Alan, think. Your raincoat is hanging on a peg, right? Now, try to think of someone who had a coat on a peg near yours, perhaps next to yours. Someone who went home just after Melrose shouted about losing his money and before Wallace the deputy head came in. It might be someone you know doesn't get much pocket money. He had a coat near yours, and he went home as soon as Melrose raised the alarm. Well?"

Hesitantly Alan mentioned a name. "But he's my friend, he wouldn't—"

"I don't think he meant to, just got scared. Leave it to me now, Alan, and don't worry."

He asked Alice the number of the Peakes' house, walked round there and persuaded a surprised but slightly flattered Brenda to let him see Norman alone for a few minutes, telling her a problem had come up in relation to school that Norman might be able to solve. He reported the result to Alice.

"He was scared out of his wits, thought I was there to take him away and lock him up. He says he took the money for a joke because Melrose is what he called such a big-mouth, always saying how much money his dad makes. Then he was frightened when Melrose started shouting and crying, shoved the envelope in the nearest coat, which happened to be Alan's, and ran home. He says he was going to own up in the morning, and perhaps he was. He couldn't make out how I got on to him. I didn't tell him it was my Sherlockian powers of logical deduction plus a portion of luck. He didn't want me to tell the awful Brenda, but I said we'd tell her together, and we did. I can't say she was pleased, but she'll ring the school in the morning and say it was all a mistake. She doesn't love me any more than she did, I'm afraid." He laughed.

"You've told Alan." He said yes. "And you're pleased with yourself." He waved a deprecating hand. "Shall I tell you what it tells me, Superintendent Catchpole? That you don't trust anybody. When I first told you, you thought Alan had taken the money."

"It was possible."

"You should have *known* he couldn't have done it. I knew."

"So did I after I'd talked to him."

"That's what I mean. You don't trust anybody. Not even your own son."

"Anything's possible, that's what you learn in the force. Anybody can do anything—almost."

"I don't believe it."

"Good for you. But you're not a copper."

The opening of the restaurant was accompanied by some well-organized media attention. There were pieces by columnists about what one paper called "The Great British Food Revolution" while another less friendly one asked: "Is Purafood Purer Food?" Eleanor had said her name should be kept out of the publicity, but a gossip columnist discovered her connection with the restaurant and wrote a piece mentioning it. "Eleanor Midway, presiding genius over menus at the new British Purafood Restaurant, is mother of art dealer Jenny Midway, whose disappearance remains a mystery. Mrs. Midway refused to talk about her daughter, but was eloquent about the menus she has devised for the restaurant, which include Turkey and Hazelnut Soup, Glamorgan Sausages and Skuets (skewered sweetbreads plus bacon and mushrooms to you). All British, she says, and British is Best, but I doubt if Le Gavroche will be worried."

At the opening the restaurant was full of invited guests, including the Minister for Food and his shadow counterpart, an assortment of current celebrities thought newsworthy, and several self-appointed food and wine experts who wrote in the media. The meal was generally approved, except that the Yorkshire Curd Tart, a kind of cheesecake made from an eighteenth-century recipe, was thought inferior to more recent American and Israeli variations. After the opening the restaurant was full every day, bookings had to be made in advance. Bryan was delighted, Cliff Davies never failed to supply the materials asked for, and even Maggie agreed things seemed to be going well, although she just smiled when Eleanor said their success proved showcases didn't always lose money. After a couple of weeks, however, it became clear that most of the lunchers and diners preferred conventional dishes like roast guineafowl to skuets or Hindle Wakes, a dish of chicken, ham and prunes cooked in a lemon-flavoured cream stock.

The restaurant occupied Eleanor's mind, she enjoyed organizing the menus, Stella's worshipful admiration was pleasant, yet she was conscious of a worry no doubt mental yet more easily envisaged as something physical like a tumour growing inside her. Its malevolent components were Jenny's disappearance, the disturbing change in John, and more recently concern about the problems that would face David and Mary when they became parents. She needed in some way to get rid of the tumour, cut it out or vomit it up, to know exactly what had happened to Jenny, was happening to John, could be done to help her son and his wife.

In an attempt to resolve what were now her doubts about Jenny she rang up and spoke to the detective in charge of the investigation, only to learn that he was no longer concerned with the case. When she asked what was happening he told her first that Detective Superintendent Lowry was now in charge, then expanded a little.

"Mrs. Midway, I'll be frank. You can speak to Superintendent

Lowry if you wish, but I can tell you there have been no further important developments."

"The man who was on trial, Lewis—"

"There's no doubt at all that he was involved in a robbery down in Sussex at the time Jenny disappeared, and he's been sentenced for that. We're satisfied he had nothing to do with her disappearance."

"It sounds to me as if you've given up."

"Don't think that, Mrs. Midway. After Lewis's acquittal I was very much involved with other things, and it was thought somebody else might have a different viewpoint. I know Superintendent Lowry's looking at various possibilities now, and if he finds any of them likely to tell us what's happened to Jenny he'll be in touch. And if you or your husband hear anything at all that you think would be useful don't hesitate to speak to Mr. Lowry, or if you'd prefer it to me."

She understood what he was saying, saying as pleasantly as possible: We've given up, we're just waiting, and hoping for something new to turn up. As she tried now to think of Jenny she was distressed that it was hard to summon up her daughter's features. They were as if seen in a photograph taken when the subject had moved so that the effect was blurred. If she could have seen this figure coming towards her in the street she might have said *This is Jenny* and run forward with open arms, yet in the mind's eye she was now unclear, the very shape of face and expression uncertain. It was now more than four months since Jenny had gone. Had she deliberately put her daughter out of mind, knowing she would never come back?

On the day after she spoke to Catchpole there was a telephone call from John's secretary Susan, who surprised her by asking if John had spoken to her. She asked what was meant by that, and Susan said they should meet. When they did so that evening in a bar near MultiCorpus Eleanor was totally unprepared for what

Susan told her. She stared at the dumpy little woman swallowing a mouthful of bitter, and said nothing.

"I told John we couldn't go on as we were, he must speak to you. It's not right for things to be hole and corner, is it? Not fair to anybody."

"I suppose not." She looked at the glass of sherry she had ordered. It seemed impossible to drink it. "Thank you for telling me."

"John's very good in the office, but outside it he seems to be a different person. You have to make decisions in this life, don't you, Mrs. Midway? He and I, we've been together, if you call it that, for a little while now. After your daughter's disappearance. It seemed he needed somebody. I'm sorry, perhaps I shouldn't have said that."

"It doesn't matter."

Susan, whom she had never considered except as an adjunct to John, a voice on the telephone competent at taking messages, now demanded human status. What she had said appeared a kind of unintended condemnation. He needed somebody, yes, but he didn't need you. Or perhaps she hadn't wished to be needed, which would be worse. I must try to understand, she thought, I must know what it is John wants, whether I want it too, what we should do. Two men at the bar were laughing fit to bust, and she had not heard what the little fat woman, whom she could not really consider as her rival, was saying.

"I'm sorry, what was that?"

"I said I love John, always have loved and admired him. He's so good with other people's problems, finds it hard to face his own. He has to make up his mind, decide what he wants." Was the blue blouse Susan wore on this warm evening slightly grubby at the neck? "I said to him, make up your mind, don't worry if I'm upset, I shan't put my head in the gas oven, and anyway my cooker's electric." She laughed at the feeble joke, but Eleanor did not manage a smile. It took a moment for her to realize what was being suggested, that John might leave her. "I'm sorry, I'm afraid this has been a shock, but it's best everything should be in the open, don't you agree?" Eleanor said she agreed. "And you'll speak to him? Because, it seems ridiculous when you think what he's like in the office, but I don't know if he'll pluck up nerve to say anything otherwise." Yes, Eleanor said, yes. "No reason why it shouldn't all be friendly, is there? I mean, we're civilized people."

On the way home—although "home" seemed no longer quite the right word—she wondered how John could possibly have gone to bed with a woman not perfectly clean, then realized she didn't mind who he went to bed with, and thought that was the worst thing of all. When John returned she told him Susan had spoken to her. He sank into a chair and said it was his fault, all his fault, he was so very sorry. She repeated what seemed her line for the day, that it didn't matter. His head jerked up, big nose in air, lower lip thrust out and wobbling. How could she ever have thought him a strong, decisive man? He said this was something that had happened, just happened, these things did happen, it was all terribly banal, what was there to say that didn't sound banal? She found herself annoyed by this. There were, she said, decisions to be made, they must make up their minds what they wanted.

He gave a kind of groan, shook his head miserably. "You've changed."

"*I've changed.* I'm not the one who's been sleeping around."

"Not sleeping around. Nobody but Susan." That too was an irritating remark. Did he think she imagined he slept with a different woman every week? "It was because—you've been so unfeeling about everything. As if you didn't care about anything except your restaurant."

"Ah."

"What do you mean, *ah*?"

"I thought it would come to that. You don't like me doing something on my own, something I enjoy."

"That's ridiculous."

"So you get back at me by going to bed with your secretary. I can't say I admire your taste."

"Eleanor." He gave the groan again.

Like a sick animal, she thought, wondered at her own hardness, and made an effort to subdue irritation and anger. "I don't mean to quarrel, we shouldn't quarrel. But you have to decide what you want, and tell me." Why was she talking like this as if she bore some responsibility, when he was the one who'd been sleeping around? Her tone sharpened again. "But if you've got some idea about me giving up the Purafoods restaurant job, forget it."

Another groan, or perhaps a sigh. Then he said again she had changed and went on slowly, stumblingly. "Jenny's death seems to have meant different things for us. Because you wouldn't accept it I turned to somebody else, someone who offered comfort. And now you have accepted it you've escaped from me, from the memory of Jenny, into this job." He gave the wave of the hand she had in the past found so impressive. "It's not a question of blame, no use blaming anybody. We both need help, but we can't help each other."

She considered this for a few moments, then said: "Balls."

Another wave of the hand. "You see. You can't talk to me without abuse."

"In the first place I haven't accepted Jenny's gone. It's a long time now, but, still I just don't know, and you don't either. At least I try to be optimistic, but if she's gone when did you ever say a word that might help me to bear it? As for the restaurant, I didn't go looking for it, it came out of the blue, but yes I enjoy it and think I'm good at it. Other people seem to think so too, but when did you ever show the slightest interest? When you talk about us helping each other it's one-way traffic you've got in mind, that I should be sitting here all the time thinking of ways to console you."

Lower lip thrust forward he said, with a touch of the belligerency she had admired in the past: "Just abuse. Useless to talk to you."

She laughed. "It's wonderful, really it is. Your secretary comes to me and says she's been going to bed with you, and you behave as if it's *me* who should be apologizing because I don't appreciate your tender feelings." He began to protest, but she overrode his words. "When I say *we* have to decide something, your Susan was right to say you can't do it. All right then, I'll tell you what I want, and what I'm going to do. I like the restaurant work, I feel I'm doing something on my own for the first time in my life, and I'm going on with it. If you still feel you want to go to bed with your fat secretary you should tell her to wash her neck—" She stopped talking because her sick-animal husband suddenly sprang out of his chair, lunged forward and hit her on the side of the face with his big right fist. She staggered, almost fell, sank into a chair. She was pleased that her voice sounded normal when she said: "You'd better go to her."

He stood looking down at her, lower lip thrust out. "If that's what you want."

"Oh no, you decided it when you hit me. If you don't leave this house tonight I shall."

He said nothing more, nodded and went out. She heard him moving about upstairs, then the front door closing. She looked at her face in the bathroom, soaked a flannel in cold water and bathed the red patch where his fist had hit her. Then she went to their bedroom, saw he had taken only a few clothes, and looked into the other bedrooms thinking of the children when they were small, outgoing Jenny and shy reticent David. Down in the kitchen she opened the refrigerator, poured a glass of milk and sat staring at it. Tears came like the turning on of a tap, and ceased when she said aloud: "Why did it happen? I've done nothing wrong." She thought of John, not as he had been tonight, but the masterful figure always concerned to do the right thing, the man she had respected for thirty years. It seemed all that had gone with Jenny, gone through Jenny. Sipping the milk, she yearned for her daughter.

Catchpole had detached his mind successfully from Jenny Midway, so that when the call came he could not for a moment place the man who said: "Louis Meyers. You thought I'd hear nothing further. I'm happy to tell you you were wrong."

Then he remembered. "You've got news of the Renoir?"

"Better than that. I'm looking at it now, and a very fine painting it is."

"You collected it yourself?"

"No. It was collected from customs by the agent here Fraschini's deputed to deal with it, Antonio Moreno. I know him a little and can assure you he's perfectly respectable. And I am respectable too." He laughed. Catchpole dutifully laughed back. "Now. I've already told you my client's name, and you understand I expect you to treat that as private information. I have arranged for him to see the picture next week. It will be in person—he likes to see what he is buying. Very wise." A chuckle appreciated his own humour.

"But he'll want it authenticated?"

"Of course. He will be accompanied by Professor Tufts, an adviser to the National Gallery who has written a monograph on what we may call the painter in question." Another chuckle. Meyers's spirits were evidently high. "I am telling you this because you have asked me to do so, but it can have nothing at all to do with our dear Jenny. I am sorry for her, but with this sale, if it should take place, she can have no possible connection."

Without commenting on this Catchpole said he had a request to make. "I should like to look at the painting."

Elation had been replaced by doubt as Meyers said: "Why?"

"I can't tell you. What I can say is I shan't need to see it for more than five minutes."

"Mr. Catchpole—Superintendent—it seems to me you are pursuing me, this is a vendetta. The girl worked for me, yes, for a short time, but she had no connection with this picture. This is a very big deal for me, I don't think you understand the importance of it . . ."

They talked for several minutes before, by a mixture of wheedling and vague menaces, he obtained reluctant agreement to let him look at the painting. The pictures round the walls of the gallery were all of gigantic men and women playing with balls of various shapes, sizes and colours. The painter was named Frans Hals Junior, and the exhibition's title was "The Eroticism of the Circular." Catchpole wondered whether the dung paintings had been rejected because of their smell.

Meyers, who wore today a one-piece plain black outfit that zipped up from neck to crotch, took him into an office and said he wanted to protest at what he repeated was a vendetta. Catchpole responded mildly that he only wanted to see the painting. They went down into the basement, Meyers unlocked a door and switched on spotlights. The painting was on an easel, the light beamed onto the men, the trapeze, the horses. Catchpole glanced at them, removed the picture from the easel, saw the label saying "For M. Chocquet," replaced the painting and said: "I congratulate you."

"What do you mean?"

"Or perhaps I should congratulate Angus McCracken. He will become the owner of a genuine Renoir painted between 1878 and 1880, the kind of painting on which it's impossible to put a price. As you'll no doubt tell him."

"That's all? You don't want to see anything more, ask any questions?"

"Don't forget I've seen it before. And we're all art experts at the Yard. If I say it's genuine it is."

He returned to the Yard in high spirits and sought out Higginbotham, whom he found looking at photographs in a girlie magazine, and prepared to maintain that if the *Rokeby Venus* was art these were art too. The Yorkshireman roared with laughter when he heard what Catchpole had to say.

"So when they're all talking about this Renoir at the farmhouse you snuck around behind it and made a cross on the label at the back. And nobody noticed?"

"They were all too busy listening to the Harvard professor telling them why it was genuine to worry about what his assistant was doing. I don't really know why I made the mark, I just knew there was something wrong about the deal."

"You're not as big a fool as you look." Higginbotham put the magazine into a drawer. "But what is it worries you? The deal in the farmhouse fell through, the picture's come over here, it's got your cross on the label."

"Just think about this. Fosskind and Grayson are both strapped for money, so I'm told on good information. Fraschini knows it, and knows Grayson has got this mobster for a client who collects pictures and keeps them down in the cellar. You tell me Fraschini's a crook—"

"It comes naturally to him, laddie. If he was playing patience he'd try to beat himself."

"Whatever he is, he puts the idea to them. The picture gets sold twice. It's authenticated by Professor Gifford, then Fosskind switches it for a copy—who would Fraschini get to make a copy?"

"I could name one or two here who'd do a good job, and friend Ettore would know half a dozen. Mind, when I say a good job that's not saying it would fool your professor for more than ten minutes."

Catchpole waved the tentative objection aside. "Don't you see, the beauty of it is the forgery needn't be that good. The picture's been authenticated and that leaves the Californian gangster happy. Providing they can find a client over here who's equally concerned to keep the deal secret, nobody will ever know a copy exists. It's the absence of publicity that's vital, hence the picture goes to little Meyers and his client Angus McCracken. It's the scam of a lifetime, one that will leave everybody happy and all of them much richer. Even the Count in Italy will be pleased, and who suffers? Only a retired gangster in California, and he doesn't know it."

"And all because you put a little cross on the back label of a picture. You're a clever fellow, Catchers." Higginbotham's Yorkshire accent broadened, as it did when he was being sarcastic. "But before ye try seeing if ye can pat yourself on the back with both hands, just bear it in mind ye may be wrong. Maybe Fraschini notices the cross on the back of the label and puts it on the fake."

"He wouldn't have had the chance. I saw the painting leave the house and go into Fosskind's car."

"Ah, it's still a possibility." Eyes twinkling with malice Higginbotham fired a parting shot. "I wonder you bother your head with this when ye've no longer an interest in the puir lassie that disappeared."

Was it his business to do anything about this art scam, if it was a scam? But the case itched like a mosquito bite, all the more because of his feeling that there was something enigmatic, unsaid, in the attitudes of Grayson and his wife. He put in a call to New York, to be told that Captain O'Donnell was unavailable, and spent the rest of the day catching up on a quantity of paperwork, and trying to understand a book-thick White or Blue or Green Paper called the Projected Revised Organizational Structure of Regional Development in Policing. He was about to leave for home when the green light on his telephone flashed and the switchboard girl asked if he would take a call from Captain O'Donnell. Catchpole said it was good of Rory to call back, told him the Renoir painting was now in London and why he believed it was genuine.

"You're saying if the Matresca deal went through he got a fake?" O'Donnell sounded sober, even serious. "Unfortunately Carlo came to the same conclusion. Seems our informant bedding a girl in the elephant bird's office had a long tongue, and it wagged too much when he was out on a watering expedition with Hymie Rubinstein. Hymie never loved Carlo Matresca like he loves his mother, so he makes sure the story gets back to Carlo. I think maybe I shoulda been more careful, put a padlock on our informant's tongue. Do you read me?"

"So what's the result?"

An elephant's sigh came down the line. "Carlo gets the message Hymie's pissing himself laughing because he's been done for a donkey over this French picture. He calls in some expert geezer from Berkeley who tells him sorry but that's so, what he's got for his five million dollars or whatever is worth five hundred. Carlo doesn't like it. It's not so much the money you understand, though that too, but he doesn't like being played for a sucker. And he doesn't have a doubt who's done it, the ones who negotiated the deal."

"What's happened?"

Another elephant sigh. "We'll never see our Lew behind bars now. He was taken out as he left his favourite restaurant, Angelo's on Amsterdam Avenue. Car was waiting down the street, came alongside Lew, sprayed him with bullets so he bled like a watering can."

"How about Grayson?"

"Bomb under his car, set to explode when he turned on the ignition. But he was lucky, they got the adjustment wrong—so the bomb boys say. It went off when he opened the car door, blew him a few feet away into a rose bush. He's in hospital now, minor burns and shock. Lucky for now, and could be his luck will last. My understanding is Carlo only made a down payment on the picture, so could be he'll think Providence didn't mean Grayson to meet his maker just yet. Still, I was Grayson I wouldn't sleep easy for a month or two. Does this help you any with the missing girl?"

Without answering that question Catchpole said it had solved one bit of the jigsaw, and many thanks. Any time, O'Donnell said, any time. Afterwards Catchpole wondered if it had solved anything at all, and then wondered why he was wondering when he was off the case. There had been something about the way Sally Lou had looked at her husband when Jenny was mentioned . . . He looked in on Lowry, who seemed surprised when asked if there was anything new on the Midway disappearance, then said all quiet on that front. Catchpole gave up and went home.

There Alan said his form master would be very pleased if he would give a talk about being a detective. He indignantly denied he had been boasting about his father being at Scotland Yard. "Mr. Hughes saw your picture in the paper. I never said anything, Dad, honest."

Desmond looked up from his plate of baked beans. "Anyway nobody likes the fuzz, they call them pigs." He beamed at his father, who gave a snort that might have been thought porcine.

"Don't be such a clot, Des, that's only Lenny, his father's a car dealer, everyone knows they're all crooks. Aren't they, Dad?"

"Some are, some aren't."

"So will you do it, Dad? Will you? Mr. Hughes'll write you a letter asking you."

"I shan't know what to say, and it'll be very dull. But all right, I'll do it."

Alan said smashing. Desmond snorted into his baked beans. "Honk honk. I'm a pig too."

10. Family Problems

Why did it happen? The words Eleanor asked herself after John walked out of the house had dried her tears, and when she asked them again, searching her behaviour for things she could have done differently, she found no reason for self-reproach. Had it been wrong to appear on television or to believe Jenny was still alive? She could not think so. And certainly it had not been wrong to take the job that gave her a sense of fulfilment she had not experienced since the children left school. However she looked at it, blame rested with John. He did not telephone, but a few days after he left she found he had removed the rest of his clothes. She rang the office, telling the switchboard girl she wanted only to speak to Mr. Midway, not his secretary. She felt no emotion when she heard his voice. She said he might have told her he was coming to the house.

"What would have been the point? I came to collect some things, that's all."

"You've moved in with her, then?" She could not bring herself to mention Susan's name.

"Obviously. I really can't discuss it on the telephone, you must realize that."

"It sounds as if there's nothing to talk about."

And he put down the telephone, leaving her indignant. How was it possible that he should behave as if she had deceived him or behaved badly to him, when the opposite was true? She made no further attempt to get in touch, and found a sense of freedom in being alone. When she closed the front door in the morning and walked down Sapphic Street to the bus stop in the Fulham Road there was no need to worry about getting back in time to prepare a meal. She could give her whole attention to the running of the restaurant and the arguments with Maggie Lomas about costs. Not that there seemed to her any need for argument, since the restaurant was usually packed out at lunchtime, and evening bookings still had to be made in advance. In the evening she could go to a cinema or theatre after talking to the chefs about the menu, and if she didn't want to go home and cook she could eat out. Twice Bryan Connors had taken her out to dinner, and had said how delighted he was by the success of what he called their joint enterprise. He repeated that this Chancery Lane restaurant would be the first of many, he had agents out looking for suitable places. Something about Bryan made her uneasy. He spoke of the Purafoods restaurants as if they would be the means not just of changing national eating habits, but of converting the whole nation to a different and higher plane of living. "We shall be the spearhead of a healthier Britain, Eleanor, and a healthier nation is a better nation," he said. The intensity with which the words were uttered made her uncomfortable.

Yet upon the whole she enjoyed her freedom. When she got back from a day at the restaurant she sat down in front of the television with a cup of coffee and a biscuit and watched just any old undemanding programme, something she couldn't do when John was there because of his evident disapproval. Did she think of their parting as permanent? Perhaps not, for she said nothing about it to Bryan or anybody else connected with the restaurant, confiding only in Stella who was wide-eyed in admiration of her courage, and Mary who of course told David. He rang her up.

"Mum, why ever did you do it?" She pointed out that she had "done" nothing, all the doing had been John's. "I know, but—it's all because of Jenny, if she were still around it wouldn't have happened." That was very much her own thought, but she did not like David to say it. "It's only temporary, isn't it? You'll get back together soon."

"It doesn't depend on me, you must see that."

"You could ask him to come back, say you missed him. I *hate* it that you're not together." And she recalled, out of the distant past, how upset he had been on the rare occasions when she and John had serious arguments. Jenny had been amused, thought hearing the old people arguing was funny, but David as a small boy put his hands over his ears, even once or twice ran off to his bedroom. It struck her as odd that she should have found herself on the defensive when talking to John, and now was saying comforting things to David. Surely he might have been trying to cheer her up?

"This is Steve. And Jan. Steve and Jan, this is John. My boss. And partner."

"Hi." Steve was fresh-faced like his mother. His hair was cropped very short. He wore a sweatshirt, frayed jeans with holes at the knees, and trainers. Jan had an almost skeletal figure, and fair hair that looked as if it had been cooked and then left to dry out in the sun. She stared at John as if he were a creature from another world on exhibition.

John had been several days at Stoke Newington. He had been kept late at the office for one of the departmental meetings called every month by Horton, and named by him ginger sessions. He stared back at Jan. Susan beamed at him.

"Steve and Jan just dropped in, staying to supper, isn't that nice? There's beer in the fridge if you want it." She retreated to the kitchen. Steve went out, returned with three cans of beer, opened them, gave one to John who got a glass for himself. Steve and Jan drank straight from the cans. John asked what Steve did.

"Work in a garage. Patching up dud motors that's been smashed up, cannibalizing. Piss-awful job, get caught doing it you're in dead trouble. Gotta take what you can get nowadays. You shacking up with Mum, unusual that, innit?"

"I suppose so, yes." He noticed with fascination that Jan was chewing and drinking simultaneously. She looked at him steadily, jaws moving.

Steve continued. "What I mean is, she's been on her owneo since Dad skipped out a few years back." He said to Jan: "He was a real bastard, my dad. Went off with some bint about your age, left us flat." He brooded on this. "Ma said it was only working for you kept her going, you were so good to her and that. Don't reckon she ever thought you'd shack up together though."

Susan emerged from the kitchen, face flushed. "I heard a bit of that, Steve, and you just keep quiet. I don't want John being embarrassed. You can help pull out that table and, Jan, will you lay? Knives and forks in the top drawer of the kitchen dresser."

Supper was hamburgers out of a packet, chips from another packet heated in the oven, ice cream. Steve ate enormously, Jan almost nothing. John was aware of Susan's watchful eye. When she brought in the ice cream she said: "Not what you're used to, I know that. Just bear in mind I've been in the office all day." John protested that he had said nothing. "I know that look, I've seen it often enough."

Steve was surprised. "Nothing wrong I could see. Very tasty, what you say, Jan?"

John had been waiting for Jan to speak throughout the meal. Now she looked at a Mickey Mouse watch on her wrist and said, "We should split."

"Right." He kissed his mother, said to John: "Don't you cause Ma no grief, she had enough of that with my dad." Jan opened her mouth, revealing pallid gums and a wodge of greyish chewing stuff, said "Bye." Then they were gone. After five minutes of silence while they washed up plates and saucepans Susan said: "Come on, out with it. I know you, you were surprised, horrified, disgusted, say it."

"I admit I was surprised."

"By the way Steve talked, his taste in girls? You know what his father was? Milkman, barman, bookie's runner, meat porter, sales rep for a new sort of vacuum cleaner, you name it. He never had trouble getting a job, never kept one more than a few months. Sometimes he made money, but I never saw much of it. Very likely spent it on girls, he always fancied young girls, the younger the better. I never saw the one he took off with but Steve did, said she couldn't have been more than eighteen. Why did I stay with him so long, maybe you're wondering. Well, you could say life was never dull, you never knew what to expect. But Steve, when he was young he worshipped his father, Grev was always joking with him, making up stories, playing games. Then when he was around eleven or twelve Steve suddenly seemed to turn against him, got bad school reports, realized who kept the household going I suppose, started to talk—well, you heard how he talks." John expressed surprise that he had not known any of this. "Why should you have known? I didn't want you to know, I've said already it was working for you that kept me going. Not the money so much, more you were a sort of fixed point, something I could rely on. I did my best for Steve after Grev went, but it wasn't easy, either for him or me. I thought, he's had a bad time with a father like Grev, so I've never criticized anything, the way he talks, the sort of girls he has, the kind of food he likes, nothing. Three years now Grev's been gone, and I've never heard a word. The bastard." More beer foamed out of cans into glasses. "I know you thought I shouldn't have spoken to Eleanor—"

"I'm glad you did. It brought things to a head. I had to decide something."

"That's it. I love you, the way you deal with people in the office, advise them, I think it's wonderful. You're a good man." Her eyes glistened with the hint of tears. "But, don't get me wrong, it seems to me you can advise other people, make decisions for them, but you don't find it easy to do it for yourself. I don't say you can't, just you find it hard. I'm not upsetting you, am I?"

"No. You're right. I wish you weren't."

"About the office, don't worry, I'll be the proper secretary I always am, you won't ever have to complain. Let's go to bed."

"There's some tidying up ought to be done."

"Balls to that, we can do it in the morning."

They went to bed. In the morning there was no time to tidy up.

Forget it, consider it done, no bother. Giles was not sure why he felt such confidence in Jimmy Kelsey, but certainly he ceased to worry about Mrs. Entwhistle and her cousin. Nor was he greatly concerned when Eleanor rang to say John had gone to live with his secretary in some seedy area of North London. Apart from its being, as he said to her, a really bizarre thing to do, he failed to see it concerned him. Eleanor did not accept this. Giles could surely talk to him, make him see how foolish he was.

"Do you know this woman, this secretary? I suppose she is youthful?"

"She's a few years younger than me. Plain. And fat."

Giles said he would do anything he could, adding that he was not optimistic. He had considerable legal experience of middle-aged men leaving their wives for young women, and a smaller one of middle-aged women leaving their husbands for young men, but John's abandonment of Eleanor for a fat plain secretary was beyond his understanding. However, he talked to John over lunch at his club, as he expected without result. John was perfectly reasonable, a quality Giles both admired and oddly enough resented in his brother. He said he had been under a lot of strain. Eleanor had too, their separation was a good thing in the circumstances, and something they must resolve themselves. No doubt it was the kind of safe advice he gave as a personnel director. When Giles said it was surely unwise to be cohabiting with his secretary John took offence, and said that was his affair. Only then was there any reference to Jenny.

"I sometimes think it's unhinged Eleanor," John said. "I'm glad she's taken up this cooking business because it takes her mind off Jenny. She has to accept we shall probably never know what happened to her."

Giles agreed. "There was the fiasco of the man Lewis. I think I may say he was successfully disposed of at the Crown Court." He gave a small self-appreciative laugh. Nothing further was said either about Jenny or the secretary, and they parted on good terms, although Giles did not cease to think of his brother's behaviour as bizarre. He often marvelled at how foolishly men and women behaved towards each other, and congratulated himself that he avoided such problems.

He was reading a book about Victorian murder trials, which seemed to have been far more dramatic than any over which he had presided, when the bell rang. He opened the door to be faced by Mrs. Entwhistle, her body as it seemed thinner, her hatchet features tighter, than when she had worked for him. She said nothing, merely stared at him. Surprise was succeeded by annoyance. It was to be rid of the Entwhistle problems that he had enlisted Jimmy Kelsey. He asked what she wanted.

It was as if the words released a spring. Mrs. Entwhistle let out a screech and launched herself at him. He felt her nails at his face, was pushed back into his tiny entrance hall, found himself struggling with a virago who mouthed unintelligible words. They grappled, knocking over an occasional table on which stood a china spaniel given to Giles when he had been persuaded to open a fair in a town where he was officiating at a Crown Court. The ornament was of little value and he disliked dogs, but the sound as it was crushed beneath an Entwhistle foot moved him to vigorous action. He directed a blow in the direction of her stomach, she gasped, sank to the floor. Giles pulled her up and into the living-room, pushed her into a chair, then said: "Now, tell me the meaning of this attack before I call the police to arrest you for assault."

"You'd never dare."

"If you think that, you are even more stupid than I imagined."

"You know. My Fergie. He's in hospital. Where you put him. Two broken ribs and internal bleeding. Where they kicked him." In a few more spurts of speech she told him what had happened. There had been a telephone call arranging a meeting, Fergie had been set on by thugs, taken into an alley, kicked and beaten into insensibility. The photographs he brought along had been taken, he had been told if he wanted to stay healthy he would forget they existed.

So Jimmy Kelsey had done what he promised. Giles heard her out, then asked what she expected him to do about it. She picked up from the floor a large black bag in mock animal skin which she must have dropped during their brief struggle. The catch opened with a snap. She took out a brown envelope, gave it to him. The envelope contained another half-dozen Watching photographs, most of them taken in the street, with negatives.

He waited for her to speak. When she did so the words came unwillingly, drips from a rusted tap.

"Fergie don't want any more to do with it. Not worth it, he says."

"Very wise. But how do I know there aren't more pictures that he's kept back?"

"No more. This is all, nothing else. I told you, he don't want any more to do with it. I said to go to a lawyer. What's the use, he said, what could they do? You are the bleeding law."

"I'm glad he's seen the light, and sorry he has had this trouble. Of course I know nothing about it, had no connection with it, I hope you understand that?" Her little eyes glared at him. She stayed silent. "I'm afraid he must have some undesirable associates. However I'm sorry to hear of his trouble, even though he has brought it on himself. I should like to help." He felt for his wallet, took out a twenty-pound note, laid it on the table between them. "With my best wishes for a speedy recovery."

She snatched the note. The big bag snapped open, closed. Then she was gone.

Giles looked again at the photographs, then carefully burned both them and the negatives. He did not doubt that Mrs. Entwhistle and her Fergie had learned their lesson. He thought warmly of Jimmy Kelsey although he did not deny, even to himself, that Jimmy knew some very naughty boys.

At first Mary thought the man who had taken the seat opposite her in the snack bar was trying to pick her up, because a couple of other tables were free. When she looked straight at him, however, it was into the slightly vacant eyes of Rupert Baxter.

"I hope you don't mind." She shook her head. "I thought you might be in here, didn't want to beard you in the torturer's den. There's something I want to ask."

She took a forkful of her Florida salad. "Ask away."

"It's just, you seemed to be so frightfully sensible when I came to you with that silly query about Jenny giving up one sort of life for another. You said don't go to the police, I might just have been imagining things, and I'm sure that was true. And you said stop worrying about it which I did, more or less. There's no news of Jenny, I suppose?"

"If there is I haven't heard it."

"I still hope she's in the Arctic, or South America, or somewhere like that. She's such a smashing girl." She acknowledged this with a nod. "But this is not about Jenny."

Now she looked directly at him. "In case you've got any ideas to the contrary I should remind you I'm married."

He choked slightly on his sandwich. "Good Lord, I'm sorry if—I mean, I think you're very attractive and all that, but it wasn't—"

"Just thought I'd avoid any misunderstanding."

"Oh, of course. Good idea. It's just that I was so jolly impressed by you in the torturer's den, you were so—so *unassumingly* sympathetic. I'll come to the point. I'm an executive advising on finance at Bridges, dare say you don't know of them but they're a rather important firm of brokers, and though you might find it hard to believe I've been promoted and I'm looking for a P.A., that's personal assistant. So—well—I wondered if you'd consider the job."

She put down her knife and fork. "You'll think I'm very rude. I'm sorry."

"Not a bit of it, shouldn't have broken it to you like that. Just wanted to know if you'd even consider it. Not necessary to know anything about the business, you'd pick up all you need in a week. The important things are tact, being able to deal with people, encourage them, or give them the brush-off when necessary—you could do that all right—and generally being an aid and prop for a young executive. I won't insult you by talking about money, except to say these brokers are filthy rich, just it would be marvellous for me if you said yes, or perhaps."

She finished her salad, then said composedly: "You've taken my breath away."

He laughed. "It doesn't look like it."

"I really like working for Mr. Megillah. He's very friendly, not a torturer at all. But he doesn't pay that much. More money would be very welcome." He was about to speak but she stopped him. "I don't want to talk about money, it might be too tempting. But I need to speak to my husband. That's David, Jenny's brother, I don't think you've met him."

"No, but if he's anything like Jenny—"

She shook her head. "He's not. You might say she was always bubbling over, David's still water running deep. And there's something else I have to consider—no, I'm not going to say what it is. If I let you know by the end of the week, is that all right?" He said that would be fine.

When she told David that night he said it had to be her decision.

"It would mean more money, quite a lot more I imagine." He nodded. "But you don't want me to take it?"

"Christ, how I hate the smell of that fucking Indian cooking. We need to get out of here." She said this would help. "But don't you see, I should be doing it, not you, I don't want to be a failure all my life. And what about the baby? Would you want to go on with the job after he was born? Did you tell Baxter?"

"That I'm pregnant? No, I didn't. I thought I'd talk to you first. He really wants me, maybe if I tell him that'll be the end of it but I doubt it, he's very keen. It's quite possible, you know, you take a few weeks off, then make an arrangement about looking after the baby. Don't look so miserable, as if I'd got it all worked out. I haven't, I can say no tomorrow."

Feet drummed on the floor above them. David looked at the ceiling. "I don't want you to say no for me, I want you to say it for yourself. He mustn't be born here, I don't want him born in this place." A shudder went through his body.

"Let's talk about it tomorrow. I don't want anyone but you, don't love anyone but you. You know that, don't you?"

"Yes, I know that. Although—" He shuddered again.

She said softly: "I've said no before. I believe you know that too."

What were ten- or eleven-year-old boys and girls like, what interested them, how tough were they? Catchpole would have agreed that he really had no idea, wasn't even sure what Alan thought of him when they weren't talking about Arsenal. What he knew of juvenile delinquency was disturbing. Kids as young as eight did quite a bit of petty thieving from shops as they had done in his own youth, but they extended this to well-organized breaking and entering into houses after keeping watch to make sure the occupants were out or away from home. When discovered they sometimes turned violent, ten-year-olds using knives to force information out of householders about where money was kept. If there was no money they tied up and stabbed their victims, nursing a particular hatred for the old, infirm, or partially helpless.

These things happened all over London, mostly in areas where ethnic passions bubbled and families were packed into decaying tower blocks. Mostly, but not entirely. A few months earlier three boys in Clapham, their ages ranging from eight to twelve, had tortured a half-blind eighty-year-old pensioner, finally getting away with no more than a couple of pounds. That was not in scruffy Balham but in comparatively prosperous Clapham. Who knew what vicious little toughs might attend Macaulay Comprehensive, where he had rashly engaged to talk about being a detective?

So it was a relief to find himself confronting some forty clean and apparently expectant boys and girls, Alan at the back of the group looking resolutely inconspicuous, Mr. Hughes telling them how lucky they were that a senior officer from Scotland Yard was able to spare time to talk to them about being a detective. He spoke for around half an hour, taking them through an average day with its conferences, paperwork, checking of information through the computer, and then describing a robbery that had involved the breaking down of an alibi that placed the guilty man in a pub five miles away at the time of the break-in.

There was a lot of clapping at the end, but perhaps they had expected something more exciting, more gory. There were immediate questions about when they carried guns, and who gave the order to use them. A big boy with a shock of uncombed hair said: "What about bribes? My dad says the police take backhanders from crooks, work with them." Catchpole said mildly that a serious accusation of that kind should be supported by facts, and that if it was he would certainly investigate thoroughly.

The boy persisted, with a complicated tale about his family being evicted from their home by a landlord who was in cahoots with a local police inspector. The eviction had been made allegedly to make way for another family, but the house had now been standing empty for months, and his father said the landlord and the Inspector and the Council were all in it—at this point Mr. Hughes stopped the boy, as Catchpole thought he might have done earlier, and said they were grateful to Detective Superintendent Catchpole for his fascinating talk.

That evening at supper he asked Alan the name of the boy. "It was Lenny, the one Des was talking about. His father sells dodgy cars, he's always in trouble with the fuzz, the police. It was a smashing talk, Dad." Desmond said he wished he could have heard it. "You're too young, you think it's all guns and car chases like *The French Connection*."

"It is in America."

"Well, we're in England, in case you don't know. Dad, that case about the girl who disappeared, you never said anything about that."

"We haven't found her. There wouldn't have been much to say."

"Clues," Desmond said. He mashed the food on his plate into a congealed mess, looked at it with pleasure. "You must have clues, there are always clues."

"I expect you're right. I just wish we'd found them." It was at this moment, he believed afterwards, that some hint of the truth moved in Catchpole's mind. As he noted in his journal later it was the kind of perception that could be called subliminal, in the sense that it had no obvious connection with Jenny Midway.

Perhaps, anyway, what occurred to him would have been no more than an interesting speculation moving into his field of perception (or whatever name the psychologists gave to it) and floating away, but for the call put through to his office the following day. It was a surprise to hear Grayson's slow voice saying: "I guess I owe you an apology. I wasn't exactly candid over that deal."

"That's putting it mildly."

"I must have been pretty well out of my mind to go in for it. Believe me, I'd never have let Ettore talk me into it if things hadn't been just desperate financially, and the deal—"

"You mean the scam."

"All right, yes, but it was one where nobody would get hurt except a gangster who lost his money, and even he'd have been left happy. So when you looked like barging in and maybe wrecking the deal, well, a little deception was kind of forced on me. I didn't like doing it. And you may have heard, I suffered for it."

"I heard you had a lucky escape. And I should say you're luckier still not to be under arrest for attempted fraud. But that isn't my concern. What do you want? You didn't call me from across the Atlantic to apologize, or chat about your health, I'm sure."

"Why, no. But I'm not the other side of the Atlantic, I'm in Cork Street. In Louis Arts."

Catchpole stared at the telephone as if it were telling him lies. "But Meyers—"

"If you can spare a couple of minutes I'll explain. I really have been lucky, twice over you could say. First of all that bomb exploding before it should have done, then Sally Lou's Uncle Marvin died. Have you heard of Marvin's Fast Fries? They're the second biggest selling potato chips in the States, the leader in a whole range of Marvin Fast Foods. Marvin was in his eighties, a wonderful old man, played eighteen holes a couple of days before he dropped dead. Dropped dead, just like that. Well now, Sally Lou was his only niece, so she kind of expected to be remembered in the will. But, Mr. Catchpole, he left her two-thirds of his estate. That really is a lot of money." His voice lowered reverentially as he repeated: "A lot of money." Then in a higher key. "And money has paved the way. That unfortunate deal I agreed to with Ettore and Lew Fosskind, that's all settled. Matresca has his money back, and he also has one of the gems of my own collection, a little Corot landscape."

"You mean he was still ready to deal with you after what happened?"

"No no, it was a gift. One I was happy to make. Tactful, you might say, a peace offering. And it's been accepted that way. So my problems are solved."

"And Fosskind's problems are solved too."

"Why yes, that's something I don't like to dwell on. Louis's deal with his client here has gone through without a hitch, and as of next week I shall be his partner. Louis Arts is a fine gallery, but it needs a cash injection which happily, with Sally Lou's agreement, I shall supply."

"And perhaps you feel London is healthier than Massachusetts. But Mr. Grayson, I still don't understand why you've called me."

"It's a little embarrassing." If you're not embarrassed by what you've been telling me, Catchpole thought, this must be something tremendous. What's he been doing, selling fake crown jewels to an American collector? But he was surprised by Grayson's next words: "It's about Jenny. There's no more news of her?"

"I'm afraid not."

"I suppose I might be called puritanical." Apart from selling a fake picture or two, Catchpole thought. "And it seems to me what I'm going to say can't have any possible bearing on Jenny's disappearance. But Sally Lou says it might. She says what we told you was misleading, and it's ridiculous to be secretive in this day and age. Maybe she's right, though my own feeling is in favour of discretion."

"Mr. Grayson, what are you trying to say?"

Grayson told him. Catchpole was inclined to laugh, but refrained. A few minutes after he had put down the telephone it occurred to him that perhaps there was no reason for laughter.

11. *Final Resolutions*

Alice's voice was always calm, but her husband heard anxiety in it as she asked what time he would be back. He asked if there was trouble with one of the boys. She said no, they were fine.

"Something's up. What is it?"

"I don't want to say on the phone. Come as soon as you can."

"Things are quiet. Back in an hour." On the way back to Clapham he thought of Patsy Malone's relationship with Jenny, and wondered if her account of their reason for parting company was the whole truth. In the chapel he found Alice preparing to put a beef stew in the oven. The boys, she said, were playing a computer game.

"So what's up?"

She washed her hands, dried them carefully. "Brett's been arrested."

Whatever he had expected to hear, it was not this. "What for?"

"Smuggling drugs. It's ridiculous. Some awful mistake."

"Tell me."

She told him. Brett had done his swing through Scandinavia, Finland, Sweden, Denmark, in his big Vauxhall Carlton. Then he had gone to France, seen potential buyers of Ivorine in several places including Lille and Paris, come back on the ferry. At Dover the car had been given a standard search with no result, but the customs officers had then gone further, unscrewed the door panels, taken out the seating. They had found bags of heroin behind the doors, inside front and back seats, and in the spare tyre. When she repeated that it was some sort of awful mistake he shook his head.

"No mistake, they were looking for it. Brett may have been set up. What do you know about his partner, this Santoro?"

"Nothing except what Brett told me. He's Spanish, Brett said he was wonderful, has contacts in every country, said they'd make their fortune out of Ivorine."

"How did Brett meet him, you know that? Was he the one who introduced Brett to Ivorine, or was that someone else?" She shook her head. "And where's Brett now?"

"He's being held at Maidstone. It's his solicitor who told me. He doesn't want Mother to know, it would break her heart, the disgrace." He refrained from saying Mrs. Longley's heart was tougher than that, and asked the name of Brett's solicitor. "His name's Featherstone, someone Brett knows, I've got his phone number. You'll get him out, Hilly, won't you, I can't bear to think of him in prison." Her voice remained even, but her face was very pale.

"I'll ring the solicitor, find out what's happening, take it on from there." Did she realize Brett was in deep trouble? It was hard to be sure, because she looked so pleased when he told her he would find out what was happening that he lacked the heart to say this was just going through preliminary motions.

In the next couple of days he went through the motions. He talked to Featherstone, who said his client was obviously innocent, the drugs had been planted on him, and he would be applying for bail. Then he spoke to Burgess of the Drugs Squad. It was not good news that Burgess had charge of the case. They had known and disliked each other at Bramshill, and he knew Burgess regarded him as a copper who liked to keep his hands clean, did everything by the rule book. But still he talked to Burgess, a big man with yellowish projecting teeth that gave the misleading impression of a perpetual friendly grin. He had no objection to talking about the case. There was a drugs cartel called the Picpac Group, based in Colombia but with a network of European agents in firms allegedly dealing in everything from machine tools to diving equipment, toys, and spare parts for cars, but in fact covers for drug imports. Santoro, who also called himself Steiner and Markov, was friendly with one of the chief Picpac figures in Europe, a German named Max Schell, and through one of Schell's several women the Drugs Squad had learned that the Picpac Group meant to come into England in a big way.

"We had a tip off about this Vauxhall. Santoro was meant to be coming in with it, maybe Schell too, to set up contacts in the big cities, especially London and the South. Matter of fact we got a bit hasty, meant to let them go through to London in the hope we'd get bigger fish in the net, but the Customs boys at Dover got too enthusiastic. You could say it all went off half-cock, and there was no Santoro, no Schell."

"But you got the drugs."

"Plenty more where they came from." Burgess was smoking an odious-smelling pipe. No wonder his teeth were yellow. "I don't see what your interest is. Can't have any connection with the girl you couldn't find." When Catchpole told him, Burgess puffed out a cloud of blue-yellow smoke.

"You'll be opposing bail?"

"What do you think? He's all we've got and we don't want him to do a runner or be found floating. We want him to talk."

"From what you've said there's nothing that links him directly with drugs. He was trying to beat up interest in this ivory substitute."

"You buy that? What was he doing when somebody was taking his car to bits, filling it with smack and H? Tucked up in bed, the little innocent?"

"He could have been. I think he's just a patsy."

Burgess removed his pipe. The yellow teeth menaced. "I'll tell you what he is, he's a cocky half-smart champion arsehole. And we're going to squeeze him till he tells us what he knows and who he knows. And if he's the little innocent you say, which I don't buy for a moment, bad luck."

"Can I talk to him?"

"Sticking your neck out, that's not like you, I thought you always played the percentages." Catchpole made an impatient gesture. "You know the official answer, of course you shouldn't and can't. But seeing the circumstances are special and we've known each other since way back, if you want to make an entirely unofficial visit I don't know anything about it. Mind, if he bleats anything to you about names and places I want to know it."

So he went to Maidstone and saw Brett, after the request for his release on bail, strongly opposed by Burgess, had been turned down. Certainly there was no sign of cockiness in the hollow-eyed figure who clasped Catchpole's hand in both his own. All Brett's jauntiness had gone, and he appeared to have shrunk inside his clothing. For what was only a few minutes but seemed much longer he poured out complaints about the disgusting nature of prison, his treatment, the food, the coarseness and filthiness of his fellow inmates. At moments Catchpole feared Brett might cry.

Like others Catchpole had seen who found themselves unexpectedly in prison, Brett could not believe what had happened to him. It was all a mistake, he kept repeating, some kind of confusion had arisen, the promotional tour had been going so well with interest in Ivorine expressed by everybody he met especially in Germany and Holland, if they could only get in touch with Santoro he would be able to explain . . . But about details he was vague. Santoro had left him in Amsterdam he thought, or perhaps a little later in Lille, he had mining interests in Bolivia and there had been some crisis, he had to fly there for an urgent meeting but had said he would be back within a week and meet up with Brett again in London. Schell? Brett knew nobody named Schell, nor did he know Santoro had used the other names Catchpole mentioned. How had he first learned about Ivorine? Through a friend of Santoro, who had introduced him to Santoro as a man who would be able to put up or find the necessary financial backing. Where had they met? In Malaga, in a bar. Brett had been working for a time-share company, he had been introduced, Santoro had invited him back to his villa in the hills outside the town, it had all gone on from there. If only Santoro were here he would explain that there had been some absurd mistake.

Every so often, in the course of saying this, Brett's eyes seemed to roll up so that only the whites were visible, and his expression became vacant, almost idiotic. Catchpole could not decide whether he was acting or was really as big a fool as he seemed. On the whole, he thought the latter. He tried to inject some reality into the conversation.

"Brett," he said. "Santoro is a drug dealer. His Bolivian contacts are part of what's called the Picpac Group, he's a member of it himself. Did you ever hear that name mentioned?"

Brett looked at him vacantly. "No. Never. Manny is rich. That's his name, Emanuel Santoro, Manny."

"He may be rich, but his money comes from drugs. We think he was tipped off, that's why he left you in Amsterdam, Lille, wherever it was." Brett still looked vacant. "It's important you remember all the details you can about where you met him, who the other man was who introduced you and what he looked like, who else you met. Am I getting through to you? The first thing your counsel will want to know is all the places you stopped, where the car was left each night, how easy access to it was. You understand it didn't just take minutes to stash the drugs inside the seats and door panels, it will help to know when and where it was done, and the odds are Santoro masterminded it, so it was while he was with you. Remember the dates?" Brett stared at him, shook his head. "Well, try. Look, I ought not to be here, or be telling you this, so don't pass it on. Alice wanted me to come, sent her love."

"How is she?"

"Fine, except she's worried about you."

"Mother. Mother doesn't know about this, does she?"

Mrs. Longley had been on the telephone daily to Alice, expressing her outrage at Brett's arrest and detention, and expanding on the distress the affair was causing her and the remarks made about it by friends in Hove. He said to Brett only that she knew, it was in the papers.

"Yes," Brett whispered. Then he said, pleading like a child: "I can't stay here, I hate it. I must get out."

"I'm sorry, Brett. You know the magistrate refused bail."

"I'll give up my passport, anything. I promise I won't run away. This—" He waved a hand at the room in which they were talking. "The cells, you don't know what they're like. The smell. And some of the warders—" He looked at the blank-faced man by the door, didn't go on.

Afterwards Catchpole told Alice he couldn't be sure if Brett was as confused as he seemed.

"You've never liked him, that's why you don't believe him. But he's my brother, and I know he'd never have had anything to do with smuggling drugs. He simply wouldn't."

"I haven't said I don't believe him. But either he's a fool or he must have had some idea of what was going on. There must have been characters Santoro was seeing who raised his suspicions, people who couldn't have had any connection with Ivorine. Maybe Brett just didn't want to know." She shrugged. "Look, I'm trying to help. You've got to understand Brett's in real trouble. He doesn't have to talk to me, maybe it's better he doesn't, but he's got to give a reasonable story to his counsel, and if he behaves the way he did with me he won't do that."

"Oh, you and your *reasonable story*. You just want to see my brother get a prison sentence."

Alan, who took a healthy—or perhaps unhealthy—interest in newspapers, asked the following day: "Is Uncle Brett in prison?"

"Yes. He's what's called on remand, waiting to come up for trial."

"Like that man you thought killed the girl, the one who got off because he'd been robbing a post office and went to prison for that?"

"Right."

"Mum says Uncle Brett didn't do it." When there was no reply he went on. "Did you get him sent to prison?"

Desmond, who had been listening, said: "Catchpole on the case. Wow."

"I had nothing to do with it. There's a department at Scotland Yard called the Drugs Squad. The case is to do with bringing in drugs to this country, and that's illegal. But I hope your uncle had nothing to do with it."

"Crack?" Alan asked. "Nose powder?"

"Where did you hear those words? At school?"

"Read them in the paper."

"I don't want to hear you using them. And I want no more talk about it."

Life was exciting, the Purafood restaurant offered a fulfilment Eleanor had never known, yet life was also, she acknowledged to herself, in some ways empty. The emptiness was not alleviated by the worshipful attitude of Stella, who regarded Eleanor as a kind of feminist heroine. "You've done what you want," she would say when she came round in the evening for what she called a cup of coffee and a good natter. Morning coffee was a thing of the past, for Eleanor was in the restaurant by ten-thirty every morning, ready to supervise the day's menu. "And really it was through me it all began, wasn't it?"

Eleanor smilingly acknowledged that her introduction to Bryan Connors through the dinner party had sparked it all off.

"Oh, I didn't mean I was *responsible*. It's just that you've had such troubles with Jenny, and then—" She paused, at a loss.

"And John going off to live with his secretary. You can say it."

"Yes, well, and that. But you've triumphed over them, that's what's so wonderful. You've come through. You must think I'm feeble and silly, just being a housewife and a rotten one at that. You're *fulfilled*."

That, indeed, was the word Eleanor repeated to herself, and most of the time believed to be true. Yet there were things that worried her and, strangely, the fact that Jenny might be dead was not the chief of them, although it stayed in the background of her mind. Although John was so obviously and hopelessly in the wrong she worried about him, even about such trivialities as whether his shirts were being properly ironed. And she worried also about Bryan Connors.

It was not that Bryan was less enthusiastic about the restaurant or the meals served in it. He lunched there at least twice a week, generally with guests, and his praise of the menus, the cooking, and the British nature of what was served verged on the extravagant. Perhaps that was to be expected, but there was something lyrical in his praise, as if it referred not to the actual dishes brought to the table, which because the cooking was done in quantity rather than individually were in fact not quite so good as those she had served to the office luncheon parties, but to some perfect meals existing in his imagination. When she was summoned again to the tenth floor she got out of the lift with a feeling of trepidation that proved unfounded. Janetta's smile was no less dazzling than usual, and Bryan advanced to greet her with little arms open wide. A kiss was bestowed on each of her cheeks. It was not excitement he displayed for he seemed perfectly in control of his feelings, it was a religious exultation that infused him as he waved at her a sheaf of press cuttings about the restaurant, and said they were ready for the next step. His round face was smiling as he said: "Or several next steps."

"I'm sorry. I don't understand."

"I told you I had a vision, a Purafood vision, a crusade. The flag is flying proudly in Chancery Lane. Now we shall plant it all over Britain." The smile broadened. "I've had agents at work since the day our flagship set to sea, and I've now bought a number of properties all over the country. Refurbishing is going on, each restaurant is being designed with features typical of its area, tartans and Bonnie Prince Charlie for Scotland, the great feats of Welsh rugby shown in panels at Cardiff and Swansea, fishing nets and lobster creels in Cornwall. My vision will become reality, and what greater success can a man have than that? And you are a vital part of it, Eleanor, with your help we shall make a better, a healthier, a Purafood Britain. What do you say to that?"

When she asked how far the refurbishments had gone, he waved a hand. "One or two are near completion, others have been begun, some are still in the planning stage. But in a few weeks, at most a few months, they will all be ready. And when they are, Eleanor, when they are I mean to astonish the country with such a varied cornucopia of British food as the country has never seen. The restaurants will make Purafood the symbol of perfection in national food. And your part in planning the menus,

Eleanor, will make you famous." He beamed at her, his expression remarkably like that of Cruikshank's Mr. Pickwick.

It was another few minutes before she realized that he was expecting her to produce for each restaurant menus typical of the region, and that the necessary variations would involve the creation of literally dozens of different dishes. When she tried to convey the immensity of the enterprise, the time it would take to devise and test the recipes, and her doubts about her ability to do anything so ambitious, his voice took on a preacher's earnestness.

"You can do it, Eleanor. In your heart you know you can and want to. It's a matter of faith, and we both have faith in abundance, faith and the energy that has made the flagship a splendid success. Now we are moving on to greater things, much greater, and together we can do them, never doubt it." He clasped her hands in his own small ones and lowered his voice. "And even this I see not as an end but a beginning."

She left the tenth floor in a daze. She mentioned Bryan's plans to Maggie Lomas, and was not surprised when they were greeted coolly. "I heard something about it, but I'm not sweating too hard designing menu cards yet awhile. Let's just concentrate on the restaurant we've got, OK? I hear on the grapevine Derek's been approached by the Connaught, wants us to up his money fifty percent or he's off." Derek was the younger and better of the two chefs working under Eleanor, and she protested when Maggie said it looked as if they would have to let him go. Derek was good, surely they should try to keep him. Maggie patted her on the shoulder.

"You look after stomachs, I count the cash, agreed? Besides—"

"What?"

"I said before, let's concentrate on this one for the time being." Why did Eleanor have the feeling Maggie had been about to say something else?

* * *

David worked partly on salary, partly on commission when he sold a property. When the call came he was totting up the amount due to him on sales for the past quarter. The result was not encouraging. The switchboard girl said: "It's a girl called Donny. Says you know her."

When he picked up the receiver an unfamiliar voice said: "It's Donny, Donny Williams."

"I don't think—"

"From the flat above you." The orange-haired girl, of course. Had he known her name? What was she saying? ". . . called the doctor, and he says she's OK."

"What was that? I'm sorry."

"Your wife. She came home early, felt ill or something. I'm off work, see, 'cause I'm on a three-day week, 'stead of sacking some of the girls they put us all on a three-day week—"

"What's happened to Mary?"

"I was saying, wasn't I? So I'm home, got the telly on and hear this screech, thought at first it was our telly, sounds it makes sometimes, but then the screech comes again and I know it must be something else, so I go out to the landing and there she is coupla floors down, lying spread out like on the floor. So I go down to her—"

"Is she all right?"

"Yeah yeah, I was saying, I got downstairs and she's kind of buckled up, one leg under her. Seems she didn't feel too good, left her job early, came home, musta slipped on something, coulda been bit of banana I sometimes eat 'em, say they're good for you. Anyway I tried to get her up, couldn't. Saw she was bleeding a bit and I thought Donny this is one for the medic so I calls him and—right, I'm making it short, you want to know. She's OK, tucked up in bed, didn't wanna go to hospital and I don't blame her, so she's OK as I say but pregnant and lost the baby—well, you can't call it that, it was only three months . . ."

And it was Donny who greeted him when he entered the flat, Donny transformed from the shrieking virago up above into a smiling version of Nurse someone or other on TV, ready with tea and soothing words, lacking only the uniform. It took ten minutes to get rid of her. Then he was alone with the small figure in the bed who looked at him forlornly and said she didn't know how it happened, as Donny said she must have slipped on something.

"I know what happened. You did it deliberately." She stared at him, then shook her head. "You never wanted it. Not with us living here. Not the way I did."

Donny had drawn the curtains. The only illumination came from a low-wattage lamp beside the bed which seemed to accentuate the pallor of her face, leaving half of it in shadow. She shook her head again. He went on.

"You thought it would be no good having a baby here, not enough money without you working, scraping along. I don't blame you, you never really wanted it. I thought of nothing else coming back here, can't now. I can *see* our baby, I know what he looks like. Would have looked like." She put her hand over his. "You're all right?"

"A bit late asking that, aren't you? The doctor says yes. A couple of days in bed and I can go back to Mr. Megillah. Donny was wonderful, you must be nice to her. You don't know how you sound when you don't like somebody. David?"

"Yes?"

"You don't really think I did it deliberately, do you? I'd never do that."

"I don't know what I think." He removed his hand from hers, looked down at the quilt, traced one of the worn patches on it with his finger. "You were going to leave me."

"What makes you say that?" He teased with his finger at the quilt. "I don't know what you heard. Or what anybody said, but it isn't true, wasn't ever true. And it isn't true I wanted to get rid of the baby. David, are you listening to me, do you believe me? David?"

"Yes, I believe you."

"Everything goes away in the end. All the pain, the jealousy, the loss. How do you think I feel now? Empty, just a terrible sort of lightness in my body as if I could float away. But I know it won't last, nothing lasts. All those feelings, in the end they fade away."

He took her hand again. She lay back in the bed, dark hair spread around her, head turned to him, eyes searching for a response. Above them Donny's voice was raised, some heavy object rolled across the floor. "Dipak's home," she said. "Donny loves him, you know. She told me so."

It was Catchpole's view that, although loose ends always existed at the end of a case, you should try to tie them up, and it was in pursuit of a neatly tied bow that he called at Louis Arts where little Meyers greeted him with literally open arms. Catchpole avoided them, and said he understood the Renoir deal had gone through, and McCracken had bought the picture. The dealer put finger to lips.

"No names, Superintendent, no names. But you were absolutely right about the picture being a genuine Renoir. I now know there is at least one art expert at Scotland Yard. And everybody is happy." He sketched a bow, smiling.

"No American repercussions?"

"I don't want to know what happened in America. With hand on heart I can assure you it had nothing to do with me."

"No problems with your Italian friend?"

"The Count is delighted. Ettore is for the moment incognito, I don't know where he is."

In view of what he had tried to put over on Matresca Catchpole was not surprised. He said he heard Meyers had a new partner.

"It was necessary. Not desperate, my situation, you understand, but like so many other small businesses we are undercapitalized. Eversley has brought his knowledge of the American market and his wide range of contacts. And he is putting in capital." Meyers beamed. "All are valuable."

And some things are more valuable than others, Catchpole thought. "I wanted to ask a question. About Jenny Midway." The dealer's face assumed a suitably doleful look. "You've said she was quick and intelligent. Would you say she was a possibly disruptive influence here?"

Meyers shrugged. "When somebody has disappeared, someone young and beautiful, you say good things, not bad. And don't mistake me, there were not bad things to say. She picked up the right sort of approach, the right language, wonderfully fast. But—"

"Yes?"

"Maurice didn't like her. And she came to me once or twice with stories about him losing a possible sale, pricing a picture too high, that kind of thing. I tell it to you crudely and it was done subtly, but that was what she did. Maurice said she was a troublemaker. I put it down to over-eagerness, trying to prove herself. Now you ask, I tell you this. But don't think I was saying anything but the truth when I told you she was quick and clever and charming."

"I would never suspect you of doing anything but tell the truth." Catchpole paused. "Except when necessary."

"Ah, necessity makes liars of us all. Was it Oscar Wilde who said something like that? You will excuse me now, I see Maurice making signals. I shall come to Scotland Yard when next I want a picture authenticated."

* * *

The voice on the telephone said it belonged to Jack Johnson of the *Banner*, and had the confident but respectful note Giles had heard before in reporters' voices when they were keen to get his views about capital punishment, the length of prison sentences, or the frequency with which appeal judges might put right injustices resulting from verdicts that hadn't taken full account of the evidence. He was not at all reluctant to pronounce on such questions, although he had refused more than one request to comment on his niece's disappearance. If he had been pressed he would have said capital punishment was a public issue, Jenny's disappearance a private matter of family concern, which was why he had so strongly disapproved of Eleanor's TV appearance. But Jack Johnson said he wanted Mr. Justice Midway's opinion on a matter of public interest which he would sooner not talk about on the telephone. He sounded delighted when Giles agreed to see him.

The man to whom he opened the door, however, had the half-dressed look he had disliked in other newspaper reporters. His flat-nosed face was that of a chinless bulldog, a slight scrub of hair surrounded very red lips, he wore what seemed a rough workman's shirt, the collar open to reveal a sprout of hair springing up from the chest, and baggy trousers that looked tight round his ample waist. Altogether a deplorable specimen in appearance, and it was no surprise that he dropped into an armchair before being invited to sit. Giles remained standing for a moment, looking down coldly at this invited intruder, then asked if he could offer his guest some refreshment.

"Too early in the morning." Johnson looked round the room. "Looks like a gent's club, the general effect. Suits you, though, does it?"

"I find nothing unusual about it. And yes, the atmosphere is congenial to me. You may think Harkland Court old-fashioned"—he permitted himself a long look at his visitor—"but then I am an old-fashioned man."

"Like most judges?"

"I can speak only for myself."

"Do you see the *Banner*? No, broadsheets are more your line, I guess, *The Times* or *Telegraph*. I do special features for the paper, personal pieces, what you might call profiles, you know the kind of thing. The editor would like me to do one about you."

Giles was taken aback, but he had learned on the bench to conceal personal feelings, and now expressed only polite surprise. "I understood on the telephone that you wanted to talk about a matter of public interest. I hardly think my position on the bench is such a matter." An unwelcome thought occurred to him. "I hope you were not intending to ask my views about the disappearance of my niece Jenny. That is a private matter about which I have nothing whatever to say."

The visitor rubbed the bristles where his chin might have been. "No, I wouldn't want to concentrate on that, might just mention it. It's your career that interests us. Career and opinions."

"I'm flattered." Giles settled back in a chair opposite the visitor. "I imagine you will want to use the—ah—tape-recorder that might be called the tool of your trade." Jack Johnson grinned, took from a pocket something no bigger than a cigarette packet, and put it down on a coffee table between the two chairs. "But before we begin it might be helpful if you could tell me the general drift of the subjects you would like to discuss. I might have some rather—ah—pungent things to say, for instance about the punishment of juvenile offenders."

"We can talk about anything you like. These for a start."

There are times when one has a presentiment of disaster, the moment before the foothold on a mountain climb crumbles away, the instant before collision with a vehicle out of control and on the wrong side of the road, the fraction of time between the unwise striking of a match and the explosion in a gas-filled room. Giles Midway felt no such warning. He had noticed the folder brought in by the visitor without speculating as to what it might contain, so that the shock when Johnson produced the photographs from it was total. He felt a terrible constriction in the chest, gasped for air, then managed to get up. He poured a tot of whisky from the drinks cupboard in the room next door, then started as he heard the hateful journalist's voice behind him saying he had changed his mind, would it be OK if he poured his own? Then they were back in their chairs, and Johnson was saying he could see these had come as a bit of a shock, but obviously he recognized them.

"Where did you get them?" Giles would hardly have known the voice as his own.

"Nothing unusual, kind of thing being offered to us all the time, personal pix of everyone from rock stars to the royals. Half the time they're obvious fakes, lookalikes or different heads stuck on, sometimes we can't use 'em because the lawyers say no, then nobody sees 'em but the proprietor and editor. And we always check before we buy. So we checked these, and when we'd checked we bought 'em."

"Who did you buy them from?" But he knew the answer.

"So happens I saw him, bright young lad, said if he gave me his name there'd be no point, it wouldn't be the right one. Said he knew you." He described Jimmy Kelsey, face, clothes and gold earring. "Said he borrowed them without you knowing. Friend of yours, is he? Stayed here perhaps?"

"Certainly not." He shuddered away from the insinuation. "I tried to help him once. He stole them." Almost worse than sick awareness that he must try to make some arrangement with the journalist who sat three feet away from him, drinking his whisky and obviously relishing his discomfiture, was the realization that he had been betrayed by Jimmy. This was the young man he had helped and relied on, Jimmy who had refused payment for any expenses that might be involved in teaching Mrs. Entwhistle's cousin a lesson, and had said with his bright smile: "I owe you, this one's on me." From the beginning Jimmy had smelt easy money . . . He became aware that the man Johnson had been speaking, and he had not heard what was said.

"You want to look at these, check them out?" There were perhaps a dozen prints on the table. He shook his head. "OK, you're satisfied they're genuine. Now let's talk, talk straight, cards face up on the table. First, we didn't pay a fortune for this stuff, what is it, an elderly gentleman in drag, no big deal—"

He was moved to protest. "It is not at all what you think, what you imply. I changed my clothing so that I could observe and understand the behaviour of the young without being recognized as one of Her Majesty's Judges. It is a technique, one I call Watching, that is all."

Johnson drained his glass, clapped hands noiselessly. "Tremendous, that's the kind of thing I was hoping you'd say. These pix on their own, they're just about worth using, worth seeing the sort of thing Judges get up to in their spare time. But the pictures plus a profile, plus Mr. Justice Midway's explanation on the lines of what you're saying, that's something else. It would be your story, in your own words as told to me, just what you were doing in this Watching, why you were doing it, what results you got. Nothing scandalous about it, instead it's "Mr. Justice Midway Investigates." You'd be free to say whatever you feel about modern youth and how you got to know them this way."

The constriction returned. There was a crab inside his chest, its claws clutching and relaxing, and a choking sensation in his throat. "Get out."

"You're not looking at this the right way. I have to tell you we'll be using some of this material whether or not you cooperate. The difference will be—Jesus Christ, man, look out."

Giles had risen, clutched the journalist's shirt, mouthed something unintelligible and then fallen to the floor, his grip still firm so that they dropped together to the carpet. Johnson pulled free with difficulty, saw the colour of the Judge's face and the way he was gasping for breath, and dialled 999. When the ambulance came the paramedic said within a minute "Heart attack," and two or three minutes later shook his head. He asked Johnson what the sick man had been doing.

"Being interviewed," he said gloomily.

"I'm pleased to see the matters we talked about a few weeks ago have been dealt with. I was particularly impressed by the way you dealt with the problems of Wainwright."

Perhaps John should have been warned by this approach, for Horton was known to precede the knife in the back with a pat on the shoulder: but his mind was occupied with the problem of Susan, and of Eleanor who had rung the previous day to say she missed him, and the dull ache he felt when he thought of Jenny. He was not alerted even when the gentle voice said: "And Eleanor, how is Eleanor?"

He said she was very well. "She was well when you left her this morning?" Suddenly he understood the purpose of the interview, and braced himself for what was coming as he said he had not spoken to Eleanor that morning. He added, in an attempt to forestall what he knew was about to be said, that their relationship was not the firm's business.

Horton's voice was even gentler than usual when he spoke again, the gentleness a contradiction of the actual words. "Indeed? Even, when, if my information is correct, our personnel director has left his wife and is living with his secretary? Is it really your view that that is not the firm's business? Your considered opinion?"

When John replied he was aware of repeating clichés he had

used himself often enough to people on the staff who had unburdened themselves about the strains of marriage, to the effect that they should talk things through, do nothing irrevocable, behave like the civilized people they were. He was saying Eleanor and he were trying to do this when Horton broke in.

"But, you see, we are not talking about any couple, we are talking about the firm's *personnel director* living with his secretary. I am afraid that affects the case. I would even go so far as to say it makes your department a laughingstock. The head of department is advising staff about their problems, problems of all kinds but many of them personal and marital, and what is he doing? It might be awkward if he was carrying on an affair and that was known inside the firm, but it is one with his secretary and he has gone public, set up house with her. I'm afraid it can't go on."

He said they had been as discreet as possible, although in fact he had doubts about Susan. "I agree the situation must be resolved soon, and we're both aware of that. All I'm asking for is a little time—"

Horton's tongue came out, licked his lips quickly, disappeared. The bastard's enjoying this, John thought, this is how he gets his kicks. Yet his voice was gentle as ever, the tone almost humorous. "I think you can't have heard me, John. I said the situation can't go on, and I should have thought that was clear. It damages the good order and smooth running of the firm. If you leave Eleanor, that is not my affair, although I should regret it. And if you set up house with a Turkish belly dancer that again is perhaps not my affair, but if the Turkish belly dancer is employed by MultiCorpus and works in this department—do you understand me? Do I make myself clear?"

"I understand." At that moment John Midway's long practice in the art of persuasion deserted him, and he positively enjoyed using words that had been in his subconscious for years. Nose aiming at ceiling, lower lip out-thrust, he said: "I understand it's useless to think any human problem could be considered reasonably by somebody as emotionally constipated and eager to exploit any human weakness as you. It gives me pleasure to tell you that your filthy spying practices make you loathed by everyone in the department, and that my own detestation of them is only exceeded by my contempt for the way you use them as a substitute for your lack of management skills. I won't give you the pleasure of sacking me. I resign."

Horton's usual smile changed to a blank look, still on his face as John left the room. He told Susan what had happened, and added that if she wanted to stay she had better go in now and try to make her peace with Horton. She gasped, said he was wonderful, and left with him. When they were outside he looked up at the building and said: "Goodbye, MultiCorpus, I never liked you."

"What are we going to do now?"

"Have a slap-up lunch. Then see that Meryl Streep film you keep talking about. Then back to Stoke Newington. Then who can tell?"

Afterwards a taxi took them back to Stoke Newington. As John paid off the driver a dozen youths came out of a café called the Paper Clip opposite Susan's flat. There was loud laughter, back slapping, two or three broke away and crossed the road. A car stopped beside the main group, there was animated discussion. John stood and stared. Susan pulled at his arm. "Come on."

"What are they doing?"

"Dealing, what d'you think?"

The taxi driver leaned out of his cab, said, "Sooner you than me, mate," drove off with a toot.

"Drugs? In the open, like this?"

"Of course. They used to be round the corner, pub called the King's Head. But it was raided last week, so they're here."

"What drugs?"

"Crack and E mostly, quite a bit of speed too I expect. Come on, let's get in, they don't like staring."

Up in the untidy flat he asked how she knew what drugs were being sold. "Through Stephen? You use them yourself, is that it?"

"Where have you been all your life? Everybody uses something, even if it's just hash or pills. Things get you down, you need a lift or you just want to feel good, a reefer can work wonders."

"I've never taken a drug of that sort in my life. I don't believe Eleanor has either."

"Unlucky both. But today's been lovely, John, don't spoil it. Come on." What followed was not very successful in spite of Susan's best efforts. Afterwards she rolled a reefer, wanted him to try it, but he refused. She said: "That was one of the best days of my life."

"And mine."

"What did you actually say?"

"I've told you already." But he repeated it. The smell of hash, sweet and heavy, made him feel slightly sick.

"Lovely, lovely. You're marvellous. What shall we do tomorrow?"

"Tomorrow I get in touch to negotiate the terms of my departure. I shall say Horton insulted me. He *did* insult me, my private life is nothing to do with him." He added as an afterthought: "Neither is yours."

On the following day he saw the financial director Melksham, a narrow-faced man, tight-lipped and unforgiving as Savonarola. They argued about whether John had resigned voluntarily or been forced to do so because of what was said by Horton. John made tentative noises about going to an Industrial Tribunal, but eventually settled for a year's salary. Melksham did not suggest that he should forget his resignation, but said: "What about Mrs. Cook? Do I understand that she is also leaving?"

"I suppose so, yes."

"I thought you would know. I don't think her position here is tenable, in view of the situation. We should be prepared to offer her the same terms as yourself. Perhaps you would tell her this if, as I assume, you will be speaking to her. In my view it is a very reasonable offer in view of all the circumstances."

They shook hands. Outside in St. Martin's Lane John looked up at the grey glass-faced block. The sun was shining, the air warm but not humid. He marched towards Tottenham Court Road Underground station head up, and as he passed Foyle's said: "Something ends, something begins." Yet he did not feel as if anything was beginning, but like a man walking on firm ground that has suddenly begun to quake beneath him. Not long ago he had a wife, a daughter, a home, a job. Now they had all gone, disappeared as if by their own volition in ways with which he felt he had nothing to do. Why was he now on his way to Stoke Newington, a part of London about which he knew little and cared less? Why was he going back to a dingy flat instead of his comfortable house, to Susan instead of Eleanor?

Two boys and a girl stood chatting outside the Paper Clip. They looked at him speculatively as he approached but did not speak.

He crossed the road. Susan was on a sofa, feet up, reading a paperback. She said: "How did it go?" He told her. "What d'you think?"

"I think you should take it."

"OK, if that's what you think. And you too, you'll take the payoff, no argument?" He said yes, although he felt uneasy at the way she linked their fates. "So what do we do now?"

"I shall look for another job."

"Still, there'll be a breathing space. OK if I ring them and say I agree, or should I write, what d'you think?" Suppressing the desire to say the decision was not his but hers, he said a letter would be best. "OK. Calls for a celebratory drink. There's beer in the fridge."

It would have been churlish to say there was nothing to celebrate, or that he did not much like canned beer. She drank straight from the can, he used a glass. She went back to her book, Dick Francis, he looked at the paper. After a few minutes she put down the book.

"Want to go to bed?" He shook his head. "It was you burned the bridges. Wishing you hadn't?"

"I'm sorry I involved you, dragged you into something you may regret," he said, although that was not his primary feeling.

"If we're not going to bed you might try laughing. I mean, life's funny, isn't it? The way things turn out you've got to laugh." And indeed she was smiling. "No need to worry about Susan, she's a bouncing ball that always finishes sunny side up. And a good secretary, remember? But I think you're wondering, are we really a couple? I don't have those doubts. I told you I love you. And in case you think I've been sitting on my arse all day, that's not so. I've been out to the shops. Supper will be minted lamb chops, new potatoes that are alleged to be English, and courgettes. And apple turnovers to follow. A decent meal, only lacking a bottle of something or other. Since I'll be at work in the kitchen why don't you go out and buy one?"

He appreciated the tact of this, even though there was something distasteful about a phrase like *sitting on my arse all day*. He went out, and walked around the streets of Stoke Newington for an hour, staring into the windows of shops offering TVs, radios, camcorders, all at cut prices and bearing Japanese names. The whole of one street alternated between such shops, building societies offering special interest rates for those investing over £20,000 and big loans for first-time buyers, an electricity showroom, a furniture shop containing three-piece suites, sofas that turned into beds and overstuffed armchairs, all at bargain prices, and a small supermarket. He entered the supermarket, took a wire basket and wandered down the aisles looking at frozen chicken, frozen fish fillets, a range of frozen Complete Dinners, roast beef and Yorkshire pudding with sprouts and potatoes, roast lamb, mint sauce, broccoli and potatoes, Lancashire hot pot . . . You've got to laugh, he thought, you've got to laugh. He piled four Complete Dinners into the basket, added two packets of frozen plaice fillets, and found an attendant three feet away staring at him. A plastic badge on his lapel said: *Wally*, *Assistant Manager*. "Need any help?"

John was shaking with internal laughter, unable to speak. He shook his head, put back the Complete Dinners, then the plaice fillets, moved off down the aisle. Wally, Assistant Manager, put them more tidily in the frozen compartment, then followed him, watched as he put two bottles of wine into the basket, moved forward ready for them to be put back, asked: "You buying those?" After the responsive nod he followed John to the check-out, turned away only when they were paid for in cash.

Out in the street John sniffed again at the evening air, the Stoke Newington air, petrol-laden, smog-containing, heavy with the stink of marijuana, contaminated by dirty needles. Was it different from Fulham air, was this the air that had destroyed his Jenny, the whole of London filled with it, no escape anywhere? He left the main street and the shop windows blazing with light, then lost his way walking back to Susan down roads where all the houses had antennae nosing the night air and many carried the white shield on their breasts that showed they were reaching the mecca of the Sky.

Turning at random left and left again he was aware of a figure beside him, a voice saying: "You lookin' for somethin'? You wanna buy?" His own tongue was suddenly loosened. "What?" he cried. "What?" He raised the bag containing the bottles with the vague intention of swinging it at the figure's head. The man or youth backed away. In John's mind the bottles cracked as they hit the head, cracked then broke, wine pouring on the pavement like blood. No fear of that, he thought, the bottles are safe, what an idea, you've got to laugh.

He was opposite the Paper Clip, a couple of steps away from Susan's front door which was now his own front door, proved by the fact that he had a key. In the living-room Steve and Jan turned faces towards him. Susan said: "They dropped in, don't worry, they've brought their own supper."

The two of them stared at him, then Steve said: "Fish and chips. From round the corner. Mum and I often used to have 'em, right, Mum?"

Susan nodded, her eyes on John, watchful. She said when he put down the bottles: "Two, that's good. Enough for everyone."

Steve shook his head. "Don't like it. Red tastes sour, white looks like piss. I'm a beer man, you got beer, Mum?"

"There's some in the fridge. You've been a long time, John."

"Choosing the wine. You've got to laugh." She looked at him. "The way things turn out you've got to laugh, it's what you said. I nearly came back with four Complete Dinners, meat and two veg. That would have been just right, wouldn't it?"

Steve said: "Sooner have the old fish and chips."

Steve went out to the kitchen and returned with two cans of beer. John opened one of the bottles, poured wine into two glasses. Susan brought in the food, a large plate of fish and chips for Steve, a smaller one for Jan, the chops and vegetables.

There was a silence. Steve ate with intensity as he had done before, head rather low over plate. Jan picked at the fish, pushed it aside, picked up chips in her fingers and put them in her mouth one by one. Susan said the chops were overcooked and that was John's fault because he had been out for so long, but afterwards did not speak. It seemed to John that she watched him uneasily. He refilled his glass and hers, then his again. They finished the bottle. Steve ate the rest of Jan's fish, then both Steve and Jan declined the apple turnover.

"Both packed your jobs in then," Steve said when they were drinking coffee. "Don't blame you, can't stick those big places myself, tried it once. You too, Jan, you packed it in, right?"

Jan nodded. Her jaws moved rhythmically although there was no sign that she had eaten any gum.

Susan said: "Steve and Jan will be staying a few days. Till they find somewhere." She spoke so casually that at first John did not take in the words. Steve expanded on them.

"Yeah, we had a bit of an argument where we were."

Jan spoke for the second time. "Our squat. Some bastard tried to rape me."

"You were in a squat?"

She glared at him. "What's wrong with that?"

What *was* wrong with that? It was simply outside his experience, that was all. Steve elaborated. "It was a commune like, everyone paid something, more if they were in work, and we made like improvements. It was all right, a good place. Only this Gladiator, what he called himself, took a liberty, said Jan was asking for it."

"Why wasn't the Gladiator thrown out?"

Steve's round face was worried. "Yeah, well, there's two or three sort of run the place, they kind of said the Glad was right. Course Jan's attractive, they all wanted to get in the sack with her."

John looked at the frizz-haired skeleton who stared back at him, jaws moving. There was a very small spare room, but it contained no bed. His clothes were there, stuffed into a chest-of-drawers-cum-wardrobe already filled with junk Susan refused to get rid of. He asked where they would sleep, and Susan answered.

"For the time being in here on the sofa. Later on we can see, maybe get a bed."

Steve said with a gallant making the best of it smile: "I'll be off early each morning, no bother. And Jan'll be around to help, anything you want, shopping and that."

Jan'll be around: that brought the enormity of it, the horror of it, home. Jan would be around all day, and he and Susan would be around all day too. Jan would infect the flat with her gum, her pot, her whole presence. She would be there in the morning half-dressed, her clothes and Steve's strewn about this room or put into the cupboard in the spare room with his. If a second bed was bought or borrowed they would take that room for their own and his clothes would have to be crammed in with Susan's so that his suits soon became creased and crumpled, his shirts mixed in with her bras and briefs—it was too much. He said loudly: "No."

Silence. Susan said quietly: "What does that mean?"

"I won't have it." He became suddenly conscious that if this situation had been put to him at MultiCorpus he might have said he was forcing Steve and Jan out onto the street. He put the thought away from him. "This place is too small."

"I think you've forgotten something. It's my place. And Steve's my son. He asked if he could stay, and I said yes. Let me ask you. Suppose it was your home and I was telling you what you could and couldn't do, what would you say?"

"That would be different. There'd be plenty of room and—oh, this is ridiculous." As he saw the firm set of her mouth he knew there was no possibility of agreement between them, but felt bound to make a last effort. He summoned up the ghost of the personnel director who had so often solved other people's problems.

"Susan, we've got overheated about this. What I suggest is that tonight Steve and Jan should stay in a hotel at my expense. In the morning we can talk about it, look for a bigger place—" He stopped because she was shaking her head.

"I thought you understood but you don't. You just pour out your soothing syrup. I said I'd do anything for you, that's why I left the job, just like that, because you had. But when you have to suffer a bit of inconvenience for me—" She shook her head slowly, looked down at the carpet. "You'd better go."

As he put clothes in a suitcase hurriedly, like a commander

retreating after a battle, he felt relief and shame. Had he organized this departure, was it really what he wanted, an escape? In the living-room he was aware of the looks directed at him by Steve and Jan. There was no hostility in their gaze, only curiosity, as if they were looking at a creature of another species. Susan sat head in hands. He paused at the door. "I'll be in touch."

"Don't bother."

He stayed the night in a small hotel near the British Museum, racked by guilt, unable to decide whether he should return to Fulham. He had forgotten to pack pyjamas, and slept badly.

Catchpole rang Patsy Malone. He noted with dispassionate interest the slight shiver that shook him when he heard her voice. Her words were not welcoming.

"Not again. I thought I'd heard the last of you."

"This is just a question. About Jenny. Did you like her?"

"What sort of stupid question is that? Would I share a place with a woman I couldn't get on with?"

"I'll put it another way. Did she set out to get Gabriel away from you?" He went on before she could answer. "I know you say it didn't worry you, that isn't what I'm asking. Did she set out deliberately to show she could get him?"

A pause. "Could be. Not the sort of stuff I notice. I told you she was keen on the equipment. And Gabby certainly has it."

"What I'm getting at is this. Is Jenny the sort of girl who can't settle down to a steady relationship herself, and feels she wants to break them up when other people have them? Just to show she can do it."

"Ah, you're too deep for me. I don't go for all that stuff, I don't have *relationships*. If you're asking could Jenny be a mean bitch, the answer's yes, but so can I."

"Were you parting company because you'd had enough of her, didn't want her making trouble?"

"You could say that, except maybe Jenny had had enough of me. It was she talked about moving out, the way I told you, though I won't say I was sorry. Tell you something, you're going in for this psychological stuff. I'm happy, know what I mean? All sorts of shit happens, makes me miserable, but down deep I'm happy. Jenny it was the other way round, she laughed a lot and was fun to be with, but really she didn't know what she wanted except she hadn't got it and maybe someone else had. So then she tried something else, and could be that's why she wanted to move out of here. Deep stuff, eh?"

"It could be a help. Thanks, anyway."

"Helping the filth, I must be losing my marbles."

Her laugh echoed in his ears after he put down the telephone.

Two weeks after Bryan had revealed to her that vision of a Purafood Britain Eleanor got to the restaurant at her usual time, just before eleven o'clock, to find it closed. She knocked on the door, looked in the window. The tables were unlaid, there was no sign of life. She took a taxi to the glass and steel block, asked for Bryan, sat for ten minutes in the vast entrance hall. Then the receptionist whispered something to her assistant, who gave Eleanor a mechanical smile, led the way to the lift, and did not reply when Eleanor said she knew her way up. They went not to the tenth but the twelfth floor. When the lift door opened, there was Maggie Lomas.

"Eleanor, come along." She led the way to an office smaller and less luxuriously carpeted than Bryan's, but with an impressive battery of differently coloured telephones on her desk. She lit a cigar. "Tried to get hold of you this morning, but you'd left.

Apologies, you must have had a bit of a shock going to the restaurant. Things have been a bit hectic here. Bryan's gone."

"Gone?"

"Last year's sixty-million profit's turned into a ten-million loss, somebody's head had to roll. Bryan wanted us to expand our way out of it, the other directors said no, so it was Bryan's head. He had some crazy ideas, like the hotels and restaurants he was buying. He did it on his own for a while, till I found out. Then I tried to stop him, but he wouldn't listen. We're going to have to unload them at a loss."

"But the restaurant was doing so well."

Maggie shook her head. "Bryan arranged to subsidize all the supplies. No problem filling a restaurant if you make a loss on every meal you serve and the cooking's good. The other directors decided to close down Chancery Lane immediately. I paid off the staff yesterday afternoon. Bryan agreed his golden handshake, cleared his desk and went. He tried to ring you, had no luck."

"I'd been to see my daughter-in-law. She had a miscarriage recently, it's left her rather depressed." She sensed a certain complacency about Maggie Lomas. "You were always opposed to the restaurant, weren't you?"

"If Bryan wanted one as a sort of plaything, all right, it would lose money but I could go along with it. But a whole chain of them—crazy stuff."

"So you stopped it."

"I did what I had to. Nothing personal." She stubbed out the cigar. "About your contract. It runs to the end of the year, and of course we shall honour it."

When John Midway let himself into the house, his own house, it was mid-morning and the telephone was ringing. He knew, quite simply knew, that the call would be for him and would offer a solution to the problems that faced him, so why did he cry: "Eleanor?" There was no reply, the telephone rang inexorably, and he stood in the living-room placing hands over ears and unable to answer it. The sound stopped, he sighed with relief, called Eleanor's name again, then went out to the kitchen where the first thing he noticed was the telephone on the wall. The sound began again and this time he overcame fear and he lifted the receiver. Disappointment blended with relief when the voice he heard was Susan's.

"John? Are you all right?" *Was* he all right? She gave him no time to consider this, went on. "It's bad news, I'm afraid. The police have been trying to get hold of you, at home and through the office." *Bad news . . . the police . . .* that could only mean Jenny. The voice at the other end was still talking when he said: "Where is she?"

"I don't think you've heard what I was saying."

"Jenny, where is she? What's happened?"

"I said nothing about Jenny. It's your brother Giles. He had a heart attack. He's dead, they couldn't do anything for him. John, am I getting through to you, do you understand what I'm saying?"

With a flash of old Midway vigour he said: "Of course I understand. Do you think I'm a fool?"

"I don't know. But last night you were right about one thing. You don't belong here. I'll send the rest of your things on. Don't come here, I don't want to see you."

The connection broken, telephone replaced, he looked round at the calm order of the kitchen, saucepans on wall, kitchen knives in rack, cups on hooks, plates stacked on dresser, and wondered how he could ever have left it for the chaos of Susan's apartment. He made a pot of tea, filled a cup but did not drink from it, stared at a print on the wall that showed a stylized scene of men fishing, fish of all kinds and sizes leaping out of the water to reach the baited hooks. David had loved the print when he was a small boy, and had asked if the fish really liked being caught. Big nose in air, lower lip quivering, he remembered brusquely checking the boy's endless questions, remembered too that he had never been similarly brusque with Jenny. Had he treated them differently, and so behaved badly to them both? And Giles, had he ever tried as he might have done to probe beneath the calm surface his brother showed to the world? Should he not now be feeling more emotion than he could muster at a sibling's death?

Eleanor found him still at the kitchen table when she returned from the interview with Maggie Lomas. She had seen the unopened suitcase in the hall, so that his presence did not come as a surprise. She asked why he had come back.

His lower lip wobbled. "I've been thinking. I've made a lot of mistakes. I don't know if you want me back, not much of a bargain, given up my job. I couldn't stick Horton, and told him so."

"Wonderful. I wonder you didn't kill the greasy little swine years ago." Her voice was high, hysterical. "Oh, John, I said on the phone I missed you, you don't know how much. I'm so glad you're back."

"Something else." He told her about Giles. "I've been thinking, I never really knew him, never much liked him. My fault, I expect. And Jenny—"

"Jenny's gone. I've accepted it now, or I think I have. Don't talk about her." She opened a packet she had put on the table. "I bought some sandwiches at Marks and Sparks, couldn't be bothered to cook. Have one?"

He was halfway through the sandwich when he said: "Shouldn't you be at your restaurant?"

"I've got news too. It's packed up. Kaput. The man who wanted it has gone. I'm out of a job."

"I'm sorry."

"Don't be. It was a sort of dream anyway, I see that now. I should have known it wasn't real."

They both began to laugh.

The surge of excitement Catchpole felt about the Midway affair was tempered by worry over Alice's unreasonable behaviour. She had been to see Brett, and returned indignant about everything from the attitude of the warder to what Brett had told her about the food, but what upset her more than anything else was what she regarded as her husband's reluctance to take Brett's part. He got back one evening to find her with Mrs. Longley, and it seemed to him Alice stared at him with something of her mother's dislike, as she said Laura was staying the night.

He nodded. They were drinking sherry. He poured himself a large gin, asked for the boys, was told they were upstairs doing homework, and made a strategic retreat. Upstairs Alan said: "When's Gran going?" Told she was staying the night he groaned. "I don't like her, she's bossy."

"She's stopped me watching TV," Desmond said. "*The A-team*. Can she do that, Dad? Why did Mum let her?"

"Because you watch too much." He helped Alan with what seemed to him an extremely difficult math problem, and went downstairs again. Mrs. Longley looked at him severely through rimless glasses.

"I've been talking to Brett's solicitor, Mr. Maddox—"

"Maddox?"

Alice said: "Featherstone said he was out of his depth." When he asked who suggested Maddox she shook her head and said she didn't know. Her mother coughed, demanding attention.

"Mr. Maddox tells me the police are being most obstructive over everything connected with Brett's defence. If my son were allowed bail he would be able to get in touch with friends who could explain the absurd mistakes that have led to all this."

"As you know, bail was refused." He took a swig of gin.

"And you did nothing about it." That was Alice. Mrs. Longley took up the attack again.

"He is suffering in that prison, Hilary." She rarely used his Christian name. "Alice has told me how much. Surely it is possible for you to make some arrangements to improve his conditions, even if you are not able to arrange his release. After all you are a Superintendent, not a Sergeant."

Her intonation conveyed the feeling that the ranks were almost equally undesirable. He restrained the dislike of her he felt in his reply.

"As far as I know Brett's in the position of any prisoner on remand. He'll be there until his trial. If he's ill he'll be removed to the prison hospital."

"If you speak to Mr. Maddox he can tell you—"

"There's no way in the world I can talk to Curly Maddox about this. He's a brief, a solicitor, employed by some of the biggest villains in London." Mrs. Longley gave a gasp at *villains*. "As Alice knows or should remember. If I started cooperating with him I should be in trouble up to my neck. And it would be no help to Brett."

Mrs. Longley barely spoke to him during the rest of the evening. When they were alone in their bedroom Alice said: "It comes to this, you won't lift a finger to help. Don't tell me you can't, you've told me a dozen times about deals being done."

"That's different. If somebody coughs and gives information that helps you to catch bigger fish you can do a deal. Doesn't apply to Brett."

"If he was out on bail he might help you to find Santoro." He shrugged. "And what about that man forging bank notes you told me about, Chadwick? He gave evidence for the prosecution, you didn't charge him at all."

"He helped to put other people inside, broke up a whole gang. Burgess doesn't believe Brett would do anything of that sort, he thinks if he was on bail he'd run for it, try to get to Spain or somewhere else he can sit back and laugh at us."

"Would that be so terrible?"

He took off tie and shirt, flung them on a chair. "You're talking crap. Brett's not helped us in any way, his case is he knows nothing about any drugs, they were planted—"

"And you don't believe him?"

"Doesn't matter what I believe. That's Brett's story, he's sticking to it, Burgess says it's incredible. I don't know who's right, it's not my affair, and Burgess wouldn't welcome me sticking my nose in any further—" He stopped. She was shaking her head.

"Don't give me that. If you wanted to be more involved you could."

"You mean ignore Burgess, try to get the rules bent some way or other because he's my brother-in-law?" She looked at him with eyes wide, nodded. "First I don't think I could do it, the case looks too open and shut."

"If Brett was the AC's brother-in-law he'd be out on bail and it would all be hushed up."

"I'm not so sure you're right, and I'm not the AC. But anyway there are lines you draw, things you do to help out, others you don't. I couldn't live with myself if I tried to fiddle this. Brett's got one of the best shyster lawyers in London, I don't doubt he'll get a smart counsel. He'll have to take his chances."

"And that's it? I tell you, he's mouldering away in prison, he *hates* it, and you won't even talk to anyone who might help?"

He felt like saying Brett shouldn't have tried to take a cargo of drugs through Customs, but refrained. The emotional temperature was frigid enough.

At three in the morning Alan cried out. Alice was sleeping peacefully. He went in to the boy, who said: "I was in goal, I fumbled the ball, they kept scoring, and Arsenal players were watching, they laughed at me." He wept. Catchpole comforted him, went downstairs, poured a large brandy and sat down to think what he should do, not about Brett Langley but about Jenny Midway. By the time he finished the brandy he had decided.

At breakfast the atmosphere remained frigid, the ice melted only a little by Alan's recital of his goalkeeping nightmare. "When Dad woke me up I thought he was George Graham. That's the Arsenal manager. But he wasn't." His father laughed appreciatively, Alice gave a wan smile, Mrs. Longley's features remained as if set in stone. Alan sensed something was wrong. Desmond said: "You're a silly bugger," and Catchpole told him not to swear.

When he left Alice offered her cheek, not her mouth, to be kissed. Told that he might have a lead on the Midway disappearance she said: "I thought you were off that, it wasn't your problem. Like Brett. Only I suppose the girl is more interesting."

He could have hit her. Instead he said: "You're being unreasonable."

"Am I? It's my brother."

At the Yard he saw Lowry, who said nothing new had come up and he was thinking of passing the case on to AMIP, the Area Major Investigations Pool, where as they both knew it was likely to stagnate. Lowry made no objection to his taking away the bulky file. "Got a bright idea?" he asked, and nodded resignedly when Catchpole said perhaps. With retirement beckoning Lowry wanted nothing to do with bright ideas.

Catchpole explained the way things had linked up in his mind to Charlie Wilson. "I was giving a talk at my son's school and one of the boys went on about his family being evicted from their home, I suppose because they were in arrears with mortgage payments. Then the house stood empty for months. It occurred to me Jenny had told Patsy Malone she was moving out, starting a new life. We interpreted that as meaning she was going off with a new man to a new place, maybe another country, but suppose it was some other sort of new life, and she was looking for another place in London?

"With me so far? So she's looking at this other place and she's murdered. If she was killed when looking at a house or flat and the killer didn't remove the body, it's likely the house was empty. An empty house is the perfect place for a murder"—he continued before Wilson could object—"if it's likely to remain empty, as you were about to say. Now, who'd be likely to know about empty houses with a demolition order on them, or scheduled for reconstruction, or something similar?"

"Local Council employees? Building workers?"

"Possibilities, yes. But they'd have to be in a position of fair importance to know how soon reconstruction or demolition was likely to take place. Or if anyone was likely to be looking over the house."

"Come on, guv, you've got something in mind. Let's have it."

"How about an estate agent? And who do we know that's involved who works for an estate agent?"

"David Midway." Wilson stared at him. "Why would he want to kill his sister?"

"I don't know, but people in families do kill each other. And I've been hearing things about Jenny. They suggest she may not have been quite the person she appeared. Call it a hunch, Charlie, but I want to explore it."

Wilson looked dubiously at the folders beside Catchpole. "I thought we were supposed to be off Midway."

"Nothing to stop us occupying spare time instead of twiddling our fingers. You got any spare time, Charlie?"

"If you twist my arm. What am I supposed to be looking for?"

"I want to check through all the London sightings we had. See if any of them were connected with empty houses, or had a possible link with David Midway. Maybe not an empty house, possibly one with a flat for sale, especially a basement flat. Basically, anywhere a body could have been put with a fair chance it might stay hidden."

A few hours later Wilson came back with a faint stirring of excitement in his manner. "It's not exactly what you were talking about, governor, but you might be interested." It was one of the early sightings, in which the driver of a milk float had seen a man and woman get out of a black VW Golf, thought the woman looked like a photograph of Jenny shown to him, but saw only the back of the man. The sighting had been followed up, but the milkman added nothing to the story, and house to house enquiries brought no results. The sighting had been in Rodders Road, Parsons Green, an area covered by Wayne, Mendelson where David Midway worked. Wilson's enquiries revealed several flats for sale. There were one or two empty houses, but nothing due for demolition according to the Council.

It took a while to find the milk float driver, a man in his fifties named Bert Henderson who had taken the job after being made redundant when the children's home where he had been something called a group leader was closed down. Henderson was delighted to talk. He had now lost the milk float job, his wife went out to work as a cleaner, and he kept the house tidy.

"Seems funny that, she's a cleaner but I keep the house clean. Still, gives me time to watch the telly." He remembered the Rodders Road sighting, but was the kind of witness to make a detective's heart sink. "The woman, now, I'd swear it was the girl who disappeared. No, I tell a lie, I couldn't *swear* to it, but it was very like the picture they showed me." And the man? "Ah now, there you've got me. I'm with me float, see, getting out the old pint bottles and putting 'em in the tray when he gets out of the car. She was driving, I can tell you that, not him. He's in the front passenger seat and they start to walk up the road, so all I see is his back. Height? About the same as me I should say, five eight or nine, wearing an overcoat, couldn't say the colour, and some bright coloured scarf."

Catchpole pointed out that if the man's back had been turned to him he could hardly have seen the scarf, let alone its colour. Henderson instantly agreed. "Funny the ideas you get in your head, aren't they?" He had not noticed the number of the car. Where had he been in the road at the time? He thought around number forty. He had then gone further up the road, and had not seen the couple again. So they must have gone into one of the houses below number forty? Henderson amiably agreed, but added: "Course, they might not have gone in any of the houses, just stopped for a minute, looked at the outside, driven off." No, he had not seen the car again. He wagged a finger at them. "I could say I thought I had on my way back down the road, and it might be true, maybe it was there and I never noticed, but that'd be no help to you, would it, me saying something I mighta seen but never noticed?" Another few minutes of Henderson, Catchpole said to Wilson, would have driven him mad.

The original house to house enquiries made in Rodders Road had produced no results. Nobody had seen the car or noticed two young people going into a house or in the road looking at one. The small flame of excitement in Wilson had been almost extinguished by talking to Henderson, but Catchpole's nerve ends were still tingling with the feeling that he was near to a solution, and those tingling nerve ends led him to what he afterwards considered his only important mistake in connection with Jenny's disappearance.

Bert Henderson lived near the Wayne, Mendelson offices. Catchpole sent Wilson back to the Yard to dig further in the Midway file and went to the estate agents' offices instead of telephoning. The receptionist said Mr. Mendelson would see him, and on the way through to Mendelson's office he saw David

Midway at a desk. David half rose to greet him, then dropped back in his chair as Catchpole nodded and passed on.

Mendelson was breezy, sharp, curious. Catchpole explained the Midway file was still open, and he was following up a possibility that she had been seen in Rodders Road on the day of her disappearance. Did they have any houses or flats in the road on their books? A girl brought in files, the agent looked at them.

"There are two flats and two houses, but I think only the flats would interest you, a flat at number fifty-two and a maisonette at seventy-five."

The detective shook his head. "No good, the numbers are wrong. What about the houses?"

"They're empty. We don't have our usual board up and don't normally show them to prospective clients. They're next to each other, a semi-detached couple, need a lot of work done to them, and the owner won't undertake it because he expects to do a deal with a builder who'll convert them into luxury flats. The owner lives in the Channel Islands, pays us a small fee to keep an eye on them, make sure they're not vandalized or taken over by squatters. So, although they *are* on our books, the owner's asking an absurd price in view of their condition. I can't remember the last time we showed anyone round—" He stopped when he saw Catchpole's face. "Numbers twenty-six and twenty-eight."

"Can you check on the date when someone was last shown round?"

"I could check that with David."

"Not necessary. I'd like to look at them if you can let me have the keys. No need to tell anyone else, perhaps you wouldn't mind getting them yourself."

Mendelson looked hard at him, went out, returned with two sets of keys. "They're kept on a board out there. It would be easy to take them down. Or to see me taking them down, you understand me?" Catchpole nodded. When he left David Midway's head was bent over his desk. He did not look up.

The houses looked similar to their neighbours. The windows were dirty, but net curtains kept away the curious. There were roses and primulas in the small semi-circular front garden flower-beds. Wayne, Mendelson took their caretaking duties seriously. Like most of the houses in Rodders Road these were late Victorian, with front parlour, back sitting-room, small kitchen and scullery, bedrooms on two floors above, the top ones tiny, a cellar into which coal was originally shot from outside. No doubt there had been a hip-bath put in the kitchen on Saturday nights. But that was long ago . . .

He entered the hall of twenty-six, stepped over the pile of junk mail that accumulates in all empty houses, went upstairs, then down to the cellar. The place was in a poor state of repair. In one room the wainscot had come away from the wall, in another a marble mantelpiece had cracked or been broken almost in two, part of the ceiling in one of the top bedrooms had come down and in the other room the ceiling bulged ominously. In two rooms plugs had been pulled away from the wall, so it was perhaps a good thing that the electricity had been turned off. At the back there was a patch of garden, separated from the similar patch in twenty-eight by a four-foot-high wooden fence that had collapsed at one end. A door from the kitchen led down to the cellar, and when he opened it the smell was unpleasant. Catchpole made his way down cautiously with the aid of the small torch he carried. It ran from front to back of the house, and a film of water covered the concrete floor. He dabbled fingers in it, smelt decaying faecal matter. The sewer was leaking back into the cellar. Evidently Wayne, Mendelson's caretaking had its limits. He wished he had not sent Wilson back to the Yard.

Twenty-eight was almost identical to twenty-six except that the roof seemed in better condition. He went out into the patch of garden, but saw no sign of digging. Finally he braced himself and opened the kitchen door to the cellar. A gust of air came up at him that seemed no more and no less foul than that in the other cellar. He put a handkerchief over his nose and went down. His shoes puddled in water. He shone the torch around. There was more water here than in the other cellar, and in one corner stood an armchair, bits of wood, and what looked like old clothes. As he approached the smell became stronger. He pulled aside the armchair, and something that had been propped by it fell. The torchlight showed the remains of a face. When he bent down to look more closely the stench was overpowering. He straightened up, restrained an impulse to vomit, went upstairs, called Wilson who said: "What's up guv? You sound a bit shaky."

"We've found Jenny Midway." He did not say "I think," although the face was unrecognizable. He knew.

Knew also that time might be important if the mistake in letting himself be seen by David Midway was not to have unhappy consequences. Mendelson anticipated Catchpole's question as soon as he came on the line. "David's not here. He asked the girl what keys you'd taken, she told him, he just walked out."

"What's his home address?"

"My secretary will have it. Is it what I think, Superintendent, is David—"

"The address please, Mr. Mendelson, no questions."

On the way to Stamford Hill he spoke to Wilson again, ordered a check made on airports, a couple of men sent to Stamford Hill, photographs and forensics to Rodders Road.

"You think he'll try to do a runner?"

"It's possible. I shouldn't have gone to his office and alerted him. It was stupid."

One thing about Miss Hilly, Wilson said afterwards, if he made mistakes he admitted them, never tried to get out from under by shifting the mistake on to someone else. Miss Hilly, he knows he's made a mistake and he says it out loud, Wilson said almost admiringly.

This time it didn't matter. The end of what the papers called the Midway Mystery was undramatic, like much in police work.

When Catchpole rang the bell the woman he recognized as David's wife, though he had seen her only once, opened the door and said: "David's expecting you, though not quite so soon. He's told me." He might have been a guest for dinner who had turned up a little late.

David Midway was sitting at a table with a writing pad in front of him. He said: "I've told Mary. She knew nothing about it, nothing at all. You believe that, don't you? I was writing it all down, how it happened. You don't know, do you, you don't know what Jenny was like."

In a tone conversational, almost friendly, Catchpole said: "You'd have been right about that a couple of weeks ago. These last few days I've been finding out."

"She wanted everything. Anything other people had got. Oh, she'd do things for you, give things away as long as *she* was giving them. But anything you'd got, anything that made you happy, she wanted. I didn't have much, only Mary, that was enough for me. So she wanted Mary."

For the first time his wife showed signs of emotion. "It wasn't serious, don't you understand, just something that took her fancy. I wouldn't have told you if it was serious." She said to Catchpole: "She made what I suppose you'd call a sort of pass at me, said it would be fun to try living together, she was fed up with men. Then she said, let's go away for a trial weekend. It was just something new, a love affair with a woman."

Catchpole nodded. "I think you're right. Eversley Grayson's wife Sally Lou told me Jenny suggested they should go away for a weekend together, if they liked it set up house afterwards, she'd leave her husband. Sally Lou thought it was a tremendous joke."

"So did I. But I should have known better than to tell David." He stared at her. "She wasn't a serious person, don't you see? Everything was a joke to her."

"She deliberately tried to break up our marriage, and Eversley's, and you say she was joking. And you were attracted, you said so to me, you might have gone."

"Only because—you don't understand, she made everything seem fun. She said to me once that was all she wanted out of life, that it should be fun."

The bell rang, kept on ringing. Catchpole said: "That will be the police car. You'll have to come with me, David." He nodded, stood up. "You too, Mrs. Midway. We shall need a statement from you."

The confession David Midway made was quite short. It read:

Some time early in February, I can't be sure of the exact date, my wife Mary told me my sister Jenny had suggested Mary should leave me and set up house with her. I understood this would be in a lesbian relationship. Mary told me she wouldn't do this but the idea of it greatly upset me, although I concealed this from my wife and am sure she did not realize it. When we were children Jenny was my parents' favourite, and now she was trying to wreck my life. I determined to tell her this must stop, she could do what she liked with her own life but must leave me and Mary alone. The chance came when she told me she was moving out of her flat anyway because she was bored with her black friend, and asked if I could find something through my firm. It was typical of Jenny that she should ask me this, and at the same time try to take away my wife. When I asked her to leave Mary alone she laughed at me, and said Mary would leave me and go to live with her if she lifted a little finger. It was then I made up my mind.

I told her my firm had one or two places that might be suitable, and met her on that Monday. She picked me up at a pub I named in the King's Road, because of course I didn't want her to come to the office. I asked again in the car if she would leave Mary alone, and she just laughed. So

I took her to the house in Rodders Street. When we were inside she said it was no good, and I was a fool for wasting her time. I attacked her then, strangled her, and put her body in the cellar. Then I took the keys of her car and drove it back to Balham, leaving it near where she lived. I had no particular purpose in doing this. I intended to remove the body from the cellar and throw it in the Thames, but the opportunity never seemed to arise. Also I could not bring myself to return to the cellar.

My wife Mary knew nothing of what I had done. I deeply regret the suffering I have caused her and my parents, but wish to add that Jenny was a bad person and deserved to die.

"That seems to sum it up," the Big Man said. "Do you think the wife was an accessory? It seems to me she must have known."

"I think she guessed but didn't want to know. I think Midway will plead diminished responsibility. He shouldn't get away with it—he wiped his prints off the car carefully enough—but I understand a psychiatrist has said he's severely depressive, and also an anal-retentive type."

"I understand depressive, but the other sounds as if he suffers from severe constipation. What does it mean in English?"

"You might call it mental constipation, sir. Emotion bottled up, in this case jealousy of his sister and something like hatred for her. Then one day the bottle bursts."

"Sounds nasty. Anyway, Catchers, congratulations are in order. Give you a rest from a case and you solve it." Catchpole said thank you, although he felt the compliment had an edge. The Big Man said casually, "Sorry to hear a relative of yours is in trouble. Drug smuggling, yes? Nothing to concern you personally, I hope."

"Not directly. He's Alice's brother."

The Big Man made a clucking noise. He liked Alice. "Pity.

Burgess seems to think there's no doubt he's in it up to his neck. Kind of thing one wants to steer clear of, but if you think there's anything I can do—"

Catchpole interpreted the unfinished signal as a warning. "I wouldn't think of asking you, sir."

"Do it by the book. Quite right."

The warning had been heeded. Or of course you could say the possibility of high-level intervention had been hinted at and turned down.

Giles's funeral was well attended by legal eagles, falcons and kestrels. There was even a vulture in the shape of the *Banner*'s Jack Johnson, although his editor had rejected the idea of running a feature using some of the pictures showing Giles in Watching gear alongside the shots of legal dignitaries at the funeral.

"Not a question of taste, just they're not that tasty," the editor, who fancied himself as a wit, said. So the heading was THE MIDWAY TRAGEDIES, with the distinguished career of the Judge set against the fact that his nephew would shortly be tried for the murder of his niece. The misfortunes of John and Eleanor also came to the notice of the *Sun*, who spread themselves on THE CURSE OF THE MIDWAYS. The curse had in fact been lifted a little by the fact that Anglo American Universal, a quasi-governmental organization set up to make the English and American languages second only to native tongues everywhere in the world, had offered John the position of Programme Forwarding Director, and he had accepted.

But John and Eleanor were conscious of the curse. They were conscious of it even as they sang "He who would valiant be" and "The day thou gavest, Lord, is ended," and deeply aware of it as they listened to the Lord Chief Justice, who took as his text a theme from St. Matthew: "Think not that I am come to destroy the law . . . I am come not to destroy but to fulfil." The Lord Chief Justice praised Giles's excellence as a Judge, the care with which he weighed evidence, the wisdom evident in his judgements and the way in which when he felt it appropriate he tempered judgement with mercy, exemplifying in his own person the standards and purpose of the law. And the curse of the Midways was still in their minds as they heard the passages read from the nineteenth chapter of Revelation: "For true and righteous are his judgements . . . And I saw heaven opened, and beheld a white horse; and he that sat upon him was called Faithful and True, and in righteousness he doth judge and make war."

They came out from the church and stood there in warm sunlight in the middle of London, an awkward-looking man with his nose in the air, and a woman still elegant, who yet looked somehow shrunken and faded. The legal dignitaries did not speak to them, indeed did not know them, and they took what comfort they could from the presence of their daughter-in-law. Mary said she was going to see David, but when she asked if she could give him a message John shook his head.

"He'd like it if you went to see him."

Eleanor said: "Not yet. But give him my love. I don't understand why it happened. We loved our children. We were such a happy family."

John shook his big head again. "Not true. We were playing happy families, that was all."

In sports, in academia, in the arts—and in the Met—nothing succeeds like success. Catchpole found himself slapped on the back, congratulated, stood drinks by people who had never been friendly in the past. Higginbotham said he was going to call in Catchers next time a Goya went missing, Wilson told him a WPC said she fancied him something rotten. It would have been nice if some of this praise had been replicated in Clapham, but Alice's thoughts remained fixed on the idea that Brett could be got out of prison. Catchpole gave evidence in an insurance fraud case where Curly Maddox was involved in the defence, and the solicitor stopped him as they were leaving Court, and told him his wife's brother was taking remand hard. It could be in everybody's interest, he suggested, if he were released on bail.

"It's not my case. But nobody I know thinks so."

"He's the sort you might get what you want by relaxing instead of squeezing, and you're the flavour of the month."

"I said it's not my case. I'll tell you what other people say. Let him show some goodwill, lead us to Santoro or at least give us some names and places, then we might play Santa Claus." Maddox shrugged and gave up.

He told Alice, who said: "How can Brett give you Santoro or lead you to anybody when he's innocent? He's Santoro's victim, wants him found as much as you do."

He sighed. "To accept that, you've got to say Brett's a fool, such a fool he didn't realize the Ivorine business was a con job, a fool who didn't know he was in a car full of drugs. But Brett isn't a fool, he's quick and clever, you've always said so. They've checked the car's movements, and there's no way Brett could be clear of knowing what was in the car."

"And you won't do anything to help him?"

"He won't do anything to help himself."

"You're saying you've got no influence even after this great success you're so pleased about."

"I'm saying there are things you do and things you don't if you're a copper, and this is one of the don'ts. Brett must take his chances."

She made no attempt to keep her voice down in these arguments, and Alan said: "You and Mum aren't getting along very well, are you?"

"Not at the moment. It does happen, you know."

Alan nodded agreement. "Will you separate? Some kids at school, their parents are separated. They like it, most of them." He considered. "I wouldn't."

"Nor would I. Nor would Mummy. So don't worry." Alan nodded again.

A week before Brett's trial, with Santoro undiscovered, Burgess came to see Catchpole, his expression gloomy, his dark eyes malicious. "Bit of news," he said. "Thought you should have it. Your brother-in-law won't come up for trial." He paused. Catchpole waited. "Topped himself. Last night."

Catchpole kept voice and face free of expression as he asked how it happened, and heard that Brett had managed to tear his sheet into strips, make a loop round his neck and improvise a gallows with the help of his window bars. It was important to give no hostages to Burgess, and Catchpole merely said: "He was always ingenious."

"Pity about it. Wife'll be upset too, I suppose."

"Thanks for telling me." He rang Alice and told her, afraid that if he did not she might hear first on the radio news. She made a muffled noise, put down the telephone.

When he opened the door of the chapel forty minutes later the first thing he saw was the two boys huddled together at the foot of the stairs. Desmond ran to him, clasped his knees. Alan said: "Mum's in the kitchen. She won't talk."

Desmond said: "We haven't had our tea."

He went into the kitchen. Alice had been sitting with her elbows on the table, head in hands. "I heard that. I'll make their tea."

"Alice. I'm truly sorry."

"I expect so. Bad for promotion prospects."

"I don't deserve that."

"Don't you? You'd know. You're always right."

"What you wanted, getting him out, was impossible."

"But if it had been you wouldn't have done it."

He thought, then said: "You're right. If it had been I wouldn't have done it."

She carefully buttered the bread she had out. "You're always right, you know what's right and then you do it. We don't have anything to say to each other anymore. I'll finish making tea, then pack some things. I'm going to Mother for a few days, but I'll be in touch, get something settled. You like that, don't you, having things settled."

He stared at her. She began to spread paste on the bread. It was crab paste, which the boys always liked.